Aberdeenshire
COUNCIL

Aberdwww.aberde

KT-478-983

0 8 SEP 2017	− 4 JUL 2018
	2 8 DEC 2019
2 9 SEP 2017	1 1 JAN 2019
− 2 DEC 2017	1 1 FEB 2019
− 3 JAN 2018	
1 5 JAN 2018	− 1 JUL 2023
− 5 FEB 2018	1 0 AUG 2023
0 2 FEB 2018	
2 8 FEB 2018	

WITHDRAWN
FROM LIBRARY
ABERDEENSHIRE
LIBRARIES

Aberdeenshire

3211169

Isabel Ashdown was born in London and grew up on the south coast of England. The opening of her debut won the *Mail on Sunday* Novel Competition, going on to be published as *Glasshopper* and being named as one of the best books of the year. Today, she writes full-time, walks daily, and volunteers in a local school for the charity Pets as Therapy. Isabel lives in Sussex with her carpenter husband, their two children and dogs Charlie and Leonard. Follow Isabel on Twitter @IsabelAshdown

By Isabel Ashdown

Flight
Summer of '76
Hurry Up and Wait
Glasshopper

Little Sister

A missing child. A broken mother.
A sister who doesn't remember a thing.

ISABEL ASHDOWN

First published in Great Britain in 2017 by Orion Books,
an imprint of The Orion Publishing Group Ltd
Carmelite House, 50 Victoria Embankment,
London EC4Y 0DZ

An Hachette UK company

1 3 5 7 9 10 8 6 4 2

Copyright © Isabel Ashdown 2017

The moral right of Isabel Ashdown to be identified as
the author of this work has been asserted in accordance with
the Copyright, Designs and Patents Act of 1988.

All rights reserved. No part of this publication may be
reproduced, stored in a retrieval system, or transmitted
in any form or by any means, electronic, mechanical,
photocopying, recording, or otherwise, without the
prior permission of both the copyright owner and the
above publisher of this book.

All the characters in this book are fictitious, and any resemblance to
actual persons, living or dead, is purely coincidental.

A CIP catalogue record for this book is
available from the British Library.

ISBN 978 1 4091 6794 5

Typeset by Born Group

Printed and bound by CPI Group (UK) Ltd, Cryodon CR0 4YY

MIX
Paper from
responsible sources
FSC® C104740
www.fsc.org

www.orionbooks.co.uk

For my sister, Bec, with love

'Whoever is careless with the truth in small matters cannot be trusted with important matters'

Albert Einstein

Prologue

You were perfect; unblemished. Innocent of ill thought, with a light that radiated from you like sunlight. You brought meaning to everything, and, with you in it, my world had become a warmer place. Until I went and ruined it all.

The house was silent, and for a while it was just you and me, alone, without the distractions and noise of the others to unsettle our peace. You were special, and from the first time I held you I knew we had a connection that could never be put into plain words or easily broken. Everyone said I was spoiling you, that I should stop with all the little presents – spend my money on myself instead – but they didn't understand that all I ever wanted to do was make you happy. And to protect you. That evening I sat in the lounge for an age, staring beyond the muted movements of the television screen, willing you to wake for a while, so I could fill my eyes with your love, feel the reassuring thump of your heartbeat against mine.

'Try not to wake her,' James had said as they headed off for their party earlier that evening, dressed up in their black-tie best, looking quite the glamorous pair. 'Just pop your head in every now and then – but don't pick her up straight away if she wakes! She'll drop off again if you leave her for a few minutes.' At the front door I saw her button up her neat fawn coat and whisper something to him – and he'd rushed back in with a tub of chocolates, sliding them across the coffee table towards me. 'Babysitter's perks!' he'd said, and, checking his reflection in the mantle mirror one last time, he'd dashed from the room and out into the night.

At some point it felt as though hours had passed, but I'd started to feel strange by then, and it was hard to know if my sense of time was out, as so often happens. The clock said it was gone one in the morning, but that couldn't be right, could it? Surely I hadn't been sitting here alone for that long? I was certain I had heard you cry out, and, although I remembered your dad's words and knew I mustn't go to you yet, I couldn't help myself and I rushed up to fetch you down. You were so pleased to see me, waving your soft arms and grabbing at the air, and I scooped you up and brought you into the kitchen, strapping you into your high chair so you could watch me make up your warm milk. I dropped a couple of bread sticks on to your tray and you babbled and waved them in the air, and I felt light-headed with the joy of you. I was hungry too, and as your milk warmed in the bowl I made myself a sandwich, carving the last of the turkey breast from the Christmas joint, and laying it out in a slow, careful pattern on a slice of the crumbly organic loaf that James always insisted on. I often wondered if he'd be so popular with the women if they knew what a fusspot he really was – and in an instant I lost my appetite and I tossed the sandwich at the dog bowl, where it flopped open and spilled messily over the polished floor. The kitchen lights overhead felt suddenly too brash and I flinched, swallowing my anger as I snatched up your bottle and slopped milk across the counter. I was so cross, I reached over to the light switch, flicking them off so I didn't need to squint any more, and as I did so my arm swept across the worktop, sending the bread-board and meat knife hurtling into the sink with a clatter. When I heard you gasp in the dimness, I was sorry again, so sorry, and I reached out to put my hand on your shoulder, to soothe you and let you know I was there. I paused, my pulse racing, as I listened out for any signs of them coming home, as by now I had no grasp of time and it seemed possible they could be back at any moment, ticking me off for getting you up, for waking you unnecessarily. But the silence remained, broken by nothing more than the gentle whistle of wind passing the windows that looked out across the drive. They wouldn't understand: all I wanted to do was hold you. I felt shaky as I stood beside your high chair in the half-light, watching the whites of your eyes blinking up at me, marvelling at the porcelain perfection of your dimpled fingers and rounded cheeks. And then, as I went to lift you up, I heard the sound of tyres on the gravel outside and the room grew instantly brighter, briefly bathing you in light, and in the seconds before the lights dipped I saw your closed eyes and the blood on your sleep suit – fresh blood, bright and wet. I cried out – screamed – staggering in my panic to get to you, to save you. But I couldn't save you, could I?

The great gulf of darkness opened up again like a silent roar, wrapping its weight around me and crushing my breaths as I went under.

PART ONE

1. **Jess**

Emily is across the room, her shape made silhouette by the earthy glow of lamplight beyond the front window. There's someone with her; their head is tilted in concern, their hand resting on her shoulder, and even through the vapour of my dazed mind I can see that she is crying, from the way her chest rises and falls with each shuddering breath. It's a tiny movement, but one I remember from earliest childhood, the way she'd turn inwards as she tried to keep it together, tried to hold it all inside. I see her now, aged four or five, casting aside her new red scooter, wanting instead my purple one; I was bewildered as she turned her back to me and stood at the low garden wall, unspeaking, taking these same shallow breaths, trying to contain herself. *Like a volcano*, that's what Dad used to say. *She's about to blow.*

The paramedic tells me to stay still for a while, and I'm so tired I don't argue. I just close my eyes and drift, and wait for them to tell me what to do next. I'm rocking, standing alone on the deck of the ferry, seeing the island for the first time, the sea sunglass-bright, sailing past cheerful yellow buoys and bobbing yachts as the densely wooded land and stony beaches come into clear view, a picture-postcard setting for idyllic grand houses and country-quaint cottages. Behind me, beyond the white spumed wake of the vessel, dark Napoleonic forts rise up through the distant waters, and I'm afraid. What is this, I wonder, this strange meandering train of thought? I can feel the hard surface beneath me, and my fingertips move listlessly, recognising the rough furrows of the kitchen floor tiles. Am I drunk – or dreaming – or dying even? My head feels submerged, as though I'm looking up through water, yet at the same time there's a feeling of clarity that frightens me. I feel the weight of a hand on my wrist, of fingers tugging at my eyelids, the assault of bright light on my retinas, and I gasp for air, my memories suddenly, horrifically breaking through the surface: awake, aware, *remembering*.

'There's a doctor on the way,' the plain-clothes officer says as she passes me a glass of water, indicating that we should move into the living room. I've been perched on a chair under the archway of the open-plan kitchen, a blanket draped around my shoulders as I gaze out into the dining room where James and Emily answer questions, their eyes drawn back to me from time to time, their faces distraught. 'Are you sure you wouldn't rather have a tea or coffee?'

I shake my head, almost afraid to speak, as I attempt to take in the reality of the situation. Daisy has gone. *Gone*? I want to feel more, but I can't, my senses deadened by the impact of the fall, my thoughts and emotions slow to respond. It seems impossible that life can change so swiftly, so entirely, from one moment to the next. Already my mind is crawling over what I can remember – and scrabbling for what I cannot – and I pray to God that I'm not responsible for this in some way, that there wasn't something I could have done to prevent it.

As we leave the clean light of the kitchen and pass through the dining room, I glance back at Emily and James, now seated around the family table with two other officers, a photograph of Daisy placed starkly in the space between them. Emily's neat dark bob has lost its party sheen of the night before, and she looks tiny beside James, whose posture is like that of a great wide-shouldered boy. His youthful peaks of hair seem incongruous in contrast with his abruptly aged expression. 'What now?' he asks the officer opposite him. His voice is husky, his tone softly urgent. '*What happens now*?' The pain that exudes from him and Emily is unbearable. They look drained of life, transparent beneath the bright glare of the dining room lights, and I know she's aware of me standing there, but my sister won't look up, she won't meet my eye.

'It doesn't look as if anything's broken.' We're in the living room, an open doorway separating me and my traumatised sister, and the woman is looking at me for a response. She points to the sofa, and I sit.

'What?'

She gestures towards my bloodied shirt as she takes out a notebook. 'It looks like a nosebleed to me. But we'll get you checked out all the same. So, Jess, I'm DCI Jacobs,' she enunciates carefully, and I realise she's told me this already, that she's not sure if I got it the first time.

They don't always send a detective out straight away, do they? But what do I know? I have no idea what's normal, or who arrived here in what order tonight. My gauge of time is completely out. I look beyond the inspector, out into the empty space of the doorway towards the dining room as another officer passes by. The place is thrumming with people. Did they all arrive while I was lying on the kitchen floor? Or did I just not notice them turning up as I sat on that hard chair, trying to bring my mind back into focus?

'Jess?' the inspector repeats, and I snap to attention, trying to blink myself towards some sense of clarity. She's older than me, maybe nudging fifty, and her hair is cut in a close ear-tucked style, entirely grey. She's not vain, I can tell, but there's an attractive energy in her dark eyes, a sparkle of life. She stares back at me, as though trying to work me out, and then the questions come. Were you alone all evening? Did you hear or notice anything unusual? Was the back door locked? Are you certain? When did you last see your niece Chloe? How old is she? Fifteen? What time did she go out? Are you sure? Do you get on well with your sister? And your brother-in-law? When did you last look in on Daisy? When did you last *see* Daisy? I try my best to answer them all, but I'm sure I must come across as guilty in some way, because I can't quite seize all the details, and even in my confused state I can see how some of the gaps seem oddly placed.

'So you can't remember *anything* from around 7pm until your sister and brother-in-law returned home together at 2am? Did you speak to anyone on the phone? Or maybe you watched something on television?'

I turn my head towards the TV and close my eyes, recalling a remote image, barely a memory at all. 'There was something with a dragon in it,' I say. When I open my eyes she's looking at me as if she doesn't believe me, or else she thinks I'm insane. 'A film, I think,' I press on. 'Animated. But I wasn't really watching it. It was just background noise. I remember thinking I was hungry. Maybe I made a sandwich.'

Her brow crinkles as she scribbles in her notebook. 'What kind of sandwich?'

I think for a moment. I've no idea what kind of sandwich; I just said it, for something to say, to make her stop looking at me like that. *Shit.* Why do I do this? Why do I keep getting it wrong? 'Turkey?'

After making another note, Jacobs rises and returns through the dining room into the kitchen, and I trail behind her, wishing

I could shrink myself down to nothing and slip away through a crack in the floor. I hover in the entrance as she takes a tour of the kitchen, peering at the few dirty items in the sink, opening the fridge and scrutinising the contents. On the kitchen wall beside me an old photograph of Chloe looks down – not the funny, fawn-legged Chloe of today, but the little Chloe of years ago, long before I ever knew her. Her eyes are the same eyes, the exact startling blue of her father's, but here they are unadorned, not yet blackly lined and painted like those of the teenager I've come to know so well. My heart lurches at the thought of her, of the pain she has yet to feel, of the gaping hole that's about to open up in her world. She adores her baby sister, loves spending time with her on the play mat, an unspoken return to toddler-hood. She'll pile up the bright wooden blocks, higher, higher, until Daisy can resist no longer, reaching a chubby hand forward to send the tower toppling. 'Daisy, you dodo!' Chloe will cry out in mock surprise. Emily hates that. 'Don't call her a dodo, Chloe! It's horrible!' I have to cover my mouth and turn away, and Chloe will catch me and shoot me a little smile as she scoops Daisy into her arms, allowing her baby sister to tug at her long copper-dyed hair with softly grasping hands. I love those girls.

DCI Jacobs leans out to speak to Emily and James, who are still being interviewed at the dining table. 'Sorry to interrupt . . . Mr and Mrs King, do you have any turkey left over from Christmas?'

Emily looks confused – offended even – and shakes her head. 'We threw the last of it out a few days ago.'

'Thank you,' the officer replies, and she jerks her head for me to return to the living room with her. 'So,' she says when we are seated again, her voice low and controlled. She rests her elbows on her knees, and leans in so I can hear and see every word formed on her narrow lips. 'Let's start again. And this time, if the answer is *I don't know*, then you say *I don't know*, OK? There

13

is a one-year-old child missing, and I'm keeping my voice down for the sake of your sister out there but in child abduction cases time is of the essence. The baby isn't walking yet, so we know she hasn't simply wandered off. *She's been taken.*' She pauses, staring at me closely, making sure I'm getting the severity of the situation. 'Everything you tell me will be followed up on, and we can save a lot of time if you can resist the urge to make up what you don't know. Do you understand?'

Her voice is solid and reassuring, and I feel her eyes drilling right down inside me, as if she's lifted the top off my head and peered in. She's giving me a second chance.

'I'm sorry,' I stammer, and my voice sounds pathetic. 'I just – I just panicked. I'm trying to remember, honestly. But I was out cold earlier. It's a heart thing – they call them "episodes" – and I haven't had one for years, and I thought I was over them, but they – they can hit me like a sledgehammer. And afterwards, there are these small chunks of time missing, and my mind feels like sludge, and I thought if I didn't say *anything* you'd think I had something to hide, and Daisy – *Jesus*, Daisy—'

And that's when it really hits me. My niece is gone. Sweet, beautiful Daisy is gone.

2. Emily

She hadn't expected to see her at the funeral. After all these years, Jess had faded until she had begun to take on the sepia tones of a distant memory or of a film watched long ago, the images patchy and incomplete. It wasn't that Emily never thought of her; she *was* aware of her in the world, but just – during the past sixteen years at least – not in hers. And so it took her by complete surprise, the lurch of yearning affection she felt when she spotted the unmistakable outline of Jess sitting alone at the far end of the empty front pew. From the doorway, she appeared unchanged, the sharp downward light from the stained glass windows outlining her narrow shape. Emily would have known that shape anywhere: the sun-streaked hair that bordered on messy, the modest tilt of her head, the delicate frame of her shoulders still evident beneath a heavy mannish coat. How must it be for her, returning to their gentle home town after all these years away? Emily finds it strange enough on her yearly visits, but to have been absent for the best part of two decades? It must feel like walking among ghosts.

Instinctively Emily reached for James, slipping her arm through his as she scanned the farther rows of the small church.

Chloe trailed awkwardly beside them, visibly shivering in the cold stone building, the cuffs of her coat pinched down into tight fists. Emily searched for familiarity in the faces of her mother's friends and neighbours, and her glance lingered briefly on her old schoolfriend Sammie Evans over on the far side, but apart from her she recognised no one. Many of them seemed to know her, though, to nod and smile sympathetically as she, James and Chloe passed mutely along the aisle towards the front seats, reserved for immediate family, reserved for them. *That's Emily*, they'd all be thinking. *That's Emily with her widower and their baby, and that's the teenage stepdaughter. SO sad; the mother died when she was just a tot. SO sad. Amazing how Emily took them on. He runs his own business, you know.* Oh, yes, they'd all know who they were: Mum would have shared every proud little detail, passing it on over church tea and cake, her talk of them a poor substitute for the visits they should have made more often. When did all these people get so *old*? Emily wondered, her eyes taking in the sea of silvered hair and mourning grey, not one of their faces recognisable as the younger versions from her childhood. Is this the way it will go, for all of us? Daisy wriggled on James's shoulder and he extricated his arm from Emily's to soothe and reposition her. Even the baby was silent, as if she understood the gravity of a funeral, the need for solemnity in the House of God. That was what Mum and Dad used to call it, the *House of God*, and Emily and her sister would try not to smirk or roll their eyes or any of those other things that teenagers falling out of love with religion so often did. Mum never got used to the idea that neither of her daughters wanted to carry on in the Catholic faith, and Dad, though silent on the matter, was saddened by it too, missing the presence of his daughters by his side at Sunday mass. Of course, Jess was gone long before Emily had the courage to pull away completely, but over the years she and her parents found a way to skirt around the subject, to avert their eyes from the disappointment in the room. Not that it mattered any more, because now both their parents were dead. Perhaps that was why Jess felt able to come back; perhaps it's always easier to face our loved ones once they're gone.

Daisy reached out towards her and Emily felt a pang of regret that she hadn't brought her to see Mum in the past six months or so. She had only been three or four months old the last time Mum saw her, and she probably wouldn't have recognised Daisy now, her early wisps of dark downy hair having morphed into soft blonde curls; they change so quickly in that first year. People are always saying that, aren't they: *make the most of these early days, they'll have grown up and left home before you know it*. When Mum last saw her she was barely rolling over, and now she had a whole world of her own: favourite toys and television shows, best friends and funny little habits. Only last week she had them all in stitches when they caught her leaning out through the old cat flap, desperately grasping for a dropped toy she'd spotted on the other side. Mum would have loved that story. Emily thought of all the other things they'd never discussed. Jess's disappearance. Dad's indiscretions. Emily's desperation to break away. Should she feel bad about these things? These missed opportunities to know her mother better, to love her more? Maybe it was just being in church again, the source of this guilt. Or maybe it was seeing Jess, sitting there, so alone, without family or friend by her side. Of course, she thought, we Catholics do a good line in those things – shame, anxiety, remorse. In reality, Emily didn't think of herself as someone too blighted by these emotions, but even as they drew closer to the front of the church, towards the elevated coffin at the centre of the aisle, she wondered if God had been watching when she shuddered in disgust at her mother's request for burial, still wedded as she was to the old Catholic rites. When drawing up their own family wills, Emily had firmly stipulated cremation for herself and James (along with a hilltop scattering, to go the whole hog), and she wondered what God thought of that – or what he thought as she popped her daily contraceptive pill, and consciously supported the concept of a woman's right to choose. *Bless me Father, for I have sinned – it has been twenty-one years since my last confession, and I've broken all the rules.*

She started to worry what the rest of the congregation would think if she didn't join them to receive communion, and as they drew closer to the coffin she became aware of the force of her breath pushing against her ribcage, straining to be released. She exhaled, slowly, silently, and when they came level with the front pew Jess turned and looked at her, as if she'd known she was there all along and could sense her anxiety. Jess smiled, gently, and Emily slid into the seat beside her and, without thought, slipped a hand into hers. And that was how easily they glided back into each other's lives: a simple moment of understanding, a shared point of grief in their adult lives.

And now here they are, three months later, in what feels like a scene from a nightmare parallel universe, small clusters posed around the house in the soft rising light of morning. They gather like portrait studies: the devastated parents bent over the dining room table, a police officer on either side; the huddle of strangers through the archway, poised to photograph the island worktop, the bloodied kitchen floor; the barely functioning aunt, a blanket around her shoulders, hovering in the doorway to the living room. Emily glances at James before she replies to the officer's question, giving an answer that accurately matches his. 'We arrived home together. At around 2am. That's when we found Jess on the floor.'

She can feel her sister's eyes on her; she feels the need in them, the way they implore her to turn in her direction, to look up and offer her hope. But she won't do that, can't do that. She stares at a dark knot in the wood grain of the table, focuses on the streaks and whorls of it, until she hears the faint tone of Jess from the other room, answering the inspector's questions in an oddly blunted voice. Now feeling strangely composed, Emily knows she only has herself to blame. *She* brought Jess back into this family, despite everything that went on before. She trusted her. She *forgave* her.

3. Jess

I'm sitting in the interview room at Newport police station, and all I keep thinking is, do they suspect me? Am I under arrest? The officer said not, that they just thought it was better to continue our interview at the station, out of respect for Emily's and James's feelings. But still, they bagged up my clothes, ran a pick beneath my fingernails and took my fingerprints.

'We'll be doing the same with James and Emily,' DCI Jacobs says. She has barely left my side since we departed Emily's house, helping me as I signed in at the police reception desk, busy as it was in the murmuring, restless aftermath of New Year boozing and brawling. She's told me she'll be in charge of the investigation. *Investigation*.

'You'll be bagging up their clothes?' I ask.

'Well, no. But then their clothes weren't covered in blood. It's all straightforward procedure. We need to analyse yours to establish whether that's your blood, Jess – or someone else's – or *Daisy's*.'

I feel sick every time they mention her name, every time a suggestion floats into the air, an unspoken implication that she could be hurt, or worse . . .

Another officer enters the interview room and places a cardboard cup of coffee on the table in front of me. I take a sip and wince: no sugar. I have a vague sense of him, a tall man in his forties, bearded, but my attention is focused on DCI Jacobs. She's the one I have to convince. He takes a seat beside her and fiddles with the recorder as she turns to a fresh page in her notebook, jotting down the date and some other words I can't make out from my position across the desk. And so the interview begins, going over all the same questions as before, and all the while I do my best to follow DCI Jacobs' advice, slowing down my thoughts before I answer, trying to visualise the scene. But it's hard, so hard, with these great slices of it missing.

'What time did James and Emily leave for their party?' DCI Jacobs asks, seamlessly returning back to the beginning again. Her expression is unreadable, the sharp lines of her face showing no clues as to what she really thinks of me, what she believes might have happened here.

'Just after seven,' I reply.

'Do you know where the party was being held?'

I look back at her blankly. 'No. I mean, I know it was at Marcus and Jan's house, but I'm not sure exactly where they live on the island. Somewhere near Shanklin, I think? *Fairbrother*. That's their surname.'

The inspector makes notes, even though the lights on the recorder show it is all being captured on tape. 'And how do your sister and James know Marcus and Jan Fairbrother?'

'He's one of James's oldest friends. And they're business partners – they joined their two IT companies together a few years back, I think. You'd have to ask James for the exact details.'

'So, you say they left for the party at 7pm? How can you be sure of the time?' She's clearly checking how reliable I am with the simple information, because she's asking so many of these kinds of questions.

'It was definitely close to 7pm – I know that's right because Emily had been stressing about leaving on time, and Daisy was still not quite settled. I was in the kitchen, and James was putting on his coat and locking the back door. Emily was standing at the foot of the stairs, complaining that Daisy was still babbling away in her cot, and I told them to get on their way, that she'd be fine with me.'

DCI Jacobs nods for me to continue.

'I've been looking after her since October, so I'm used to getting her to sleep.'

'Three months ago. So, that was when you first moved in with your sister's family?'

'Yes. Emily only recently went back to work. She's a teaching assistant at the local primary school. She'd interviewed lots of nannies and childminders but she hadn't found anyone she was happy with, so when I offered she jumped at the idea.'

'Are you a qualified childminder?'

My stomach lurches at the question; surely they suspect me, if they're asking questions like this? 'Not as such. But I did a bit of nannying on my travels, and I'm Daisy's aunt, so I guess Emily felt she could trust me –' The bit about nannying abroad is a lie and I flush hotly, wondering if they can tell. Suddenly the initial fib I told to Emily seems enormous, at once of great importance, but of course it's too late to go back on it now, all these months later. What would Emily think?

'And you say Emily hadn't been able to find a suitable childminder – why was that?'

'What do you mean?'

'What reasons did she give for their unsuitability?'

'Oh. I don't know – she's got quite high standards – dietary requirements, weaning plans, that kind of thing – and I guess some of them felt they couldn't work with that; and others just weren't, well, her cup of tea, I suppose. She's a really good mum, really conscientious. You've got to click with the person who's looking after your children, haven't you? You've got to be able to trust them.'

DCI Jacobs nods slowly. 'Have you ever had children of your own, Jess?'

I shake my head, finding it hard to meet her eyes. I don't like the feel of these questions at all.

'And what about Emily's stepdaughter, Chloe? She's, what, fifteen? I understand she was out for the night. How do you get along with her?'

'Chloe? She's a great kid, I love her. We get on really well.'

DCI Jacobs refers to her notes. 'I believe Chloe's mother died when she was very young – and Emily and James got together a year or so later?'

'Yes. I think Chloe was maybe two or three?'

'Does Chloe get on well with your sister – her stepmum?'

Is this a trick question? 'Yes,' I reply, but she registers the pause in my voice and instantly I feel as though I've betrayed Emily. I'm so bloody exhausted and I know I'm getting it all wrong; even when I'm telling the truth, my voice says I'm lying. How am I supposed to behave? How are you meant to arrange your hands on the desk – to focus your gaze – to pitch your tone of voice – when all the while you know they're on the lookout for tiny signs of nervousness and deceit? The despair washes over me and for a moment I can't even remember what she was asking me.

'Emily and Chloe?' DCI Jacobs' eyes widen slightly, urging me to elaborate.

'They're just a normal family – they get on one minute, fall out the next. I was the same at that age. Chloe's a teenager, it's what you'd expect!'

'But Chloe gets on well with you?'

'Yes, of course, but I'm not her mum, am I? It's easy for me. I try to spend a bit of time with her at weekends, to give Emily some space with Daisy. Em gets really tired; it's hard going back to work after having a baby.'

'How is she when she gets tired? Does she ever lose her temper?'

'No!'

An expression of disbelief is fixed on DCI Jacobs' face. '*Never*?'

I want to scream, the way she's turning me in circles. 'Well, of course she does *sometimes*,' I reply, irritation showing in my voice. 'She's not a robot! But not with Daisy, if that's what you're suggesting. Daisy's such an easy baby, Emily would never have cause to lose her temper with her. She's a *baby*, for God's sake! Ems might occasionally lose her temper with James or Chloe – me even – but never with Daisy.'

The questions keep coming. 'And what does Chloe think of Daisy? Is it possible she might feel a bit sidelined?'

I laugh, and I can tell from their expressions that it's not appreciated. 'No! If you think Chloe has anything to do with this . . .' I can hardly believe what they're implying. 'Chloe loves her sister! And anyway, she was staying with a friend last night. She wasn't even there. She was at Beth's house.'

The other officer jots down a few notes.

'So,' DCI Jacobs continues, 'let's get back to last night. After Emily and James left, did you check on Daisy at all?'

I think hard, walking myself through the unremarkable moments of my evening, careful to get it straight in my head before I answer. 'Yes, I did. I remember now, Daisy carried on chattering away in her cot for a while after they'd gone – I had the intercom on in the living room – but after about half an hour it turned into crying and I could tell she wouldn't stop unless I went up to her. As soon as I went in I could smell she needed changing, and I ended up having to give her a quick bath, she was in such a mess. I changed her sheets and put her in a fresh sleep suit, and then I sat with her on my lap for five or ten minutes before she eventually dropped off. Then I put her in her cot and went back downstairs.'

'Could someone have been in the house during that time, while you were upstairs?'

'No-o,' I reply cautiously, pausing a moment while I consider it. 'No, I really think I'd know. I definitely didn't hear anything, or notice anything different when I got back downstairs. And if someone had got in, then they would have had to hang around for, what, another four hours or so before snatching Daisy?'

But now I'm thinking, *could* there have been someone in the house with me all that time? Watching, listening, waiting for their moment?

'So when you got downstairs, what did you do?'

'Nothing – I told you, the TV was on, but I wasn't really watching it. I flicked through a few magazines; I probably snoozed a bit. I ate a few chocolates.' Both officers are staring at me, waiting for more. I don't know what they want me to say; what should I say? 'Quality Streets, I think.'

'Did you drink at all?'

I think about the bottle of prosecco that James opened in the kitchen before they left, surreptitiously pouring me a glass while Emily was starting the car. He handed it to me with a little smile, an *our-little-secret* kind of smile, and he returned the bottle to the fridge before racing out after her. 'No,' I reply. I know they will judge me more harshly if I tell the truth; that they'll suspect me. More than anything, I couldn't bear for Emily to know, for her to think that my having a drink was the cause of all this. I wasn't even drunk, I mean, not *drunk* drunk – just

26

a bit looser around the edges. It was New Year's Eve, for God's sake! Who doesn't have a few drinks at New Year? 'No, just tea,' I say. 'I remember making a cup of tea around eightish. Maybe 8.15.' I know I finished the bottle, because I remember going out through the back door to carefully push the empty far down into the recycling bin, to conceal it beneath the milk cartons and mustard jars and cheese cracker boxes. *Did* I lock the back door again? Yes, I'm certain, because I remember testing the handle before I went back to the living room, and then I know I dozed off for sure.

'And after that? Do you remember anything at all?'

'Nothing,' I tell DCI Jacobs, because, after that, I really don't remember a single thing.

I like to think of myself as the kind of person who finds it difficult to lie, but, if I search myself, I know that's a lie in itself. We all lie, don't we? Little fibs, everyday untruths, the tweaking of facts to help us sail through life more smoothly. We lie to our dentists about daily flossing, to doctors about our units of alcohol, to friends about why we arrived late; and, let's face it, daily to ourselves about how we're really feeling, what we're really thinking. Are they lies? Not if they harm no one, surely? It must be true that if their intention is only to make others feel better, to reassure, to remove the prospect of disappointment – surely that has to be a good thing? Not lies, perhaps, but mere fine-tuning. Take the lie about my nannying experience, for example: it was at Mum's funeral, when both Emily and I were giddy with the joy of our effortless reunion, that Emily had impulsively blurted out her idea that I could care for baby Daisy. My stomach had flipped over – *yes*, I knew, I would love that – but, as quickly as Emily had suggested it, a flicker of doubt or regret passed across her face like a dark cloud.

'I was a nanny in Canada for six months,' I said, so convincingly that I almost believed it myself. 'They were a lovely family, with a four-year-old and a young baby – the mum said I was a natural! I would've stayed if it hadn't been for my air ticket home.'

Emily's face had relaxed into a delighted smile, and I didn't feel bad about the lie; I knew I'd said the right thing. 'Leave it with me,' she said, and her eyes searched the room for James, finding him standing over at the fireplace talking to some of Mum's elderly neighbours. The trio of white-blonde women were animated, clearly entranced by this handsome man who chatted and laughed with ease, including every one of them in his attention. There was something boyish about him, and in the short few hours since I had met him I could see what the women found so enchanting about him. Already I liked James; he was one of the good ones.

'Will James be all right with it?' I asked, wondering how he would feel about me – essentially a stranger – moving into his home. I was startled by how anxious I suddenly felt at the idea of this spontaneous plan not becoming a reality.

Emily cupped her hand beside her mouth, and the conspiratorial gesture was so familiar that I wondered for a moment if I was dreaming. Could I really be here with Emily? Emily with her flawless fair skin and her glinting chestnut eyes, so like my own – Emily with her glossy dark hair and long manicured nails, still every bit the bigger sister, the grown-up. God, how I had missed her – how I had missed the things that made us so different; the things that made us the same.

She had smiled deviously. 'I'm the boss when it comes to all things childcare – he'll be *fine* with it.'

Of course, it did all work out, and within a fortnight I had packed my meagre belongings, sailed across the sparkling Solent waters to the Isle of Wight and moved into Emily's lovely family home. I must have got better at lying, I think now, because Emily didn't flush out the fib the way she usually would; either that, or my sister's inner lie-detector had weakened over the years. Or perhaps she had sussed me out straight away, spotted the lie, but wanted me anyway. Perhaps she needed me in her world again, wanted me entwined in her life as I had been before, when we were young, young enough to forgive each other our differences. Young enough to forgive each other our mistakes.

4. **Emily**

Emily can hear their voices through the nursery wall; she's sitting in Daisy's nursing chair, a small velour cat in her hand, her eyes resting on the shadow of cot bars cast across the carpet by the mid-morning sunlight. On a normal day off she might have been leaning into the cot right now, putting Daisy down for her first nap, smoothing down her patchwork blanket and twisting the clunky dial of her mobile until the moon and stars begin to turn and play. On a normal day, she might be heading downstairs, to put soup on to warm for lunch as she tidies away Daisy's scattered toys and James lays the table and pours the wine. On a normal day, her sister wouldn't be down at the police station making a statement, and Emily wouldn't be staring at the inkstained pads of her own fingers, and Chloe wouldn't be standing in the room next door with a hangover, about to hear the worst thing she's ever heard. Until this moment, Emily realises with sudden clarity, she has never really thought much about Chloe's relationship with Daisy. She knows she loves her, that she thinks she's adorable, that she cuddles her and plays with her and gently bops her on the nose every time she passes her sitting in the high chair.

But it still seems strange to Emily to hear Chloe talk about her 'little sister', when they're not *really* sisters, are they – not like Emily and Jess were, not brought up alongside each other since the youngest age, with the same mum and dad, the same grandparents, the same schoolfriends and childhood experiences. The only thing they really share is their dad, but everything else is different. How can they be like real sisters when so much is different, when their lives are so profoundly not the same?

Chloe's bedroom is next door. James is in there with her now, breaking the news to her that Daisy is missing. *Our baby is missing*.

Emily speaks the words, barely a whisper, '*Daisy is gone,*' and she wonders why she cannot cry in the way she would like to, in the way she ought to. There's no doubt that the sensations of shock and grief are fiercely at work within her, and yet Emily now feels incapable of giving life to them, powerless to let them out in either tears or words.

In contrast, she hears Chloe's grief exploding next door, the keening shriek of disbelief, the tumble of words and questions, set against the low, soothing tone of James's voice as he pulls her to him, muffling her cries.

Emily doesn't remember her little sister arriving, as she wasn't even a full year old when Jess was born, and so ultimately they grew up more like twins, with Emily reaching every milestone first and Jess trailing slightly behind. It was no wonder Emily was sometimes a bit harsh, a bit bossy with Jess; Jess wasn't younger enough for her to mother, but neither was she old enough to keep up and match Emily's pace. It wasn't Jess's fault, Emily knew, but it didn't stop her from feeling irritated at times, held back by Jess's unsteady feet or hesitant temperament. There were so many differences between them, not only in the physical sense

– Emily being fair-skinned and dark-haired to Jess's luminous complexion and golden locks – but also in the very core of their beings. Where Emily joined up to dance class and drama club and choir, Jess would rather seek out solitary pursuits like drawing or tending the garden or walking Victor the poodle for Mrs Shaw along the road. Jess's quiet nature was so often the cause of irritation in the outgoing Emily, and only now, when she looks back on her childhood, does she realise it was at the same time one of the qualities she most valued. They were close, of course, and if Emily concentrates hard enough she can remember the way in which Jess would sometimes mother *her*, talking her down when she got carried away with an idea, or when she lost her temper with a friend or got herself into bother at school. Jess had a quiet way of calming Emily as no one else ever could, and in her gentle manner she could be quite forceful. Emily recalls a fight with one of the rough lads down the street, when she was seven or eight, started when the boy – Connor Drake – threw a stick into the spokes of her bicycle, causing her to be jettisoned on to the grass verge at the edge of their suburban road. Emily had been furious, enraged with embarrassment – and she'd leapt to her feet and taken after him, knocking him to the ground, a knee pinning down each of his puny arms as she pummelled him at close range. She had despised him for humiliating her like that, for hurting her, for mocking her, and in that heart-racing, deafening moment she had wanted to pound him out of existence. When Jess caught up, his nose was already bloodied and he was crying for his mother despite being nearly ten years old. Jess had bent close and whispered, 'Let's go home,' but Emily had wanted to carry on, to punish him thoroughly. When she went to throw another punch, Jess caught her fist and drew it back, hooking the fingers of her other hand into the neck of Emily's shirt and gently reeling her off. 'Let's *go*,' she whispered again, and before Emily knew what she was doing she was trotting alongside her younger sister, fetching up her scratched bike and leaving the trouble behind without so much as a backward glance.

'Em?' James is standing in the doorway looking down at her, and she starts with a lurch, ashamed at her ability to sleep at a time like this. 'Are you OK?'

His face looks grey, and she can see the pain written through him, and she envies his ability to display his emotions so openly.

'I was just resting my eyes,' she replies.

The shape of Chloe passes on the landing behind him, and James and Emily stare at each other as the muffled tread of her feet descends the carpeted stairs. It's such a bright and beautiful day outside; the rest of the island will be busy congregating along the beaches and promenades now, for the traditional New Year's Day walk, as they build up an appetite for lunch, calling a cheery *Happy New Year* to every group they pass, commenting on what a wonderful start to the year this is. *Such a beautiful day.* She thinks of the holiday parks and amusements around the island, now shut down and vacant for the winter months, their Waltzers and Spinning Cups and Lazy Rivers standing idle, gathering moss as the locals reclaim the landscape. She thinks of herself as a local now, she realises, no longer a visitor. No longer a tourist.

They had said they'd drop by for a quick drink at Becca's in the evening; who would phone her friend to say they weren't coming? Not Emily – how could she even start to form the words? The loopy island swimmers will already have towelled themselves off after the annual Big Swim, and they'll now be propping themselves up in various local pubs, downing a well-earned pint of lager or a white wine spritzer or better still a warming brandy to thaw themselves out. Fleetingly, Emily craves a stiff drink. Who would blame her?

34

Her mind rushes over the confrontation she had rehearsed for when James arrived home last night. She'd planned to demand an answer to why he had insisted on staying at the party a little longer, encouraging her to return alone. As she had collected her coat and left the party, she'd scanned the room and its remaining guests and wondered, is *she* here? His mystery woman? Is he hanging back for her, waiting for his boring wife to piss off and leave them to it? But it was impossible to work out which one it could be. All the women love him, they all fawn over him as if he's the sweetest man they've ever encountered. *Wonderful James!* was what Jan had exclaimed when she and Marcus welcomed them in earlier that evening. *Wonderful James!* If he had just come with her when she wanted to go home last night, if he had just said *yes*, maybe she wouldn't be sitting here now; maybe they would have got home together in time to stop this happening – to save Daisy. The ghost of last night's anger presses against her chest and she suppresses it; none of that matters now. Nothing but Daisy matters now.

'What time is it?' she asks James.

He checks his watch, running his other hand through his hair so that it stands up in crazy peppered peaks. She wants to leap from her chair and straighten it out, to put him back the way he should be, but at the same time she knows she can't bring herself to touch him. Not now; not with Daisy missing. She can't imagine touching another human being for her rest of her life, if she can't touch Daisy again.

'Nearly one,' he says and Emily struggles to remember what they were talking about. Her eyes linger on the solid bones of him, his wrists, his shoulders, the clearly defined lines of his neck, and she wonders if she knows him at all. Does he know her? How strange to think of the places our choices take us; if she'd never met him all those years ago, she wouldn't be sitting here now. There would be no Daisy to go missing, no nursery to sit in, no pain to endure.

'Any news about Jess?' she asks after an awkward beat. She's been gone six or seven hours now. What are they asking her? It seems incomprehensible that they would think her a suspect, but she's been away so long. 'Why are they keeping her?' These last words come out in a rush, surprising her with their force.

James shakes his head. 'The family liaison officer says it's just routine – easier to interview her there than here, you know? To spare our feelings, I'd imagine.'

'Liaison officer? Is he still here?' Emily's pulse quickens at the thought of someone else in the house. She'd completely forgotten there was anyone else here. 'Where is he?'

'In the kitchen. His name's DC Cherry. I left him down there with a coffee and some toast.' His voice is weary, dull. 'He says he wants to ask us a few more questions when you're down, to build a picture of our lives. Friends, family and so on – our routines. He says he'll be one of our main contacts during the investigation.' James crosses the room and straightens the curtains. He stands at the window looking out across the drive, over the distant rooftops towards the blue horizon of the sea. The smart grey shirt he donned last night now hangs crumpled and loose. 'Chloe's home,' he says. She nods, and he turns, not hearing her reply. 'I went and picked her up outside the Albion – she'd walked there from Beth's house.'

'I heard you come in,' she says.

He looks hard at Emily, impatience creeping into his tone. 'I told her.'

Emily stares at him, wondering what he wants her to say; his expression is hurt.

He turns back to the window. 'She's devastated,' he says, pinching the bridge of his nose and taking a deep lumbering breath. 'I've never seen her so distraught. She's growing up so fast, and just now – well, she reminded me so much of Avril –' His shoulders rise and fall, and again there's a pause as he waits for some response, but Emily can't find one. She's stunned that he should bring his first wife's name into this. His *dead* wife's name. 'She adores Daisy, you know? She just kept asking me question after question after question – and Christ, a dad's meant to have all the answers, isn't he? But all I could say was, *I don't know, Chloe, I don't know* – and she looked at me like she was waiting for me to say it was all going to be all right –'

He turns back to face Emily, and she sees disappointment in his eyes. He wants her to reassure him, but she can't, no more than he can reassure Chloe, and she hates him for wanting it from her, for *expecting* it from her. As she unflinchingly returns his gaze, Emily senses his warmth draining away, and then suddenly he's shaking his head, shock-faced, and striding from the room.

'I'm going down to check on her,' he says, and he's gone.

Emily remains in the warmth of Daisy's room for another hour, maybe two, until the sound of the police car arriving on the gravel drive stirs her, and Jess's voice floats in through the front door, coaxing her out of her room. She wants to ask Jess if she'll phone Becca, to explain that they won't be coming, but at the top of the stairs she finds herself fixed to the spot. She can see Jess crossing the dining room, her arms outstretched. Chloe steps into her aunt's embrace, and sobs against her shoulder.

'It's going to be all right, Chloe,' Jess tells her.

Across the room is James, leaning up against the sideboard, one hand clasped to his mouth, tears spilling from eyes that are locked on his daughter and Jess. As Emily furtively observes this intimate scene she wonders, what is it she can see in his expression? Chloe turns from Jess and moves into her father's arms, and, as she does so, Emily reads meaning in the glance that passes between James and Jess. It's more than just simple gratitude, or reassurance; it's understanding. *They understand each other*, Emily thinks with detached certainty, and the old suspicions rise up in her like tiny flickering flames.

5. Jess

There is an unreality about returning to the house. Through the open window of the car I hear gull cries drifting in from the shoreline, and as we pull up on the driveway the dazzling light of early afternoon spills out across the gravel. Along the roadside outside the gate there are several cars and vans parked up on the pavement, and the officer driving gives a disgruntled *humph* noise at the sight of them. DC Piper, his name is, and as he drove me home he was friendly enough, allowing me to sit in the front seat beside him while he made small talk, acting more like a taxi driver than a man of the law. His beard is dark and full with a bold streak of silver running through the centre of it, like the markings of a badger, and I find myself staring at it, wondering if anyone has ever commented on it before. I'm told he's one of two family liaison officers assigned to Daisy's case – two because it's a major crime, a crime of great urgency and significance. *A major crime involving a minor.* These phrases fill me with dread, making my head throb with the harsh sounds of their words in my ears. Major crime investigation. Forensics. Witness statements. Abductee – *abductor*. Victim profile. I feel emptied out after the hours of questions, as DCI Jacobs went over and over the same events, probing me endlessly as if with each repeat I might suddenly remember more than I had the last time. In fact she had been right, because at some point I had a sudden flash of recollection – of a *sound* – and, while I couldn't be sure whether it was dreamt or real, I decided to tell her anyway. I was feeling a bit more trusting of her by this point, since she'd just received confirmation that my heart condition was real. The doctor who had checked me out on arrival was kind – spoke to me in the familiar language of blood pressure and capillaries and irregular rhythms. I felt safe as he pressed his two fingers to my wrist, peered studiously into my eyes with his little torch, listened carefully to the sounds I created through the earpiece of his stethoscope.

'Well, I'm happy with your account in the main part, Jess,' DCI Jacobs had said. 'I've seen your medical records, and I understand that you have a history of this kind of thing – a long-standing condition, I think?'

'It's fairly rare –' I started to say, but I saw the notes in front of her and I knew that wasn't what she wanted to hear about. We weren't there to talk about my health.

'So I understand that the fainting is a symptom of your condition, and that there can be various triggers to set it off, such as stress – or shock?'

'Well, yes, but not always.' *Stress.* The word made it sound so wishy-washy, as if it's not a real thing. As if I'm just a hypochondriac, or one of those people who passes out at the sight of blood. 'It hasn't happened for a while, but the doctors think I'll need a pacemaker if it continues – if I start to have more than two episodes a year.'

'Yes. Thank you, Jess, that's helpful.' I could see she was just being polite, eager to move on to the real subject. 'Now, we're going to need as much as you can give us. Can you think of anything unusual at all that happened last night? Anything that may have triggered your reaction? Any strange phone calls – visitors – smells or sounds?'

And it was that word – *sounds* – that triggered my memory, the flash of it rushing to the front of my mind the very moment she said it. After I'd drifted off on the sofa, I told her, I thought I was roused by the sound of glass, a bit like the sound of bottles clinking against each other in a carrier bag. When I say I *thought* I was roused, it really was as vague as that, as if I had been dreaming – a frustrating dream about being in a busy pub crowd in which I was pushing and pushing and never quite reaching the bar – and so as I was waking I just thought the glass sounds were part of that dream, because they stopped as soon as I focused in on them. DCI Jacobs wrote this down, but she looked slightly perplexed, and I wondered if I shouldn't have mentioned it at all. Now, I think maybe it just makes me look even more unreliable than I did before. She asked me again if I'd been drinking at all, and again – that bottle of fizz looming large in my mind – I said no.

'Why is that so important?' I asked her.

'Because people behave differently when they've been drinking,' she replied.

Not me, I thought, though of course I know that's not true. *Everyone* behaves differently when they're drunk.

It seems strange to be knocking at the front door now, rather than using my own key, but I'd been taken to the station with nothing more than my coat and gloves, my only thoughts being of Daisy and my growing panic over what might have happened to her. There's a rushing sound of feet over gravel, and I turn to see half a dozen men and women with raised cameras and notepads coming at us, calling my name. *My* name. Fear surges up through me, and I want to hammer at the door and scream out to Emily and James, *Let me in! Let me in!* But instead I freeze, the flat of my hand against the door, staring at it mutely, waiting for what feels like forever.

'Jess? Give us a picture?' One of the reporters is right up next to me, sweaty-faced and reeking of body odour and snapping a photograph as I bring up a concealing hand a second too late.

'Jess! Who do you think took Daisy?' They've got me surrounded. I'm vaguely aware of DC Piper, who puts himself between us, holding up his palms in a 'back off' gesture, trying and failing to shield me from their cameras and questions. 'Jess! Is it someone you know? How's Chloe? How are Emily and James coping? Jess!'

As the front door is cautiously opened from the inside, DC Piper gives me a light shove in the back and we stumble over the threshold, shutting the mob outside. *But she's only just gone*, I want to scream back at them. *How do you people know about it?* This thought vanishes in a moment when I see Chloe, standing by the kitchen table, her hand curled beneath her chin, thumb hovering at her lower lip, her face shrouded in pain. When she raises her eyes to meet mine, I rush to her, holding on tight as she weeps against me. James stands at the closed door, talking quietly to DC Piper, and I wonder where Emily is; the house feels so quiet without her in the room. The dread weight of bereavement hangs over the house. There's a tall, thin man I assume to be another officer on the far side of the kitchen, and he raises a hand to me in polite greeting as he stirs sugar into a cup of coffee and heads out through the back door with a packet of cigarettes.

'That's DC Cherry,' James tells me. 'Family liaison officer.'

So he's the other one, I think, as the shape of him disappears beyond the frosted glass panel. A *family liaison officer* – until today a term I'd only ever heard used in TV and books – never in real life, never an actual person drinking coffee at your dining room table or smoking cigarettes in your back garden.

'You poor love,' I whisper, so only Chloe can hear, and I smooth the tangled hair from her wet cheeks and hold her like a child. She stinks of stale booze, and of course I know she hasn't been with Beth all night; she's probably not even been to sleep yet. Fifteen, nearly sixteen. So young, but so much the person you'll always be. So ready to make reckless mistakes for the sake of new experience and adventure. 'Have you eaten?' I ask her, still holding on.

Chloe shakes her head, and when I look beyond her I see the dark expression on James's face. He's destroyed; he's leaning back against the kitchen worktop, one hand gripping the counter behind him, the other covering his mouth, and tears stream down his cheeks as he watches Chloe wrapped in my embrace. They're lost without Emily at the centre of things, organising them, sorting everything out, leading the way. Where is she? I wonder, knowing even in this moment that her competitive instinct would begrudge my stepping in to offer comfort in her absence. It's true it's not my place, but I can't let go of Chloe, this girl who needs a mother more today than she ever has in her life. DC Piper is still standing in the doorway, and I turn my head towards him with a nod of thanks which he takes gratefully as his cue to leave. As the door clicks shut behind him, I hang on to Chloe, cradling her head against my shoulder, and silently I watch James until he finally looks up and meets my gaze. 'It's going to be all right, Chloe,' I say, but it's James I'm looking at, James I'm trying to comfort.

When we were old enough, Mum and Dad bought us guinea pigs, one each. Mine was white and tufty with pink eyes, and Emily's was a smooth patchwork of brown and tan with jet-black eyes. I decided to call mine Doctor Who, which Emily thought was stupid, and she named hers Taz, which I thought was a good name as he was made up of similar colours to the cartoon Taz.

It had taken years to convince our parents to let us have any pets, until Emily quite rightly concluded that if we started nagging for a dog, then a cat, eventually they would give in and allow us some smaller pet. We brought them home in the springtime, and at first we played with them all the time, letting them out of their wooden pen to run about in the open garden, while we raced ahead setting up obstacles and tunnels, luring Doctor Who and Taz through with trails of carrot pieces and kibble. Sometimes we made a competition of it – 'Piggy Crufts', Emily named it – where we would construct two identical courses in which the guinea pigs would race to complete the run in the quickest time. Doctor Who never won; he wasn't as streamlined as Taz, and, while he was just as motivated by food as his slim brother, he liked to take his time over it, nibbling each new discovery with dignified care, while Taz simply stuffed his treats down and raced on. For the Piggy Crufts grand finale, Emily invited all the neighbourhood kids along to watch, and by the end of it Taz had achieved an unblemished hundred-per-cent win rate. Emily was delighted, swinging her glossy ponytail as she allowed everyone to hold him, pronouncing hers the Champion Guinea Pig. She was always more competitive than I was, and, while I really didn't mind that Doctor Who wasn't as fast as Taz, her endless bragging that afternoon started to fray my nerves, and more than anything I felt sorry for Doctor Who.

Everyone helped themselves to the beakers of orange squash Mum had brought out. I jumped up on the edge of the crumbling rockery and clapped my hands, feeling a flutter of nerves at drawing attention to myself so boldly. The group turned towards me and for a moment I was lost for words. 'Now it's time for the beauty contest!' I blurted out. It was as much of a surprise to me as it was to Emily. I guess I just wanted to give Doctor Who a chance at winning *something*. Emily scowled; this wasn't part of the plan.

The dozen or so children all gathered closer, and it was agreed that we should pass the two guinea pigs around the group so they could each take a good look at both contestants before casting their votes. When we were ready, I stood to the left of the hutch with Doctor Who, and Emily stood to the right with Taz. In order to vote, our friends simply had to walk over and stand by the guinea pig they judged to be the cutest.

Undeterred by my improvisation, and still buzzing from Taz's recent victory, Emily kissed her guinea pig confidently and cried out, 'Cast your votes!'

Our friends rushed forward, and to my amazement all but one of them was standing on my side. Next to Emily and Taz was the lone figure of titchy Sammie Evans, Emily's most loyal friend, but even she looked as though she might have preferred to be standing with the rest of us. Ben Christie scooped Doctor Who from my hands and held him skywards. 'The Winner!' he shouted dramatically, and the crowd broke up, the game having come to an end.

The next morning when I went to feed the guinea pigs, I found Doctor Who huddled in the corner of the hutch, his face an indigo mess where he had been trying to lick clean his darkly stained hind quarters. Lying on the floor beside the hutch were two fountain pen cartridges, both of them pierced and entirely emptied of their contents.

6. Emily

Emily lies in the bath, wishing she could disappear into the steam altogether. It's coming up to forty-eight hours now since Daisy disappeared and the police don't seem to be any closer to finding her, to finding out what has happened. She tries not to think about the significance of the passing of time: in the hours that followed the discovery of Daisy's disappearance Emily sat at her PC, robotically Googling 'missing children' in a bid to find something, anything that might provide clues to bringing her back home. But everything she found seemed to relate to either runaways or parental abductions, and the few statistics relating to unknown kidnappers were chillingly spare. The one message that came through loud and clear was this: the first twenty-four hours were crucial. After the first twenty-four hours, a child's chance of being found alive plummeted dramatically. But twenty-four hours has been and gone, and now they are approaching forty-eight hours, and the odds are stacked against them. In all that time, Emily has barely slept, apart from these occasional minutes of deep slumber from which she finds herself waking with a start, as she remembers it all again.

This afternoon, after the doctor had been called out to see her, Jess had persuaded her to take a bath, to brush her teeth and wash her hair and freshen up. 'You'll feel a lot better after a bath,' she'd said gently, sitting across the table from her, trying to coax Emily into making eye contact. But Emily was mesmerised by the glow of Jess's hair in the window light; the blonde locks of her childhood had transformed into darker sun-kissed waves that rested untidily around her shoulders, unkempt, unadorned. It was this that Emily always envied: her carelessness.

'Ha!' Emily had retorted, as though it was Jess's fault she was like this, filthy and near-insane with worry. She could see Chloe sitting in the corner seat of the room, her attention fixed resolutely away from the rest of the family, her thumbs scrolling up and down the screen of her smart phone. She's barely said a word since she heard the news, and Emily wishes she could gather up some feeling of compassion towards the girl, but she can't, not when all her thoughts must stick to Daisy. '*What are we going to do, Dad?*' she had heard Chloe whispering to James on the landing late last night. '*We can't just go to bed, can we? Shouldn't we be doing something? How can we sleep?*' Her voice was urgent, childish, and yet in those few words Emily was shamed by her own lack of agency, as she lay in her bed, staring helplessly at the ceiling. When they rose this morning they had discovered that Chloe had been up all night, launching a #findDaisy campaign on Twitter and Instagram and countless other forums, and, while Emily's immediate emotion had been one of fury at the public intrusion, Jess and James had convinced her it was worth a try. She had no fight in her, and she'd sat as she was instructed, and waited for the doctor to arrive.

Though her body is inert, hands floating loosely in the hot bathwater, Emily's mind jumps from thought to thought, back and forth over the past two days. It tangles and writhes, never ceasing, even through the welcome fog of these tablets.

'How many of these are you meant to take?' Jess had asked James, scanning the leaflet that came with the perscription. It seemed strange to Emily how they all carried on like this, with DC Cherry the quiet, gaunt-faced liaison officer constantly there, hearing their every word, their every breath. There was no point in asking James, Emily had wanted to say, bitterly glancing across the room where he stood at the kitchen window, staring out over the wintry garden. This man was barely recognisable, so unlike the confident, light-hearted James that she'd left at the party just days ago, mingling like a pro and topping up the glasses of the good and the beautiful. 'Emily, he's an *angel*,' Jan had called over to her that night, as she passed him two more bottles of champagne from behind their marble-topped drinks bar. 'Marcus has buggered off somewhere, so I've commandeered your good man. I adore him!' James had laughed, taking the two bottles in one hand and blowing them each a kiss, one after another.

In the absence of an answer from James, Jess had continued to read the instructions to the end of the page, before fetching her sister a glass of water and sending her off to the bathroom with a clean towel.

'Thank you,' Emily had whispered before shutting the door behind her, but she wasn't sure if Jess had heard her or not. She didn't even know if she'd spoken it out loud. Thank God she's here, Emily thinks, smarting with guilt over her earlier ill feeling; who else would talk to James and Chloe otherwise? Who else would make them eat, and ask them if they're all right, and check if they needed anything? Who else would answer the endlessly ringing phone and chase off the reporters who have started camping out on the street and knocking at the door at all hours? It's hard enough for Emily to listen to her own thoughts and horrors, without having to live through their tortures too. James is as broken as she is right now, and Emily can find nothing to say to him, nothing of any value. She can gather no sense of feeling for him; for Chloe; for herself even. *Eighty per cent*, she thinks, visualising the number in her head. That was another of the statistics she uncovered online yesterday. The number of relationships that break down after the loss of a child. *Eighty per cent*.

Her skin has turned pink, leaving two pale circles where her knees protrude from the hot water. She presses her toes against the hot tap, topping up the bath, sending more steam billowing out into the room. The police said they'd like to do a television appeal tonight, and they want her and James there, to speak to the cameras. *To make a statement, an appeal to anyone who might know something.* Emily replays these words in her mind. These aren't the kind of sentences a parent should ever have to hear; they belong in TV dramas or the ten o'clock news – they belong to other people. If she didn't feel so subdued by medication, Emily knows her heart would be racing now, with the fresh terror those words bring. 'Will it make a difference?' she had asked DCI Jacobs. She knows how the public view these appeals; she's not stupid. How were you meant to conduct yourself in a situation like this? In the face of such horror, how could you gather the strength to address a room full of cameras and journalists, to speak the words aloud, without publicly breaking down? And at the same time, she knows, it is impossible to appear blameless in the absence of such an open display of grief. It's what the public *want* to see. They want to measure up the parents, assess their emotional responses for authenticity. Every person in every household around the country will be watching them speak, and they'll be wondering, *are they behind it? Is he guilty? Is she?* She's thought it herself, when watching some poor beggar or other imploring their missing teenager to make contact, to come home, and she realises now, with shame, that she's flippantly thought, *well, that's that, she's dead for sure.*

Is Daisy dead? She thinks of the photograph the police took away on that first night, the one of her snapped by a pop-up baby photographer in Portsmouth on a Christmas shopping trip last month. It's this photograph that is now the official image of Daisy, the picture that every news channel and newspaper in the country has featured, heading up the daily news along with its horrible nod to modernity: Chloe's #findDaisy hashtag. It's not even the best picture of her, but it's the clearest, a close-up portrait, well-lit, with an ugly mottled backdrop that makes her soft baby form stand out starkly. She's a little too pale in it, and her smile not quite full, but her blonde curls and clear blue eyes are captured exactly. My Daisy, Emily thinks now. My little Daisy. 'This is perfect,' DC Piper had said, and he'd smiled at the photo, adding, 'She's a bonny little thing, isn't she?' Emily stares into the memory of that photograph. Is it conceivable that her beautiful, smiling Daisy is dead?

'*She's not.*' She hears the answer, spoken clearly into the vapour-filled room, and slowly it dawns on her that she said the words. These tablets are strong, she thinks with more clarity; she must be careful when taking them. At the same time, it feels good, the numbness she's experiencing now, the way in which she can think it all through, dispassionately; rationally. She has a sense of profound understanding tickling beneath the surface of her conscious thoughts, as though *she* holds the key to Daisy's disappearance, to her whereabouts, as though the answers lie within her alone. She draws her hands up and over her face, pressing the tips of her fingers into the dark hollows of her eyes, concentrating hard, trying to unravel it all. Her mind rests on James, on the freeze-frame image of him as he entered the house that night to find her stooped over Jess's blood-stained body, screaming at her to talk, to tell her what happened. Already the police were on their way; after charging up the stairs and finding

51

Daisy gone she had phoned them – it was the first thing she had done. She remembers the emergency operator telling her to slow down and speak more clearly, and when she asked if anyone was hurt Emily found herself back in the kitchen standing over Jess, looking down at her prone body, at the golden mess of hair fanned out around her side-turned head, and she'd said *no*. Why had she said no? She focuses hard on that image, trying to get herself back into the moment. She had been used to Jess's fainting fits, ever since they started in childhood, and she'd been known to have the occasional nosebleed too. But Emily would have thought all that would've stopped long ago, that Jess would have grown out of it, so why wouldn't she have taken this seriously, finding her sister in that state?

In her mind, she repeats the sequence and tracks back again to that first moment when she walked through the front door. She was completely sober, as she'd offered to drive that night so that James could have a few drinks with Marcus and their various colleagues, but in the event she'd driven home alone as James had insisted on staying on for a nightcap. So, she'd walked in through their front door, surprised not to find Jess curled up on the sofa watching TV in the living room, and while nothing was obviously out of place she had immediately sensed something wrong; a *stillness*. And then she had seen her through the open archway to the kitchen: Jess, or at least her legs, stretched out on the hard floor, just visible beyond the island unit that dominates the large room. Throwing down her bag and keys, Emily had rushed to her – yes, that was the first thing she did – and straight away she'd felt for Jess's pulse. Thank God, it was there, a strong beat, and she'd shaken her roughly, calling out her name, even slapping her cheeks with a light hand in an attempt to bring her round. And she *had* come round, with a gasp of shock, but she had looked dazed and she'd whispered,

'Daisy?' – and instantly Emily had smelt alcohol on her breath, and thought, *she's pissed*! She had been so angry, she'd shaken her again, furious that she would even contemplate drinking when looking after their child, but Jess had grabbed the sleeve of her coat and tugged her closer, repeating, 'Daisy!' with such urgency that it had sent a pinch of cold fear right through her, and Emily had recoiled and rushed for the stairs.

That was why she'd told the operator no one was hurt; she had really thought Jess was just drunk, that she was OK. And if she's completely honest with herself, she thinks now as she hooks the plug chain between her toes and allows the bathwater to drain away, the moment she discovered Daisy was missing, she couldn't have cared less what happened to Jess.

The first time Jess was rushed into hospital, Emily travelled in the back of the ambulance with her and Mum. Jess was nine, Emily ten, and as there had been no one else at home they had all had to go. Emily remembers the flutter of excitement she felt as the paramedic tended to Jess, fitting her with a breathing mask and strapping her arm up in a tight blue band. Emily clung to her mother, sitting on her lap as the vehicle sped towards the hospital for the first, it turned out, of many visits they would make over the next few years.

To begin with, having no concept that Jess would be anything other than fine at the end of it, Emily enjoyed the thrill of the hospital. Together they were rushed into A&E, where Jess was looked at by an endless stream of concerned and smiling doctors and nurses, and Emily and her mother were swept along like special guests with a backstage pass. For a while there were three or four medics squeezed into the side room where Jess was, so to make space Mum told Emily to step outside the booth to sit on one of the plastic chairs facing the open doorway. Emily could still see everything that was going on; Jess was now fully awake and quietly answering their questions, lying perfectly still on the trolley bed as they listened to her heart, shone lights into her eyes and talked among themselves. Briefly, Emily thought *she* would like to be one of those doctors in a white coat, that she would perfectly suit the medical setting with her clear-thinking mind and her ability to organise things. Her last school report home had said, 'Emily is an outgoing, responsible and hard-working member of the class. She's a pleasure to teach, and a good example to others.' She could remember it word for word, so proud was she. Jess would be no good in a hospital at all; she'd get horribly upset every time someone couldn't be fixed or, worse still, if they died. Her school report had used the words 'sensitive and thoughtful,' so she'd probably be better off working in a library or a nursery school or something quiet like that. But Emily would be perfect as a doctor! She would cure people and save their lives, and they'd forever remember Dr Emily, perhaps even naming their girl babies after her like they did in the movies. The A&E corridor was busy, with occupied wheelchairs and trolley beds passing by every couple of minutes, parents carrying crying infants, teenagers limping past on crutches. She made a point of smiling at them all, practising to achieve an effect of sympathetic confidence, but her smile faded quickly when the victim of a road traffic accident was rushed past her on a gurney, the surgical wadding doing nothing to hide the damage inflicted on the poor man's face.

'Emi!' her mum called from Jess's booth. Emily could see that Jess was now sitting up, beckoning her sister to join them. She had a slightly bemused expression on her face, but the colour had returned to her skin and she was smiling.

'Is she going to be all right?' Emily asked, only now feeling a flood of anxiety that had earlier been completely absent. Her gaze returned to the empty corridor where the crash victim had just been, and she burst into tears.

Jess reached out and pulled her on to the bed to lie beside her. 'Don't cry, Emi,' she said, patting her shoulder reassuringly. Emily felt good lying there in Jess's warm embrace, the focus of concern having suddenly shifted to shine brightly on her. She nestled in beneath Jess's arm where the hospital smells of bleach and metal mixed contentedly with the scent of Vosene that still lingered in Jess's freshly washed hair. 'I'm going to be fine,' Jess told her. 'It was just a funny turn, that's what the doctors said, didn't they, Mum?'

'That's right,' Mum said, and Emily looked up to see her mother tugging at her bottom lip as she stood and watched her two girls curled up together on the hospital bed. 'Just a funny turn.'

But time would show them all that it wasn't just a funny turn, and, although Emily couldn't imagine it now, the initial excitement of the hospital ward would soon wear thin. She wasn't accustomed to Jess soaking up the full light of her parents' attention, and, when her sister's 'funny turns' threatened to become a regular occurrence, Emily sought out their sunlight in the only way she knew how: by casting a few shadows.

7. **Jess**

Last night I sat in the living room and watched the early evening news with James and Chloe, the three of us awkwardly spellbound by the TV screen as a miniaturised James and Emily, bleached out by grief and the white flash of cameras, appealed for the safe return of their child. Across the front of their press desk was a white banner emblazoned with black lettering – #findDaisy – and I wondered how many tweets and retweets that little phrase had prompted, and how likely it was that anyone out there would ever read it and think, *yes, I know where Daisy is, I can help you find Daisy*. Did these things work? Were they a waste of time, a waste of hope? I was conscious of DC Cherry, standing discreetly behind us in the doorway, and of the light creak of the stairs as Emily took herself to bed, unable to face the horror of her life being played out to the television viewing public. 'Can I get you anything?' DC Cherry asked, but we shook our heads, not looking round at him, all of us nervously transfixed by the TV. He's slept in the spare room the past couple of nights, and he's said he's happy to stay as long as we want, but I know Emily can't bear it, can't stand the idea of him observing our every move as we wait for something to come to light. Between him and DC Piper, we're covered around the clock, and while that should be reassuring to a family in our situation, to have someone on hand to help field the media intrusion and liaise with the investigating officers, it's actually deeply unsettling. The sense of being under scrutiny is intense; Cherry and Piper work for the police, after all. So it goes to reason they're investigating us, no matter how supportive they might appear to be. I give them twenty-four hours before Emily puts her foot down and they're out.

The on-screen Emily described what Daisy had been wearing that night, spoke of the bright red strawberry birthmark still visible on her right shoulderblade, and the velvety grey elephant that had disappeared with her. 'She can't sleep without it, so I'm glad she has Ellie with her . . .' she said, trailing off, her expression suddenly bewildered by the reality of her words. Gone was the polished, confident woman of just a few days ago; this sallow, lank-haired version was unrecognisable. Chloe was sitting between me and James on the sofa, and I felt her bring a hand to her mouth, heard the gentle gasp of anguish that escaped her lips as she watched, and I eased my arm around her shoulder to pull her close as she silently wept. James too reached out for her, slipping his hand into hers. 'OK, Chlo?' he whispered, and she nodded, though of course we all knew she was not.

On the screen James was reading from a sheet of paper on the desk in front of him, and he spoke slowly, carefully, looking into the cameras every few seconds, his calm exterior belying the inner turmoil he was surely experiencing. 'Please, please, if you know where Daisy is – if you think you know anything about her disappearance – I beg you to contact the police and let them know. All we want is our little girl back home. She'll be missing her mummy and daddy, and her big sister Chloe, and all the other people who love her. All we want is Daisy back home where she belongs.' His appeal complete, he lowered his eyes to the sheet in front of him. To me, he looked as though he was trying to hold it together, to keep from breaking down. But to the rest of the world, I thought, with his measured words and his clean-cut, faultless delivery, he could almost look guilty.

This morning I slept late, waking sluggish after sharing a bottle of wine with James last night. Emily hadn't come back downstairs for supper, and when Chloe headed off to bed at nine DC Cherry did the same and I found myself sitting across the table from James, wondering what it was I needed to do to help him. He seemed to have aged in the space of three days, his skin grown slack, with dark circles etched deeply beneath his eyes. For several minutes we sat there, unmoving, he seemingly spellbound by the tightly clenched knot of his own fingers on the table before him, me looking on, unable to unearth the right words. The soft click of Chloe's bedroom door closing upstairs seemed to snap us both into some kind of activity, and as his eyes looked up and met mine I said the first thing that popped into my head: 'How about a glass of wine?' God, he looked so grateful, I could have cried. So I opened a bottle, and we drank and talked, not just about Daisy, but about all sorts of things – we talked about his work, about the places I'd been on my travels, the places we'd still like to go, the things we'd always wanted to see. He spoke warmly of his great friendship with Marcus, his oldest friend and business partner, gently mocking his lavish but chaotic lifestyle with glamorous Jan and their six unruly children. *Six*, James repeated, incredulous, and I ached for his loss. He described Chloe in words of such affection, and I saw him in a whole new light, and I was touched by the way his later love for Emily had never diminished his first love for his daughter. One bottle led to two, and it was only my sense of sisterly duty that stopped us from opening a third, as my eyes swept past the clock and saw it was gone one o'clock. Emily wouldn't thank me for a hungover husband in the morning. I fetched James a glass of water, watched him neck back two paracetamol to ward off the hangover and sent him up to bed as I blearily cleared away our glasses. Without thinking, I unlocked the back door and pushed the two empty wine bottles to the bottom of the bin, instinctively knowing that Emily wouldn't like the thought of James sitting up drinking with me. None of us needs any further cause of upset at this dreadful time.

As I lie in bed staring at the ceiling, I trace over the past few months living here with Emily. I'll never forget that ferry crossing, as I stood on the front deck watching the island come into view, gradually drawing close enough to pass the affluent houses dotted along the coastline, those sprawling residences sheltered by surrounding woodland to create mini island retreats of their own. There must be some money here, I thought, as I watched two small children bouncing on a netted trampoline at the top of a lush tended garden that meandered down towards the stony shore below. It was October. Already autumn was turning the leaves to rust, and the bright sunlight on the water had taken on that cool, sparkling quality that feels clean on the eyes. I was a foot passenger, and, as I disembarked with my travelling rucksack and single holdall, I felt the overwhelming sense of life starting over. Seabirds screamed noisily overhead, ducking down to pick up crumbs outside the terminal café, and I scanned the ferry loading area for sight of Emily, walking out towards the exit road as she'd instructed me. When I saw her, my breath caught in my chest: there she was, my big sister, waiting for me. She was standing beside a showroom-clean Range Rover, her figure neat and composed, her dark bobbed hair whipping around her head in the seafront breeze. On spotting me, she threw up her hands with a joyous shriek and raced to meet me. I dropped my bags and we embraced as if we might never let go – as we used to as children – and I thought, she really has forgotten everything that happened before. She really has forgiven me.

When I get downstairs, I find everybody is up already. James *does* look a little jaded, but I can tell he's trying to inject some normality as he places a bowl of boiled eggs on the table in front of Emily and Chloe. He indicates for me to sit down and help myself. I take the seat opposite my sister and offer to help her to eggs, but she puts up a declining hand and instead reaches across the table for the coffee pot. Her face looks drawn; I swear she's lost half a stone in the past few days.

'You ought to eat something,' I say quietly.

She doesn't reply. She doesn't even look up.

'Ems,' I persist, 'I'm worried you're going to make yourself sick. Please try to eat just a little bit. Even if you don't feel like it, those pills of yours aren't meant to be taken on an empty stomach.' I butter a slice of toast and reach across to place it on her plate. 'Just a few bites?'

A flicker, a little nod, and she picks up the toast, taking a small mouthful and washing it down with coffee, continuing until she's eaten half of it. Chloe is sitting beside me, and I chop the head off her egg and pass her a slice of white toast. I know she's fifteen, but still she likes to have the top chopped off for her. Emily always says she refuses to spoon-feed a teenager, and I wonder if she's forgotten how much our mother used to do for us when we were that age. And then I wonder if it was just me that Mum needed to help, because, now I think about it, it seems Emily was born capable, able to master anything she puts her mind to without anxiety or fuss.

Chloe gives me a little smile, and dunks a soldier into the top of her egg. The yolk is hardening; she'll be sad about that.

61

We've had many a conversation about the perfect consistency for the perfect boiled egg – about how much Marmite is too much – about which chocolate is best, Dairy Milk or Galaxy; which smells nicer, baking biscuits or rising bread. From the moment I moved in we hit it off, finding we could chatter away for hours on seemingly inconsequential subjects, discovering our shared pleasures in life and bonding over a mutual love of the ridiculous. While Emily was busy with Daisy or having an early night, Chloe and I would often sit up late for a box-set marathon, both of us glad to watch the recommendations of the other, happy for James to come in and join us, to catch the tail end of our laughter and tears. I guess our relationship felt more sisterly than niece-aunt, and that was fine all round. Perhaps I was enjoying playing the older sister for once. I don't know; you could analyse these things until the end of time and still be none the wiser. All I know is that Chloe and I had a close bond, that she trusted me, and loved me, and that was why I kept her secret. Now, though, sitting at the breakfast table, Chloe's phone bleeps and she leaps up to retrieve it from the kitchen sideboard. And, as she stands in the cool morning light that streams in through the back door, a sudden thought hits me, and I feel sick to my stomach, because this thought – this recollection – means I'm going to have to betray her trust. I'm going to have to tell Emily and James about Max.

8. Emily

Emily can barely find breath for the rage that is roaring inside her. Her fingers worry away at the sore, gnawed edges of her thumbnail, the weekly routine of her French manicure now abandoned in anguish.

This morning, as soon as Chloe had left the table and headed upstairs, Jess said she had something to tell her and James, insisting that Emily stay seated at the table when all she wanted to do was crawl back upstairs and into bed. As Emily registered the anxious strain on Jess's face she felt a lurch of nausea as the unbidden thought *she knows something* sprang to the front of her mind.

'About *Daisy*?' The words barely made a sound in the suddenly quiet dining room.

Jess's eyes darted from Emily to James, and she bit down on her bottom lip the way she would when she was little, when she was embarrassed or ashamed – or guilty. She leant back in her chair to check on DC Cherry, pacing up and down the garden having his morning smoke before DC Piper arrived to take over. What was the point of him? Emily wondered, her mind lurching away from whatever it was Jess was about to hit them with. DC Cherry with his gently probing questions and continual log-keeping. He writes down everything – who visits, who calls, what time they go out, when they return – and he's constantly asking subtle questions, casually dropped in as he offers to make coffee or volunteers to drive them about. All his presence does is add to her overwhelming anxiety, to her daily sense of having her life ripped from her. To her sense of having done something wrong.

Emily's thoughts were broken as James leant in to the table, his expression grave. 'Jess?'

'It's about Chloe.' Jess looked over her shoulder towards the stairs, and turned back to them, her voice carefully lowered. She paused, and, though Emily could clearly see the turmoil she was in, her patience and escalating fury was threatening to boil over.

'*Jess*,' she hissed. 'For *God's* sake, spit it out!'

Jess held up her hands and shook her head, as though trying to clear her thoughts. 'Sorry – I'm sorry. It's just I promised to keep her confidence, and I feel like a complete bastard for betraying her. But it's just something I remembered a few minutes ago, when I was sitting here at breakfast – and, well, it might be relevant.'

'Relevant to what?' asked James.

Jess blinked, the words hesitating at the edge of her lips. 'To the night Daisy disappeared.'

To Emily's astonishment, Jess went on to tell them about Max. It seemed that a few weeks into Jess's stay with them she had discovered that Chloe had been keeping a secret, in the form of boyfriend Max, and for some reason had agreed to keep quiet about it, until Chloe was ready to introduce him. James and Emily had absolutely no idea about him, and in fact had often talked about the fact that Chloe seemed singularly indifferent to the opposite sex; she'd *told* them she wasn't interested in going out partying like so many of her peers, preferring DVD nights in with best friend Beth, cosied up in their pyjamas with a bowl of popcorn instead. It all made for a reassuringly wholesome picture of their daughter's independent life, perhaps a picture neither of them had wanted to question too closely. Was it all a lie?

'How did you find out about him?' James asked. He was stunned; he reckons he knows his daughter so well, Emily thought, and now he's having to recalibrate his mind to accommodate this different version of her.

Jess looked down at her hands, choosing her words carefully. 'There was one afternoon, in early November I think, because I remember the fireworks had been keeping Daisy awake at night and she was a bit off colour. We were meant to be at our Friday soft-play that afternoon, but Daisy had grizzled all the way through the first half-hour – so we'd come home early. I'd literally just got through the front door and hung up my coat when I heard the key turning in the back door.'

Emily could feel the steady pounding of her heartbeat. She nodded impatiently for Jess to continue.

'I didn't move. I suppose I was momentarily scared it was a burglar or something – and I watched them come tumbling through the back door – Chloe and this boy – laughing, and I thought, *he's been here before.* They still couldn't see me round the corner, and I watched as he went straight to the cupboard for a glass – he knew where it was – and then helped himself to orange juice from the fridge. When I stepped into view Chloe nearly had a heart attack.'

'How long has it been going on for?' James asked.

'I'm guessing every Friday afternoon,' Jess replied. 'Soft-play runs from 2.30 onwards, and I'm rarely back home before five. Until that day, there'd been a clear month or so when the house had been empty pretty much every Friday afternoon.'

'How old is he?' James asked, as Emily's impatience strained closer to the surface.

'I don't know. He wasn't in school uniform, but he looked fairly young to me – not much taller than Chloe and quite slight. He had freckles like that kid on the front of *MAD* magazine. Seventeen, perhaps?' Jess's attention moved between James and Emily, as she tried to gauge their reactions, anxiety in her expression. 'Chloe says he's a nice guy.'

James looked pale. 'Are they sleeping together?'

The force of Emily's fists slamming down on the breakfast table was violent enough to send the knives clattering. 'Jesus! What the hell does it matter if Chloe's shagging her boyfriend, when Daisy's missing?'

Jess flinched, her disapproval instantly written in her eyes, and Emily hated her as she saw James and her exchange a fleeting, horrified glance.

'Of course it matters!' he rounded on her in suppressed anger. 'How can you even think like that, Emily? She's *fifteen*. I know Daisy's missing – don't you think my world has fallen apart too? But Chloe's still here – and we're still her parents. I'm *still* her father!'

Emily's heart hardened a little more, and, with no acknowledgement that James had spoken at all, she turned to Jess. 'I don't understand why you're telling us this now, Jess. And, more to the point, I don't see how it has anything to do with Daisy's disappearance.'

Jess frowned. 'But don't you see? Chloe had forgotten her front door key, so they had to come in through the back.' She paused, waiting for Emily and James to catch up. 'And the only way through the back door is with the spare key you keep in the greenhouse, isn't it?'

They both nodded, still clearly struggling to understand.

'Which means that you, me and Chloe aren't the only ones who knew where the spare key is kept. Max knew about it too.'

'The spare key,' James murmured. 'Shit, how could we have forgotten about the spare key?' In a heartbeat, he was on his feet, sprinting through the back door and up the garden to the greenhouse, to retrieve the spare back door key from its hiding place, inside a gardening glove beneath a flowerpot, tucked out of sight behind the aluminium shelving.

'Is everything OK?' DC Cherry appeared in the back doorway, alerted to the fresh panic. 'I've just seen James running down the garden – what's going on? Has something happened?'

Both women shook their heads, not wanting to speak until their suspicions were confirmed. DC Cherry fell silent, knowing better than to press them, his attention on the greenhouse at the far end, waiting for James's reappearance. Long minutes passed, and the sisters sat gazing at each other across the table, one glaring, the other on the brink of tears, with nothing but the whirring buzz of the fridge freezer to break the silence.

As the phone started ringing again, James reappeared in the doorway, panic radiating from his tautly held figure. 'It's gone,' he said, breathing heavily, turning to DC Cherry, preparing to tell him everything. 'The key's not there.'

Now, as Jess fills the kettle for what seems like the hundredth cup of tea, all Emily can do is wait for the police to return. She stands at the kitchen counter, a pill in one hand, a glass of water in the other, averting her gaze from Jess and James and the ever-present DC Cherry. She doesn't know how much more of this she can take. She swallows the tablet down; swallows down her feelings of heartbreak, of terror, of betrayal. And waits.

It had been easy for Emily to love Chloe when she first met James. She was the sweetest little thing, not yet two years old, and the way she adored her father would have thawed even the coolest of hearts. When James first introduced them, it was over Sunday lunch at his house, and Emily marvelled over the ease with which he prepared and served the roast meal, carving and pouring wine, all the while tending to Chloe in her high chair at his side. When she needed spoon-feeding, he did so with minimum fuss; when her face wanted cleaning he vanished her mess with a quick swipe of the napkin, chucking her under her chin to turn her objections into a smile. They were a delight to be around – not only James, but Chloe too. It wasn't just James Emily fell for; it was the pair of them, the whole package. Being part of it made her feel warm and complete – wanted, needed – and gradually, she knew, indispensable.

And of course, it was her tacit appreciation that they came as a package that helped James to fall for Emily so easily. Secretly Emily acknowledges this as clearly today as she did back then, and she wonders how different things might have been if she hadn't so embraced the role of mother that had been implicit in James's invitation to start a new life with them over on the island all those years ago. It was a such a happy time when they set up home together, Chloe no longer having any need of a nanny, and Emily stepping effortlessly into the caring role. Not once had she felt envy at the little girl's devotion to her father, or his to her, and for the first ten years, at least, they had been a tight unit, happy in their small family clique, really needing no one but each other for happiness and companionship. Each morning, when James headed off to work, Emily and Chloe would busy about like long-time companions – Emily clearing dishes, filling sandwiches, sorting the laundry, Chloe racing up and down the stairs, searching for misplaced shoes and homework – and then they would set off for school together, walking along the coastal path in all weathers, their hands linked and swinging between them.

Emily thinks of those simple days, of that sweet little Chloe, and she wonders where she went. Who could find her in the Chloe of today, with her secrets and silences, with her glowering moods, her hidden thoughts and long absences? That lovely little Chloe gradually shrank away inside the impostor who now inhabits the bedroom beside Daisy's; vanished inside the thorny, black-eyed gazelle who now trails down the staircase behind her hollowed-out father. *This* Chloe is not so easy to love.

DCI Jacobs tells James she thinks it best initially to interview Chloe at home, with her parents present, where she might feel more relaxed about opening up. Chloe is sitting in the living room, waiting, as they speak in whispers in the kitchen, agreeing how to proceed.

After James discovered the key missing, he had first phoned Beth's parents, only to hear that Chloe hadn't stayed over at their house in months, and then DC Cherry had taken over, phoning around until he tracked down DCI Jacobs, who'd said she would come over straight away. Although none of them said it, they were all taken aback at the speed with which Jacobs reacted to the new information, and the three of them had waited anxiously for her arrival, delaying the moment they must call Chloe out from her room. Strange how they have become three: Emily, James and Jess.

'If we don't get anywhere with her this morning,' says DCI Jacobs now, accepting a cup of coffee from Jess, 'we'll interview her again at the station. We're not out to scare anybody, but sometimes the formality of the police station environment can be enough to extract the truth, if it's a little slow in coming.'

James agrees, and Emily leads the way through to the living room, glad to leave Jess alone to clear up in the kitchen. Ever since Daisy went missing, Jess has become a spare part, and with no specific job role to fulfil it seems she has clung to the new responsibility of 'carer', automatically taking over the household duties of cooking and cleaning, running errands, and making sure everything and everyone is all right. On the one hand Emily is grateful; on the other, she wishes she'd simply vanish into thin air – as if she'd never returned at all – and leave them to moulder in their grief. Emily is growing impatient of her sister's constant presence, however helpful; no one should be able to bear such close witness to a crisis of this kind – it should be something private, sheltered within the confines of family, between a husband and wife. Not that she and James are *actually* married. This has always bothered her, and his excuses that he doesn't see the point, that it would bring up painful memories of the past, don't wash with Emily. 'As far as I'm concerned, you *are* my wife,' he had said to her at that New Year's party, his eyes heavy with drink. 'As far as I'm concerned, *I'm not*,' she had replied. 'You married *Avril*,' she'd added, knowing this would hurt him. '*Avril's dead*,' he'd said in a hushed whisper, his expression aghast, shaming her. She had seen the dark film of sadness pass across his eyes, and she'd fetched her coat and left. Those were her last words to him before the nightmare unfolded; those were her last words to him before Daisy disappeared.

Whenever that same argument comes up, James reminds her he is more than happy for her to call herself Mrs King, to refer to them as husband and wife, in the same way as she refers to herself as Chloe's mum. If she was worried about what the outside world thought of them, wasn't that enough? To be Mrs King in name, if not on paper? No, she thinks now, as she takes her seat on the sofa beside James – no, it's not enough. A wedding ceremony sends a message to the rest of the world – a message of significance, of devotion – of belonging. Why wouldn't he want to do that with her, *for* her?

'So, Chloe . . .' DCI Jacobs begins. She has pulled her armchair closer to Chloe's, so that the leather arms are touching. Emily notes with irritation how the inspector didn't even think to ask her permission, just went ahead and moved their furniture, exposing a nasty great carpet indentation where the chair had previously sat. 'I'm sure you're feeling a bit worried right now?'

Chloe nods, her face drained of colour. She looks tall and gawky, too big for the school uniform she still has to wear.

'Well, there's nothing to worry about, so long as you're truthful and clear in your answers. You're, what, fifteen? OK, so your parents are here to make sure they're happy with everything – but you're old enough for me to talk to you like the young adult you are. So if everyone's ready to start –' she turns and looks to James and Emily for their approval '– we'll chat as if it's just us in the room, Chloe, just you and me. OK?'

Chloe nods again. There's a defensive air about her, and she looks like a cornered animal, her eyes restless and furtive.

The inspector smiles at Emily and James, a closed-lipped businesslike smile, to acknowledge that they are starting. 'Let's start with Max Fuller. Would you describe him as your boyfriend?'

'Yes,' Chloe mutters. Her gaze flickers briefly towards Emily and James, but she doesn't hold eye contact. She's ashamed, thinks Emily. As she should be.

'And Chloe, how long have you been seeing Max?'

'Since the end of the summer holidays – just before the start of school.'

DCI Jacobs makes a note. 'So, it's quite serious, then? That's four months. That's a long time to keep it a secret.'

Chloe shifts in her seat. 'It's not a secret; I just didn't want Emily and Dad to know about it.'

Emily bristles. She still hasn't got used to Chloe using her first name, having adopted the habit about a year ago, and it still hurts.

71

'Why not? It's the kind of thing most parents would want to know about.'

Chloe shrugs, fixating on the seam of her jumper cuff.

'Is he older than you, Chloe?'

No answer.

'Chloe?'

'A bit.'

Emily turns to look at James, who has the appearance of a man about to vanish inside himself. She watches the rise and fall of his throat as he swallows, his eyes never leaving his daughter.

'Just so you know,' DCI Jacobs says, her gentle tone giving way to the subtlest threat, 'my officers back at the station are running checks on Max as we speak. So we'll soon have all his details – how old he is, where he lives, whether he has a criminal record of any kind. Are we likely to find anything we don't like the look of, Chloe? I'm not asking you to betray him; we *will* find out anyway.'

Chloe shakes her head violently. 'No! He's a nice person.' For the first time she looks directly at her father. 'You'd like him, Dad – I just didn't think you'd like me going out with anyone while I'm in the middle of my GCSEs.'

'How old is he?' James asks. Emily notices how strangled his voice sounds, as if he might cry.

Chloe doesn't speak for a moment, lacing her fingers together, over and under, as she gathers her reply. Then she juts her chin out, a challenge. 'He's nineteen.'

James half rises from his seat, but Emily reaches out a stilling hand and he sits again, dropping his forehead into his hands. 'For Christ's sake, Chloe – *nineteen*?'

Chloe starts to cry, and, when James moves towards her, both Emily and DCI Jacobs react to prevent him. He drops back into his seat, his face awash with unease as he distracts himself by rolling up his shirt sleeves, smoothing out the trouser creases along his thighs. His shirt looks barely ironed, his manner dishevelled and restless. The vertical furrows that mark out his jaw as strong are clenched, the blue of his eyes more startling. It reminds Emily of how he was when they first met, of the strength she gathered in response to his vulnerability, and she shuts the memory down as quickly as she thinks it.

'Can we just stick to my questions for the time being, please?' DCI Jacobs asks, regaining control of the situation in a second. She raises a flat palm towards James. 'Everyone, please, just take a deep breath. There'll be plenty of time for you to talk together after this. For now, we just need facts.'

Chloe wipes away her tears, visibly trying to compose herself. 'OK, he's nineteen, but he's been really respectful – you know, about me not being sixteen yet.' She looks at Emily meaningfully, clearly hoping she'll understand, but Emily looks away.

'But you've been staying over at his flat, haven't you? When you told your parents you were staying with Beth, you were actually sleeping at Max's house?'

'Yes, but we've never – you *know*. I swear!'

'OK, so you're not sleeping together?'

'No.'

'So what *do* you do together?'

Chloe looks lost.

'Do you go out, to the cinema for example, or for pizza?'

Emily can feel her heart rate increasing; what the fuck is this woman going on about? *Pizza*? Why isn't she asking her about Daisy?

'Well, mostly we stay in and watch films together, and we like walking on the beach late at night, after everyone else has gone home. Max hates sharing the beach, he says. He likes it when it's completely empty and we have it all to ourselves.'

'And you, Chloe? Do you like that too?'

'Yes. It's peaceful. Max says the world is too full of stuff that doesn't matter – that if we wanted to we could all live with less stuff, less money, and just do the things we want to do, make up our own rules. Look at this place,' she says, her eyes casting around the large, plush living room, at the Christmas tree still standing tall by the bay window, its lights unlit. The look on her face is pure disdain. 'We've got far more than we could ever need. It's obscene.'

James looks shocked.

'*His* words, I presume?' Emily says, biting down on her fury, containing herself with shallow breaths.

'*He's* right,' Chloe retorts, and a flash of hatred passes between the two women.

DCI Jacobs throws a reproachful glare at Emily, and shifts round in her seat, drawing one leg up under the other, in a more intimate pose. 'Max knew about your spare back door key, didn't he, Chloe? He knew where it was hidden?'

Chloe's panic breaks through and she's on her feet. 'I know what you're all getting at! You're looking for someone to blame for Daisy's disappearance, and Max is just the person! You've got it *so* wrong!'

DCI Jacobs remains cool, indicates for Chloe to sit down with the briefest jerk of her chin. Chloe obeys.

'Of course that's not what we want. We want to find Daisy, and in order to do that we need to establish the chain of events that night. So again, Chloe, did Max know about the spare key that was hidden in the greenhouse?'

Swiping tears from her cheek, Chloe gives a little nod of her head. 'Yes. Just once, I forgot my front door key and we went round the back and let ourselves in. He was with me when I fetched the spare from the greenhouse – but, when we got inside, Jess was home, and Max went pretty quickly when we saw she was there. I doubt he even remembers about the spare key. It was ages ago.'

'Did you put the key back?'

'Yes. When Max had gone, Jess told me to return it to its hiding place, and we could forget all about it.'

'Forget all about it?' asks Emily. 'About what?'

'About Max being there. Jess promised she wouldn't tell you and Dad.'

Emily turns to James, hoping to exchange a moment of united anger, but he won't look at her. Out in the hallway, the phone is ringing again, and Emily glances towards the doorway, sees the briefest flash of Jess as she sprints past to grab it. It's not a reporter, Emily can tell, by the way Jess wanders back past again, the phone held casually to her ear. Another bloody well-wisher, she thinks, another friend wanting the inside scoop. Why can't they all just leave them alone? Another blur of movement, and DC Piper passes the door, having just arrived to take over from Cherry; Emily must tell DCI Jacobs she doesn't want them here any more, at least not staying overnight. It's too much; it's just too much.

'So, Chloe,' continues DCI Jacobs, 'where do you suppose that key is now, if you or Max haven't got it?'

She looks affronted. 'How should I know? Dad or Emily probably used it – or Jess.'

DCI Jacobs turns to Emily and James for their response.

'No,' they both reply.

'And I've already checked with your aunt, and she says she hasn't used it either. So, we'll need to get to the bottom of that, won't we? We'll be checking with Max once we've taken him in.'

'Taken him in?' asks Chloe, aghast.

'Yes, of course – we'll need to talk to him –' DCI Jacobs breaks off as a call comes through on her mobile phone, sounding out the alarming ring tone of an old-fashioned telephone. She mouths an apology as she steps out of the room to take the call, leaving James, Emily and Chloe sitting in silent and suppressed fury.

When the inspector steps back in it's clear that the interview is over. 'That was one of my officers,' she says. 'They're off to pick up Max now. It seems he does have a criminal record, Chloe, whether you knew about it or not, so we're going to need to interview him as a matter of priority.'

'What for?' James calls after DCI Jacobs, jumping up to follow her to the front door. 'What's the criminal record for?'

Emily can hear the urgency in his voice, the fear, and she thinks, please, God, let it be a driving offence – a pub brawl – drugs. Please, God, let it not be to do with children – anything but that. She stands in the doorway of the living room, watching her husband and DCI Jacobs, their shapes darkened against the glass panels of the front door.

Lowering her voice, the inspector tells him, 'It looks like nothing more than petty theft and an old caution for possession of cannabis, but let's keep that from Chloe for now, shall we? She might give us a bit more information on him if she thinks he's been dishonest with her. Might encourage her to volunteer something useful?'

James turns to look at Emily, his eyes searching for something – support, affection – love? Whatever it is, she can't give it to him, and, as DCI Jacobs exits the house to the snap and flash of the waiting press, Emily heads up the stairs alone and returns to bed. Her last lucid thought is: Chloe has concealed this from them for all this time; what else could she be hiding?

9. **Jess**

This morning I set off early to walk the Tennyson Trail alone, driving out to Alum Bay before dawn and reaching the hilltop monument in time for the Solent sunrise. There's rarely anyone to be seen at this time of day, and the peace and serenity of this natural spectacle expands in my chest as I wrap my coat closer, pulling my scarf up over my nose and mouth. Somehow the crisp beauty of moments like this seems to sharpen the pain of losing Daisy; in the mundane, everyday grief of her absence, sensations are dulled, like sounds heard from below water. But the recurrence of these natural events, events that continue day after day in spite of our human tragedies . . . somehow such beauty has the power to illuminate and intensify feeling, and for the first time in days I allow my tears to fall.

At Emily's house, I can't do this. At Emily's, I must be strong and solid, the person they can depend on to keep life ticking along. There, I can cook, clean, drive Chloe around, field unwanted phone calls, see off doorstep reporters, run the gauntlet of the weekly supermarket shop. I can listen quietly, give approval, make gentle suggestions, empty the laundry basket, discreetly fold Daisy's clean baby clothes and slip them away. I can put out the empty milk bottles, open up my arms for needful embraces, switch off the TV when the inevitable news updates appear. But I can't cry. To do so would be cruel, self-indulgent, when James and Emily have lost so much. Of course, I am heartbroken too at the loss of Daisy; that precious child inhabits my every waking thought. But I don't have the right to show my grief. Not in the face of Emily, who conceived Daisy, gave birth to her, held her to her breast as an infant, and hadn't yet even seen her take her first tottering steps. To cry would be an insult. She needs protecting as much as possible, when she has so much to bear.

I think about the phone call from Sammie yesterday afternoon. Apart from a few brief words at the funeral, she and Emily have barely seen each other since their teens, and Emily said it herself, she's fed up with all these 'friends' calling to get the latest gossip on the case, to draw themselves into the drama of it all. Sammie means well, of course – she'd seen the TV appeal and wanted to see if we were all OK. She did ask to speak to Emily too, to let her know she was there for her if she needed anything, anything at all. And I told her, thank you, it will mean a lot, and I'll pass it on, but not to expect a return call straight away because Emily's not in much of a state to talk at the moment. Sammie said she'd try again in a week or so, and I told her it was probably best if she waited for Emily to call, when she was ready. I hope she wasn't too upset by my fobbing her off, especially after everything she did for me around my mum's funeral, putting me up when I had nowhere else to go. She's a precious friend, but the family needs shielding, and I'll do whatever it takes to protect them from more hurt.

I narrow my eyes at the red-pink horizon, willing my mind to clear, to move momentarily away from the nightmare of the here and now. But it's impossible, and I hate myself for even trying.

It's been two days since DCI Jacobs came and interviewed Chloe, since they took Max in for questioning. It seems an age away now, and in that time it seems the fractures in the family have deepened, with each of them retreating to their chosen corners of the house, into their own private state of misery. Emily is popping pills like there's no tomorrow, and I am certain she's taking more than prescribed, knocking back the wine when she's supposed to avoid alcohol altogether. But who can blame her, who can take that small comfort from her, when all she wants to do is sink into dreamless sleep to escape the dreadful reality? James is in his own private hell, masking it as best he can, making small talk with Cherry and Piper, plying them with endless hot drinks and sandwiches, treating them as much like guests as Emily treats them like visiting salesmen. The liaison officers are clearly used to this; they accept James's hospitality for what it is – the desperate time-filling attention of a devastated father. They ask easy questions, listen to James's concerns, making notes and following up on any queries the family might have. They *liaise*. Chloe, for now grounded from leaving the house – even for school – only leaves her room to fetch food or use the bathroom. I've been popping in and out of her bedroom to check on her, but now she's even uncommunicative with me, who she usually sees as an ally. I know she's finding it hard to forgive me for blowing the whistle on Max; but I didn't have any choice, did I? I would *never* have betrayed her trust, but Daisy's disappearance has changed everything. When James found that key to be missing, the police had to know, didn't they? After all, I wasn't foolish enough to think that I wasn't still under some kind of suspicion myself, and, if the missing key was enough to give the police another lead, then I had to let them know. If there was any chance – however remote – that it could bring Daisy back, Chloe's secret had to come out. I've told her this, and I know the rational, caring part of her understands; I know she'll come round to me again.

How do the police ever get to the bottom of these things, I wonder, when everyone lies so routinely? Look at Chloe, how effortlessly she told DCI Jacobs she wasn't sleeping with her boyfriend, even embellishing the untruth by saying he was 'respectful' of her age. I was in the kitchen when the interview was going on, but the door remained open and in the frozen silence of the house I heard every word spoken. Perhaps she would have found it harder to lie if I had been in the room, if she had had to look at me. Me, who sat down with her after that first encounter with Max, who asked her if she was being careful. 'Careful?' she had repeated, knowing exactly what I meant. 'You don't want to get pregnant, Chloe,' I'd replied. There was no point in being anything other than direct in these matters. She had laughed, and after I'd finally got the truth out of her – that they'd been sleeping together for a couple of months already – I persuaded her to let me take her to the family planning centre to get checked out and arrange some reliable form of contraception. She begged me not to tell her parents. 'Emily will literally KILL me,' she had fretted, as we left the clinic, a white pharmacy packet secreted in her school rucksack. 'Believe me, Chlo,' I'd replied, 'I've got more to worry about on that front than you. I think Emily would kill me first.' We had laughed, and hugged, and never spoke another word about it again.

Maybe some lies are best kept. I don't know; I'm no expert on the matter. When it comes to secrets and lies, sometimes I worry I'm so full of them that one day they'll just come spilling out of me, in such a rush of shame and torment that they'll wash my new life away, Chloe and all.

*

I was seventeen when it happened, and yet, when I think back on it, I remember myself as so much younger than Chloe seems now at fifteen. Was it because of my heart condition, and the kid gloves my parents used to handle me after I'd started having my episodes? Or was I just naturally quieter, shyer, less bold than others? It was something that came up at every parents' evening – the teachers' coaxing suggestions that I should be more ambitious, put my hand up more, *be more like Emily*. It was impossible to avoid the comparisons; we were in the same class, after all, Emily one of the eldest, me, the youngest. I was smaller, quieter, less visible all round – and to be frank I was perfectly happy that way. 'We can't all be in charge,' Emily once told me as I sat cross-legged in our shared bedroom, following her instructions to line up our soft toys in tidy classroom rows as she set up her miniature teacher's desk. 'It would be chaos if we all tried to be in charge.' She must have been eight or so at the time. What kind of eight-year-old uses the word 'chaos'? But she was right, we *couldn't* all be in charge. Emily and I had always been treated more like twins than sisters, and, with less than a year between us, that was how we behaved. I was the subordinate ape to her silver-backed gorilla. And I was fine with that; Emily's extroversion gave welcome shade to my quiet ways.

It carried on this way right into our teens, and when Emily worked out that I was pregnant she kept it to herself for a week or more, her rage bubbling deep, before she finally confronted me on a rainy Tuesday morning as I got ready for college. Despite my remorse and fear – and my abject terror of what the future might hold for me now – I remember a tiny part of me thinking, *she doesn't like it when I do something first, no matter how awful that thing is. And she doesn't like it when I keep secrets.*

She was waiting for me when I got out of the shower, sitting on my bed, her hands folded neatly on her lap.

'Bloody hell, Ems! You scared the life out of me.' I nearly dropped my towel at the sight of her, but my startled smile quickly faded when I saw the hard line of her mouth, the seething shine of her eyes.

The party loomed large in my mind – both the bits I remembered and the bits I did not – and I'd known right from the start, deep in my gut, that things could never be the same again between my sister and me. How could they be? When terrible things like that happen, they change the way you look at the world, the way you look at each other, and you're altered permanently, with no hope of return to the state of life before. Our relationship had been strained for weeks, ever since the party, ever since that horrible, terrifying blank hole that opened up around me at Sammie's house. At the time, we'd been over it again and again, Emily worrying away at it like a child at a scabby knee, demanding that I try harder to remember the exact sequence of events that night, to remember what really happened in the bedroom while she was dancing with Sammie and the others downstairs. The fact that I couldn't recall any of it didn't take away my grotesque sense of disgust at what must have occurred while I was absent from myself – and still, night after night, I would wake, my breath caught in my throat, the helpless sensation of being paralysed overwhelming me, threatening to send me under.

But how could I explain any of this to Emily? She wouldn't believe me; didn't believe me. As far as she was concerned, I was to blame for what happened that night. 'You're a tease,' she had said again, the morning after the party, talking to my back as I stood at the kitchen worktop making tea with shaking hands. 'You give off this virginal not-interested vibe, Jessica, but all the time you're loving the attention.' She was leaning up against the kitchen table, the stains of last night's mascara still streaked down her cheeks.

'*What* attention?' I had whispered through my tears, still not turning to face her. 'I never wanted any of his attention.'

'Well, you got it!' she'd hissed, and for several weeks that had been the very last thing she said to me.

When she got mad like this, all I wanted to do was put my arms around her until she stopped thinking bad thoughts about me, and in the old days that was just what I would have done. But not now. These days she didn't want my arms about her; she wanted Simon's.

'Close the door,' she whispered now, as I stood shivering in my towel. Mum and Dad were still in the house, bumbling about, Dad getting ready for work, Mum in the kitchen taking her rota turn at preparing the floral arrangements for weekend mass.

I drew my towel closer, quietly pushing the door closed behind me. I really didn't want to be alone with her. I knew that expression; I knew I wouldn't like what was coming. She barely moved as she spoke, and my gaze became transfixed on her lips, as the damning words flowed from her, floating into the room like black smoke.

'So, when were you going to tell me?'

I gawped back at her.

Really? her expression said to me. *Really, you're going to deny it?* She jerked her chin towards my belly, the movement aggressive, disgusted. 'You're pregnant,' she said simply.

I couldn't speak. I just *couldn't* speak, and I crumpled to my knees, pulling my towel tighter, my sense of nakedness suddenly overwhelming. I shook my head – I wasn't denying it but trying to shake it away, to expel this horror from my thoughts. To give it words was to give it life.

'You're trying to tell me it's not true?' Her words came out incredulous, a nasty scoff punctuating the question. 'Jessica – I know you better than anyone knows you – better than you know yourself. Do you think I haven't noticed the change in you? The nibbled breakfasts. The pale skin, the shaky hands in the morning – the dry-heaving in the bathroom. My room's right next door, for God's sake. I can hear everything!'

'I'm sorry,' I said. It was all I could think of. It was what I thought she needed to hear, though I'd said it a hundred times since that dreadful night, when she'd dragged me out of that room and away from the party, mortified at the behaviour of her pathetic little sister, her sister who gets into God knows what state and shows her up and lets her down. Her little sister who spoils everything. 'I'm sorry,' I said again, because there was nothing else available to me. *I'm sorry. I'm sorry. I'm sorry.*

Beyond my bedroom door, Mum was saying goodbye to Dad on the front step, something she'd done every morning since I could remember, a strangely formal ritual that seemed to belong in the 1940s: he in his shapeless grey solicitor's suit, she in her pinny.

'Will you look at me, Jess?' The hard edge in Emily's voice had softened. 'Jess?'

I hadn't realised I was crying until this moment, and I wiped the palm of my hand across my face. The action felt dragged out, like a film on slow-play.

'So I take it that it happened there? At the party? Unless you'd been at it before then too –' Her words stung – they were intended to, suggesting I was some cheap slut who slept with anyone who came her way. How could she even think it? Before that night, I'd never even kissed a boy.

I gasped. 'I – I haven't – it's –' There were no words to convey what I wanted to say, the shame and fear I felt.

Emily's face was starting to harden again, her hate for me expanding in the face of my cowardly blustering.

'Yes,' I said, defeated. 'It was that night. But, Emi, I don't remember a thing!'

In a rush, she was on the floor beside me, her arms encircling my bare shoulders, her face pressed into my damp hair, and she was crying and rocking me, and I never wanted her to let me go.

'It's OK, Jess,' she whispered into my neck. 'I'm here for you. I'm sorry I'm so hard on you, but you can't go on pretending nothing's happened, can you? We'll get this sorted, OK? We'll get this all sorted and no one ever needs to find out about it.'

And that's how I found out I was having an abortion. My big sister told me, and that was that.

When the sky has morphed from pink into blue, I leave my hilltop bench and continue along the Tennyson Trail, aiming to reach Carisbrooke by one o'clock, where I can grab a sandwich in town and catch the bus back home. The gulls are flying high, soaring to great heights before bombing down towards the choppy waters, and the great expanse of open grass and gorsey meadow spreads out before me, giving me the sense of being the last person on earth. From here, there are no houses to be seen, no cars, no litter, no noise but for the screech of birds and the rush of wind and ocean, and when I turn in arm-flung circles there is only blue and green stretching out all around me, reaching fingers of rich colour towards the white rocks that tether the island to the sea. As I approach the stile, the goats appear, startled and staring on the path ahead. So I'm not alone, I think, and I step up on to the wooden strut and jump over, but the goats aren't taking any chances and they bound towards the cliff edge and disappear with a graceful leap. I gasp in shock at their sudden demise, and in a beat I'm after them, racing towards the wire-chained precipice, leaning out as far as I can go without falling, and I see them: two white horny heads huddled together on a narrow ridge not five feet below. I marvel at their nimble art, the way in which they must know this landscape, to leap so fearlessly from the rock face, confident that they will thrive.

My phone rings in my jacket pocket, the sound of it startling as it breaks through the tranquillity of my escape. I don't recognise the number, but I can't just let it go, in case it's something, *anything* to do with Daisy. 'Hello?'

As soon as I hear her voice, I recognise it as DCI Jacobs. I scrabble to my feet and return to the trodden path, now marching with purpose, as if this might somehow help me to think, help me to answer her questions correctly, to not get it all wrong.

'Is it a good time to talk, Jess?' she asks.

A whistle of wind howls past the mouthpiece, and I tug up my collar to shield our conversation. 'Yes – yes, it's just a bit windy. I'm walking.'

'Well, I won't keep you too long,' she says, her tone brisk as ever. Strangely, I realise it's one of the things I like about her: she is who she is, and that's reassuring. 'There are two things. Firstly, you and your sister, Emily. It's only just come to my attention that until recently you two had been estranged for many years. Is that correct?'

'That's right,' I reply, a knot of nervousness balling up in my gut. 'We met again at my mother's funeral last year.'

'So I understand. My condolences. And, before that, it was sixteen years since you'd last seen each other?'

'Uh-huh.' I really don't know what else there is to say.

'Jess, I'm wondering why neither of you thought to tell me about this estrangement?'

'Why would we? I don't see how it –'

DCI Jacobs interrupts. '*Everything* is relevant in a case like this, Jess. Everything. Family disputes, disagreements with colleagues, suspicious neighbours – anything that might lead us towards reasons – possible motives – for Daisy's abduction.'

Abduction. The word is so violent in its simplicity. It conjures up faceless men in the night, cloaked figures who spirit babies away, pied pipers with evil intent. I mustn't cry, I tell myself, I must stop this constant desire to cry, and pull myself together – for Daisy's sake, if for no one else.

'Yes, of course,' I reply, trying my best to sound like a good, trustworthy person. 'Of course.'

'So, Jess, can you tell me the reason for your separation from your sister for those sixteen years?'

I know that she will have already asked Emily the same question, that she will have phoned the house first before trying my mobile phone, and my mind scrambles to find the answer that Emily will have given her. What would she have said? What would Emily do in this situation? She won't have told them the truth, that much I know. She won't have told them the real reason for my leaving home – she won't have told them how she blamed me for everything, how she couldn't be near me, how we didn't so much as speak to each other in sixteen years.

'I guess we just drifted apart,' I say, gaining confidence in my answer as it arrives. 'You know how it is – I went off travelling when I was seventeen or eighteen, and got wrapped up in that, I suppose. And Emily was always the more academic one, so she stayed on with Mum and Dad, went to uni – and after a while we just stopped writing and got on with our lives. I know it's a bit of a dull answer, but that's it really – we simply drifted apart.'

There's a pause, before DCI Jacobs speaks again. 'Yes. That's pretty much what your sister said. Still, it's a long time to lose touch, isn't it?'

She's not going to let this go as easily as I hoped. 'Well, I suppose we were never that close as kids,' I say. 'Not like now.'

'I understand,' DCI Jacobs replies, but judging by her tone I'm not sure she's completely satisfied. 'OK, Jess. Thank you.'

I think she's about to hang up, but then I remember she said there were two things she wanted to talk to me about. 'Oh, yes,' she says, as if it's an afterthought. 'Your brother-in-law, James. Do you know where he was last night? Around 7pm?'

'No,' I answer, knowing he didn't arrive home till late. 'He got home about nineish – he was meeting up with Marcus and some of his team from the office. Why?'

'Max Fuller was attacked last night. He was given a pretty nasty going-over – he's in St Mary's at the moment. A couple of broken ribs and a lot of bruising. He's not saying anything, but we're pretty sure James King is behind it. You wouldn't know anything about that, would you?'

I think of James arriving home last night, looking unchar-acteristically unkempt and smelling of beer. Emily was already in bed, and I warmed up a plate of food for him, noticing the purple bruising that had started to snake around the knuckles of his right hand.

'Jess?' DCI Jacobs repeats.

'Sorry,' I reply, my eyes fixed on the undulating winter ocean, on the bright liquid sunlight that ices its shifting surface. 'The signal dropped off for a second. No, I'm sorry – I don't know anything about it. James seemed fine when he got home – completely ordinary. And I'm sure he wouldn't do a thing like that; he's not capable of that kind of violence.'

DCI Jacobs releases a small, humourless laugh. 'You'd be surprised what the most ordinary of people are capable of.'

10. Emily

There are days when she thinks perhaps she has died, and this place she now inhabits is hell. There are days when she creeps about the house, timing her movements with theirs, occasionally managing to avoid them altogether. Her senses are dulled by the welcome medication, and she strains to listen out for the scrape of chairs on the dining room floor, the weary tread of bare feet on the carpeted stairwell, the clunk of the front door closing behind them. She longs to be alone in her sorrow, yet she never is. Even when the others leave the house, her home is surrounded by photographers, journalists – predators waiting to pounce, to strip the flesh from her scrawny bones. She knows she is growing scrawny; she sees it in those moments alone behind the bathroom door, when she lets her dressing gown slip to the tiles, to stare at her stranger's nakedness in the reflection of the full-length mirror. There wasn't much of her to start with; she'd always been so careful to keep a neat figure. And of course, it was torture after Daisy came along, because all she wanted to do was eat. The more Daisy fed off her, the greater Emily's hunger raged, and the more she longed for all the worst things – sponge cake, biscuits, fatty chips and sauce. But she never gave in to those cravings, instead focusing her energies on tiresome fitness DVDs, pulling on her pristine trainers the moment Daisy went down for her twice-daily naps, sweating it out in the living room before recharging with a fresh smoothie from the Juice-A-Matic she'd invested in a month earlier. It was all in the planning, her return to pre-baby fitness, and the greatest compliment she could receive was, 'Gosh, you'd never think you'd just had a baby.' Now, as she sits on the edge of her bed remembering the gruelling nature of those days, she flushes as she realises remarks of that kind meant more to her than 'what a beautiful baby' or 'isn't she *just perfect*'.

'There's no excuse for letting yourself go,' she says aloud now, and she drops her face into her hands. She releases a moan, a deep, guttural cry of disbelief at what she's so quickly become, at the never-ending misery of her new life. Is this it now, is *this* her life? Will Daisy never return? Will they have to do that thing that others so callously suggest to the recently bereaved – will they have to *move on*? It's only been a week, she reminds herself, as she runs ragged fingers through her lank hair. It's only a week, and Daisy could be found at any minute. Right now, the police could be snatching her out of the grasp of her kidnapper, preparing to rush her back into the bosom of her family. But what if she's not found? What if they do find her, but she's – a shutter comes down, and Emily is on her feet, rushing into the bathroom to run the shower, to deny the worst thoughts that chase after her, snapping at her heels. Unthinkable thoughts. A strange contradiction, for surely you must think these thoughts in order to name them unthinkable. She stands beneath the shower, disappearing into the steam, digging her nails deep into her scalp and allowing the hot water to scald her pale skin pink.

*

When Jess first moved in, it was clear she was going to do everything she could to help, to be a useful member of the family. They hadn't been home for more than an hour when she had said, 'You go and have a shower, Ems. I'm happy playing with Daisy for a while, and if I need anything Chloe will show me – won't you, Chloe?'

It's strange, thinking back, how easily she accepted Jess's help – so unlike herself, who was normally loath to reach out to others, for fear of displaying weakness. But she had been exhausted, and so grateful for those precious moments to herself, suddenly able to take a long shower instead of a rushed one with Daisy in the bathroom with her, babbling in her play cot like a ticking clock. She supposes she has come to take Jess's help for granted now, but she knows she couldn't have managed without her here over these past months. And Chloe – well, Chloe took to her so instantly, it was like a crush of sorts, and Aunt Jess could do no wrong in her eyes. *She's so cool.* That was what Chloe had said to Emily on that first night, and she can't help but admit that it hurt a little. Perhaps *I* would still be cool, she thought, if I hadn't given the best years of my life to rearing you, Chloe, to being a good wife and mother – to having Daisy. Maybe if she too had spent the past two decades free of family responsibility or adult commitment – maybe in those circumstances even Emily would have had time to work on her cool rating. But we make our beds, don't we? And let's face it, hers has been a much more comfortable bed than Jess's, cool or not. After everything, now that Mum and Dad were both gone, Emily was glad to be able to help Jess out. Poor, aimless Jess. She'd made so little of her life – no career, no family, no real place she could call home. What kind of sister wouldn't want to help, wouldn't want to open up her arms and welcome her in?

And James had liked her straight away, and Emily had been pleased, because Jess was a part of her, and she knows he felt happy that she had let *him* in a little more, shown him a part of herself that had previously remained hidden away.

When James returns from wherever it is he's been, Emily is watching from the nursery window. It's around four and already dark outside, and she stands in the unlit room, hidden behind the curtains, scrutinising his every movement, trying to decode the expression on his face, his gait as he glances over his shoulder in search of the press vultures. But the reporters have all gone for the day, too lazy to hang about after dark, when a well-earned pint or a family meal calls or a tastier tragedy comes knocking. The police have been on the phone again, asking about James's whereabouts the night before last, because they suspect him of attacking Chloe's boyfriend. Did she know anything about it, they'd asked? 'No,' she had replied, automatically adopting the tone of offended wife. 'That's a ridiculous idea – did Max *say* James did it?' The liaison officers were quick to reassure her: no, she really mustn't worry, Max hadn't made any kind of allegation – he hadn't got a good look at his assailant – but they *had* to ask, 'under the circumstances'.

Of course it was James, she knows, and it strikes her, with a certain sense of fear, that he has that in him, this hitherto unseen rage. Through the fog of her exhaustion she recalls the demented way in which he paced the bedroom after DCI Jacobs had been round to interview Chloe about Max, all his fear and horror surrounding Daisy transferred to thoughts of Chloe in the blink of an eye. 'I don't care what she says, there's no way she's been staying over at that boy's house without something more than hand-holding going on.' He had waited for Emily's response – standing at the foot of the bed, hands on his hips, with her lying back against the pillows, longing for sleep. He had wanted her to disagree with him, to say all the right things and soothe him as she used to. His stubble was now bordering on a beard, she'd observed. Perhaps he should just go with it and see how it suits him.

'So what?' she'd heard herself say, and she had known he would go crazy.

'So WHAT?! So – she's fifteen and he's nineteen, for fuck's sake, Emily! She's a child and he's a grown man! There's no way Chloe would have lied like that without someone pressurising her into it.'

She'd laughed – she had actually laughed. If he only knew what young people were capable of, what lies they could tell, what secrets they could keep.

'You haven't got a clue about kids, have you, James? No idea what they can get up to when left to their own devices.' She wouldn't open her eyes again, felt protected from his wrath by not looking.

His voice, after a beat, came out softer. 'So you *do* think they've been having sex, then?'

Emily had dragged her arm across her face. The overhead light was so bright, and all she'd wanted to do was disappear into the darkness of night-time. 'Of course they're having sex.'

She had heard the bedroom door slam shut behind him, and crawled beneath her duvet, muffling the raised voices of her husband and stepdaughter as their hearts broke in fury and regret in the room across the hall. Thank God DC Cherry isn't staying in their spare room any more, she'd thought; thank God they were free of that scrutiny in the evenings at least.

Now, she hears the front door closing behind James as he returns home, the gentle chink of his keys on the hook, the dull sound of his unlaced shoes hitting the carpet, and she sprints back across the hall and slips beneath her bedcovers. She doesn't want to see him. She doesn't want to hear where he's been, what he's done, how he's feeling. She just wants to slide into nothing, and she forces herself below the waves of darkness, holding herself down until sleep takes over. Only in the deeply medicated shade of nightfall can Emily shut out the worst of her thoughts: the fear, the anger, the *guilt*.

11. Jess

Tonight there's a meeting at the town hall, to mark a week since Daisy went missing. The police are keen to keep her disappearance fresh in people's minds, and they think bringing the community together might uncover some forgotten detail, some piece of information that will lead us to find her. I'm relieved that they're doing something tangible, that there's some active evidence of the search, lest she be forgotten as last week's story, no longer headline news. For the first few days, Daisy *was* headline news. Her image, along with a picture of a stuffed toy just like her velvet Ellie, took over front-page spreads across the country, dominating both local and national news, and it was grimly heralded as the latest heinous crime to shake the nation. She headlined radio updates, television news, and, so the police tell us, social media feeds around the world. There was even that hashtag, #findDaisy, accompanied by a silly little flower emoji, a tiny emblem floating out there in virtual space, fruitlessly willing members of the public to remember something, *anything* that might bring Daisy home.

She still makes the news, but in the past couple of days she's slipped to page two or three, recent developments in the investigation clearly lacking the sensational drama the red tops favour. The last one of worth to them was a couple of days ago: DAISY SISTER'S BOYFRIEND HELD FOR QUESTIONING. The phone rang off the wall that day, and to James's distress it seemed the press were more interested in Chloe's underage relationship with Max than they were in helping to find Daisy.

As we arrive, I have the feeling that we're trespassing on to the set of some television drama, where anxious locals fill the seats and line the walls, a hubbub of chatter trundling around the place like a train, the sound of it filling the hall to its rafters. *Isn't it awful? Isn't it awful? Isn't it awful?* When we walk through the open doors, we feel the collective pause as eyes turn upon us, and the chatter is sucked from the room in an instant. DCI Jacobs is on the stage at the front, and she spins to face us, sensing the change in atmosphere. I'm so grateful to her as she raises her hands, beckoning us towards her, causing the crowd to part and let us through, and I'm glad to hear conversations start up again once we've passed. She hops off the edge of the stage, and to my surprise she embraces first Emily and then me, before clasping James's hand between hers.

'How are you all feeling?' she asks, and her eyes are sincere, warm. 'This is a good turnout. That's a really good sign that you've got the community on your side.'

James and Emily do their best to look pleased, and we take our reserved seats at the front of the hall, directly facing the stage, with Chloe sitting between James and me, the icy atmosphere between the girl and her parents having temporarily thawed for this public outing. DCI Jacobs steps up on to the stage, along with DC Cherry, DC Piper and two other officers who have been dealing with the investigation over the past week.

The room falls silent.

'Thank you all for coming.' DCI Jacobs addresses the crowd from her position behind the table. Their arrangement reminds me of the television appeal, and I wish they had chosen a different way to sit, a less intimidating pose. She has a strong voice, though, commanding and clear. 'Firstly, let me say that a case like this, of a missing child, always has the power to provoke strong feeling in a small community like yours – feelings of fear and even anger – and those feelings can cause us all to take our eye off the ball, can distract us all from the job at hand.' She pauses, a well-timed moment to add weight to her message. 'And that job is the task of finding Daisy. Agreed?'

Around the room people nod in agreement, a few clap hands, along with an encouraging, 'Hear-hear!' from the far corner.

DCI Jacobs continues. 'Already this evening, a few of you have expressed frustration that the police force aren't working fast enough – and I ask you now, each and every one of you, to please be patient, be vigilant, and let us do the job we're trained to do.'

I run my eyes around the edges of the room, where people are propped against walls or perch two to a chair, listening intently. She must have had an ear-bashing from some of the more militant locals before we arrived, for her to start the evening with this kind of plea.

'You've had a week now, mate.' A deep male voice carries over from the back of the room. 'I dunno about anyone else, but I can't see you've made much progress.'

A growing murmur of assent ripples through the audience: you can feel it, see the confrontation move through the crowd like a gently undulating spring tide.

DCI Jacobs holds a hand up, trying to contain the sudden volley of questions that are fired at her. 'We *are* making progress. There are a number of leads coming in as a result of the television appeal, and several new lines of enquiry have opened up to us in the past week. What we want to ask of you – Daisy's friends and neighbours – is that you go back home from here and think really carefully about your movements on that night. It shouldn't be too difficult, with it having been New Year's Eve, but we also want you to think about the week or so leading up to it. Have you noticed anyone different hanging around – any strangers, anybody asking questions about the King family, or taking an unusual interest in local events? Has anyone you know been behaving strangely, perhaps more stressed or upset than usual, or has anyone you know gone away lately, unexpectedly or otherwise?'

'So you think it's a stranger, then – not someone in the family?' This from a man in a fur-hooded parka near the front right-hand wall – a Scottish accent, I think. I'd heard that large numbers of the islanders are incomers, immigrants from the mainland, many of them looking for new lives, new hopes, new futures. Does *he* look like a kidnapper? I wonder. Any one of these people could be guilty of unspeakable crimes. They all look ordinary, blameless, but that doesn't mean a thing. And then I understand that this is the way it could be for us, forever wondering – *is it you, is it you, did you do it, are you a kidnapper, or worse?*

'We're not ruling anything out,' DCI Jacobs replies. 'We're considering every possibility – so it is vital that you provide us with any information you have, no matter how small it might seem. No one will be made to feel foolish or disloyal if they come to us, and my colleague at the door there will be giving out the direct contact number you can use if you want to talk to us confidentially.'

I turn to look back over heads to see the officer at the open double doors holding up a handful of contact cards to make himself known among the gaggle of locals. It's dark outside, and the white mist of breath lingers in the space above their heads. I notice James's business partner Marcus at the edge of the group, and he nods gravely when we look in his direction, clearly trying to convey support to his friends. James returns the gesture; Emily turns back sharply, impatiently, and I wonder if she even saw him, if she even cares.

Somewhere in the middle of the seated area, a woman stands up. I don't know any of these people, and I wonder if Emily and James do, if they are friends or acquaintances or if they've never even met before. 'We've all heard about Max Fuller. Being beaten up.' Her voice is nervy, indignant. 'I heard you'd had him down the station beforehand.'

More murmurs, louder and more excitable this time. I'm aware of James along the row, his head lowered as more voices join in the discussion, his jaw clenched.

'*Druggie*,' another angry voice adds to the growing alarm, and I recognise its owner as the woman from the fish and chip shop at the end of our road.

Someone right behind me asks, 'Why did they let him go?'

Beside me, Chloe covers her nose and mouth with a mittened hand. I see the tears streaming into the bobbled purple wool, the taut effort of her presence, and I feel relief as James silently reaches for her hand and she allows it.

DCI Jacobs looks annoyed. 'OK! Calm down, everyone, please. Yes, I *can* confirm Max Fuller was taken in for questioning – along with a number of other people – and he was released, for the very good reason that we were satisfied he was not anywhere near the King household on New Year's Eve.'

'But he's got a record for drugs, hasn't he?' demands the fish and chip woman. 'He got done for possession last year. Everyone knows that.'

'We have several witnesses that prove Mr Fuller was nowhere near Daisy's house that night,' DCI Jacobs responds firmly. She points across the hall to a young woman with her hand in the air, waiting to ask a question. 'You, at the back?'

'What about local paedophiles?' the woman asks. Her broad Yorkshire accent lends a softness to the harsh noun. I can't bring myself to look at Emily; I don't want to see what this question will do to her. 'There are a few of 'em living nearby – you only have to go online to find out who they are. Have you questioned them all?'

DCI Jacobs tries to maintain her calm demeanour, but she senses the crowd gaining volume and vigour, their individual fears gathering momentum as the woman at the back lights the touch paper.

'*Here*?' another woman calls out. 'Who are they?' It's becoming hard to distinguish the voices, as thrown sentences jostle and tangle with each other, obscuring words.

The Scottish man in the parka again. 'You're telling me we've got these perverts living on our doorsteps and the police don't think to warn us about them?'

'And the thing I would very much like to know –' This from a woman sitting in the front, several seats along from me, pronouncing the words carefully in a heavily accented voice. Spanish, perhaps? 'Where were the parents when this child was taken?' She leans out, fixing her attention firmly on Emily. 'They were *out*! At a party!'

DCI Jacobs tries to bring the room into order, but it's too late: James and Emily are on their feet, pushing through the crowded aisle towards the exit doors at the back, Chloe following close behind. I turn to look at the young woman before I leave, and she clutches her scarf to her broad neck in a briskly self-righteous motion, narrowing her eyes at me before looking away. It's only when we get outside that I learn this woman is Marta, Emily's ex-nanny, and by the sound of her she's got an axe to grind.

*

For most of our childhood, Mum was a constant presence, the archetypal stay-at-home mum, always there to greet us after school, to help us with our homework and put dinner on the table at six. I remember my friends saying how lucky we were, that we didn't know how awful it was to have a working mum, to go home to an empty house. We were in the minority, with nearly all the other mums going out to some kind of work or other, and once the difference was pointed out to me I wasn't sure how I felt about it. Sammie would regularly come back with us after school – an unofficial arrangement – for the company (and the food, it had to be said), and over the years she grew as close to my mum as she was to us girls. She was a tiny little thing – delicate as a fairy, Mum would say – and more often than not she would hop up and sit in the windowsill like one of Mum's Staffordshire figurines, and chat with Mum while Emily and I mooched about the kitchen grazing on freshly baked biscuits.

'Saves *us* having to chat to Mum,' Emily said one evening as we all headed out into the garden to top up our tans.

Sammie told her she was horrible and she should think herself lucky to have a lovely mum at home baking biscuits.

'I'd rather have one like yours,' Emily said.

'What's "one like mine"?' Sammie asked, stretching out on the blanket between us and hoiking up her little skirt.

'Invisible and loaded,' Emily replied, and we all laughed, because it was so awful, so deeply insulting to both mothers in wildly different ways.

Sammie would always head off home around half-five, before Dad got back for dinner, and often my mum would stand at the door and sigh, and say again, 'Poor mite – she misses having her mother around. It's all well and good having that lovely big house and all the trappings, but a girl needs family. Especially when she's an only child.'

But I wasn't sure it sounded so awful. Sometimes I would lie on my bed and imagine how it might feel to take the bus from school, to travel along the high street, out towards our leafy suburban road, to walk the last few steps home alone with no chatter from Emily or Sammie rattling in my ears. I imagined how it would feel to arrive on the doorstep and turn the key in our front door, opening it into dimmed silence. I saw myself walking through the hallway, breaking through sunlit dust motes, and throwing myself across the sofa, where I would recline and pick out shapes and faces from the ceiling swirls above. I would tune in to the drip-drip-drip of the kitchen tap; to the chitchat of birdsong in the garden beyond; to the distant rumble of the train track several streets away. I would lie there for hours and hours and hours, and, when I'd had my fill of solitude, there would be Mum and Dad and Emily in the doorway, home for supper and happy to see me. That was the fantasy, though I never told Emily – she would never be able to understand it, never see how I could wish for something so strange as a little time alone.

At the end of our last year at primary school, Mum had to go away for several weeks in the summer holidays to care for our grandmother. Her mother was in heart failure and it was agreed that it was no place for us girls, and so a nanny was employed to care for us at home for the month of August, while Dad was out at work. When I look back on it now I wonder if Mum purposely chose an ageing, mousy little woman for fear of her catching Dad's eye; his eyes always twinkled a little more when a pretty woman entered the room. While she was lovely, and sweet, and a wonderful cook, Dad's eyes never twinkled when Lizzie Glass was in the room.

Lizzie Glass didn't lay down too many rules for us, but, as it was the summer and we wanted to be outside all day long, she merely insisted that we come home by midday for lunch and then again in the afternoon in time for tea. With Mum away, we were now eating at five with Lizzie, and Dad was eating his dinner later alone, to allow him longer at the office. Emily hated the arrangement, hated the change.

'Why can't we eat with Dad?' she asked Lizzie one teatime. Lizzie had cooked a fish pie, with an apple crumble for afters. Both were delicious.

'Your dad has lots of paperwork to catch up on at the office,' she replied in her softly lilting Scottish accent, patting Emily's hand.

Emily snatched it away, and Lizzie Glass did her best not to let on she was hurt.

After a week or so, Emily started to find reasons to make us late home for lunch, dragging her heels when I tried to hurry her along, making up diversions for us before we reached our street. She'd insist on a detour to the duck pond to poke around for newts, or to the library on the corner of the high street to hang around in the children's section until the librarians had to ask us to leave so they could shut up for half-day. I knew Emily was punishing Lizzie for being there instead of Mum, but nothing I could do would speed Emily home. Every day we were arriving later and later, until one day we didn't get in until gone two o'clock, to find Lizzie sitting at the kitchen table, the hem of her apron clutched in her papery hands, tears of frustration pricking at her eyes. I was mortified and I moved to comfort her, but Emily grabbed hold of my wrist and I stopped where I was.

'Girls?' Lizzie asked. She rarely showed disapproval, and even now her voice was soft and unthreatening. 'Where is it you get to? I've been worried sick, and I don't want to bother your father, but I'm going to have to let him know. You come in later and later every day. He would be so cross to think I'm letting you run around all over the place, and me with no idea where you are. I don't know what to do!'

Emily threw herself at her, wrapping her arms round her neck and saying, 'We're sorry, Lizzie. We're sorry, sorry, sorry!' Emily held on with such affection that the little woman seemed to melt before us.

'Oh, darling, I *know* you are!' Lizzie Glass cried out, and she mopped at her wet eyes and agreed not to tell our father as she set out our egg sandwich lunch and poured our milk.

That evening, as Lizzie served up our father's dinner, Emily beckoned me into the hall. I watched her take a twenty-pound note from our father's wallet and push it into the pocket of Lizzie's cardigan where it hung in the hallway. I shook my head at her, but she brought her finger to her lips with a fierce scowl and sent me into the living room to watch TV.

We never saw Lizzie Glass again.

12. Emily

There's a dreamlike quality to Emily's waking: the winter sun streams in behind James where he stands at the window knotting his tie. When she stirs, his attention turns towards her as he flips his collar down, fastens his cuffs. These feel like the everyday actions of normality, of before – the time before Daisy disappeared – and for a few seconds she's filled with hope that it's true, that this whole black episode was a figment of her imagination. The police, the interviews, the town meeting – and, she remembers with a gasp, that terrible Marta woman – all just a horrible waking dream. She tries to speak but finds her mouth slow to move, her reactions still sluggish from the sleeping pill she took before bed last night.

'Stay in bed,' James tells her. 'Jess is already downstairs and she said she'll get Chloe off to school.'

'What?' Emily asks, baffled by this sudden burst of domestic activity.

He picks up his mug of coffee and takes a sip, a cautious tone creeping into his voice. 'I think it's best if I get back to work – there's no point in sitting around here for hours on end, just waiting for the police to call. We're all driving each other crazy, sitting on our hands day after day, wondering and worrying.' She knows he's still mad about the family liaison officers; he thinks not letting them stay overnight makes the family look guilty. *As far as the rest of the world is concerned*, Emily told him, *we already look guilty. The parents always look guilty.*

Emily doesn't speak, doesn't even blink. A few days ago she emailed the head teacher at the school where she works, informing her that she can't contemplate returning to work until Daisy is found. How could James be doing exactly the opposite? Her fingers curl over the edge of the duvet and she feels she must hang on tight for fear of falling.

'Don't look at me like that, Ems. I'm going out of my mind too. I feel so helpless – at least at the office I've got something to do, and things are starting to grind to a halt down there without my input. It *is* my business, after all. I can't leave everything to Marcus, it's not fair. He needs me back on board.' He tries to smile at her, but she sees his insincerity as the warmth fails to reach his eyes. He's just looking for an escape, she knows.

'Well, if *Marcus* needs you, you'd better go,' she replies, hating him, hating that he isn't hurting as much as she is. Doesn't he feel distraught? Doesn't he feel guilty too? She feels reduced by their relative positions, he up and dressed and ready for the world, she cowering vulnerable beneath the bedcovers, puffy-eyed. 'Don't worry, James,' she says above the hammering pain in her temple. 'You run off to work and I'll stay here and sit around feeling helpless for the both of us. And if Daisy happens to come home while you're out, I'll send you a text message.' She curls on to her side, not wanting a reply.

And he doesn't reply. He picks up his mug and his jacket and exits the room, leaving the door open just enough for her to hear the distant cheery tone in his voice as he puts on a positive front for Chloe and Jess downstairs. Groggily Emily rolls on to her back and looks around the material objects of the room, remembering the brief glow of pleasure they'd imprinted on her at the time of their purchase: the expensive Conran drapes and glass-drop lampshade she'd talked James into buying soon after they'd moved in, the wall-to-wall cupboards that had cost a fortune to have custom-built. Cupboards that contained thousands of pounds' worth of clothes and shoes and handbags and boots, most of which had only been used once or twice but which had seemed so important to own at the time. She was lucky, she knew. James's IT business generated enough income that she had never really *had* to work, and he never begrudged her using his money as if it were her own, never questioned how much she spent or what she spent it on. It was one of his most attractive qualities, his generosity, and she recalls his surprise when she announced she was starting a part-time job as a teaching assistant at the local school Daisy would eventually attend. Emily shakes her head, trying to get her thoughts straight. No, that was all wrong: when she took that job there was no Daisy – she wasn't even pregnant, she didn't even want a baby, though she'd never said as much to James. James had said he didn't understand why she wanted to take on more work when Chloe still needed her around, and she'd replied, *Chloe's old enough to look after herself*, and he had said, *But we'll have another child before we know it and then what?* By that point Emily really, really wanted the job and before she knew what she was doing she had said, *It's the best school in the area and there's a lovely nursery attached which feeds straight in, and we'd definitely get a place with me working there so it could be perfect, couldn't it?* And James had hugged her and agreed, yes, it could be perfect, because he was so happy, so completely thrilled that for the first time she was making the same noises as him about having a baby together, and that was what *he* wanted more than anything. She had been able to stall for another couple of years, secretly popping her contraceptive pills, but when he started suggesting fertility treatment she silently conceded defeat and gave him the child he longed for. Now she lies alone in their bed, her sadness and disappointment weighting her limbs like rocks, and she wonders how he would feel if he knew she had deceived him for all those years, if he knew Daisy – their beautiful, profoundly loved child – might never have been. Would that have been better? To have never loved her, never held her, never felt the pain of her loss, like a limb being wrenched from the body, the ache of it endless and raw.

By the time she has showered and made her way downstairs, Emily finds the house empty. James is at work, Chloe now back at school, and Jess, who knows? It is strange to Emily to realise that, without Daisy to care for, Jess now moves about independently, with no requirement to tell the family where she is going, what she is doing. She's taken to heading off on long hikes across the island, always returning early enough to sort out supper and clear up after them all. She's probably conscious of still needing to earn her keep, Emily supposes, and she feels instantly tight for having even thought it. Why must she always think the worst of people; why wouldn't Jess be caring for them simply because she loves them, because she wants to make things easier on them? Thinking about Jess's sudden freedom makes her realise how restrictive it is to have a small child in your care; it makes Emily yearn to return to *her* work, to escape from the prison of her empty home. To do so would seem shameless, though. What would people think? But she can't just sit here doing nothing, slowly losing herself in grief and darkness; she has to do *something*.

Without a thought, Emily grabs her winter coat from the hall and pulls on the first pair of boots she can lay her hands on, before banging the front door shut and heading for the first of her neighbours' homes along the street. Out in the street the first of the media cars is arriving, but she passes them unnoticed as their attention is diverted by DC Piper arriving on the drive. She breaks into a run, her heart hammering against her ribcage in alarm at her sudden fit of action, feeling astounded at the ease with which she's slipped past her jailors. She intends to call on every house along the street, whether she knows the inhabitants or not, and ask them if they recall anything about the night Daisy disappeared. She knows the police have interviewed everyone already, but if they saw *her*, understood what it means to them as a family, perhaps it might provoke them to remember something important. It's got to be worth a shot, surely.

Mrs Bowen next door looks alarmed to see Emily standing on her doorstep. 'Emily, dear,' she says as her delicate hand rests on the door frame, her expression one of grave concern. 'How *are* you – how's James?'

Emily doesn't have time for platitudes. 'Fine. Well, not fine, of course.' She suddenly realises how hard this is going to be, that they will all ask the same of her, and what is the right answer? What *is* the social protocol for parents of snatched children when responding to concerned neighbours? 'It's just, I wanted to ask you – ask everyone – if you saw anything at all that night, anything that might help, the night when –' And then the words simply won't come, and she blinks hard at her elderly neighbour, her jaw stuck in mid-sentence, her lower lip limp.

'Oh, *goodness* – the police have already been and asked me, dear.' She reaches towards Emily with that papery pale hand and Emily withdraws, again repulsed by the thought of human contact. Mrs Bowen flinches, and Emily notices but can't feel anything for the woman and she turns and marches back down the path towards the main street without another word. 'I'm sorry, dear!' Mrs Bowen calls after her, but Emily's mind is on other things.

The idea was foolish, ridiculous. She can't even spit the words out, let alone coherently interview the thirty-odd families along the street. Of course the police have been to see all the neighbours. What was she thinking of? There's a harsh wind sailing up from the coast and Emily pulls up her collar, securing the top button and dipping her head against the cold as she continues to walk, veering away from home and down towards the town. She has no idea where she is going until she is standing beneath the burgundy canopy of Becca's Café, gazing at her own hopeless appearance in the polished glass of the front window. The swelling sea behind her is reflected sharply and her eyes follow the rise and fall of the gulls in the sky overhead, as they make their way out over the water, occasionally dipping below the surface in pursuit of their prey before rising skywards again. Her normally groomed hair is airborne, swirling around her face as though in a vortex, and it's only when Becca appears in the open doorway, her mouth shaped into a worried little 'O', that Emily realises she looks quite mad.

'Becca,' she manages, and she folds into sobs, allowing her friend to help her inside, where she sits her at a window seat in the empty café and fetches some drinks.

Emily's crying is under control by the time Becca returns and places down a tray laden with coffee, cake and a small shot of brandy. She pushes it towards Emily with a curt nod. 'Knock it back.'

Emily does as she is told and takes a long, slow breath as the heat travels through her. 'Thank you,' she says in a small voice, and she reaches for the coffee to wash away the harsh tang of the liquor.

'You look terrible,' Becca says. She always was one to state facts plainly, and in this moment Emily loves her for it.

'I feel so bloody useless,' she replies. 'And there's nothing from the police. Nothing at all.'

Becca watches her closely, as though trying to assess how best to proceed. Again, she goes for the plain approach, sparing Emily the insult of small talk. 'What about Chloe's boyfriend – Max? Is it true it was James that had a go at him the other night? Todd said he heard he was in hospital with a couple of broken ribs. James wouldn't do something like that, would he?'

'I don't know what I think, Becca. You read about things like this all the time: how people can be together for years without ever really knowing anything about their partner – anything about their hidden side. Think of the Yorkshire Ripper.'

'Emily!' Becca says, and Emily shrugs, unconcerned at the effect her words have had on her friend.

'Either way, it's not Max Fuller, they're pretty certain. He's got alibis for that night.' She breaks off a small piece of sponge cake and puts it to her lips, trying to decide whether to eat it or not.

'It's coconut,' Becca says, eyeing her hesitation, and Emily feels duty-bound to eat at least a little of it, out of politeness.

'Jess says I should tell the police about Marta. You know, that horrible nanny I had for a couple of weeks?'

Becca nods. 'I heard she spouted some bile at the town meeting the other night. Sorry I wasn't there, by the way – Todd was ill.' Beyond the window, an elderly couple walk by, raising their hands to Becca. She waves back. Emily thinks how nice it would be to be like Becca, right at the centre of the community. She remembers the early days when they arrived on the island, meeting Becca at playgroup, their friendship cemented by Todd's and Chloe's instant affection for one another. They would joke that they might have a wedding to plan in a few years if the toddlers' relationship continued to flourish beyond their infant crush. Back then, Emily was surprised to learn that Becca also had two older children, twin girls, and she wondered how she managed it all – running the business and home, ferrying the kids about everywhere – doing it all with such easy enthusiasm and humour. She's a better mother than me, Emily thinks, hating herself for the comparison when her own daughter is God knows where.

'Do you remember what she was like? *Marta*. I never trusted her, and thank God I was around for most of that trial fortnight or anything could've happened to Daisy.' She pauses, realising how stupid it sounds, realising that 'anything' *had* happened – the worst possible thing *has* happened.

'Yeah, you said she was a nightmare.' Becca picks up Emily's cup and takes it to the counter for a refill.

'I just always got a bad feeling about her. The way she looked at me – like she was jealous or something, all attitude if I asked her to do anything around the house, and then all charming when James came in. I swear she fancied him. And she wasn't caring enough with Daisy. One time I came in from a trip to the shops and caught her sitting at the dining room table, drinking coffee and texting, while Daisy was crying in her cot upstairs!'

Becca raises her eyebrows, and Emily is reminded that Becca is of the 'controlled crying' school of parenting, so she couldn't possibly understand how awful something like that felt to Emily at the time. Emily knows it doesn't sound as dreadful as she wants it to, but she was there, she knows what it was like – Marta was *horrible*. Predatory, even.

'Anyway, we got to the end of the two-week trial and I told her we wouldn't be keeping her on. She was furious because she'd given up another job to take this one. But that's the risk you take, isn't it, especially if you're no good at your job? And then we found that dead seagull lying on the driveway a week later, and I'm convinced it was her.'

'Oh, I don't know, Emily. I'm sure that was just a coincidence.'

'No. I'm positive. It was sinister.'

'But didn't James say the gull looked as though it had flown into the top window? He said there was a crack in the glass.'

'Yes, but I'm sure that crack was already there. She did it.' Emily chews at her lip, her thoughts whirring noisily, and she wishes she had remembered to take one of her tablets this morning, just to take the edge off. 'I think Jess is right, you know. I'm going to call the police, tell them about her.'

Becca frowns, clearly unconvinced, before she breaks into a smile as a new subject comes to her. 'How is your sister, by the way?' she asks, and Emily can tell she's trying to steer the subject away from Marta.

'Fine,' Emily replies, but she doesn't want to talk about Jess. 'She's helping to keep things ticking along at home. When she's not out *walking*.' She puts a slight emphasis on the word 'walking' and she's surprised by her feelings of irritation. Why shouldn't Jess go out walking? She's a free agent, isn't she? Perhaps it's because she associates the starting of these walks with Daisy going missing. Before, Jess never had the time; now she has all the time in the world.

'Yes, she certainly seems to love a walk,' Becca says. 'I wish I had the self-discipline to get myself out there like she does. She never misses a day, does she?'

'What, walking?' Emily says as Becca stands to load the empties on to the tray.

'Yes, she must be *really* fit. Probably how she keeps so bloody slim!'

'Well, to be fair, she's only just started, hasn't she?' Even now, Emily's jealous streak rears its ugly head. 'She'll grow tired of it before you know it.'

Becca looks confused. 'But she's been doing it for weeks – ever since she got here. She passes by the window just about every weekday afternoon, rain or shine. I always notice her because it's around the time Todd gets back from school.'

'With the pram?' Emily asks. She gets to her feet, a sense of disquiet swelling in her chest as she fishes about in her pocket, apologising for not having brought a purse out with her.

Becca steps aside to let a customer enter the café. 'No, on her own. I wondered if she had a fancy man tucked away,' and she laughs to let Emily know she isn't really serious.

Emily doesn't know how to respond to this new information, and she utters a simple, 'Huh,' before hugging her friend briskly and saying goodbye. As she lowers her head against the wind, she visualises a past image of her sister sitting at the dining room table when she returned home from work, Jess spooning baby food into Daisy's smiling face, the pair of them looking as if they haven't left home all afternoon, the house clean and tidy, the delicious smells of supper wafting from the warm kitchen. Jess has never mentioned these walks. Why not? And where was Daisy when these furtive excursions were taking place? Emily's pace quickens until she's nearly running, desperate to get back home, desperate to work out whether she's missed anything else, whether there's more she doesn't know about, more that her sister is keeping from her.

It's evening by the time Emily wakes, and she's stirred by the sound of activity in the kitchen, and the smell of cooking in the air. Jess must be back. The last thing Emily can remember is arriving home to find the house empty, before washing down her medication with a large glass of lukewarm wine and trudging upstairs with the phone in her hand. She heads downstairs and passes Jess without a word, taking a new bottle of white wine from the fridge, and a glass, and returning to sit in the single armchair in the corner of the dining room, where, while she is obscured by the table and chairs at the centre of the room, she can still see through to the kitchen. If Jess has picked up on Emily's silence she doesn't show it, but then she's probably grown accustomed to her erratic moods over the past week and a half – the way in which she shuts them all out for fear of what she might say. She hasn't mentioned those secret walks to Jess yet; she'll watch and wait a while. For now, she is content that the police are on to Marta, having phoned DC Cherry the moment she arrived home from Becca's this morning, and she's confident they're taking it seriously, that they're considering her a viable suspect. *That bitch.* To say those things in front of the whole town, to suggest that *they* are to blame, that they're bad parents. She feels a hard knot of hatred forming in her gullet, like a blockage that she must force down with another glass of wine. She's glad of the way the hard edges of the room grow softer with each glass, until James arrives home, passing through the dining room, oblivious to Emily's quiet presence, into the kitchen where Jess potters at the hob.

'What's this?' he asks, lifting the lid, his voice sounding as though he hasn't a care in the world.

Jess lifts the spoon and holds it between them. 'Bolognese. Have a taste.' And, brazenly, she moves it to his lips and he takes it, his mouth closing over the spoon and drawing back in a languorous movement. Jess is smiling at him, like the cat that got the cream, like a woman who's just pleasured her man, and she lowers her eyes to the stove-top and replaces the lid. 'You'll have to wait for the rest,' she says, and she throws him a coy look as she reaches for the spaghetti jar on the top shelf.

James laughs. 'I've got time for a shower, then?'

She looks at her watch, tells him he's got ten minutes, tells him to let Chloe know on his way past her room. As he turns to leave the kitchen, he spots Emily in the dining room, tucked up small in her corner armchair, an empty glass in her hand, and there it is! A flash of guilt sprinting across his eyes, as though she's caught him stealing. A look that says he's untrustworthy; a look that says he's cheating.

13. **Jess**

I don't know what happened while I was out yesterday, but when Emily came downstairs in the evening she was vile. She sat curled up like a seething cat in the corner seat of the dining room, knocking back wine and spying on me through narrowed eyes, and I knew that it was best to leave her alone. It took all my self-control to resist the urge to ask her if her muted fury was aimed directly at me or at the rest of the world for all it has thrown at her. When James arrived home, I noticed he responded in much the same way, turning a blind eye to the darkness that radiated from her so that they barely exchanged a word until I placed supper on the table and Chloe came down from her room. Once we were all seated around the dining room table it became clear just how drunk she was, whether through the wine or the tablets or a mixture of both. I made a mental note to check on how many pills she's taken; I'm certain she's not following the instructions properly, just taking them as and when she feels like it, and that can't be good for her. She could overdose.

Chloe ate silently, aware of the strained atmosphere, and poor James did his best to make conversation, to ask about school, to share a bit of news from his office, but it was no use at all and in fact, it seemed to be the very thing that provoked Emily to thrust her rage towards me.

'Tell us about these daily walks of yours, Jess,' she said, dropping her fork with a clatter, her jaw set hard.

'What?' I glanced at Chloe and James, but they seemed as bemused as me.

'These walks you've been taking. Apparently – before Daisy went – you've been spotted walking out through town, towards the beach, *every single day*. On your own.' She turned to James, clearly expecting him to show some sense of shock, but his expression remained blank. '*Without Daisy*,' she added with emphasis, though none of us was any clearer on the significance of her words.

I stared back at her, uncertain of the right response. It's true, I am in the habit of walking daily, and I hadn't mentioned it before, but why the problem? 'Ye-es,' I tried, but Emily cut me off.

'So where was Daisy? What did you do with Daisy while you were off on your own doing God knows what?!' She was screaming. James reached across the table to calm her but she threw her arms in the air, as if burnt by his touch. 'Where were you, Jess, when you should have been caring for Daisy?'

'I was just walking, Ems, that's all.'

'And is that by any chance what you were doing on New Year's Eve, when you should have been here? Out walking?'

I was so confused, and even Emily didn't look entirely convinced by what she had just said. 'Ems, I was here at New Year, you know that. I was here when you came home, remember? And the walks – it's just an hour each day, isn't it, Chloe?'

Emily shot her stepdaughter a vicious look. I leapt in, desperate to save Chloe from Emily's wrath. 'It's no secret, Emily, really. Each day after school, Chloe simply takes over with Daisy for an hour so I can have a walk on the beach. It keeps me sane! You know it's pretty full-on all day long with a child, and it just gives me a little break before I come back to start on supper.'

I realised my mistake before Emily even replied.

'*Gave*,' she says. Her eyes are unfocused. 'Not *gives*. It *gave* you a little break. Past tense. Daisy's not here any more, is she? No need for you to *take a little break* any more, is there?' And, with that, she shoved back her chair and took herself to bed.

This morning she remains in bed, even after DCI Jacobs phones to say she'd like to pop round with an update. Only when the doorbell goes does she come to the top of the stairs, making her way down in her dressing gown, her face slack with hangover. I've never seen her look so dreadful.

DCI Jacobs accepts a cup of coffee and asks us where Chloe is as we pull out chairs and gather round the dining room table.

'She's upstairs,' James says, glancing at the clock in the kitchen. It's only just gone nine; Chloe always sleeps in on a Saturday.

'OK, well, it's probably best if you hear this first, as it concerns Max Fuller, and I'm sure Chloe will find it upsetting.'

Emily and James put down their mugs, and lean in to the table in a mirror of concern.

'While Max could provide alibis for New Year's Eve, the most concrete one was from Chloe, and because they've been in a relationship together we have to treat her word with a certain degree of caution. We've since spoken to a number of young people who were also at the party they attended, and several have said that Chloe and Max couldn't be accounted for for the *entire* evening. There was at least an hour – maybe two – when they weren't accounted for at all.'

The colour has drained from James's face. 'You can't think . . .' he starts, but his mouth seems to run out of strength.

'I'm not suggesting Chloe had anything to do with Daisy's disappearance, but we have to cover everything. You understand? So, with this in mind, we decided to take a closer look at Max Fuller, and we got a warrant to search his vehicle, his home having turned up nothing.'

Emily is rapping her knuckles against the table top, signalling her impatience; she's unaware she's even doing it. 'And?'

'And we uncovered a number of things that we'd like you to look at, to see if you recognise them.'

My heart lurches – I've seen these scenes in television dramas, where the police pull out a child's mitten or a significant toy, and they lay it down before the parents and it can only mean one thing –

'Jess, are you all right?' DCI Jacobs is looking straight at me and I realise I'm clutching my shirt front, barely breathing.

I exhale, and nod for her continue, and she places four transparent evidence bags on the table. The first contains a House of Fraser store card – with Emily's name printed on the front. The remaining bags contain items James and Emily confirm as belonging to them: an ornate silver cigarette lighter, a mobile phone and a gold necklace. All items that hadn't even been missed, the phone being broken and long since replaced, the store card rarely used and the Victorian lighter small enough for its absence to go unnoticed. James's expression has shifted from concern to silent fury, the muscles in the side of his jaw working mechanically as he stares at the objects, digesting what it might mean.

None of us hears Chloe descending the stairs, and she walks in just as DCI Jacobs is telling us that they've taken Max back to the station for further interview.

'Of course he could have stolen these items when he was here with Chloe – but the fact that he was with her when she used the spare key means that he knew where it was kept and he *could* have had access to your home without her. We're now officially treating Max Fuller as a suspect.'

'Max?' Chloe asks, her face breaking into despair, and she looks so young and fragile, and I can't bear to see her so broken.

I go to her, wrap my arms tightly about her, desperate to take away her pain. As I hold her I am shocked by the way Emily's watching face is shifting, and I think, *she hates me, she really hates me*, and then calmly she turns back to DCI Jacobs and says, 'Chloe's fifteen, you know? And he's nineteen – Max Fuller?'

I feel Chloe gasp and she pulls free to face Emily, to face James. 'What do you mean?' she says through halting breaths.

'I want him charged with statutory rape,' Emily continues, and it's clear that as far as she's concerned Chloe might be too young to consent, but she's certainly old enough to experience her cruelty. I recognise this cruelty in Emily; I've been on the receiving end of it before.

When I was eighteen, when a full year had passed, I wrote home, addressing my letter to Emily – my first contact with the family since that day we parted. 'I'll write,' I had said at the time, but she had been adamant we should leave it a while, *let the dust settle*; and, bowed of spirit, and turned inward with remorse, I had agreed.

That first letter of mine was written while sitting cross-legged at a coffee table in a beachside bar in Thailand, where I had come to pause after travelling around Australia for six months and getting swept up with the onward travel plans of a trio of fellow travellers I'd met in a hostel in Cairns. I had never been one for groups, so it had been strange for me to attach myself to these other women, but I think there was something we recognised in each other that was reassuring, an unspoken kind of solitary support. Our ages varied, me being the youngest, Sandy the eldest at thirty-two, and Britta and Angela somewhere in their mid-twenties, and the thing we most clearly had in common was the fact that we were travelling alone, none of us in contact with family at home. On my first night at the hostel, just hours after first chatting with them in the communal kitchen, we had headed off to the Scratch Bar together and bonded over a shared bottle of tequila and a bowl of tortilla chips, exchanging stories of home and history and by the end of the night making plans to journey onwards to Bangkok together, once we'd all managed to earn our air fare. It's like that when you travel: somehow the usual conventions don't apply with new people, if you encounter others you connect with. You're lonely, I guess, and when you find these people you hang on to them, open yourself up to them, and ultimately let them go again with just as much ease. That evening we learned that Sandy had been married and sep-arated, and that she had left a two-year-old child behind in New Zealand, because, in her words, she was 'no kind of a mother'. Britta confessed that at home in Sweden she had been indulged by overbearing parents, and was running away from their limit-less expectations of her, and, instead of investing in an education she was blowing her grandparents' trust fund on flights and adventure. Angela spoke curtly of a childhood of abuse and neglect in rural Aberdeenshire, going into little enough detail to suggest she was running from the horrors of her past, hopeful of a future on the furthest side of the world. Me? I told them my truth, the truth as I believed it to be then: I had betrayed my sister; I'd broken my parents' hearts; I didn't know who I was, or what I was, or where I belonged in the world. We were all four of us Seekers, and we liked each other, and as easily as that we agreed that would follow the next leg of our escape route together: seek out the paradise beaches of Thailand.

By the time we reached Krabi two months later, such effort-lessness had developed between us that we behaved more like siblings than recent acquaintances, and when I look back now I realise that, with the exception of my sister Emily, I had never before felt such kinship with other human beings. At Tew Lay bar, a wooden shack set upon stilts overlooking the glistening waters of Krabi beach, I told them how much I yearned to hear news of my family, and how sorry I was about the way things had ended with them. Sandy persuaded me to write. She was working behind the bar there, and she brought to my table paper, pen, a bowl of floating candles and a bottle of iced lager with a lime slice pushed into the neck. I can see and feel that moment even now: the dark humidity of the Thai night, the moonlight shifting across the lilting water, the smell of candle wax and the industrious percussion of cooking and chopping drifting in from the kitchen next door. The place itself was half-full, the atmosphere relaxed, and Britta and Angela had taken themselves to the bar, where they chatted with Sandy, giving me space to think, to write. To hope.

'Now you just have to wait for a reply,' Britta encouraged me as I handed over my letter at the post office in Utarakit Road. 'They're your family. Of *course* they'll be glad to hear from you.'

In the weeks that passed, we all found casual jobs in local restaurants and bars, combining long hours of work with long hours of play, either whiling away the evenings at Tew Lay, or sunbathing and snorkelling in the clear blue waters of Railay beach. When Emily's reply arrived it quite took me by surprise, some four weeks later, and I barely had the courage to open the letter myself. It was Sandy who tore open the envelope in the end, passing me the folded letter across a table laden with Pad Thai and empty beer bottles.

The reply was short, the contents delivered like a sharp blow to the sternum. My father was dead – the funeral had already

125

passed – and my mother was still not ready to see me. *Just leave it a bit longer, Jess*, Emily's letter told me. *Let her get over Dad first. She's had a terrible shock and she doesn't need you adding to it.* There was no warmth, no love, and, in those few lines, no words of encouragement to hasten me home.

I wake in the night, my skin drenched with the sweat of nightmares, tangled dreams of Thailand and home and Emily and James and Daisy, all mixed up to set my heart racing in panic as sleep slips away. The moonlight beyond my window has crept in through a sliver in the curtains and it slashes across my torso, cutting me in two where I have kicked the bedclothes clear. I'm on the cusp of grasping something, some kind of knowledge, and at first I think it must be to do with Chloe, so unsettled am I by the news that Max Fuller is now a suspect. But I realise I'm wrong when it comes to me sharply: a clear memory of New Year's Eve, which causes me to question everything I thought I knew about that night. Emily – and James – told the police that they had arrived home together at 2am that night, when they found me on the floor of the kitchen. But I can see that moment now, as clearly as if I am reliving it, and I know it was *only* Emily who found me. There's the sensation of her hand against my cheek, her shaking me, repeating my name over and over – and then silence, before the terror of her screaming from the landing above – *God*, the sound of her screaming. But there was *no James*. Can that be right? I lay there on the kitchen floor, in much the same position as I lie here now – and I know I'd had one of my episodes, as my consciousness desperately clawed its way back up to the surface – and I heard the sound of my sister talking urgently on the phone, and felt her shaking me again, and shouting at me to wake up and tell her what happened – and *then* there was James coming in through the front door, and the distant chugging sound of a taxi turning on the gravel to drive away. Now, I recall his voice, his distress, the rasp of his shoes against the floor tiles as he tried to revive me, before everything shifted again and the police were at the door and the house was alive with voices and light and sound.

Emily and James *didn't* come home together that night. So why did they lie about it?

14. Emily

Back in the early days Emily had trusted James completely. Had she been right to? she wonders now. She had only been twenty-two; ten years younger than him, and she had wanted to save him. She'd wanted to be saved. Was it all a mistake? Was it all a big, nasty mistake? She stares at her ghostly reflection in the dressing table mirror, willing herself to pick up the hairbrush, to get dressed, to pull herself together. Beyond her bedroom door the phone rings again. It's Sunday morning, for God's sake. The Sabbath; the day of rest – is nothing sacred?

'Ha!' she laughs, a hard plosive sound as she hears her mother in that last sentence. Since when did Emily care about 'the Sabbath'? She draws the brush through her hair, scraping it back into a tight, neat ponytail, and reaches for the jeans and sweatshirt that lie in a heap on the floor where she dropped them yesterday. She's done with vanity; she doesn't have the strength for it any more. What use are manicured nails and waxed legs when all she wants to do is curl up into a ball and disappear from the world?

Taking a deep breath, she dresses, slips her feet into her slippers and opens the bedroom door to head downstairs where the rest of the family will be having breakfast. This last thought – *the rest of the family* – comes close to flooring her, and she stops dead on the landing, pausing to gaze at the black and white photograph of Daisy, the one James took of her on her first birthday in November, in which she's sitting up in her high chair, a wonky party hat balanced on her downy head. Her hands are held up, chubby fingers splayed, and her face is full of delight, her dark eyes alive with laughter. Behind James and the camera Emily was waving Daisy's toy elephant, making her smile for the perfect picture.

The rest of the family. If Daisy doesn't return, she knows, there will be no family. Not in the way it should be. It will be broken forever.

'Is that you, Ems?' she hears Jess, calling up to her.

Emily swallows her thoughts away and descends the stairs, making her way into the kitchen where James and Jess are cooking breakfast together. Chloe is in the dining room, silently laying the table, her phone playing a favourite track from its position on the sideboard. It's as though nothing has happened, as though everything is just the same as before. This seems impossible to Emily, obscene. Only last night they'd all sat around this table – she and James along with Jess and DCI Jacobs – interrogating Chloe yet again, James's voice soft and coaxing, Emily's fury rising so violently that at one point DC Cherry had offered to escort her from the room.

'Do you want to help me make another cuppa, Mrs King?' he'd asked her, and she hadn't even answered, pointedly ignoring the fact that he'd spoken.

Chloe had denied it all at first, until finally she'd admitted, yes, she and Max *had* left the party for a couple of hours but they'd only gone to the pier at Yarmouth, where they'd sat together on a bench overlooking the water, just the two of them and had a few drinks.

'Yarmouth is only a short distance down the road,' DCI Jacobs had said, direct as ever. 'You could easily have come back home, taken Daisy, and returned to the party without anyone there really noticing you'd gone.'

'We didn't!' Chloe had cried out, and she was a mess, a sobbing, snivelling mess, and Emily didn't believe her for a moment.

Eventually, the inspector left, assuring the family that they would be following up Max's version of events, along with a check of all the CCTV cameras in the radius surrounding Yarmouth, their home and the party at Freshwater. She or DC Cherry would be back in touch in the morning with an update.

'Was that the police?' Emily demands of Jess, flicking her hand towards the phone, and even she is surprised at the brusque tone of her voice.

'No,' Jess replies, trying not to scowl in response. 'It was just Sammie. I told her you'd call back when you were up to it.'

'Up to it?'

Jess looks apologetic. 'I mean "up". I meant you'd phone back when you were up.'

Emily pours herself a coffee. She's sick of these sympathy calls. Marcus had phoned last night, wanting to speak to her, but she'd told James she didn't want to talk. She didn't care if he was James's best friend, if he was only trying to show support – she couldn't stand to go over it all again. If it hadn't been for Marcus's party that night, they would have been here, and Daisy wouldn't be missing now. Let James fill him in on it all.

'Well, anyway, I'm not phoning her back. We barely exchanged two words at the funeral. Why would I want to speak to her now? She probably just wants all the juicy gossip, like everyone else.'

'Oh, I doubt it,' Jess says, tilting her head in a pose of compassion. 'People just want to see how you are – to let you know they're thinking of you. Everyone's shocked, you know, Ems? But I'll field the calls, don't worry.'

131

Emily can't look at her sister. She knows that Jess is saying only kind things, but her presence is a constant reminder of everything she has lost. She's robbed Emily of so much, of so many things. *Jess* was the last person to see Daisy – the last person Daisy saw. That should have been Emily, her mother, shouldn't it? Jess was the last to kiss Daisy, to tuck her into her own bed. Jess's was the last voice to say night-night; Jess's were the last hands to smooth Daisy's sleeping head. Those rights belong to a mother, surely? Not an aunt she's only known five minutes – a drunk one at that.

'You were pissed on New Year's Eve,' Emily snaps, stopping in the doorway to turn as she says it. 'I could smell it on your breath.'

Jess's mouth drops open. 'No, I wasn't.'

'Your fainting thing was always worse if you'd had a few drinks. I remember, from when we were younger. The doctors told you that you shouldn't drink too much – that it did something to your capillaries – made your episodes more likely.' Emily surprises herself with how much of this she remembers. But then it was such a major factor in their life, how could she forget?

'Yes, that's right . . .' Jess stammers. 'But I wasn't *pissed*, as you put it.'

'You reeked of it. Stale booze.'

Jess looks sheepishly at James, and she seems ridiculous, standing there with a spatula in one hand, an unbroken egg in the other. 'I had one drink,' she says. 'A glass of prosecco at the very start of the evening.'

James nods. 'It's true – I poured it for her,' he says, as if that makes it any better.

'So what happened to the rest of the bottle, then?' Emily demands, and she feels triumphant when she sees the look of doubt cross her husband's face, and he turns to Jess as though *he* wants to hear the answer too.

Jess turns away and cracks the egg against the side of the pan. 'God knows,' she replies, too casually. 'We probably polished it off over the next few days without realising it.'

'When?' Emily shouts, throwing her arms wide. '*When* did we "polish it off"? We weren't exactly in celebratory mood during the first few days of New Year! I think I'd *remember* drinking prosecco while the police scoured the country for my missing child!'

James steps between them, ever the peacemaker, and then the phone rings again and they all turn towards the sound, startled, anxiously hopeful once more. They see Chloe pass the doorway to catch it, and they wait, frozen, breathless for news.

Chloe reappears, holding out the receiver, and Emily snatches it from her as the sound of blood rushes in her ears. 'It's DCI Jacobs,' Chloe murmurs, her expression uneasy.

'Hello?' Emily says, and she leaves the kitchen and walks along the hall, suddenly terrified that this will be the news they fear the most, the worst possible news.

'Emily? DCI Jacobs here. We've got a brief update for you and James. Two things, actually. Firstly, we've had to release Max Fuller on bail – for the time being we've just got the charge of theft. The CCTV cameras picked up him and Chloe on Yarmouth pier, exactly when she said they were there. Judging by the timings, it's not *impossible* that they could have stopped off at home on the way past, but in my opinion it's unlikely. They look pretty relaxed in the video footage, not like two people with something to hide. We've nothing further to hold him for at the moment, but of course we'll keep you fully updated as we continue to investigate him.'

It's not a body, Emily thinks, her relief so profound that she fears her legs might give way beneath her. She eases herself down, to sit on the bottom step of the stairs as she tries to regulate her breathing. 'You said there were two things?'

'Yes. The second thing relates to Marta Alvarez – your ex-nanny. We've just picked her up for interview – I'm on my way to the station now. Look, I don't want you to let your imagination run away with you, Emily – but we've followed up on a couple of her previous employers and it turns out she was sacked from an earlier job on the mainland.'

Jess and James join her in the hallway, and they stand over her, their expressions questioning. Emily switches the handset to speakerphone.

'For what?' Emily's voice is small; she knows what's coming. 'Why was Marta sacked from her last job?'

There's a slight pause, as DCI Jacobs carefully chooses her words. 'For harming a child in her care.'

Emily drops the phone and lets her body crumple against the stairs. It's the Sabbath, she thinks, her mind flitting absurdly. Don't people know not to phone on the Sabbath?

When Emily first headed back home after graduation, she had intended only to spend the summer there, a well-earned couple of months being mollycoddled by Mum, while she polished her CV and started to consider the prospect of work and life in the 'real world'. Back home, the town felt too small: the shopping centre in the high street unsophisticated, the cafés and bars too provincial; even Minxies was on its last legs, its striped canopy now faded and tattered. All of these places seemed lacklustre and suffocating. And, worse still, their tree-lined street, gently affluent on the outskirts of town, appeared completely unchanged, as though time had simply stood still in that tiny part of the world. Of course she'd been home many times in the two years since Dad had died, but those had been just short visits, a week or two at most, and this time she was struck by the physical change in her mother, and by the perceptible absence of her father in the house. She supposed Mum's ways were magnified now that she wasn't shaded by Dad always taking the limelight, and her carefulness, her timid voice, her unspoken sadness were sometimes more than Emily could bear. She seemed so *old*; so dismal. Of course, Emily hardly had to lift a finger; Mum was overjoyed to have her daughter back home, to cook for and clean for and love and support – and for many a young person it would have felt like a welcome sanctuary, a place of comfort after three years of frugal student life. But for Emily it was suffocating. Her mother's faith, ever-present throughout Emily's childhood, had swelled in fervour since her dad's death, and the rituals of mealtime grace and Sunday mass were more tangible than ever. In recent years Mum had taken on additional church duties – she was in sole charge of the weekly floral arrangements, and to Emily's horror she was now the approved Catechism teacher at St Peter's, meaning she was responsible for the extended religious education of small Catholic children for whom an hour and a half of mass was deemed insufficient worship on their precious weekend off school.

'You know we hated it?' Emily said one Sunday afternoon, after her mother had returned from church, regaling her with some dull story about the children and the fourteen Stations of the Cross.

The words appeared to paralyse her mother, who stood quite still for a moment, a serving spoon full of carrots poised over Emily's dinner plate. 'Hated what?' she asked eventually, apprehensively.

'Me and Jess,' she had replied, knowing how her sister's name would push the wound deeper. 'We *hated* Catechism. As if it wasn't bad enough being the only Catholics among our friends – we then had to give up half of Sunday to the church, no matter what. Do you remember how we weren't allowed to go on sleepovers on a Saturday night, in case we missed Sunday mass? Our friends' families used to go on Sunday picnics – day trips to the beach – or, heaven forbid, have a *lie-in*. We got to sit in a dusty church hall. It felt like a punishment.'

Emily didn't feel a thing when her mother's eyes filled with tears, when she dropped on to her seat clutching a napkin to her mouth. Actually, she hated her a little more, for her weakness, for her blind faith, and she knew then that she had to find a way out of this, find a life of her own.

The solution presented itself quicker than she could ever have imagined when she took an admin job at a successful young IT firm in Fleet, as personal assistant to the branch manager, working in the swish environment of their first-floor offices overlooking the high street. It wasn't quite what she'd had in mind when she had signed up for a degree in English and politics three years earlier, but her final grades had been mediocre, and, to be honest, by the time she graduated she had found herself entirely lacking in political ambition and uncertain of where to go next. All she knew was that she couldn't keep living at home *and* retain her sanity, and the best way she could see out was to get a job and save enough money for a first month's rent somewhere. She'd live anywhere, she thought, so long as it wasn't with her mother. When had she come to resent her so? she wondered. Perhaps Mum had always been this awful, this pathetic; perhaps, distracted by the bright presence of Dad, Emily just hadn't noticed.

Her first day at work came as welcome relief from the monotony of home life, and after a morning's induction across the various departments of the firm she was introduced to her boss, James, a handsome, gently charming man, a decade older than her and, it turned out, recently widowed with a young child. Emily was captivated: by his calm demeanour, by his tragically romantic situation, by the way in which everyone who worked for him seemed equally entranced. Rumour had it that before arriving in Fleet he had taken a few months out to care for his daughter and get over the shock of his wife's death, the word *breakdown* hinted at in hushed tones across in-trays and coffee cups. His charisma was a strange thing – not born out of narcissism or a knowing quality or sexual appeal – it was something rooted in his goodness, and his quiet sorrow. He was a good man, a kind man, and everyone loved him. Within six months he and Emily had embarked on a covert affair, which continued in secret even after James announced that he loved her and wanted them to share a life together – a life somewhere else, a fresh start for him, Emily and little Chloe. He had had enough of his job, knew he possessed the resources to go it alone, and for the next year they quietly plotted and organised, until they were ready to announce their plans and leave. It was the most exciting time of Emily's life – those clandestine weekend trips over to the island with James and Chloe, searching for the perfect house, the perfect town, the right office space, the best schools – all the while telling Mum that she was off meeting some old uni friends, or staying late at the office for a business meeting. None of their colleagues had a clue that they were a couple, so careful were James and Emily to avoid meaningful eye contact or anything more than very public conversation. One of the IT consultants even asked her out to dinner during that period, and when she turned him down it took great self-restraint not to laugh at him, tell him, 'Don't you know? I'm sleeping with the boss?'

And so it was almost an anticlimax, a disappointment, when the time came to tell everyone, to go. Perhaps the most exhilarating part of a secret is the keeping of it, greater than the secret itself. Their colleagues were surprised and delighted for them; Emily's mother was quietly heartbroken all over again.

*

All the time the others are in the house, Emily does what she can to avoid them. She is so full of hate and resentment, and only the tablets seem capable of taking the edge off these feelings of anger and blame, so that she can operate in anything close to a normal fashion. She hates them all: James and Chloe – Jess – the journalists – the police force – her poor dead mother. She knows it's irrational and wrong and unfair, but, if she doesn't give way to hatred, what will she give way to? She can't stand to be around the members of her family, and yet, when Monday morning comes around again, she is left bereft in their absence. James and Chloe are the first to leave, setting off at eight, and by the time Emily makes her way downstairs Jess is already putting on her coat to head out for her daily walk.

'You must be getting fit,' Emily says as she passes her at the foot of the stairs. She takes in the athletic form of her sister, still managing to look attractive in faded black jeans and scruffy man's coat.

'Why don't you come, Ems?' is Jess's reply, but Emily just tuts and carries on towards the kitchen.

'I'll see you later?' Jess calls after her. 'I've bought ingredients for lasagne, so I'll do that for supper tonight. OK? It's Chloe's favourite.'

'And *James's*,' Emily mutters as she hears the front door slam shut behind her sister.

This train of thought sparks something alight and continues throughout the morning, as she sits in her corner seat nursing the same cooling cup of bitter coffee; thoughts of James and Jess together in the kitchen, the little looks they share, the way Jess touches him on the forearm when he says something funny, the way he defends her whenever Emily is vicious-tongued. She thinks about the dining room and the natural seating positions they adopted when Jess arrived to live with them: James between

Chloe and Jess, Emily opposite. She sees the three of them in a warm, smiling cluster, and her, a long way away, shut out from their easy conversation and laughing eyes. The more she thinks about it, the more convinced she grows that they are sharing secrets, that they're shutting her out purposely, making their plans together. There's no hard evidence, she knows, but she's certain. But then she's been certain in her suspicions before – both of Jess and James – and she hasn't always been right.

By late morning Emily is dressed and pulling her trainers on in the hallway. She opens the front door to test the air and reaches back inside for her jacket and hat. There's been a hard frost overnight, and although it's nearly midday the frost remains, coating the gravel drive, the pillars that flank the entrance, the leaves of the rose bush that cling to the trellis. Her breath billows out white in the quiet driveway, and she's relieved to find the road free of journalists for the first time in days. Checking her pockets for keys and purse, she pulls the door closed and sets off to pick up the bus into town, getting off at the Carisbrooke stop so she can walk for a little longer, think a little more clearly. The sharp air feels good on her face, and she pushes her hands deeper into her pockets and quickens her pace, only slowing down when she reaches the street where James's offices are located. There are a few people about, mostly shoppers and young parents on their way to and from playgroup. That would have been me once, Emily allows herself to think, but then she realises that even that is wrong. That would have been *Jess* once, while Emily was out at work. What had she been thinking, letting someone else look after her baby? She runs her fingers over the keypad of her phone and thinks about phoning DCI Jacobs, to ask if there's any more news about Marta, but somehow she knows there is none. Marta is a spiteful bitch, and someone who should never be left in charge of young children, but, standing here on the high street in the cold light of day, Emily fears that Marta is no more guilty of taking Daisy than she is.

Crossing the street, she ducks her head down and rushes along the path, darting into Rosa's Café directly opposite James's office. It's risky, she knows, as the café is used by members of his staff who pop in and out for takeaway coffees and buns, but James never comes in himself and Emily is pretty sure she won't be recognised if she keeps her hat on and sits close to the window with her back to the door. The only other danger is Marcus – she's pretty sure *he* would spot her straight away, but she decides it's a risk worth taking. Marcus never struck her as the tea-and-a-bun type; he probably has a cordon bleu platter yachted in from the mainland every lunchtime. She orders coffee and a shortbread biscuit, more for appearances' sake than from hunger, and settles at a small table looking straight out across the street. The office building is set between two retail units, a print shop on one side and a nail bar on the other. The ground floor is the reception area, but Emily knows the desk is set far enough back that she won't be noticed through this steamy window; and James's desk is on the first floor, with no view of the street.

She takes a sip of her coffee, which is still too hot to drink. What is she doing here? She has no real plan; she just felt compelled to come, to sit and spy, perhaps to see how it feels to be in the outside world, out from under the all-consuming weight of home, to gaze in on James's life and make some sense of it all. Perhaps she wants to understand how they can all get on with their lives so easily, when hers has come to a standstill? An elderly woman passes the window, walking a small dog, and Emily feels an unexpected stab of loss for her mother. She should have been a better daughter. She should have visited her more than once a year; she should have made it easier for her mother to be a part of their lives. She's losing her thread again. It's the tablets; she couldn't do without them right now, but at the same time she resents the way in which they buff off the raw edges of feeling, when she knows somehow that she ought to *feel* the feeling in order to find the answers.

The front door of the office opens and her breath accelerates in anticipation, but then a pair of young women walk out on to the pavement and head in the direction of the main street. Emily looks up at the clock: it's 12.15. Does he have lunch at his desk? He doesn't take a sandwich, so he must go out for one, or send someone out to fetch lunch. And then, just as she is thinking how strange it is that she doesn't know the details of her husband's day-to-day life, Jess appears, pushing open the office doors and wiping her sandy boots on the doormat before letting the door fall shut behind her.

Jess? What the hell is Jess doing there? Emily feels herself rise from her seat, but thinks better of it and drops back again, her heart pounding against her ribcage. 'Can I get you something else?' the owner calls over, alerted by Emily's sudden movement. 'Another drink?'

Emily, not wanting to tear her gaze from the building across the street, raises her hand to decline, throwing a distracted, 'No, thanks,' over her shoulder. She hunkers down in her seat, cradles the mug to her face, and waits. Five minutes later, the door swings open again and James comes out, laughing – he's *laughing*, head thrown back, eyes bright – and he reaches an arm behind him to hold the door open, and Jess steps out alongside him. He gestures towards the town, and she smiles, and as though they are synchronised they turn together in that direction, and then they are gone.

15. Jess

I promised Chloe I'd meet her after school today, so with a couple of hours to kill after lunch I wandered along Newport high street, half-heartedly window shopping until I was drawn into H&M with an unexpected urge to buy something new. Ever since I'd arrived on the island, I'd adopted a fixed uniform of jeans, sweatshirt, and comfortable shoes. There seemed little point in trying to dress up, when your day was made up of childcare, housework, cooking and soft-play. This must be the way new mothers feel, I think, and I decide that I don't want to feel that way any more. I'm not a new mother; I'm a single woman, in my early thirties, and I should make more of an effort.

The shop is fairly quiet, as it's a weekday, and I meander along the aisles, running my fingers over fabrics, holding dresses and tops against myself, gradually accumulating an armful to try on in the changing rooms. Behind the cubicle door, I undress, pausing to meet my own gaze in the full-length mirror. Why do I feel as though I'm doing something wrong, I wonder – as if I'm bunking off school or being deceitful? When I met James for lunch today I felt the same, though I had no reason to, and I'd only suggested meeting up so that I could ask him why he hadn't been truthful about coming home later than Emily on New Year's Eve. But when it came to it he took me to this lovely little bistro, and we were having such a nice time, I couldn't bring myself to say anything. Selfishly, I didn't want to break the illusion that we were just two people out for lunch, enjoying the food, enjoying the conversation, enjoying an escape from it all.

Daisy's face rears up in my conscience, and I blink it away, guilt biting at me as I do so, hating myself for all the times I've denied her absence. But life can't just grind to a halt, can it? I love that little girl with every fibre of my body, and God knows how many tears I've shed into my pillow – but we have to stride out, surely, to make a pretence at normality? To make a pretence at life. *Don't we?*

I slip my arms into a cherry-red puffa jacket, and stand before the mirror looking at my reflection. It's close-fitting and warm, with deep pockets, and a flattering hemline that just skims my bum. I know I look good in it, and I want it so much that I don't even bother to try on the other things, still wearing it as I make my way to the till, asking the cashier to snip off the label once I've paid, and bagging up my old coat. Checking my watch, I see it's nearly time to meet Chloe, and I realise that what I'm feeling is gladness: I'm looking forward to seeing her, to hugging her and chatting with her on the drive back home.

Despite everything, today is the best I've felt in the almost two weeks since Daisy went missing, and as I turn my face towards the cool bright sunlight of January I decide that, for today at least, I'm going to let myself feel that way.

As soon as Chloe gets in the car I sense she needs to talk, so I take a detour on the way home, stopping off at the Beachview

Hotel for a bowl of her favourite Minghella ice cream, served up in knickerbocker glory glasses at a table for two, overlooking the dimming horizon of the sea.

'Shouldn't we tell Dad?' she asks, looking suddenly concerned. 'He might worry – you know?'

He never used to worry, I think, not before Daisy disappeared. 'It's fine. I saw him in town at lunchtime and said I might take you for a treat after school.'

She relaxes, her shoulders dropping slightly as she leans in to take a first taste of her ice cream. She looks so young, despite all the grown-up things she's been getting herself into – the boyfriend, the drinking, the secrets and lies – and it's clear to me that she's still just a little girl, vulnerable to life's ills.

'How are you doing, Chlo?' I ask.

She shrugs, refilling her spoon. 'Pretty shit. Some of the kids at school have been saying I'm going out with a paedo. That I'm *shagging* a paedo. Yesterday, one of my best friends tried to defend me to someone by saying that they should cut me some slack because *I* was the victim. Which was nice.'

I don't know what to say, and I stare at her across the table, shocked.

'And some of them think Mum or Dad did it – took Daisy and killed her or something – because of the papers, because of all the bollocks the newspapers say.'

I can see the headlines, running across my mind's eye like a newsreel ticker: WHO TOOK BABY DAISY? . . . DAISY'S PARENTS – MORE QUESTIONS ARE ASKED . . . DAISY SISTER'S BOYFRIEND BEATEN – *IS* HE GUILTY? . . . DAISY NANNY INTERVIEWED IN POLICE PROBE . . . a fresh one daily, it seems; it's no wonder her classmates are saying these things, when there's a new line of enquiry every day, a new dead end, a new flare of hope, a new false start.

'Today this one little dick in History said, *It's got to be one of you – it's* always *someone in the family*, and I swear I would've kicked him in the nuts if Sir hadn't come in at that moment and broken it up.' Chloe jams her spoon into her ice cream and I realise I haven't touched mine yet.

'They're all just idiots, Chloe, you know that?' I take a careful spoonful, building up to asking her about the one thing I know she doesn't want to speak about. 'So, what's the latest with you and Max?'

Chloe puts her spoon down, and for a moment I think she might just walk out. But instead she takes a deep breath and begins to talk. 'You might not believe this, Jess, but he's beside himself. He says it's the worst thing that's ever happened to him – worse than his parents' divorce, or when his cousin died of cancer – *the worst thing*. He's had "nonce" scratched into the side of his car and death threats on his Facebook page – and, since he got beaten up, everyone assumes he must be guilty and people are openly talking about him on Instagram. Like he's already been convicted of it, like he's a sex offender. He had to delete his accounts in the end. Why are people like that?'

I let the silence hang between us for a moment, hoping she'll carry on.

'And I can't tell you how many times he's told me he's sorry about those things he took. I mean, they weren't even important things – they weren't even worth anything.'

I frown at her across the table. 'That's not exactly the point, is it, Chloe? You invited him into your home, and he stole from your family. He stole from *you*. You've got to agree, that's pretty crappy?'

Her eyes remain downcast and she nods, and I hope she won't cry, I couldn't bear to be the cause of her tears when she's going through so much already. Eventually, she looks up and says, 'I

146

hate him for that – but I love him too, and I just don't know what to do, Jess?' She says it like a question, as though she thinks I have the answers. But I don't. She lowers her voice, her eyes flickering across the faded Art Deco dining room. 'I know he took those things – *stole* those things – but that doesn't make him a kidnapper, does it? Or a *rapist*!'

She's referring to Emily's words on Saturday, when she told DCI Jacobs that she wanted Max charged with rape. Chloe hasn't spoken to her stepmother since, and I've watched them in the days that have passed and wondered, is this it for them – can they never be close again? Has too much been said, too much hurt been inflicted? Or would Daisy's safe return heal it all, wash it all away? I'm not sure; I'm not sure Chloe can ever forgive Emily for the things she has said. And I'm certain Emily will never forgive Chloe for bringing Max into their lives.

'I know he's not, Chlo. I met him – he seems nice – you seemed good together. But it's probably best if you keep a low profile when it comes to Max at the moment, until Emily's forgiven you for lying to them about New Year's Eve. Just keep out of her way a bit, until she's in a better place.'

'A better place? I *hate* her. It's not just this, not just since Daisy, you know? But then, you wouldn't know because you weren't here before, when she used to be nice – she used to be like you. I don't know what it is, but gradually she just changed towards me, got colder. She stopped hugging me or wanting to do things together, and she didn't want to know what I'd been up to at school or anything, and she'd always be complaining to Dad about how lazy or messy or ungrateful I am. And I know I'm not *that* bad –'

'You're not bad *at all*, Chloe! You're a wonderful, precious girl. Please remember that. Don't let other people lure you into thinking otherwise. You're a good person.'

I think about Emily in our childhood years, and the way she could punish, pushing me away with such frost that in the end I'd do anything to return to the warmth of her embrace. She could make me feel that I was all kinds of things I wasn't, make me question everything I thought I knew about myself. But I understood Emily better than anyone – and I knew how it worked. Chloe doesn't know how to play this game. It's not a level playing field.

Chloe is plaiting her fingers together on the table between us, and I'm suddenly worried that it sounds as though I'm bad-mouthing Emily. 'You've got to understand, Chloe, Emily's going through hell at the moment. She had her heart ripped out that night Daisy was taken – and she's suspicious of *everyone*. Even me.'

Chloe pulls a face. '*You*?'

'*Yes*, me! She watches my every move; haven't you noticed? But it's not just me. It's you, your dad, the nanny, Max – I guess what I'm trying to say is, don't take it personally. We've all just got to concentrate on staying positive until we get Daisy back, and then we can all get back to normal again.'

Now Chloe does cry, a tear coursing down the side of her nose as she pushes her half-finished dessert away. '*Will* we get her back, Jess? What if she's – I couldn't stand it if she's . .'
And then the words run out because Chloe can't say the words either; none of us wants to say the words.

'Of course we'll get her back,' I say, and I know in that instant that I'd give my life for Daisy's in a heartbeat. I reach across to cover Chloe's hand with mine.

With her other hand, Chloe runs a finger beneath her lashes. 'I wish you were my mum, Jess,' she says. 'I wish we could get Daisy back – and I wish Emily would vanish – and I wish you could stay with us forever.'

'Three wishes?' I laugh, patting her hand as I catch the waitress's attention for the bill. 'Careful what you wish for, Chloe-boo.'

*

On the drive home we share a companionable silence and I think about Chloe's shock at Emily's suspicions, my mind returning to an afternoon in late October, not long after I'd moved in, when I walked in on Emily rifling through James's paperwork while he was out at work. It was a stormy, cold day, and the rain was lashing hard against the windowpanes of his study as I pushed open the door to wheel in the vacuum cleaner, surprised to find Emily standing over James's desk lifting papers from his in-tray. I wouldn't have thought much more of it, had she not looked so overwhelmingly guilty and embarrassed.

'Jeez, you made me jump!' she said, after that first wordless pause of shock, and she dropped the papers back into their tray and tucked the chair beneath the desk with purpose. 'I was looking for some of the solicitor's papers to do with Mum's will,' she blurted, but I knew she wasn't telling the truth. 'You haven't seen them, have you?'

'Which papers are you after?' I asked.

She stared back at me, stumped. I plugged in the vacuum and was about to get started when instinct made me reach out and touch her arm as she went to leave. 'Is everything all right, Ems? You look a bit, I don't know – freaked out.'

At first I thought she wasn't going to tell me, but then it all came spilling out: how she had nothing concrete to go on, nothing more than a gut feeling, but she thought James could be cheating on her. That he could be having an affair.

Of course I talked her round, told her she must be imagining it because James was one of the *nicest*, most trustworthy, loyal people I'd ever met. And I was glad when she seemed reassured by my words, and she thanked me for listening and we hugged, and the subject never arose again. Was I right to reassure her?

I wonder now, my thoughts lighting on his late arrival home on New Year's Eve. Where had he been, and why would he actively lie about it to the police? If he *was* having an affair, surely Emily would have brought it up again, and I'm certain she would have told the police that they didn't arrive home together that night, out of anger if nothing else.

Unless . . . I think with a shudder as we pull into the driveway and park in front of the house, the thought faltering as I unbuckle my seatbelt and see James smiling at us from the open doorway. Chloe is craning her neck to look up at the gap in the curtains of the nursery window, and there is Emily; pale and haunted, a ghost in her own house. *Unless,* the thought returns to me, *unless they* both *have something to hide.*

16. Emily

The banging at the front door is so loud that Emily's first heart-pounding thought is *they've found her, they've found Daisy!* James is out of bed before she is, throwing back the covers and leaping to his feet to stand naked in the gloomy morning light, hooking back a small gap in the curtain to look out on to the front drive. There's a short pause, before the knocking resumes.

'Who is it?' Emily whispers, easing her heavy legs from the bed and reaching for her dressing gown.

'Dunno,' James replies as he drops the curtain drape. He picks up his jeans and hurriedly begins to dress. 'There's a whole load more journalists outside the gate, though. Something must have happened.'

Emily follows him as he rushes from the bedroom and down the stairs, passing a bleary-eyed Chloe on the landing as they go. They jog down, one after the other, so that when Jess opens the front door they are a welcome party of four, looking their morning worst, not caring about the snarling photographers who trespass on the driveway to snap their reactions to the police officers standing on the doorstep.

DCI Jacobs steps over the threshold, beckoning DC Piper and another officer to follow suit, swiftly shutting the door against the media intrusion.

'What is it?' Emily asks, her desperation laid bare in a strangled voice. *Please God, please God, please God.*

DCI Jacobs' expression is steely and she casts her gaze over every one of them, assessing the situation, clearly weighing up what she can say in front of them all. 'Mr and Mrs King, can I speak to you alone in the kitchen?'

Emily and James exchange anxious nods, indicating for the detective to follow them through, leaving the two officers to hover in the dining room with Jess and Chloe. The worktop is a mess, its surface strewn with Jess's cereal bowl and milk slops. There's a coffee cup and a left-out juice carton – and, beside the sink, two wine glasses, their ruby-stained dregs dried on from the night before. Emily's eyes linger on the empty wine bottle. She took a sleeping pill last night and went to bed early, leaving Jess and James to clear up after supper. As she headed for the stairs, Jess had told her to sleep well; James told her he'd be up soon.

'What's happened?' Chloe calls after them from the dining room, and Emily steps out to shoot her a warning message. *Back off,* she wants to say. *Back off, Chloe.* As she returns to the main kitchen, she hears her stepdaughter's complaining voice against Jess's reassuring murmurs, and then the sound of Chloe's light footsteps retreating back up the stairs. Emily wants to know where Jess is; it makes her uneasy when she's out of sight, listening, spying on their business.

'Tea?' James asks, distractedly opening up the dishwasher to clear away the dirty pots, and with a violent passion Emily wants to lash out at him. *Tea, for Christ's sake!*

'Is it about Marta Alvarez?' Emily asks, desperate to steer DCI Jacobs straight to the vital information. 'You were interviewing her, weren't you? What did you find out?'

The inspector shakes her head dismissively. 'I'm afraid we hit a dead end with Miss Alvarez. While she has a poor track record as a nanny, she had a clear alibi for New Year's Eve – she was babysitting for her new family, while they entertained at home. So she was there all night, with plenty of witnesses to back up her statement.'

Emily stares at her, a mixture of emotions buzzing through her veins. Disappointment? Relief? Anger? It's all of these things, and more. 'Did you tell her new employer about her past, about hurting that child? She's clearly a danger around children!'

DCI Jacobs nods, curtly, indicating she won't speak further on the matter.

'And Max Fuller?' James asks, his eyes flickering towards the archway into the dining room.

'Chloe's gone back upstairs,' Emily mutters. 'Yes, what about *him*? What about Max – or Chloe, for that matter?'

James is horrified. '*Emily?* What the hell are you talking about?' He looks at the detective, his bright eyes a study of confusion.

'She's hiding something, James, and if you can't see it you're blind! Creeping about all the time, asking questions – trying to deflect suspicion with that bloody hashtag-find-Daisy campaign. You don't want to see it – but she's not telling us everything.'

James puts his head in his hands, raising his face as he gathers a breath. 'I'm sorry, inspector, I really don't know what Emily's saying. Chloe's not under suspicion, is she?'

DCI Jacobs takes a moment to answer. She's assessing us, Emily thinks, she's trying to read us, but she'll never be successful. There's too much going on here, too many secrets, too many half-truths and downright lies.

'Chloe's not a suspect, no.'

Emily doesn't like the way she puts emphasis on the word 'Chloe', as though something else is coming, and it *is*, it *so* is coming –

'Chloe's not a suspect because she can pretty well account for her movements for that night. You two, on the other hand – well, we received some information last night that suggests you haven't been entirely honest with us in the statements you've given.'

'What?' James is incredulous. 'About what? What information?'

'*Both* of us?' Emily interjects, the panic rising up in her like a flush of nausea. 'I don't understand!' She grips the worktop with one hand, the other coming instinctively to her mouth, to gnaw on her ragged thumbnail as she waits for all the answers she doesn't want to hear.

'Yes, both of you.' DCI Jacobs pauses in that horrible watchful way she has. She seems to be soaking up their thoughts, gauging their responses for signs of deceit. 'I can't go into it here, Mr and Mrs King. But I can tell you that this new information has also been backed up by independent sources – other people who were at the party with you on New Year's Eve – so naturally we're going to have to interview you further to make sure we've got all our facts straight.'

'Both of us?' Emily asks again. She can't believe this is happening. Most chilling of all, she lights on the use of 'Mr and Mrs King'. No more *Emily*. No more *James*. Now it's *Mr and Mrs King*.

James is shaking his head. Emily looks on, barely able to blink as she tries to process what's happening in her kitchen. Her mind is in overload. *Do they think we took Daisy? Do they think we are guilty? Do they?*

'*Who* has given you this information?' James demands, raising his voice, his arms folding across his body, his stature growing large. '*What* information?'

'I can't go into it here,' Jacobs replies firmly, unruffled. She's not a woman who is easily stirred, and she continues, businesslike, matter-of-fact. 'We'll interview you at the station this morning, and hopefully clear it up once and for all. Do you need a few minutes to get dressed?' She looks at Emily in her dressing gown. 'To gather your things?'

We're not under arrest. Emily feels as though her legs might give way beneath her. *If we were under arrest they wouldn't say 'gather your things', would they? They'd just bundle us into the police car and take us away. We're not under arrest.*

James appears suddenly crestfallen. Emily and James take it in turns to ascend the stairs, to swiftly dress and brush their teeth, to 'gather their things'. For Emily, there's no time for make-up, or to brush her hair, and she glances in the mirror as she leaves her bedroom, and barely recognises the rag of a woman who returns her gaze.

Downstairs, she meets James at the front door, where he's talking to Jess in quiet tones, instructing her to look after Chloe, to make sure she gets to school OK, make sure she eats properly. Could Jess phone Marcus for him, let him know the situation, get him to reschedule their morning meeting? Chloe sits silently on the bottom step of the stairs, small and pale in her unicorn-print pyjamas, studying her own feet. Emily extends a hand towards James, but he shakes his head, before casting his gaze about the room and grabbing his keys and mobile phone, indicating to his police officer that he's good to go. DCI Jacobs informs them that there are two vehicles on the drive, and that they are to travel separately, Emily with her and DC Piper in the unmarked car, and James with the other officer in the marked police car.

'The press are really pumped up out there today,' Jacobs says. 'So, on the count of three, I'm going to open the door and we will all move directly to the vehicles and get straight in. Minimum fuss, OK?'

Emily and James nod dumbly, and in the space of a few seconds the five of them are out through the front door, sprinting across the gravel towards the cars, ducking beneath the baying cries of the gathered press. 'Mrs King! Is it true you lied about your whereabouts on the night Daisy disappeared?' 'Mr King! Can we get a photo?' 'Emily! James! Do you know where Daisy is?'

Their questions are shattering.

Jess shouts out to Emily from the open doorway, unheard words, not loud enough to make out over the noise of car doors slamming and journalists calling and jostling for a scoop. From her seat in the back of the car Emily sees Jess hold up her arm, swivelling her hand into a thumbs-up, a look of naïve encouragement on her face.

Emily turns to her right, to look directly at James through the glass window of the car beside hers. His eyes don't meet hers. They're locked on Jess and Chloe in the doorway, and she sees him nod, an expression of gratitude radiating from his face as the engines start and the cars move away. As her vehicle turns on the gravel and passes the front door, Emily sees Jess's face, a mask of concern. She looks as though she might cry.

At the station DCI Jacobs keeps Emily waiting for hours, shut in an interview room with a blank-faced PC on duty, with nothing more than a cardboard cup of stewed tea and the promise that they 'shouldn't keep you waiting too long'. She is asked if she would like a solicitor present, and she declines without hesitation. What does she need a solicitor for? She can't possibly be under *real* suspicion. They're just clutching at straws.

As time ticks by, her initial indignation turns to anxiety. Why are they taking so long? Are they interviewing James yet? Why wouldn't they be interviewing them simultaneously? They must be getting his version first, so that they can check if their stories match up, and of course they won't, will they? Emily now knows that James's reasons for lying were purely practical, and entirely innocent: he was pissed as a fart when he left the party, and after waiting an age for a taxi he shared the ride with some bloke he'd only met that night. He couldn't remember this man's name, or even what time it was when he left Marcus and Jan's house, and he had panicked, that was all – thought it was less complicated if they said that they'd left the party together, that they'd arrived home at the same time. And of course, that suited Emily too. No need to explain where she'd been or what she'd been up to if they both said they were together for the whole evening. Even now, James thinks Emily got home at least an hour before he did, but the truth is, it was a matter of minutes, twenty at the most. He's so mortified about being drunk that night – as though he thinks he could have changed any of this if he had been sober – that he hasn't questioned Emily's version of events at all. Why should he? She's never given him reason to mistrust her. She's never done anything like this before.

DCI Jacobs enters the room with another officer, and the interview begins. It's 3pm and she's been waiting for six hours. Outside it will be starting to get dark again soon; they've kept her locked up like a prisoner for the best part of a day. Surely they suspect her? Why else would she still be here?

'Apologies for the delay,' the inspector says, pushing a packaged cheese sandwich and a coffee across the table.

'Am I under arrest?' Emily demands, bringing the drink to her mouth, savouring the burn of it against her tongue. 'You've had me here for hours. Am I under arrest?'

DCI Jacobs appears perplexed by the question. 'No-o-o,' she replies, sounding out the 'o' so that it's long and considered. 'We wanted to follow up some of the details of your husband's statement first. He's now given us a slightly amended version of events, and we'd like to see if you want to do the same?'

Emily sits across the table, her focus moving between DCI Jacobs and the young man at her side, and she thinks, *I can't. I can't ruin it all now. I can't risk everything I have for a moment of madness.* And quickly, she adapts her story to one she believes will work, one she hopes they will accept as true: she left before James, she got waylaid chatting to other guests in the hallway, and then she headed home, alone, arriving to find Jess on the floor of the kitchen and Daisy gone. James, in a taxi, arrived ten, maybe twenty minutes behind her. That should do it, she tells herself. Why wouldn't they believe me? I'm a respectable mother, a good mother, a law-abiding citizen with a flawless reputation.

When Emily has finished talking, DCI Jacobs rests her pen on the table between them, takes a sip of her own coffee and clears her throat. She looks at her watch; it's getting late. 'So, Emily, after you left James at the party on New Year's Eve, you *didn't* go down to Shanklin beach and have sex with Marcus Fairbrother before returning home?'

'*Oh*,' Emily sighs, and then she starts to cry.

Emily was so angry at James when she left the party that night, she could feel the rage churning inside her, like a small volcano ready to erupt. She hated him, for not loving her enough to marry her, for asking her to be his wife in everything but law, for the raw emotion he lets slip whenever Avril's name is raised. *Avril, Avril, Avril* – she wanted to shout it in his face. *She's dead, you idiot! She's dead, and we're all here – me and Chloe and Daisy – we're all here and you've never got over it, have you? You've still got one foot in the past.* He was stuck in a time that filled him with self-indulgent sadness and seclusion. Did he love his first wife more than he loves her? How much better it would be if he were divorced, if he'd left his wife acrimoniously, so he could now view the woman with a healthy dollop of bitterness and suspicion. So much better than this, because what kind of a person utters harsh words about a dead woman – feels *jealous* of a dead woman, when there's no way to compete, no way to be what she will always be: a sainted mother, preserved in memory, robbed of her life too soon.

As she left the Fairbrothers' house that night, Emily breathed in the icy night air, taking in the sharp, salted scent of the sea, the sounds of carousing and laughter fading behind her as she walked, weary on high heels, towards their family car, parked beneath the giant palm at the entrance to Marcus's ostentatious driveway. The moon was just off full in the clear sky, coating the expansive gardens in a luminous film of milky light. Already, frost was settling, and she checked her watch: 12.30am. She was glad to get away early, glad to be sober and heading home without James. Let *him* have the hangover. Let *him* struggle to get a taxi home on the busiest night of the year.

She reached the driver's side door and paused a second, fishing around in her bag to locate the car keys, worrying for a moment that she'd have to return to the party, stern-faced, to ask James if he has them in his pocket. But, there!

Just as she laid her fingers on them, she heard her name spoken, close by, and she looked up to see Marcus standing in the dark shadows of the palm tree, just half of his face exposed by the light, a cigarette held loosely between his fingers.

'Off so early?' he said, a smile in his voice. 'You always used to be the last one standing, Emily.'

She smiled, pushed her hair from her face. 'Well, that was before I got well and truly tied to the kitchen sink.'

He took a step forward, so that his whole face could be seen. He's not handsome, not in the way James is, but there's something unmistakably *male* about his heavy face, his strong nose strikingly broken, his cupid's bow mouth sharp and sensuous. There's an affluent carelessness about his appearance that is quite captivating.

161

'By James?' he asked, surprise in his voice.

'No!' she laughed, pressing her key fob so the central locking popped open. 'By Daisy! You know what a new baby is like, Marcus. You've had enough of them.' This is a standing joke between James and his business partner, Marcus's great fertility having spawned not one but six children in the space of the past ten years.

Marcus took a final deep lungful of smoke, turning his face skywards to exhale a cool white stream before dropping the stub and grinding it out beneath his polished chestnut brogues. He'd left his jacket inside, and his grey linen shirt was rolled halfway up his muscular forearms, revealing winter-tanned skin.

'Aren't you cold?' Emily asked, a sudden shiver running through her.

'Want to look at the beach?' he said in answer, as he took another step closer, casually planting his hands in his pockets. 'Shanklin will be quiet, down by the Fisherman's Cottage. It's a beautiful view on a moonlit night. We can walk from here if you like?'

In that moment, standing on that driveway with Marcus beneath the starry sea-crisp sky, Emily didn't want to go straight home. She didn't want to be a mother; she didn't want to be sensible. She wanted to be the last one standing. She *wanted* to be wanted.

17. **Jess**

It's just after 9pm when James is dropped home by DC Cherry. The press clearly think they're on to a good story here, because there are still a large number of them just beyond the driveway, and I've been fielding their phone calls and door-knockings all afternoon.

After the police took Emily and James first thing, I told Chloe I thought it was a good idea if she stayed home today, and we spent the day baking, and ordered takeaway pizzas to eat on the sofa as we watched old Disney films and pretended that none of this was going on. After supper I made her a hot chocolate and sent her to bed early, and I could tell by the weary weight of her movements that she was happy to go up, that the poor girl had had enough. Upstairs, I tucked her in, much as you would a child years younger, and she closed her eyes immediately, and I knew how much the care and attention meant to her, how much she needed it. As I switched off the main light, a strong memory jolted me, from when we were not much older than Chloe: a memory of Emily tucking *me* into bed with a hot water bottle, a glass of water by my side. She'd kissed me on the forehead and told me to get some sleep. 'It's all over now,' she told me, smoothing the hair back from my face. 'You can get on with your life.' We had just returned from the clinic, my baby aborted, our problem solved.

As I click Chloe's door quietly shut, I hear the car on the gravel outside, and lightly I jog downstairs to have the door ajar ready for Emily and James to bolt through. But James is alone. He slides in through the gap and pushes the door shut with a muffled thud, immediately grabbing me in a tight and unexpected hug.

'Christ, I'm glad to be back home,' he sighs into my hair, and then he releases me, his arms dropping like anchors as he lets out a long, exhausted sigh. 'Got any wine open?'

We settle on the comfy seats by the open fire in the living room, and, as James eats reheated cottage pie and downs a second large glass of wine, he tells me everything. He explains why he lied about returning home with Emily on New Year's Eve, and it's so obvious, so heartbreakingly simple that I feel dreadful for having doubted him. He was drunk, more drunk than he liked to admit, and he'd been worried that it wouldn't look good. He was worried the police would think he was a bad father.

'So, what did they say about Emily? You said they haven't finished interviewing her yet?' I think about her, sitting in a cell, growing hungry, tired, and angrier with every passing hour. 'Surely, now you've cleared up your movements that night, surely they'd just let her go too?'

James reaches out for the wine bottle, distributing the last of its contents between our two glasses. 'That's what I thought,' he replies, leaving his seat briefly to fetch a second bottle from the wine rack at the far end of the room. He places it on the coffee table with the corkscrew. 'But I'm guessing that if our versions still didn't match up, if Emily was still trying to cover for me, they'll just keep going at her until they believe she's telling them the truth. And you know how stubborn she can be, Jess – she'll stick to her story if she thinks she's right.'

James draws one leg up on to the sofa between us, twisting slightly so that his head can rest on the arm, the toes of his socked foot slipping casually beneath my thigh. I reach out and place a friendly hand on his knee, giving it the lightest squeeze. 'Are you all right, James?' I ask.

He lifts his head a little to smile sadly at me, but he doesn't reply.

'I worry about you,' I say. 'I worry about all of you, but especially you. Everyone's keeping an eye on Emily, because she's more obviously – well, you know. She shows it more easily, and we're all trying desperately hard to keep her head above water. But just because you're not falling apart, James, it doesn't mean you're not feeling it just as much, that you're not equally devastated by all this, does it?'

His eyes glint with unspilled tears. 'Do you miss your mother?' he asks me, quite out of the blue.

'I – of course,' I say, because I don't know how to talk about it, it's so complex and unspeakable. 'What about you? I've never heard you talk about yours.'

He nods, and for a moment I'm not sure if he will go on. 'We fell out – over Avril – and I've never got over the guilt of that. We never made up. I just left, the way I always do when the going gets tough.'

I shake my head. 'Don't be so hard on yourself. These things happen.' God knows, *I* know that much.

'But we were always so close, me and my mum. I was quite a mummy's boy, I'm ashamed to say – the much-celebrated only child.' He smiles, and a tear drops heavily on to his shirt. 'She was so critical of the way I dealt with Avril's illness; she thought I should have been stronger, more *there* for her. But I didn't know how to deal with it. I was scared, and barely keeping it together myself. I regret that I left things the way I did with Mum, and I regret that Chloe's missed out on having her grandmother in her life. Maybe things would've been better for Chloe if my mother had been around too.'

'Have you ever thought of trying to make up with her – you know, it's never too late? It's one of my biggest regrets, not sorting things out with my parents when I still had the chance. Maybe you should try to make contact?'

He looks at me, his expression hard to read. 'I don't think so. I feel so bad about leaving it this long, I wouldn't know how to begin to put things right. You must think I'm a coward?'

'I'm hardly in a position to think that,' I say, and I think, we're the same, James and I. We're both on the outside looking in.

We sit quietly for a moment. 'You know Chloe's going to be OK, don't you?' I say. 'She's got you to talk to, and me. I adore Chloe, and I'll always be there for her. But I just want you to know that *you've* got me too, if you need to talk, James, or cry, or shout, or rant – or anything!' I feel self-conscious, awkwardly offering up my support in so vocal a way, because really, we don't know each other that well yet, not like this.

James's phone buzzes in his shirt pocket, and he has it in his hand in a second. 'It's a text,' he says, the disappointment evident in his posture the moment he reads it. 'It's just Marcus. Wants me to call him ASAP. He'll be chasing me up about that meeting I had to cancel yesterday.'

'Bit late to be making work calls, isn't it?' I feel vaguely irritated at Marcus's insensitivity. Doesn't he know what James is going through right now? 'Let him wait till morning.'

I've forgotten that my palm is still resting on his knee, until he places his hand over mine and the pad of his thumb circles the small bone of my wrist in an oddly intimate gesture. 'I know, Jess. *Thank you.* Just having you here, I can't tell you the difference it's made. You must know that? Of course, it's been hell, and Emily – she –' He halts, dropping his head back against the sofa again. 'You know what she's like. It's hard. That's all.' He looks over at the obsolete Christmas tree and sighs. 'That evening – when we put the tree up with the girls – thank you for that. I've got such good memories of that night – the way you were with Daisy and Chloe, and me –'

I remembered it all too well, the way Emily came home in a foul mood and refused to help with the decorations, taking herself to bed with a 'headache'. At first I'd thought it was something I'd done, until Chloe told me they'd fallen out over breakfast that morning. 'She's trying to punish me,' Chloe had said. 'She knows I was looking forward to putting up the tree tonight.'

'She *does* love you,' I say now, gently drawing my hand out from under his. I busy myself opening the second bottle and refill our glasses as James considers his reply.

'I think so,' he eventually says. 'But I don't know so. She's so changeable – always has been. It's sometimes exhausting trying to keep up with her moods.'

I laugh, a small utterance of comradely understanding. Oh, yes, I think, I understand how that feels. And he's right – exhausting is the word for it, is exactly what you feel when you're constantly on the watch for those small shifts in atmosphere, eager to stay on her right side, to please her, to make her happy. I'd never seen it with such clarity, until tonight: the disabling power of her disapproval and the way in which it has, almost single-handedly, marked out the path of my life.

'She's difficult to read,' I say, simply. I don't want to say any more, don't want to put her down or muddy the way James sees her. And at any rate I wouldn't be telling him anything new; he knows. He's lived with her for over a decade now, good and bad, and he knows what she's like.

'She's more than difficult.' James reaches out for his glass, our knees bumping as he does so, and he drinks deeply before settling back against his corner of the sofa. He looks at me squarely, seriously, and says, 'She's bloody ruthless, Jess.'

The day I left home was a bright, uncommonly warm day in March. It was a Sunday, and Mum and Dad were at mass, Emily and I having feigned illness in order to stay behind and get me to the train station. On the platform, the sun streamed down through the corrugated awning, creating strips of bright white across the chewing gum marked concrete. Emily stood at my side, a foot apart from me, her mouth fixed in the polite, social smile she had adopted from Mum, to be called upon in moments of public stress or discomfort. And I, desperate for Emily's approval as always, chattered inanely, making small talk that skimmed over my terror, that ignored the momentous ripples we were about to cast off into the future.

I didn't want go; I was just seventeen – too young, too inexperienced and too naïve to simply head out into the world alone with nothing more than a rucksack and a little money. But Emily was right: I had no choice. I'd made my bed, as she put it, and life could never return to the way it was before. Not now. I had screwed it all up, ruined everything, thrown it all away.

After the party, after Emily had caught me with Simon – in bed with *her boyfriend* Simon – she'd separated herself from me, any remaining affection reduced to nothing. He had been *her* boyfriend, not mine. How could I have let that happen? I tried so hard to tell her, to convince her that I didn't remember a thing about it, *nothing* – that the last memories I had of the evening were of sitting on the top step of the stairs in Sammie's house with my head in my hands, feeling the cold, dread drop of my blood pressure as one of my episodes threatened to take me down. Sammie had passed me on the stairs, on her way down from using the loo, and she'd asked me if I was all right because I looked so pale, and then she had helped me to my feet as Simon pushed by, laughing and reeking of lager and cigarette smoke, and I remember thinking, *Emily won't like that. Emily hates it when he smokes.* And as Sammie helped me up I could feel my breath stalling, and I saw how Simon wrinkled his puggy nose at me and said, 'Shit, Jess. Overdone it a bit?' And then Sammie told him to *piss off*, and she took me into her bedroom, where I sat on the edge of the bed and tried not to close my eyes as Sammie smoothed my skirt straight over my knees and felt my forehead with the back of her hand. 'I'll go and find Emily,' she said, and I was grateful. I was scared, but it was OK, because Emily was coming. My big sister was coming, and she'd make everything all right. As Sammie left, the edges of the candy-striped room closed in around me, and my consciousness dropped away.

All these years later, and still my body remembers what took place that night, even when my mind cannot. When Emily had pressed me, wanting to know if I was certain it was *that* night that I'd fallen pregnant, I was able to say, yes, *of course* it was that night, because there wasn't any other night. That had been my first and only time. But how could she ever understand that, while it had happened there, and had happened with Simon, it wasn't an act of betrayal. How could it be – when I had no recollection of it in the moment, no memory of it at all. No proof that it ever happened, except for the bits that Emily told me afterwards, and so many times since. No proof, except for the bruising, and the bleeding that only I knew about; both long since vanished, long since washed and scrubbed away. No proof, but for the rotten sense of shame and dread that now inhabited my every waking hour, and crept beneath the covers with me at night-time, never leaving me. How could I even contemplate telling her the truth of what I really feared? I had lost so much, but I knew, because Emily told me day after day – she had lost so much more. She had lost Simon.

She'd finished with him there and then, and for that, at least, I was thankful.

My reason for leaving home was simple: my parents had found out. A few days earlier, Emily had slipped into my bedroom late at night, to speak to me for the first time in the fortnight since we had returned from the clinic. I felt so glad to see her in my doorway, hope rising in me like a breath.

'They know,' she had whispered. 'I don't know the details, but they know – about you and, and about the –' She couldn't find the words, and indicated towards my belly with a flick of her hand. '*I* didn't tell them,' she went on. 'But the clinic phoned; I'm pretty sure I overheard Mum speaking to them.'

I'll never forget the rush of adrenaline that I felt when she told me that my parents knew. I felt sick, in part because I was so relieved that it had been taken out of my hands – that the truth, as awful as it was, could be spoken aloud. But that sensation was short-lived, when Emily said, 'They want you to move out. They don't even want to talk about it – but you have to go, Jess. I mean, Jesus, this goes against everything they believe in. Unmarried sex? Abortion?' Her eyes were wide, persuasive. 'I think it's for the best. And it would probably do you some good, wouldn't it? A bit of time to think things over?'

I recalled the look my mother had given me that morning as she left for church, a mixture of unspoken sadness and profound disappointment. She'd been spending more and more time alone in her room in recent weeks, emerging only to prepare our meals and clear up after us, and even then it seemed she struggled to meet my gaze. She'd been the same with Dad and Emily, but I realised now that the source of her distress was, of course, me. *Of course* they knew. How could they not?

As the train pulled in, I clung to my sister, not wanting to let her go; not wanting to go. 'How will I live without you, Emi?' I asked, my tear-streaked face buried in her hair.

She pulled back and opened the carriage door, handing me my rucksack as I stepped aboard the train. Her last words to me were spoken coolly before she turned and walked away.

'You'll be fine, Jess. Life has a way of working itself out.'

18. Emily

Emily is drained; emptied out. Finally, she told DCI Jacobs everything about that night. She told her how she *didn't* drive straight home on New Year's Eve, but instead went with Marcus, her husband's best friend, down to the sheltered beach at the foot of Shanklin Chine, where they had cold, hurried sex against the salt-corroded wood of the furthest beach hut. Emily skirted over the details, sticking to the raw facts – the time, the location, the duration – as if communicating the events with speed and brevity would somehow reduce the severity of her betrayal. What she didn't tell the inspector was just how alive she felt in those few fervent, moonlit minutes; how Marcus devoured her with such intoxicating appetite that she wishes she could return there now, if only to obliterate the horror of her reality, to give herself up again to that fleeting deathlike rapture.

Just as DCI Jacobs is wrapping up the interview, there's a knock on the window and a young woman enters the room. 'We've had a phone call I think you should know about,' she says, and her eyes dart towards Emily briefly, causing the inspector to push back her chair and follow the officer from the room.

Once again Emily is left alone with the silent officer, and, try as she might, she can't get the image of Daisy out of her head, a picture of her lying in her cot on New Year's Eve, her fists balled, her face scrunched up in wet frustration – crying to be picked up by her mummy, when all her mummy wanted to do was strap on her kitten heels and get out of the house. It was the first time in months she had actually been looking forward to a night out, and Emily had hated Daisy for slowing her down. She'd *hated* her.

Had she? Is that possible? Is that the way she is? Is that the person she has become? Or the person she's always been? Emily stares towards the glass panel in the interview room door, focusing hard, trying to see herself as better. She sees herself with James, a family, walking across the wooden slats of Yarmouth pier with Daisy in her pram when she is just days old, smiling at the passers-by who cast admiring glances at the beautiful new baby. She sees herself bending over the changing mat, to kiss Daisy's rabbit-soft forehead as she smooths down the Velcro of a fresh nappy, meeting pools of adoration in her daughter's eyes. Emily recalls the way in which, whatever they were doing, Daisy's head would turn to follow the sound of her voice, and how she loved that, that simple thing. *I'm not all bad*, she allows herself to think now, *I'm not all bad*. What on earth will James do when he hears about this – about Marcus? God, this nightmare just rolls on and on.

DCI Jacobs returns to the room and to her seat. 'Right, Emily, we'll be getting you off home in a moment. But first I've got a couple more questions I want to ask you, and then one of our officers will drive you back. Your husband, James – has he ever given you reason to mistrust him?'

Emily is stunned by the question. She's been here all night and this hasn't come up. It seems so ill placed at the very end of her interview, so weighted with suggestion that she's uncertain what it is the inspector is asking of her.

She thinks of the letter, *that* letter, the one she found on James's desk all those weeks back, but she doesn't say a thing. An affectionate letter of few words, written on floral notepaper and signed with a kiss. No, she won't tell them about that; she doesn't want to open up an entirely different can of worms. 'No. Why do you ask?'

'It's a standard question,' DCI Jacobs replies, her expression giving away nothing. 'And when you first met, what was James's situation then? He already had Chloe, didn't he?'

'We've been over this,' Emily says, curtly. How many times do they have to do this? 'He'd lost his wife –'

'Avril?'

'*Yes*. She'd died a year and a half earlier, and he'd moved to Fleet with Chloe soon afterwards. We met at work.'

'OK. And exactly where did he and Avril live before he moved to Fleet? Do you know?'

Emily's patience is exhausted. 'Somewhere in London. I'm not sure exactly where. I didn't know him back then. If you want details you'll have to ask James.'

DCI Jacobs scribbles a note and nods at the other officer. 'Interview terminated at 7.55am.'

As Marcus walked Emily back up the steep beachfront steps and winding pathways towards his own front drive, it seemed strange to her to be chatting so very casually, when something so intimate had just passed between them. He asked her how Chloe was doing at school, how Daisy was getting along, even going so far as to suggest they must all go out for lunch again soon at the Crab and Lobster – her and James, him and Jan. If anyone overheard us now, she thought, they'd never suspect in a million years that we'd just been shagging like seals on the beach. She laughed aloud at this last thought, and Marcus stopped her with a light hand, a look of alarm entering his wine-soaked features. They were concealed, standing just beyond the high perimeter of his garden wall. 'I know I don't need to say it, Em, but – this is just between us, yes?'

She had raised a wry eyebrow and shaken her head slowly. 'You think I don't have just as much to lose as you, Marcus? What happens at the Chine stays at the Chine.'

Now it was his turn to laugh, and he pulled her forward to kiss her on the cheek like old friends. And, shoving his hands deep into his pockets, he turned away from her and sauntered back towards the party. As if it had never even happened.

When the police car returning Emily pulls up outside her house, she sees Marcus is driving away. He appears to look towards the car as he passes, grave-faced, but gives no sign that he has seen her. It's just gone nine and already a few early photographers mill around the vehicles in the street, jumping to action when they see the police car arrive. James and Jess are standing on the doorstep, looking bewildered, and Emily can only guess at what has just taken place, at what they now know to be true.

'All right?' DC Piper asks her, because she's been sitting there motionless for too long now. 'Do you want me to come in with you?'

'No,' she replies. She's had enough police company to last her a lifetime. She thanks him, and steps gingerly on to the pavement, feeling the burden of her husband's eyes on her as she treads across the gravel drive, the crunching sound of it loud in the early-morning hush. Her gaze is lowered as she reaches them, and she's aware that over the past fortnight she has come to view them as a united front, as a pair, because they're so very alike in many ways, both good and gentle and honest. They say women often end up marrying versions of their father. Not me, thinks Emily as she raises her eyes to meet theirs. I married my sister.

'*Marcus*?' James asks. That's all. Just that one word.

And she wants to spit back, *And what about you and my sister, meeting for secretive lunches? What about that, Mr Squeaky Clean?* But there's no time to answer him, because then DCI Jacobs is pulling up in the entrance to the driveway, her tyres spitting up small stones, and she's out of the car even before the engine cuts out, her legs moving across the wide driveway with such purpose that Emily thinks she's back for her again, that they've let her go too soon.

'Mr King,' Jacobs shouts over to James, the urgency pouring off her. She comes to a halt facing the three of them, and places her hands on her hips in a mildly aggressive pose, inhaling deeply as though she's run all the way here, not driven. She's fired up; there's something new.

James hasn't answered. He just stands there, gaping, like a man teetering on the edge of the abyss.

'Mr King,' DCI Jacobs repeats. 'I think we'd better go inside. It's about your first wife, Avril. Your deceased wife.'

James nods dumbly.

The inspector gestures towards the house, and they step over the threshold, one after the other, until they're inside the hallway, the door sealed safely shut behind them. Nobody speaks; not James, not Jess, not Emily. They stand and wait, their inner fight collectively draining away.

At last DCI Jacobs speaks. 'Mr King, we're going to need to talk with you in more detail about your first wife, Avril King. We have good reason to believe that you've lied about the circumstances of her death.'

PART TWO

1. Avril

You were perfect; unblemished. Innocent of ill thought, with a light that radiated from you like sunlight. You brought meaning to everything, and, with you in it, my world had become a warmer place. Until I went and ruined it all.

The house was silent, and for a while it was just you and me, alone, without the distractions and noise of others to unsettle our peace. You were special, Chloe, and from the first time I held you I knew we had a connection that could never be put into plain words or easily broken. Everyone said I was spoiling you, that I should stop with all the little presents – spend my money on myself instead – but they didn't understand that all I ever wanted to do was make you happy. And to protect you. That evening I sat in the lounge for an age, staring beyond the muted movements of the television screen, willing you to wake for a while, so I could fill my eyes with your love, feel the reassuring thump of your heartbeat against mine.

'Try not to wake her,' James had said as they headed off for their party earlier that evening, dressed up in their black-tie best, looking quite the glamorous pair. 'Just pop your head in every now and then – but don't pick her up straight away if she wakes! She'll drop off again if you leave her for a few minutes.' At the front door I saw her button up her neat fawn coat and whisper something to him – and he'd rushed back in with a tub of chocolates, sliding them across the coffee table towards me. 'Babysitter's perks!' he'd said, and, checking his reflection in the mantle mirror one last time, he'd dashed from the room and out into the night.

At some point it felt as though hours had passed, but I'd started to feel strange by then, and it was hard to know if my sense of time was out, as so often happens. The clock said it was gone one in the morning, but that couldn't be right, could it? Surely I hadn't been sitting here alone for that long? I was certain I had heard you cry out, and, although I remembered James's words and knew I mustn't go to you yet, I couldn't help myself and I rushed up to fetch you down. You were so pleased to see me, waving your soft arms and grabbing at the air, and why shouldn't I pick you up whenever I wanted? Why shouldn't I hold you and kiss you and never want to let you go? A mother should be allowed to do these things. A mother shouldn't be told when and how much to love her child, should she? *His* mother said I was overdoing things. *His* mother, constantly hinting that I couldn't cope. I scooped you up and brought you into the kitchen, strapping you into your high chair so you could watch me make up your warm milk. I dropped a couple of bread sticks on to your tray and you babbled and waved them in the air, and I felt light-headed with the joy of you. I was hungry too, and as your milk warmed in the bowl I made myself a sandwich, carving the last of the turkey breast from the Christmas joint, and laying it out in a slow, careful pattern on a slice of the crumbly organic loaf that James always insisted on. I often wondered if he'd be so popular with women if they knew what a fusspot he really was – and, in an instant, I lost my appetite and I tossed the sandwich at the dog bowl, where it flopped open and spilled messily over the polished floor. Toddy heard the noise and stirred in his basket, sniffing the air and padding across the room to claim his treat. That was another thing she hated me doing – giving Toddy too many titbits – and I felt jubilant at my trifling rebellion as I watched him pick up the sandwich in his softly drooping jaws and carry it back to the comfort of his bed. *Good boy*, I whispered, and he looked at me out of the side of his eyes, his expression a confused mixture of uncertainty and gratitude. The kitchen lights overhead felt suddenly too brash and I flinched, swallowing my anger as I snatched up your bottle and slopped milk across the counter. I was so cross, I reached over to the light switch, flicking them off so I didn't need to squint any more, and as I did so my arm swept across the worktop, sending the breadboard and meat knife hurtling into the sink with a clatter. When I heard you gasp in the dimness, I was sorry again, so sorry, and I reached out to put my hand on your shoulder, to soothe you and let you know I was there. I paused, my pulse racing, as I listened out for any signs of them coming home, as by now I had no grasp of time and it seemed possible they could be back at any moment, ticking me off for getting you up, for waking you unnecessarily. But the silence remained, broken by nothing more than the gentle whistle of wind passing the windows that looked out across the drive. They wouldn't understand: all I wanted to do was hold you. They think I'm taking my medication, but I'm not. They don't know how it feels, how it takes something of me away, robs me of my ability to love you as profoundly as I can when I'm myself. When I'm myself, the connections all link up, the world is excruciatingly sharp but at the same time breathtakingly clear – and my bond to you, Chloe, is tangible, as real in the world as the cord that fastened us together in my womb. How could I give that up? How could I suppress my sense of you, of myself, of *us*? I felt shaky as I stood beside your high chair in the half-light, watching the whites of your eyes blinking up at me, marvelling at the porcelain perfection of your dimpled fingers and rounded cheeks. And then, as I went to lift you up, I heard the sound of tyres on the gravel outside and the room grew instantly brighter, briefly bathing you in light, and in the seconds before the lights dipped I saw your closed eyes and the blood on your sleep suit – fresh blood, bright and wet. I cried out – screamed – seeing the rich crimson line that flowed from my wrist, and I staggered in my panic to get to you, to save you. But I couldn't save you, could I?

The great gulf of darkness opened up again like a silent roar, wrapping its weight around me and crushing my breaths as I went under.

2. **Jess**

'Mr King, we're going to need to talk with you in more detail about your first wife, Avril King. We have good reason to believe that you've lied about the circumstances of her death.'

Is DCI Jacobs accusing James of killing his wife? I think this is what she's saying, and by the look on Emily's face, so does she. How much – or how little – does Emily even know about James, I wonder? How much do any of us know about each other? Is this just a precursor to accusing him of taking Daisy? Or worse? They couldn't be thinking that, could they? James still hasn't spoken a word, and it doesn't look good for him. It doesn't look good at all.

The detective stands at the foot of the stairs with her back to the door, facing the shocked gaggle of Emily, James, Chloe and me, and it feels as though the air has been sucked from the room. How much more can this family take? Just minutes earlier, Marcus had been standing on the front drive, frantically running his hands through his hair as he confessed that he'd slept with his best friend's wife – with Emily – on the night that Daisy disappeared. That they may even have been doing it at the very moment Daisy was being snatched; that *he* was the reason Emily was late getting home – that he's barely had a wink of sleep since he realised his part in the whole awful affair. The police had been on the phone to him yesterday evening, questioning him yet again about James and Emily's movements when they left his party on New Year's Eve, and something inside him had folded, he said. If it hadn't been for Daisy, he told James, he would never have said a word – would never have hurt James by letting him know the truth. It wasn't as if it was something they would *ever* repeat; it was a one-off, a slip-up, a lapse in judgement.

'A lapse in fucking *judgement*?' James spat. I'd never seen him this way, his face distorted with the hurt and fury that rushed into his features. 'A slip-up? You arrogant *shit* –'

I'd thought he was going to go for Marcus, who by this point was so grey that he looked as if he might vomit on the doorstep. But instead James took a backward step, and shook his head. 'You're welcome to her,' he said, and Marcus had no choice but to return to his car and drive away.

And then, there was Emily arriving on the scene, and, while no real words have been spoken since she arrived home just minutes ago, the knowledge of her betrayal hangs between them like red mist beneath the clouds of DCI Jacobs' newest revelation.

'What do you mean, he lied?' asks Emily. Her face is pale, her voice small.

DCI Jacobs looks at each one of us, her focus lingering longest on Chloe, poor bloody Chloe, who only woke at the sound of the inspector running across the drive and now stands on the bottom stair tread looking expectant and scared.

'Yes, what do you mean?' Chloe demands, her voice rising as she pushes through to stand between James and Emily.

The inspector looks directly at James. 'Would you like to explain, James?'

When I arrived here last autumn I thought it strange that Emily and James had never married. I suppose I assumed he had never quite got over the loss of his first wife, Avril. As children, Emily was always more girly than me, her games often consisting of make-believe situations such as mummies-and-daddies or mummies-and-babies, or her favourite of all, fairytale weddings. In these games, I always took the support role, and so as chief bridesmaid in Emily's marriage fantasy I was nothing if not aware of her child's-eye view of the 'perfect' wedding. There would be an enormous white cake, a horse-drawn carriage, a dress more beautiful than the town had ever seen – and confetti! So much white confetti that they'd think it was snowing in July! And as we grew older, into our teens, getting married and settling down was something that Emily talked about in so casual a way that I understood it to be an event that would simply happen for her. Strange, as at that age it was never a future I could visualise for myself – the idea of giving myself over to one person so completely that they became my world, my new family. In childhood, all I could really imagine was staying with the family I already had. But then Emily always did live with one eye on the new, happy to drop everything – and everyone – for something shinier or more fun.

It seems inconceivable to me that James is capable of – of what? What exactly are the police suggesting he's capable of? Right up until this moment, I'd have said he's one of the most honest men I've ever met. But then I think of him all those months back, when I came upon him sitting alone on the stone wall overlooking Freshwater Bay as I walked along the water's edge. I had only arrived a fortnight earlier, and I'd spotted him in the distance. It was unusual to see him out on the beach on

189

his own. He was so engrossed, reading what looked like a letter, that I was right beside him before he even noticed me.

'Jess!' he said, looking up, wide-eyed and fumbling, as he shoved the soft floral notepaper into his jacket pocket. I was sure I saw alarm in his expression, but that thought quickly disappeared when he dropped down off the wall and fell in step with me to walk over the stones below. 'So what have you done with Daisy?' he smiled.

It was a Saturday, and Chloe was babysitting her little sister while Emily drove over to Newport to spend a couple of hours at the gym. 'Oh, I left her home alone,' I replied, adopting a serious tone. 'She's what – eleven months old now? More than grown-up enough!'

James nodded approvingly, zipping the neck of his jacket beneath his chin. I like him, I remember thinking at the time, the emotion instinctively uncomplicated. He understood my humour and always went along with it. Not like Emily, who hated it when I made silly jokes, just not getting it, not understanding why I'd say something so stupid and untrue.

'Yeah,' he agreed, a small laugh in his voice. 'We'll have to start thinking about sending her out to work soon. Get the little layabout to pay her own way.'

Already the mid-afternoon sun was casting long shadows of the corroded groyne posts that stuck up through the sand like sentries. I thought how much I loved this time of day in clear weather, when the light was low and bright, everything rendered sharper and deeper – the colours, the shapes, the coast-crisp sounds of the seafront.

'What brings you down here?' I asked. 'You looked deep in thought.' I couldn't help glancing towards his jacket pocket.

'Oh, that,' he replied. 'Just an old friend. Haven't heard from them in years.'

The tide lapped at my boots, gulping its way further up the sand and stones as the tide drew in. 'I miss *real* letters,' I said.

'Somehow an email or a text message just isn't the same. Me and Ems used to write letters to each other all the time.'

'When you were travelling?' he asked.

I laughed, though I didn't know why. 'No! When we were little. We used to write secret letters and hide them beneath each other's pillows.' I felt a powerful surge of nostalgia at the sudden memory, and I wanted to cry. Emily had been more generous, more honest, more affectionate in those letters than she ever was in real life. Sometimes she was even funny. 'I loved it. It's one of the things I most missed about her, when I left home.'

'I can't imagine Emily doing something like that,' James said, and he sounded so young and pensive that I had to stop myself from reaching out to touch his face. 'There's so much I don't know about her, I suppose. But maybe she'd say the same about me.'

We continued along the water's edge in companionable silence, until we reached the stone staircase at the foot of the sea defence, where James held out his hand to help me leap over the tide that was now swelling at the bottom steps. At the top railings, we paused together to look out across the darkening horizon, where the sun was now no more than a wisp of orange watercolour in the sky.

'That letter –' James started, but I shook my head and stopped him from saying the words. In my brief glimpse of it, I had seen it was a handwritten letter on pastel flowery paper, distinctly feminine, its contents clearly significant enough to make him secretive. I liked James very much already, and I didn't need to know anything that would change my opinion of him.

'I could murder a cup of tea,' I said instead, and he smiled, relief rippling across his features like a wave.

In the late autumn dusk of October, we walked together along the leaf-strewn streets of Freshwater, until we reached our street, and I realised I felt entirely at home for the first time in years. Part of the world again. Part of *Emily's* world again. Part of the family.

DCI Jacobs indicates towards the dining room table, and wordlessly we all move towards it, pulling out chairs, sitting so that we can now plainly see each other's expressions. It's horrible.

'James?' Emily whispers, but he just sits there with his face in his hands. She turns to look at the inspector, desperation pouring from her. 'Please. Just tell me what's going on here!'

Jacobs fixes her gaze on James, who seems incapable of movement. 'Well, she's not dead, James, is she?'

At this, he drops his hands from his face and tilts his head, never raising his eyes from the table top. 'No,' he says, but it's barely audible.

This was the last thing I expected to hear – the last thing any of us expected to hear. *Avril*? James's first wife, *Avril*? Alive? How was it possible to conceal a detail so fundamental from the people you love? A whole other story; a whole other life.

DCI Jacobs places her hands flat on the table top. 'Make us a pot of tea, DC Piper?' she says and the officer disappears through the archway into the kitchen.

'Now, you're not denying it, James,' she continues, 'so I'm assuming this isn't news to you. You already know that Avril is alive and well?'

All at once Emily and Chloe snap out of their shocked silence, demanding answers, shrieking, crying, pushing back from their seats.

'What the hell is this?' Emily cries, standing, taking a backward step, as though the distance might help her to process the information. Her dark bob hangs in lifeless strands; I've never seen her so desperately unkempt. 'How could you keep something like this from me, James? How could you lie about something so huge?'

James raises his eyes in a scowl that demands *how can you*

ask me *about lying?* Emily sits again, her furious eyes downcast, her lower lip pinched between her front teeth.

DCI Jacobs reaches out a hand to soothe Chloe, letting it rest a moment on her forearm. 'This must be a shock to you, Chloe. We will get to all your questions in a moment, but for now –' she runs her gaze over every one of us '– for now, I want to talk to James directly. Without interruptions. OK?'

Around the table we all nod our agreement, Chloe's arms folding about her in a self-hugging pose, Emily's hand covering her own mouth in censorship. I'm so stunned by this latest revelation that there's no danger of interruption from me.

'James?'

James fiddles with the front of his hair, his focus indistinct, and for a moment I think he won't speak at all. But then he does, directing his words towards Chloe. 'She was very ill, mentally – emotionally – and when she was first institutionalised I really had intended to stand by her. To be there for her until she was better. Even when it became clear she wasn't getting better, I had *wanted* to stay nearby.' He now looks at the detective. 'So that Chloe could have some kind of a relationship with her mother.'

'*Institutionalised*?' Chloe whispers. Her pallor appears translucent; her fingers dig into the flesh of her upper arms as she holds herself in.

James nods. 'She had become very, very ill, Chlo. I didn't know it when I met her – and we really were very much in love – but she'd suffered with mental illness since she was young. She'd been diagnosed with a personality disorder, and had been successfully managing it with medication for over ten years – but when she became pregnant with Chloe – well, she had to tell me then, the midwife was quite insistent, and together they broke the news to me at the twelve-week scan.' He looks at his daughter, stalling while he finds the right words. 'She was scared the pills would damage the baby. She wasn't just taking medication for the condition, there were all sorts of other drugs for the side-effects of that medication, and as soon as she realised she was expecting – she just stopped taking them all. No weaning off gradually or planning – she just stopped taking them overnight.'

DCI Jacobs nods at him to continue.

'It was devastating,' James says. 'It was nothing short of hell. Avril changed so dramatically, I barely recognised her. She was a danger to herself, sometimes disappearing for days on end, turning up halfway across the country, unable to say where she'd been or what she'd been doing. Right before the birth, my mother moved in with us to help out – but really, I don't know if that just made matters worse. She tried her best, but Avril rejected every gesture of help she offered. And even after the birth she wouldn't resume her medication, because she wanted to breastfeed. She couldn't see what we all could: that she was disappearing before our eyes – that everything could return to normal if she just put the baby on to bottles and started taking the damn pills again. She wasn't in her right mind, and yet she wanted to do everything right for her baby. She adored you, Chloe.'

'But why did she have to go into an institution? Couldn't you have *made* her take the medicine?' There are tears rolling down Chloe's face, and her breathing comes in short, shallow gasps. I worry that if she doesn't loosen the grip on her arms soon, her fingers will puncture the material of her shirt, puncture her skin. I bump her knee with mine, offer her a hand beneath the table.

Across from us Emily's face is unreadable – is she angry? Afraid? Guilty? It's impossible to tell.

'In the end we had no choice, Chlo. After a few months she *did* agree to start taking her medication again, and it was such a relief because I really thought we were getting the old Avril back. She'd had a few a blips, but mostly she was doing fine. On that last evening, I went out to a drinks party with my mother, and we left you in your mum's care for the first time in months. We thought it would be OK. We thought she'd cope.'

'What happened?' I ask.

'She cut her wrist. Luckily we arrived home just in time – found her in the kitchen, bleeding profusely, and Chloe fine, but sitting up in her high chair covered in blood. And then it all happened so quickly – she was rushed to hospital and by the end of the week she'd been sectioned and moved to a secure unit where they could take proper care of her. Later, when I came back home, I searched her bedside cabinet and found all the tablets I thought she'd been taking, dozens of them stuffed into the back of the drawer. There must have been a couple of months' worth. I knew then that they were right to send her to that hospital, that it was the safest place for her.'

'And she's been there ever since?' DCI Jacobs asks.

James stiffens visibly. 'I don't think she's there now.'

'Do you know where she is now, Mr King? Has she made contact with you – or Chloe – at all over the years?'

I think we're all expecting James to say no, but now there's a weighted silence in the room as he hesitates, balling a fist against his chin, gathering up the words. With a lurch of suppressed horror I remember that floral notepaper – the letter that Emily had been searching for all those months ago. *Not* a letter from a lover, but from a dead wife.

'She wrote. A few months ago. I don't know how she got our address, but I saw from hers that she'd moved –' And then the realisation hits him and he turns to the detective with an expression of disbelief and says, 'You're not thinking about Daisy's disappearance? You think it could be Avril?'

'You didn't write back?' Jacobs asks, ignoring his question.

'No, and it was the only letter I received, so I thought she'd given up.'

195

'You haven't had any phone contact, or spoken to her in any other way?'

'No!'

DCI Jacobs turns to Emily. 'And you didn't know about this letter, Mrs King?'

'Of course not! Until a few minutes ago I thought the woman was dead! Of course I don't know about the bloody letter!' Emily has now moved away from the table, articulating her words in a low, menacing snarl. 'Are you telling me that this crazy woman has my daughter? That *Avril* has Daisy?'

James is shaking his head, trying to get her to sit, to calm down. 'Emily – back up. It *can't* be Avril, can it? We haven't had contact for over a decade, she wouldn't just . . .' He gnaws on his knuckle, his eyes roaming the table top as he tries to make sense of it all. 'I'll get you the letter! There's an address on it – somewhere in Surrey. I'll try to find you the letter – I'm not even sure where I put it – and you can speak to her yourselves?' He looks at DCI Jacobs for reinforcement. 'Can't you?'

DCI Jacobs picks up her mug of tea and takes a sip from it, carefully returning it to the table top in front of her. 'From what we know, she was in and out of hospital and independent living for several years after her first stay at St Justin's – culminating in a five-year stay in a place called Buddleia Hill when her condition became quite severe. But she was actually signed off altogether a year ago, Mr King. She's been living in a small town just outside Croydon since then, and according to her local police force the neighbours say she hasn't been seen for over a fortnight. The next-door neighbour said she told her she was taking a holiday somewhere off the south coast, visiting her baby daughter. The officer said he wouldn't have thought any more of it, but this neighbour was insistent that it didn't add up – she's never seen any evidence of a baby in the year she's known her, and apparently

Avril was very vague when the woman asked to see a photo. All she told the neighbour was the baby's name. *Chloe.*'

Emily crumples against the table, her cries pouring out, muffled and keening, incomprehensible. I rush to her side, crouching beside her to cradle her frail body against mine, and we stay like that, her slumped against my chest like a ragdoll, my eyes locked on Chloe's, trying to convey my thoughts to her. *We'll be OK*, I'm trying to tell her, *we'll be just fine.*

'Look, it's important to understand there is absolutely no guarantee that Avril has Daisy, so I don't want you getting your hopes up just yet. But we are following it up as a matter of urgency. We've already got officers checking her bank accounts to see if there's been any unusual activity – hotel bookings, large withdrawals, transactions of that kind. We've got her car registration details, and we're checking with the ferry companies to see if a matching vehicle has travelled to the island in recent weeks. And yes, James, can you look for that letter?' DCI Jacobs stands, inviting him to lead the way. She regards each of us in turn, before her voice softens a little. 'I know this is alarming for all of you. But the good news is we now have a clear and significant suspect for Daisy's disappearance. We already have the entire force out there working on tracing Avril King – checking the ferries, the bus companies, the hotels and holiday rentals. This is an island, and there are only so many places a woman and a baby can hide indefinitely. Emily?'

Raw-faced, Emily looks up at the detective.

'Trust us, Emily. We're doing everything we can to find Daisy.'

As DCI Jacobs leaves the room my sister turns back to me, with terror in her eyes. 'What if she's killed her, Jess? What if she's dead? I'd never forgive myself,' she says quietly, before bringing both hands up over her mouth, like the speak-no-evil monkey, and I swear she's scared of what she might say next.

3. Emily

Emily refuses to be part of the next television appeal. At the press conference she sits at the side of the room, close to the front, disguised under a heavy coat and hat, and she feels as though she's watching the whole thing through water. Her rational brain fears that she's becoming too dependent on the tablets that get her through each day, but the part of her that is still fighting to survive knows that she couldn't do it without them.

The conference table is arranged with DCI Jacobs and DC Piper to the left, James and Chloe in the middle, and the Chief of Police to the right. Jess isn't here; she's outside in the car park, waiting with DC Cherry to speed them away as soon as the appeal is over. Thank God for Jess.

They start with an introduction from the police chief, and Emily is zoned out, not hearing a word he says, not caring, her attention trained on that horrible #findDaisy banner – and then she regrets it, regrets not listening to every little detail, so that she will know what she's dealing with here. So she knows what's what. When DCI Jacobs begins to speak, Emily is better focused, concentrating hard, straining to take it all in amidst the fidgeting, note-taking, photo-snapping background of the hungry press row.

'What we know about Avril King is that she's a forty-three-year-old woman, five foot six inches tall, medium build, with dark blonde, shoulder-length hair, usually worn up. Given her age, she could be presenting herself to others as Daisy's mother, or even her grandmother, and if she knows she is being looked for it's quite possible she is disguising her appearance in some way. With all these difficult factors in mind, we're hoping that members of the public will be vigilant in looking out for *anyone* they feel may fit this profile. Do you know anyone who has recently been visited by a new grandchild or niece, for instance? Is there anyone new in your area, on her own with a child of Daisy's age? Have you noticed anyone acting suspiciously? We do know that Ms King travelled over in a silver 2008-reg Renault Scenic and that she arrived on the island twenty-four hours before Daisy's disappearance on New Year's Eve. Any help in locating this vehicle could be crucial to our investigation.'

Behind her is a poster-sized image of Daisy – blown up from the photograph Emily handed the police on the night she was snatched two weeks ago. DCI Jacobs half turns and gestures towards it. 'This is Daisy, taken only a few weeks before she disappeared. Details to look out for are her lilac-print sleep suit –' the DI holds up an identical romper '– and her favourite toy, a velvet plush elephant like this one, purchased from Debenhams.' She holds up a toy elephant just like Ellie, but newer, and Emily thinks how ridiculous the inspector looks – a middle-aged woman, grave-faced and composed, brandishing a bean-bottomed elephant with a droopy trunk.

Further along, behind the Chief of Police, there's another poster. It's of Avril King – 'A' she thinks bitterly, remembering the simple sign-off at the foot of that letter she'd found in James's office – but the picture is too out-of-date to be much use. It's at least a decade old, and it's a grainy, unprofessional image, blown up from a group photo taken at the mental health facility she stayed in – long before she'd been moved into the lower-security care home where she resided up until her release last year. These are the details the police have shared with them over the past twenty-four hours. The care provision details of a woman who, up until now, Emily hadn't thought existed in the world, a woman she had believed to be long dead and buried. God knows, she recognises the irony of her wish on New Year's Eve – the thought that James's first wife would be more tolerable still alive and divorced than dead and sainted. Guilt rises up in her: she could have prevented all this, she knows it. She should have worked out the truth of James's past earlier, but she never tried to, did she? Even when he was evasive about his first wife, about their home and life together, Emily never pressed him, and she wonders whether deep down she knew he was lying. She didn't *want* to know, didn't want to open up anything that might smudge the unblemished life she was so proud of. In a rare surge of self-awareness, Emily sees herself for the flawed, shallow creature she really is. *It's all her fault.* It's Emily's fault that Avril came looking for them, Emily's fault that Daisy has gone.

She clenches her fingers into fists and stares ahead.

Now, it's James's turn to talk, and, as agreed late last night, sitting around their dining table with the police officers and their media consultant, his appeal is directed at Avril. The experts fear Avril's confusion is so profound that she believes she has taken Chloe, *her* baby, and that their best chance of bringing her forward is by showing her Chloe now. Chloe the teenager. What a shock that would be, thinks Emily, and she imagines not seeing Daisy again until *she* is a fifteen-year-old, make-up-wearing, attitude-filled teenager with views of her own. The thought is appalling.

James reads from a script, careful to look up between sentences – as coached – to make contact with the camera, ultimately to make a connection with Avril. 'Avril, if you're watching this, I hope that it means you are well, and that you're caring for Daisy. I'm sure you are, because you were always a good, loving mother to our baby daughter Chloe. Avril, we don't harbour any ill feeling towards you. All we care about is having Daisy returned to her family where she belongs – and making sure that you are all right, that you are cared for too.' He pauses, and Emily wonders if this is also scripted, to make him appear more vulnerable, to pull on Avril's heartstrings, if she has any. He rests his hand over Chloe's, who sits beside him like an ivory-skinned mannequin. '*This* is Chloe, your daughter. It's been nearly fifteen years since you saw her, and we're hoping that when you bring Daisy home you'll be able to see her at last.'

Chloe doesn't move; doesn't react at all. When this line of appeal was put to her last night, she said she didn't care what they promised Avril, so long as she could bring her baby sister home. 'I'd cut off my right hand if it meant we could get Daisy back,' she'd said, and Emily had felt a lurch of self-disgust, because she knew that she couldn't be certain she would promise as much.

James turns his face towards Chloe and gives her fingers a squeeze of encouragement. She too looks directly into the camera, but she's struggling to keep her upset and anger inside and her words come out robotic and stilted. 'Please. *Mum*.' She says this last word with such weight that it could be construed either as something that means a great deal to her or as something that cost her a great deal to give up. 'Please bring my little sister back home. Please, Mum.'

And that's it. That's where they end the appeal, with the word 'Mum'. As Emily dashes from the room ahead of the gathered television crews and journalists, she wonders, will she ever get to hear that word spoken to her? Will Daisy ever be old enough to graduate from *Mama* to *Mummy* to *Mum*?

*

When Chloe was ten, she asked James and Emily about her 'real' mother, while travelling in the back seat of the family car as they drove along the old Military Road on a bright August day. Out beyond the tent-festooned fields the sun shone brightly on a sea dotted with sailing boats. Emily was wearing a new pair of designer sunglasses for the first time, enjoying the Hollywood feel of them, and she had just been silently musing that there was nowhere more idyllic than this island on a summer's day, nowhere more perfect. It was one of those rare moments in which she felt wonder – and pride – at the faultlessness of her life: she had a handsome husband, a stepdaughter who adored her, a comfortable lifestyle, and the figure of a woman several years younger. What more could she want?

'I just wondered,' Chloe asked, ever so casually, as the warm breeze whipped through the open windows and snatched up her long honey hair. 'You know my mum? My *real* mum? Is there a grave we could visit? You know, to put flowers on or something.'

Emily felt a powerful and unusual twinge of spite towards the girl, for yanking her from the indulgence of those earlier thoughts. She noticed with irritation how James's grip tightened momentarily on the steering wheel, how he paused before answering, his eyes darting up towards the rear-view mirror and back to the road again. Did the mention of Avril still upset him so much all these years later? It was nearly a decade since her death, Emily thought, and he had *her* now, didn't he? Wasn't their relationship, their stability, enough to have got him past it all? 'James?' she urged him quietly, wanting to hear his reply.

'It's a long way away,' he told Chloe. 'Too far to visit very easily.'

'Do I have any cousins?'

'No,' James replied.

'What about photos? Are there any photos of me with my mum before she . . . you know? Before she died?'

'Oh, I don't know, love. I'll have a look when we get back.' James was clearly struggling to keep his voice even, and he kept his eyes fixed ahead, ignoring Emily's attempts to catch his attention.

'Do I look like her?' It was as though Chloe had discovered curiosity for the first time; the questions just kept flying out of her. 'I mean, I know I look a bit like you, Dad – but my hair's different isn't it? I thought if I could see some photos it would be good. It would be interesting.'

Where was this all coming from? Emily's heartbeat quickened, and she wondered why she should feel so panicked by this unexpected interrogation.

'All right, Chloe! For God's sake!' Her tone was far harsher than it had sounded in her head – virtually a shout – and she turned to look back between the headrests to see that Chloe looked as though she had been slapped. Emily tried to soften her voice a little, forcing a smile on to her lips. 'Stop bombarding your dad when he's driving – we could crash if he takes his focus off the road. He'll see if there's a photo when we get back, won't you, James?'

James nodded, frowning hard, and Emily wondered if he was frowning about Chloe's inquisition or about her raising her voice so severely.

'Why all the questions, anyway?' Emily asked, attempting to bring serenity back into her tone.

Chloe shrugged, the firm set of her jaw showing she was still stung. 'We've been doing family trees at school,' she replied, turning her face away to look out across the horizon. 'That's what I took the photo album in for. Beth said I didn't look

anything like my mum and everyone agreed. So I told them –'
and now, she looked straight back at Emily '– that you're not
really my mum.'

This time it was Emily who was stung. Was that the beginning
of the end for her and Chloe? she ponders now. Was that the
moment their bond began to fray loose?

4. **Avril**

The coastal cottage is perfect, the end terrace in a row of three, nestled into the hillside overlooking the Needles in a location almost entirely abandoned at this time of year. The other two cottages stand empty, and when we return from our walks we barely see another soul on the path, save for the occasional walker or cyclist, too busy in their own solitary pursuits to take much notice of an ordinary mother and child on an afternoon stroll. I always smile and say hello, and most often people are friendly and return the greeting as they carry on by. It's nice; being outside is good for me and I know I could be happy here. The cottage itself is simple, small, and perfect for the two of us, and even though there are two bedrooms we've chosen to be together in the one at the front, with Chloe sleeping in a cushion-padded drawer I've placed between the two single beds that dominate the room. There's a little kitchen, perfectly adequate for our needs, and a small lounge with an open fire and television, although I've draped a throw over that as I know it's not good for me to spend too long gazing in at the sadness of the wider world. Initially I booked for a fortnight, and it felt like a stroke of luck when

I phoned ahead and the owner agreed to hold the reservation without a bank deposit. He was happy to accept cash on arrival, what with the holiday season being so far away and the cottages standing empty. He's a quiet sort, lives alone in the farmhouse a mile or so along the coast; he says we won't see hide nor hair of him, unless we call needing anything. This weatherbeaten high point on the island is all but deserted. At night-time, the wind howls around the building, whistling down the chimney and channelling along the courtyard that runs the length of the cottages. When the wind drops, the quiet is more eerie still, and I take comfort in the sleeping form of my girl, as I reach down to touch the curled fingers that rest like a delicate stack of slipper limpets on the pillow beside her face.

How could his mother think I wasn't fit to look after her? Of course, she never said as much, always made a good show of helping out, of *caring*, and James would never hear a bad word said about her. And, when I really concentrate on those memories of Alicia now, I can't be sure if I was right or wrong, whether my feelings towards her were fair or clouded by illness. I know I wasn't always reliable, wasn't always focused, but that was the medication, not me. And even then, my erratic behaviour never impacted on Chloe, not at first anyway. In the beginning it was simple things, like losing my house keys or leaving bags of paid-for shopping on the conveyor belt at the supermarket. I was so tired all the time; those errors were just drifts of concentration, small mistakes. But everyone made so much of them. 'Oh good-ness, you'll poison everyone!' I remember Alicia saying to me as she scraped an entire chicken casserole into the kitchen bin before I even had a chance to serve it up to James. Her small hand moved in a brisk, efficient motion, scrape-scrape-scrape into the bin. 'You can't eat that now, dear!' I'd been preparing it – and myself – all afternoon, desperate to make an effort to pull myself together, to show him I was all right. As Alicia lowered the bin lid I felt foolish to be wearing the dress James had once loved me in, ashamed of the time I had wasted on applying make-up, when all the while the meat was spoiling on the sun-drenched worktop downstairs. James must have seen I was upset, because he had tried to defend me – tried to say *it'll be fine, I'll eat it* – but she wouldn't let him. 'No, James, you really mustn't risk it. That chicken was out on the side all morning, on a hot day like today! I'll never forget the time I made the same mistake when I was young. Your poor father, James. He was sick for days.' She turned to me with her gentle blue eyes and said, 'You must be exhausted, dear,' and she reached for the mixing bowl and whipped up some omelettes.

I started to worry more and more about the things I was getting wrong, grew paranoid about poisoning Chloe, and so I decided I'd breastfeed her for as long as possible so I wouldn't put her at any risk. But, when Chloe got to ten months, Alicia and the health visitor suggested it might be better for me if I moved on to the bottle, and, incapable of resisting their power, I embarked on a fortnight of weaning that left Chloe fretful and me swollen with mastitis and anxiety. My dreams became increasingly disturbed. I imagined Alicia, creeping into Chloe's room on tiny shiny shoes, standing at her cot-side as she inhaled the baby's life force until she was no more than a wizened sack. From a distance I watched James in a passionate embrace with a strange woman, and when they stepped out of the darkness I screamed without a sound when I saw it was *her*. I knew these were only dreams, but equally, I knew it meant something. It meant I shouldn't trust Alicia, and I told James so, told him his mother was a harbinger of bad things, that she *had* to go if we were to thrive.

I never should have said that, because then the doctors came with their stethoscopes and adjusted prescriptions and softly examining voices, and Alicia stood in the doorway beyond them nodding sadly throughout, but *I* could see the victory shining in her narrowed eyes.

'You must rest now, dear,' she told me when James walked the doctors to the front door, and she kissed me gently on the forehead and smiled with warmth, but I wasn't fooled. Even if James was.

5. Jess

I'm about to turn the lights out downstairs when Emily appears at the foot of the stairs. James and Chloe have gone to bed, and we're alone. Emily falls against me, her arms clinging to my back in an embrace that takes me back, far, far back into early childhood when we would grab on to each other in a fierce gesture of affectionate play, a jaw-clenching pleasure of happiness and safety.

'I'm so scared, Jess,' she says, her words muffled against the shoulder of my sweater. The press have been hammering down the door again, and earlier this evening one of them climbed into the back garden and came right up to the kitchen window, photographing Emily in her dressing gown. It had shaken her terribly, and we were all grateful to have DC Piper here to chase them off with threats of arrest.

I run my hand over the dome of her head, kissing the top of it, moving her away from me so I can look into her face. 'I know, Ems.' I nod, and I know she understands that I mean to say more, but that no words can really convey what either of us are feeling. 'Hot chocolate?' I offer, and somehow it's the right thing to say.

Emily smiles gratefully, and we move into the kitchen, where she pulls out the stools around the island unit as I fetch mugs and milk to make the drinks. Outside, the moon is high over the house, and through the back window the garden is illuminated as brightly as if it was lit up by a street lamp. The light is so clean and clear that you can see the detail of every shrub, every paving slab, every neatly tended blade of grass. Daisy's out there some-where, perhaps even with that woman, under this same moon. When I turn back to look at Emily, to pass her her drink, I see she is gazing out into the moonlit night too, and for a moment that long-buried sisterly connection revives, the intense feeling of it stronger than ever. I know what she's thinking.

'She'll be fine, Ems,' I say. 'We can't know for sure that she's with Avril, but, if she is, she'll be safe, I'm sure of it. Avril thinks she's taken her own daughter – Chloe – and James said she'd never hurt a hair on her head.'

Emily lifts her mug with great effort, and it saddens me to note the sedative-slow responses that have become the norm for her lately. I've mentioned it to James, but the doctor says she's taking the right amount, that she's probably better off with them at the moment than without.

She looks at me directly, and it seems all the fight has left her. Before the news of Avril emerged, when we had no idea where Daisy was or what had happened to her, Emily's anger and spite lived right on the surface where we could all see it – ready to erupt into a rage at the slightest provocation. Poor Chloe seemed to have had the worst of it, as if her very presence made the absence of Daisy all the more visible.

'Jess, I'm sorry I've been such a bitch,' Emily says.

I'm startled. I can't think of another time in our lives when she's apologised like this; in childhood we'd simply move past it, pretending that any unpleasantness had never happened. 'That's

OK.' I smile at her. 'We're all allowed to fly off the handle once in a while. And these *are* pretty exceptional circumstances, Ems.'

'No, I mean it, Jess. I don't know what I was thinking back there for a while – I've been feeling so paranoid about everything. I even thought you and James – I saw you meeting him for lunch a few days back, and –'

'Oh, Emily! Oh, no, you mustn't think that! It was my idea, not his – we just met for a quick bite in town, because – well, because I've been worried about you and I just wanted to talk it through, away from here. Oh, Ems! I'm sorry!' I put down my cup and grapple her into a tight embrace.

When I release her and return to my own seat, I see her cheeks are flushed with embarrassment.

'You know I was convinced James was involved with someone else, and I've been hating him for it for months, certain he was lying about something – and then there was this letter I found, signed from "A". *With a kiss*. Oh, what a bloody fool I am, Jess. Of course, I realise now it must have been from her. From *Avril*. I completely misread the meaning in it. She said she wanted to see him, "to talk about things" – and I just thought – well, I jumped to all the wrong conclusions. It wasn't James she wanted. It was Chloe.'

I remember the day I had walked in on Emily, going through James's desk: the naked shame on her face as she tried to pass it off casually, before confessing her fears that he was having an affair. That would have cost her a lot, admitting to me that everything wasn't completely rosy in the garden. And that letter – he should have destroyed it; these things have a habit of coming back to haunt you.

'It's hardly surprising, Ems. He told you she was dead! You'd hardly be likely to think this letter you saw was from a dead wife rather than a lover!'

She manages a small laugh, dropping her face into her hands to smooth back the tension and tiredness that etches her features.

'Is that why you did it?' I ask, softly.

Emily looks up, her face scrunched in a frown. 'What – Marcus?' she replies, and I nod. 'No,' she says casually, and the old, unrepentant Emily is back. 'Well, yes, I suppose. I guess part of me *was* lashing out at James, because I thought he was playing away with someone else. But another part of me just *wanted* to, to do something for myself, something reckless. You know? None of that's important now, though, is it? And he's still lying to me, every day – I just know it.'

She's sitting upright now, her posture defiant. She brings the cup to her lips and drinks deeply, her eyes lingering on mine a second too long before she drops down off the bar stool and takes her cup to the sink. And I think, am *I* being paranoid now, or is she aiming that last comment at me?

In our first year at secondary school, we were placed in the same class. It was a large school – eight classes per year group – and really we should have been separated, so that we could spread our wings a little and develop our independent lives. We were given the choice, and we chose to be placed together as much out of fear of the unknown as from devotion to each other. Emily was far more vocal about it than me, but I was glad that she wanted so vehemently to remain with me, glad that my big sister needed me as much as I needed her. Arriving in our new classroom on the first day, where the tiny smattering of familiar faces was obscured by so many strange ones, I was relieved to have Emily beside me. But that feeling soon subsided, once Emily had gained the confidence of new friendships and the self-assurance to cut me loose.

When I look back on it now, I can see the very moment that her love for me began to strain. Two weeks into the new term, our form teacher, Mrs Emery, handed out thirty blank slips of paper in registration period and gave us just one minute to each nominate a class captain. The three pupils with the highest number of nominations would then have a week to rally votes for the final election the following Monday. There was a ripple of excitement around the room, followed by frantic scribbling as Mrs Emery walked from aisle to aisle, chivvying us along and collecting the anonymous nominations in a frayed wicker fruit bowl. She returned to her desk, silently sorting the paper slips, until finally she was ready to announce the three finalists.

'Now, quiet down! If I read your name out, please stand and come to the front of the room.' She paused momentously. 'Our first nominee is Emily Tyler.'

Emily just about sprinted to the front, her face aglow. I was so happy: class captain was perfect for her. She was clever, confident and a born organiser – everything I wasn't. I gave her the thumbs-up and she returned the gesture, struggling to damp down the wide smile on her face.

'Next we have – David Simpson.'

David took his place beside Emily and they smiled good-heartedly at each other before the last name was called. Mrs Emery held up a final piece of paper.

'And our third nominee is – *Jessica* Tyler!'

As my name was called out, Emily's expression shifted from pride to anger, and she glared at me as though I had fixed it that way, as though I had done it to hurt her. I stood, hardly aware of my legs moving, and joined the two others in front of the blackboard, smiling dully at the applause of our seated classmates. I thought it was one of the worst moments of my life until a week later, when despite my devoted lobbying in favour of Emily – something that only seemed to win *me* more votes – I was named as class captain, and I realised that *that* was the worst moment of my life. My relationship with Emily would never be quite the same again.

The hard expression on Emily's face passes as quickly as it had arrived.

'What are you thinking about?' I ask as I clear away the cocoa mugs and wipe up the milk spills I've made.

'I was thinking about Chloe,' she replies. I'm ready for bed, but Emily looks firmly settled back at the island unit, ready to talk. 'About her – and her mother – and how strange it is that Avril suddenly turned up like this.'

'What do you mean, Ems?' I return to my stool, slide in to sit across from her.

'Well, it would be natural enough for a teenage girl to want to know more about her real mother, wouldn't it? And it's not hard to find information online these days – what if she started searching for information about Avril and discovered she was still alive? What if Avril's letter to James was in response to Chloe first having made contact with her?'

I shake my head. 'No, Ems, she would have said something. Imagine if you'd discovered your mum wasn't dead after all – it would be impossible to keep that secret! She would've been demanding answers from James, not looking for Avril secretly.'

Emily looks set on her theory. 'I'm not so sure, Jess. She can be deceitful, that one – you don't know her the way I do. She's been in a real state since this all happened, behaving just like someone with an awful secret.'

'Of course she's in a state! Her baby sister's been taken!' I'm trying to keep the lightness in my tone.

Emily leans in, lowering her voice. 'All those lies about her boyfriend,' she whispers, 'and about where she was on New Year's

Eve – we believed her then, didn't we, and it all turned out to be untrue. She's a convincing liar. I wouldn't be at all surprised if it was Chloe who first caused Avril to contact James – who gave her our address.' Her tone is excited, and it seems that the more she talks about this, the more she is wedded to the idea. 'I'm not saying she meant for this to happen – *of course* she wouldn't have planned it this way – but it's not beyond the realms of possibility that Chloe may have made the first contact.'

I can hardly believe what I'm hearing. Chloe? I know Emily doesn't believe it any more than I do. She's doing what she always does when she's cornered, when the guilt is spilling out of her; she's deflecting the blame. 'There's no way Chloe's behind it,' I tell her.

'We'll see,' Emily replies. 'I know you want to think the best of her, Jess. But you were wrong about James keeping secrets – and I think you're probably wrong about his precious daughter too.'

6. Emily

Emily is aware of James shaking her for several seconds before her mind catches up with her body and she opens her eyelids, flinching against the bright morning light that streams through the bedroom windows.

'Emily? *Emily*?' His face is barely recognisable, sallow and drooped. When did this happen? Emily wonders as she stares up at him, blinking slowly. When did he grow so old? 'Chloe's gone,' he tells her, taking a step back, snatching up his wife's dropped clothes and stuffing them in the laundry basket, sharp criticism conveyed in the simple movement. 'Her bed wasn't slept in.'

With great effort Emily pulls herself to a sitting position, and runs a hand across her face, pushing the hair away. The daylight is coursing in, directly on to her face, and she shrinks from it, imagining the effort it would take to ease her legs out of bed and cross the carpet to draw the curtains closed again. Her attention is pulled back to James, whose movements are jerky and impatient. What does he want her to say?

'Emily!' He shouts it now, moving to her bedside to pick up a glass of water that's stale and bubbled.

Even in his panic James is tidying up, Emily notices. She allows herself the briefest memory of Marcus's eyes locked on hers, his wide hands hard on her hips as he thrust her against the wooden beach hut. She can't remember the last time James looked her in the eyes as they made love. She can't remember the last time they made love. She blames him for all of it – for Daisy, for Avril, for Marcus – for *all of it*.

James glares at her. 'Didn't you hear me? Chloe has gone!'

'So?' she replies. *You're still hiding something,* she thinks. *I can see it in your eyes.*

'Christ, you're insane,' he says. His eyes are bulging and she wants to laugh. 'What if she's with Avril?' he demands. 'What if Avril realised she's got it wrong with Daisy and came back here for Chloe?'

Emily snorts. Two days ago she learned that her husband had been lying to her about one of the most fundamental parts of his life – of *their* life – and now he expects her to continue playing Happy Families as if nothing has happened? He's deluded.

'She'll be with Max, James. *Obviously.*'

James's face moves through conflicting emotions, ultimately landing on relief. Max is better than Avril, his face says.

'So what if your underage daughter's shacked up with a nineteen-year-old man? It's not a big deal, James. Not on the scale of things.' Emily can't stop herself. She's woken full of hatred, and it has to go somewhere. She shrugs like a child and raises her eyebrows, inviting her husband's response.

'What do you mean, *it's not a big deal*?' he says, and he looks as though he believes he might be dreaming the whole thing. Welcome to my world, Emily thinks.

'Well, it's not as if we need to protect her chastity, is it? Max has seen to that already. Nothing to protect there.'

Even as she says it, she knows she's gone too far. At close range, James throws the water in his wife's face, drenching her, shocking her into silence.

'You'd better get dressed,' he says, calmly now. 'DCI Jacobs will be here in half an hour. They're going to give us an update.'

Emily knows herself well enough to recognise that sometimes she gets a little carried away with her emotions. She remembers a time in their early teens when a secret she had only ever told Jess started circulating around their year group – the details of an insignificant and long-extinguished crush she'd had on one of the popular boys two years above them. It was a silly thing, a tiny thing, but, by the time the rumour mill had done its worst, the story was that she'd kissed him – 'got off with him' – and worse, until it finally reached his ears and he stopped her in the corridor for a public showdown. As if he'd ever go near a Year *Nine*? What did she think he was, some kind of pervert? His girlfriend had stood beside him, eyeing her, crossed-armed and pitying, and the whole experience had been degrading in the extreme.

Jess had insisted she knew nothing about it, that she'd forgotten all about her sister's fleeting fascination with the boy, and, while her pleas had been convincing, Emily wouldn't believe her. Instead, she retaliated with her own rumour – that Jess's fainting episodes weren't real, but were merely a ruse she used to get attention. Their schoolfriends were incensed: how could Jess lie about something so serious, how could she trick them all like this? It was *disgusting*, and generally agreed that she should be given the silent treatment for a couple of weeks to teach her an important lesson about friendship. Jess tried to talk to them, but whenever she approached any of the group they'd turn their backs, swatting her away like a wasp, pretending they couldn't hear a word. After a week of this, she broke down, refusing to go to school, to eat, to speak. Mum and Dad were fretful with worry, and Emily resented Jess more than ever. It all came to a head one morning as Emily was getting ready for school, when Jess collapsed in a dead faint, resulting in a two-night hospital stay while they monitored her heart rate. While she wanted to believe her sister was faking, the doctors' reports said otherwise, and Emily had to admit to herself that she felt just a little bit guilty for her part in Jess's state of stress before the collapse. So, when it had finally emerged that the source of the original rumour was Emily's best friend Sammie, who had sneaked a read of her diary and clumsily let it slip, she had known that the right thing to do was to apologise to Jess, to make things right. But honestly, by now she'd had enough of being her little sister's guardian, and she was glad to have cause to keep her at arm's length. These fits of hers – or faints, or whatever it was she was having – were getting more and more frequent, and Emily had had enough. It was time for Jess to stand on her own two feet.

After the police have gone, James leaves for work and Jess heads off for her beach walk. She pops her head in to ask Emily if she'd like to join her, 'to clear her head', but Emily waves her away, sarcastically explaining that someone ought to be at home when Chloe gets back. She wishes she meant this, but really she just wants to be alone, to pour herself a large glass of cold white wine and stare at her own reflection in the dressing table mirror.

James had eventually managed to get through to Chloe's phone, and she'd explained she was at Max's house, telling her dad that she needed a few days to work things out, that she was still reeling from the news that her mother was alive. He couldn't argue with that, could he? He could hardly go marching around there to drag her out, not when he was responsible for putting her through something as awful as this.

Earlier, when DCI Jacobs arrived, they had drunk yet more coffee and listened patiently to the inspector's pointless update of leads they'd extinguished and avenues yet to be explored. It had told them nothing, and it certainly brought them no closer to finding Daisy. Emily had hardly been able to contain her frustration as she listened, and found herself desperate to share her own thoughts, her own suggested lines of enquiry. Much to the astonishment of James and Jess, she passed on her theory that Chloe might have traced Avril in the first place – that Chloe might have been the cause of Daisy's disappearance.

'Do you think this is possible?' DCI Jacobs asked James.

His steepled fingers grew white at the tips. 'Absolutely not,' he said through gritted teeth. '*Absolutely. Not.*'

'*I* think it *is* possible, James,' Emily said with affected patience. She gave DCI Jacobs a knowing look. 'I know James only wants to think the best of his daughter, but it *is* possible.'

'Jess?' DCI Jacobs looked to her for an opinion.

'No way. Sorry, Ems, but I think you've got this wrong. You saw Chloe's reaction when we learned Avril was still alive – I've never seen a person look so shocked.'

DCI Jacobs turned back to Emily and gave her a sympathetic but unconcerned shake of the head. 'I'm inclined to agree with James and Jess –' she began, but was cut off when Emily slapped her hands down violently, causing coffee to spill over the table.

'What is wrong with you people?' she screamed, her serene veneer cracked. 'What is wrong with you all?!' She shut herself away in the bedroom until the last of them had left the house.

Somewhere around midday, Emily stops crying and decides it would be a good idea to visit the school where she works, to discuss her return in the next week or two. If James can do it, so can she. It's not as if Daisy will return any quicker with her just sitting around here getting more frantic by the day. Work would do her good. Work would set her mind straight. Work would stop her thinking about all the things she's got wrong in her life, all the bad things she has caused.

At the front desk Violet looks shocked to see her. 'Emily, love! How *are* you?'

She hates this. Before, people used to say, 'How are things?' or 'How's it going, Emily?' Casually, as though she was one of them, the same as everyone else. Now it's 'How *are* you?' with all the emphasis on the *are* – as if she's an invalid, or a child . . . or a grieving mother.

'I'm fine,' she replies, staggering slightly as she misjudges the front step. 'I wanted to see Josie, if she's in?' She leans heavily on the reception desk, wiping the sweat from her upper lip, feeling uneasy as she remembers the man who was parked in her street earlier, the man who took a photograph of her as she dropped her door keys more than once on her way out of the house.

Violet looks concerned, and turns to make eye contact with old Mrs Hilgard in the back, who raises a hesitant wave in Emily's direction.

'Zat a problem?' Emily asks. She finds her words running together involuntarily, and she wishes she hadn't had that little drink before she came out.

Violet leaps from her seat, excessively cheery, her tiny hands fluttering at her neckline as she busies around the desk towards Emily. 'Of course not! You take a seat out here, love, and I'll see if I can find her. She's on class walkabout this morning, otherwise I'd send you straight in.'

Emily sits, thinking she's in for a long wait, but Violet returns minutes later with a concerned-looking Josie by her side. The head teacher embraces her and ushers her inside her office, where she takes a seat on the far side of the desk, offering Emily the one opposite. Staring at the little wooden block marked 'Mrs Priestly',

Emily feels as though she's in an interview, and she straightens herself up, smoothing down her dishevelled hair, moistening her dry lips with the tip of her tongue.

'I want to come back to work,' she announces. Her heart is thumping, and she focuses on Josie's thick, jowly neck, noticing the way it presses solidly against her beige roll neck sweater.

Josie is clearly taken aback. 'When?' she asks, folding and unfolding large pink hands on the desk before her.

'Soon as possible,' Emily replies, but again her words are like sludge in her mouth. She hopes Josie hasn't noticed.

'Do you think you're ready, Emily? What with everything you're going through right now?' She waits for Emily's answer, and when none comes she asks, 'Is there any more information about Daisy yet? We all saw the news about her – her . . .' Josie's words trail off.

'Her *abductor*,' Emily says, and then she leans over the arm of her chair and vomits on the head teacher's floor.

7. Avril

I saw the newspapers on the Co-op news-stand last night, and I'm glad I had the forethought to get my hair done before I boarded the ferry from the mainland. It had grown fairly long, but I used to wear it up all the time, and to be honest it was a pain to look after. Now it's short, cropped prettily around my ears so that the white whispers coming through at the temple look striking rather than dowdy. The hairdresser said it took years off me, and, seeing that awful old photograph they used on the front page of the *County Press*, I'm inclined to agree.

It's a wonderfully bright morning, and I know I'm taking a risk walking here in Freshwater Bay, so close to James's home, but I picked up a baby sling in town yesterday, one which allows me to carry Chloe on my front where I can keep her warm beneath my large jacket. Of course, up close, it's obvious I'm carrying a child, but from a distance I could easily be mistaken for an overweight walker in a big coat. I'm doing well at appearing open and friendly to the few people I pass, and I'm sure no one suspects me. I seem so normal, I presume; whatever that means. I'm not so deluded as to think I hold all the answers on that score. A woman in a red puffa jacket strides purposely ahead of me, her legs slim in tight black jeans and walking boots, her head dipped against the biting cold. When she passed me seconds earlier, she turned her head in my direction and nodded a polite hello, before overtaking me, oblivious to the sleeping baby beneath my clothing.

I remember the first time we took Chloe out together, James and I, when she was tiny, perhaps only a week old. James drove us out to Caversham for an ambling riverside walk, not too challenging for me and my still bruised body, a little stroll under crisp blue skies and a light lunch at the waterside café. He was always thoughtful in that way. He'd even called his mother to come and stay, and she was back home cleaning the house from top to bottom, 'so you young things can go out and have the good time you deserve'. It's such a muddle when I think of Alicia – his mother – because there are times when I remember loving her so effortlessly, and others when I remember only fear and confusion. As we walked by the river James told me how much she loved me, and I cried on hearing that, because it helped to know I was loved. There was a time when he could read my mind, know exactly what I needed. The sling we had was a special one for newborns – a gift from his colleagues at work – and James wore it so that I could walk at his side unencumbered for the first time in months, my hand in his, my eyes roaming restlessly between the flow of the river and the soft crown of our sleeping baby's head. James looked happy; there was no way he could know how I longed to release his hand and step down into the muscular flow of the water. On that idyllic, bright winter morning, how I longed to let myself slip beneath the river's cool surface, limbs drifting, to be carried out to sea and swallowed up by the dark, expansive ocean.

8. Jess

Kicking off my boots and hanging my jacket on the hook by the front door, I call out Emily's name. It worries me when I don't know where she is; she's so erratic at the moment, I fear for her safety. Before I get a chance to search for her upstairs, I hear tyres on the gravel outside and open the door to see Emily being dropped off in a car I don't recognise. An orderly little woman in her early sixties tiptoes alongside Emily, and stops to talk to me in hushed tones as my sister, stinking of stale booze, disappears inside the house without so much as a hello. It seems that, while I've been out walking, Emily's managed to get herself drunk and been in to school, where she's caused a bit of a scene.

'Tell her not to worry,' Violet says in a whisper. 'We all understand, and we all want her to get better. Maybe James could give Josie – Mrs Priestly – a call some time? Confidentially, of course.' With that she tiptoes back to her car and drives away, her aura of apology wafting from her exhaust pipe as she goes.

Inside, Emily is slumped on the sofa, and I see the empty bottle of white wine that she must have polished off this morning. She gives me a rare look of regret, and I slide on to the sofa beside her, hooking my arm through hers, feeling alarm at the frailty of her thin body.

'How about this?' I say. 'We'll run you a bath, get you a nice cup of tea and a biscuit, and then you can get your head down for an hour?'

'James would be so ashamed of me, Jess. Look at me. I'm a bloody mess. I've ruined everything.' She weeps into her free hand, turning her face from me.

'Forget it!' I say, trying to make out it's nothing, when I know it *is* something, it's the great-big-something of a woman going out of her mind. 'James is at work – he doesn't need to know a thing about this. While you're having a nap, I'll get started on supper. You can tell James you cooked it, and I'll make myself scarce for the evening? Chloe said she'd be staying away for another night, so you can have the place to yourselves. I'll even help you choose what to wear – just like the old days? How does that sound?'

It feels as though I've spent much of my life hoping for reconciliations with my older sister. After that awful time in our teens, when she convinced all our friends that my fainting episodes were faked, I had worried we would never be close again. I must have spent the best part of a school term isolated from the inner circle, excluded from sitting with them at break times, from walking with them to and from school, from their weekend trips to the town or seaside. Emily simply stopped talking to me. At breakfast she'd butter her toast across the table from me, her eyes down, focused on the task at hand, and at school she'd go to huge lengths to separate herself from me so that we might never be seen together. To a casual observer we might appear to be complete strangers, neither friends nor foe. At first I was crushed, but with time I slowly retreated within myself, and drew comfort from time spent at home with Mum and Dad, cooking, helping out around the house, sitting up and watching TV with them while Emily was off on some sleepover or another. I thought I was fine without her, until one Saturday morning when I was helping Dad to fix the guttering at the side of the house, and I passed out, causing him to drop the plastic gutter from a great height and me to cut my head open on the rockery as I went down. I came round in the back of the car, my head on Mum's lap as we sped towards A&E, and all I wanted was Emily. I didn't want Mum or Dad or anyone else – I wanted my big sister.

After two days of blood tests, tilt tests, ECGs, treadmill work-outs and visits from endless bedside specialists, I was finally diagnosed with a form of cardioinhibitory syndrome. It wasn't neurological, and it wasn't heart disease, but a rare condition affecting the heart's wiring, causing 'episodes' of fainting and breathlessness at random times, especially during periods of extreme stress or physical strain. It wasn't immediately life-threatening, but it was serious, and something that would have to be monitored for the rest of my life. When Mum and Dad left my hospital bedside that afternoon they were shocked and upset; I on the hand, was relieved, to at last hear confirmation that these 'funny turns' of mine were real, and not, as Emily would have it, a figment of my overactive imagination. That evening, they returned with Emily . . . Emily who had barely made eye-contact with me in months. She entered the ward clutching an armful of magazines and chocolate, and she stood at the foot of my bed, looking close to timid.

'Can you leave us on our own for a while?' she asked Mum and Dad, and, knowing how things had been between us, they slipped away for a coffee in the hospital canteen.

'Mum says you've got some kind of heart problem,' she said quietly, carefully lowering her offerings on to the tightly tucked blanket at the foot of my bed.

I shrugged. 'So they say. Cardio-something-a-jig.'

Her eyes filled with tears. 'Do you think they'd let me stay here with you tonight?' she asked in a whisper.

'I bet they would, if I asked,' I replied. 'I could tell them I'm really worried, and my heart's feeling all jumpy, but it's been better since you got here. If I said that, I bet they would.'

Emily smiled, and I budged up and she crawled in beside me, and we curled up just as we had on that first hospital visit, all those years ago when I was just nine.

Emily looks a whole lot better by the time we've finished getting her ready. We've curled and preened her hair until it shines, exfoliated and buffed her skin, and made up her face so her complexion glows and her eyes sparkle. Together we've picked out an outfit that best flatters her altered figure, one which covers up her hollowed collarbones and sharp wrists, and I've left her upstairs to finish up while I dash down to check on the casserole I've left simmering.

When James comes in through the door, he drops his brief-case in the archway to the kitchen and lifts his nose to the air, breathing in the cooking smells with approval.

I step away from the oven. 'Nothing to do with me!' I say, holding my hands up. 'It's all Emily. She's been slaving over this all afternoon – wanted to do something nice for you, I think.'

'Really?' James says, scrutinising me suspiciously. 'Are you sure? She didn't look too much like someone wanting to do something nice for me this morning.'

I remember the way she had slammed her hands down on the table and run from the room. 'Well, I think she's probably had time to calm down now,' I say. 'Give her a chance.'

James fetches a glass from the kitchen cupboard and pours himself a large measure of red wine, offering one to me as he knocks his back at speed and pours a second. I decline, telling him I'm going out, and I start laying the table with two place settings, as he leans up against the island unit and watches me, ribbing me as I get the knife and fork the wrong way round in my rush. Emily appears in the doorway, and she stands, facing us, looking tall and slim and glamorous in her tan slacks and black roll-neck, her eyes on James, hopeful for his approval. I'm standing at the table in the space between them, and I go to leave the room, to give them this moment, but James's mobile rings in his breast pocket and he turns away, answering the phone, presenting his back to Emily. There's disappointment in the set of her mouth, and, by the time her husband hangs up and turns to face her, it's been replaced by defiance.

'That was the hospital,' he says, and he sounds like a man at the end of his tether. 'It's Chloe – she's been taken in with alcohol poisoning.' He claps his hands to his mouth, a gasp of a sob rising up in his chest. 'They're pumping her stomach.'

9. Emily

Here she is again, alone, waiting for the others to come home. Is this the way the future looks for Emily – forever waiting? Forever waiting for news of Daisy; for James to come home? In the midst of this latest drama James had hardly looked at her, hadn't taken the time to notice how attractive she looked and the effort she had made. Maybe she *didn't* look attractive; maybe he has no interest in her whatsoever. The meal he thinks she cooked will spoil in the oven, because she won't turn it off or cover it with foil, just so she can make the point when he returns home. The hoped-for ambience Jess has been working on all afternoon has vanished entirely.

The moment James told them about Chloe, Jess had grabbed her coat and keys, directing him to get straight in the car. 'You can't drive, James. You've just had a big glass of wine. Will you be OK, Ems? I think you should stay here, in case there's any news about Daisy.'

Emily had nodded mutely. How could she argue with that?

'Ems? Is that OK? We'll give you a ring when we get there. Let you know what's going on.'

Emily noticed the tender way Jess rested her hand on James's back, urging him out of the door, snatching up his coat and pushing it into his confused paw. Was it possessive, the way Jess touched him? Or was it a mothering motion? It must be the latter, surely, when Jess has gone to so much effort to help Emily today, helping her get ready and setting up this romantic meal, as farcical as it might seem now. She is bewildered; she has no idea what she feels – about James or Jess or any of this. On reflection, it seems odd that Jess hadn't suggested that she, Emily, might want to join them at the hospital. She is, after all, Chloe's stepmother. She has more right to be at her bedside than Jess, who's not been in her life more than five minutes. But maybe Jess only plans to drop James there, to wait in the car while he finds out what's going on. Maybe she was just being practical, taking control of the situation when James and Emily looked unlikely to do so. Who knows? Emily stares across the room into the silent space of the family kitchen, a room previously unaccustomed to the quiet that inhabits it now. Who the fuck knows?

She picks up the bottle James left on the counter and pours wine into his used glass. At least this time there's no doubt it's all Chloe's fault. The name spikes into Emily's thoughts. *Always* bloody Chloe.

After the first glass she picks up the phone and calls Becca, knowing it will block the line when Jess tries to call her from the hospital, but suddenly not giving a damn.

'Becca?' she says as soon as her friend picks up. 'It's me, Emily. Is it a good time? I just really need to talk to someone –'

Becca tries to reply, but Emily talks over her, ignoring the clatter of the busy restaurant in the background.

'I don't know who else to turn to – I'm at my wits' end, and there's still no news of Daisy –' she refills her glass '– and James and Jess have just been called out to the hospital, where Chloe's having her stomach pumped.'

240

'God, Emily!' Becca gasps, the change in background noise suggesting she's stepped into the back room. 'That's awful. What happened? Is she going to be all right?'

Becca sounds so genuinely concerned that it occurs to Emily that this thought hasn't even entered her mind. *Will* Chloe be all right? She supposes so, but she's been so busy feeling rage at the girl's latest disaster that she hasn't even thought about the reality of the situation.

'Of course she will!' Emily replies with a snort. 'She's just trying to get attention. Probably got pissed out of her mind on cheap vodka. She's trying to show us she's the boss – sleeping with her boyfriend, staying out all night, getting drunk – she's just playing up. She hates it that all the attention is on Daisy. It's shocking, to be honest, Becca. I hate to say it, but she's a spoilt little cow.'

There's silence at the other end of the phone, and Emily knows she's crossed the line. Becca has known Chloe since she was tiny, ever since they first met at playgroup when Chloe and Todd were just tots. Becca's always said how fond she is of Chloe, what a sweet girl she is.

Eventually Becca speaks, her tone now laced with stilted formality. 'I'm going to have to go, Emily,' she says. 'The restaurant's full tonight and we're short-staffed. Give my best to James, will you? Tell him we'll stop by to see Chloe when she's feeling up to it.' And she rings off, leaving Emily staring at the wine glass on the worktop, the message behind Becca's words confirming what she already knows about herself: she's the worst person in the world.

Her thoughts return to that image of Jess's hand on James's back. There was always something about Jess that made people feel good. She was quiet, and so you had the sense that she was listening, *really* listening to what you were saying and feeling. When you meet someone like that, it makes you feel good. It makes you feel interesting and important and understood. Emily knows this as well as anyone – Jess was her counsellor, her confidante, her best friend since the earliest age, and she was the one person Emily would always turn to for support, the one person who would never judge her, never betray her trust. When they were little – in fact through most of their childhood together – Emily had trusted her implicitly, in many ways thinking of Jess as an extension of herself – the better, quieter, kinder version of herself. Strangely, these were the qualities which could provoke jealousy in her too, when she allowed herself to wish she were more like Jess, more *likeable* like Jess.

Before they separated, Emily had never known Jess to have a boyfriend, and, as their subsequent sixteen adult years were spent apart, she's never seen her sister in any kind of partnership at all. That's strange, isn't it? she thinks. To have only known your sister as a child – and then later, as an adult, solitary, with no apparent baggage to drag along. In their teens, Emily had lots of boyfriends, most of them only lasting a couple of weeks or so, and the awkwardly shy Jess tried to steer clear of these boys if Emily brought them home or they bumped into each other around town or school. Jess would be polite, say a friendly hello, raising her doe eyes to linger on them momentarily before spiriting herself away, too uneasy to stick around and say more. And Emily, so vivacious and certain of her own Snow White charm, would watch jealously as her latest crush darted furtive glances at her retreating sister, eyes hungrily following the pretty little mouse as she scuttled from view. And she was mousy, wasn't she? That was what Emily would tell herself in those moments of envy, gazing after Jess with her browny-gold hair and grungy attire. She might be pretty, but she wasn't sophisticated like Emily; she wasn't *fun* like Emily. Who would choose Jess over Emily?

'You're a tease,' she had once told Jess, after a particularly stupid boyfriend of three weeks had dumped her, then had the cheek to ask if she'd find out whether her sister wanted to go out with him. She had been incensed by the nerve of him, and she'd marched home from the swimming baths where it had happened, running over the times and places they'd encountered Jess, working herself up to the conclusion that her sister's shyness was in fact a form of passive flirtation designed to steal the limelight from her older, more popular sister. Jess had been helping Dad in the garden at the time, wearing cut-off jeans and a *Simpsons* T-shirt, with a ridiculous thumb-width smear of soil across her forehead.

'What?' she had replied.

'You're a tease,' Emily had repeated. 'You try to make out you're not interested in boys, and all the while you're sneaking them flirty looks.'

Even as she said it, Emily knew it wasn't true. Jess looked around, clearly mortified by the thought that Mum or Dad might have overheard. 'But I don't,' was all she could muster.

'Well, maybe you think you don't, Jess. But trust me, you do. Take it from someone older and wiser: you ought to be careful, because you're giving out all the wrong signals.'

Emily had sauntered away, already feeling better about the break-up with stupid Rick, only pausing briefly at the back door to look over at Jess. She was standing beside the border with a trowel in her hand, looking every bit as young as her fourteen years, an expression of panic fixed on her grubby face.

Emily is woken by the sound of the front door banging shut, her first emotion that of irritation. Jess and James enter the living room where Emily has been dozing, closely followed by a dough-skinned Chloe, whose expression sits somewhere between shamefaced and sullen.

'You said you'd phone me.' Emily directs her accusation at Jess.

Jess glances at James. 'I did try, but the line was busy. And your mobile's been switched off for days.'

James puts his arm around Chloe, but when he looks at Emily his face is annoyed. 'Aren't you going to ask Chloe how she is?'

'Sorry, yes,' Emily replies, rising from the sofa, shaking her head. 'Sorry. I've been worried, that's why I'm a bit cranky. How are you, Chloe?' She approaches her stepdaughter and embraces her, but Chloe is not yielding; she takes the hug like a tree resisting a strong wind.

'Fine,' Chloe mutters. 'My throat hurts.'

Jess extends a hand towards Chloe, and Emily feels cross when Chloe readily takes it, following her 'aunt' out into the kitchen to fetch a cold drink.

The living room feels like a strange place, still decked out for Christmas, the huge tree now wilting and bare in the corner, the tree that James and Jess put up with the girls all those weeks ago while Emily lay in bed with a headache. She remembers lying beneath the covers in her darkened room upstairs, the pain in her temple throbbing like a heartbeat, feeling grateful at the sound of their distant laughter as they unpacked the decorations and sang along to Boney M's *20 Greatest Christmas Songs*. They must have made a night of it, because in the morning Emily found two empty wine bottles on the side, the Christmas cheese and biscuits half devoured, and she'd had to stop her jealous alter ego from rearing up, enticing her to imagine all sorts of goings-on between her sister and her husband after the girls had gone to bed.

But even then Jess had been helping out more than she needed to, stepping in to lighten Emily's load, finding ways to make life easier for them all. She's a good sister. Since New Year, James and Jess have been trying to persuade Emily that it's time to take the Christmas decorations down, but she won't have it, not until Daisy is back home, not until this is all over. It's creepy, she acknowledges to herself now, the way she's saving it like some kind of shrine to her missing child, and the decay of the thing grows more disturbing to her with every passing day. But to take it down now would surely be to accept defeat, to accept that she might never come home? How Daisy adored the tree, with its angel on top! James would lift her high above his head to kiss the angel on the face, and then she'd rest in his arms as she pointed out every one of her favourite decorations for James to name. 'Big Santa. Shiny Robin. Sparkly Reindeer. Little Dog. Stripy Stocking.' She'd even started to form some of the words herself. 'Diney Oh'in.' That was her version of 'Shiny Robin'. The health visitor thought she was going to be an early talker, because she was ahead of her peers with all sorts of vocal cues, though she was a bit behind with the crawling and walking. Emily looks around the room, at the desiccated tree and its dropped needles, at the wizened mistletoe that hangs above the hearth, and wonders if Daisy has learnt any new words in the past fortnight. She hopes that woman – *Avril* – is talking to her enough. Daisy likes it when you talk to her a lot.

'What did the doctors say?' Emily asks James, for want of anything else to say. When did she get to feel so awkward in the company of her own husband? Ha! Even that's a laugh: *husband*.

He gazes through the door in the direction that Chloe and Jess have gone. 'Classic alcohol poisoning – nothing else. No drugs, as far as they could tell. Chloe hasn't said much about it, except that she just wanted to "blot it all out". She just wanted to forget everything for a while.'

Emily nods, incapable of coming up with anything worth saying. James makes a move to leave the room, clearly feeling as uncomfortable as her, when he stops in the doorway, an afterthought.

'One of the nurses on duty . . . she said something that worried me a bit.' He turns to look at Emily full on. 'She said that when Chloe was first brought in this evening she was crying hysterically, rambling on about her sister Daisy. The nurse wanted to know who Daisy was – I think she thought there might be another teenager out there in the same state – and of course I had to explain who we were.'

Emily stares at James, wishing he would get to the point.

'I asked the nurse if she could remember Chloe's exact words, and she told me she'd just said the same thing over and over again: *It's all my fault. It's my fault Daisy has gone. It's all my fault.*'

10. **Avril**

I'm so grateful for the open fire and the store of firewood the housekeeper has stacked up at the back of the cottage. Cold entered my bones during our morning walk on the beach and again I had that sense of myself separating out, becoming two: one version of me in the seeing, breathing moment, the other watching from afar, detached, as a hard-hearted voyeur. It frightens me. I fear that poor judgment will blight me again, as it has so often in the past, and I find myself checking and rechecking the roll of money I keep tucked in the bottom of my overnight bag, worried that it will run out too soon. But it only adds to my anxiety; the large amount of cash tells me I must have planned this with clear thought, to avoid having to use cash machines or do anything that will draw attention to me at all. As that woman in the red jacket passed me on the beach today, I had the fiercest pang of reality – that's the only way I can describe it – *reality*, and comprehension of what this actually is, what I'm really doing. But then I tell myself that those feelings are the wrong feelings, that the right ones are the ones that drove me to be here, to take matters into my own hands. Was that really me, slipping ghostlike through the midnight garden and in through their back door? Like a dream, it seems now, the way in which I spirited myself through the house and up to the nursery, instinctively knowing just where to find her, unguarded and waiting. It must have been me, I think now, remembering my clapped-out old car parked on the scrubby ground at the back, unused since that night when we'd returned here together. When I'd forgotten to switch off the headlights and drained the battery dead. As I sit here in the glow of the firelight, my beautiful girl asleep in my arms, I know that James would be happy to see us together, even after so long and painful a separation. I know because he said so. His words couldn't have been clearer. *Of course you should see Chloe*, he said. *A child needs to know who her mother is. A child needs to know where she came from. You'll always be Chloe's mother, Avril.* When did he say those words? I have an image of him sitting at my bedside cradling our newborn; another where he's blocking my entry to the nursery, and I'm crying, hands covering my own face; another as he soothes my head on his lap, and his tears hit my cheek and mingle with my own. I see him sitting on a straight-backed sofa in the whitewashed hush of St Justin's, without Chloe, his face furrowed and serious, his body stiffening when I reach for his hand. Beyond him I can see the great oak tree through the common room window, its leaves rippling in the damp breeze. Was it then that he said it? I don't know, it's all a jumble. I can visualise the words in my mind's eye, and I try to summon up the sound of his voice in my memory, but it's been too long; so long that the sound of him just won't play in my ears.

Outside, the winter wind is up to its tricks again, always at its strongest up here at the top of the island, its howling breath drawing the flames of the fire high and fierce so that the reflected light shimmers over the walls of the warm, dark room. I gaze down upon Chloe's gentle face, so like his, and I have the

248

strongest desire to see him again, to see James and let him judge for himself how good I am with her, how good a mother I turned out to be. He always said I would be, I recall as I close my eyes and let my memories drift. When I first fell pregnant he said that together we'd be the best parents a child could ever have. *Now* I can hear his voice, strong and gentle, and I feel so very lonely again. And all at once I'm alone on the empty beach below, my gaze on the horizon, and I'm wondering, how would it feel to simply walk out into the ocean, just me and my beloved child, to release ourselves forever, to see where the tide would take us?

11. **Jess**

Last night I put together some A4 flyers to hand out to the businesses around town. They're simple, made up of Daisy and Avril's photographs and a simple strapline and contact number:

HAVE YOU SEEN THIS WOMAN AND CHILD?
PLEASE HELP US TO #findDaisy

CALL THIS NUMBER IF YOU SUSPECT ANYTHING,
HOWEVER SMALL

I've no idea if it will make any difference at all, but I'm willing to try anything, rather than just sit around doing nothing and feeling useless. This morning Emily appears strangely detached from it all, in good spirits even. An outsider might think she's without feeling; I'm pretty certain she's taken too many of those tablets and she's artificially buoyant, which worries me just as much as when she's in her dark place. I'm glad when she agrees to let me take her out to lunch, as I'd feared last night's upset with Chloe, not to mention the abandoned romantic meal, might have set her back. DC Cherry texted James early this morning

251

to warn us that there's a photograph of Emily in this morning's news – looking more than worse for wear – and that we'd be wise to steer clear of journalists today if at all possible. James and I agree not to tell Emily, so I'm nervous about trying to make it past the baying mob outside without Emily being asked for a comment or shown a copy. When the time comes, with the help of our neighbours, Emily and I cut across the back gardens, popping out on the low road and managing to dodge the press vultures altogether. Thank God, she's none the wiser, and in surprisingly good humour. We arrive at Becca's Café just before the lunchtime rush begins, and she gives us the best table in the house, overlooking the bay.

'Can we get a bottle of wine?' Emily asks when Becca has returned to the bar, and, although I don't think she should really be drinking again, I suppose it won't do her any harm to let her hair down with me here to keep an eye on her. I want her to think of this as a nice day out, a treat, something that takes her away from the house and the absence that Daisy has left behind.

'Good idea!' I say. 'Why don't you take a look at the menu and I'll go and see what wines Becca has got?'

Becca gives me a strained grimace as I approach the bar. She reminds me of a 1940s farmer, ruddy-faced and solid. Reassuring.

'She phoned me last night,' she says. 'She was raving, and I didn't really know what to say. I was probably a bit off with her. I didn't like the way she was talking about Chloe, you know? Did she mention it to you, Jess?'

'No, she didn't. It must have been while I was at the hospital with James – what did she say?'

Becca leans out across the bar to pass a pile of menus to a new arrival. Several more customers have come in since we arrived and the volume in the place is now loud enough that our conversation can't be heard by Emily at the front of the café.

'She called Chloe a spoilt little cow. Can you believe it? The girl's having her stomach pumped, and her stepmother's acting cold as ice. As I say, I was speechless.'

I point to a bottle of house white in the display fridge, and watch Becca as she opens it and lays down two glasses. 'She's a mess at the moment, Becca – some days I think she's going to lose it altogether. I know the cause of it all is Daisy's disappearance, but the weirdest thing is that sometimes I wonder if she even misses her, if she's even all that sad that her baby has gone.' I don't know why I'm saying all this to Becca; it's not as though I know her that well, but I like her, and something tells me I can trust her. 'Of course that's not really the case, but it's just the way she seems right now – as if she's completely absent of any feeling, other than rage. I guess all we can do for the time being is to try to keep her grounded. Make sure she can hold it together until Daisy comes home.'

I resist the urge to turn and look in Emily's direction, to see if she's noticed us chatting. Becca peers over my shoulder, checking on Emily, reading my thoughts. 'She's fine. She's reading the menu. Listen, if there's anything you need, just let me know, Jess? How's Chloe today?'

I think of Chloe's tired little face when I popped up to see her earlier, how she seemed smaller and younger than ever before. 'She's OK. I took her up a bowl of soup just before we left, and the colour's coming back to her cheeks already. She just needs a bit of rest now – maybe I'll take a bit of that cheesecake home for her later, cheer her up.'

Becca picks up a knife and slices a generous portion of the strawberry cheesecake that sits on the counter top, wrapping it in tin foil and sliding it across to me. 'On the house. Tell her Becca and Todd send their love, will you? Now, why don't you take these drinks back to your table and I'll be over to take your order in two ticks?' She pats the counter and turns away, and I think that's what the world needs to make it a better place: more Beccas.

When I sit down opposite Emily I'm relieved to see the lively sparkle in her eyes, and I can hardly believe she's the same woman who staggered through the front door yesterday afternoon.

'Well, I'm not sure about mains, but I know what I'm having for pudding – look, they've got millionaire's shortcake just like we used to order in Minxies on West Street.' She waves to attract Becca's attention, turning her smile back to me, her face open with nostalgia. 'Remember Minxies, Jess? God, we used to love that place!'

Minxies was a 1950s-styled diner that had been on the high street in our home town for as long as we could remember, a place frequented by the older kids too cool for the doily-decked Olde Country Café on the opposite side of the road. We first dared to set foot inside Minxies on Emily's sixteenth birthday, when she gathered a small posse of us – me, Sammie, Jane Warren and Jo Floyd – to join her after school for a spontaneous celebration. I'll never forget the feeling of walking in there in our uncertain little group, with Emily boldly leading the way along the aisle, swinging her hips and sliding into the first free booth she came to. We all slid in around her, glad of the red high-backed stall that shielded us from the scary sixth-formers and college kids whose eyes had examined us on the way in.

A large candy-striped waitress called over from behind the glass cake cabinet, waving a pair of pastry tongs in our direction. 'It's counter service, girls. You'll have to come to the till to order.'

I blushed, and Emily tutted, nudging little Sammie to shove along so we could all trail up to the counter to choose our hot chocolates or Cokes or whatever it was that we wanted. I felt like a silly little baby under the judging scrutiny of all those older, more confident diners, but by the time we returned to our booth I was too distracted by the tall strawberry milkshake and pink iced bun Emily had treated me to, too entranced by the honeyed jukebox sounds of Nina Simone to care about the big kids on the other side of our private padded booth. I can see us all now, as clear as day: Emily with her shiny hair piled high in a swirling bun, her lips a smooth raspberry pout of colour; Sammie, in her soft pink sweater looking pretty as a princess; Jane and Jo barely distinguishable from one another with their heavy fringes and identical denim jackets; and me, boyish in a stripy T-shirt and jeans, my long sun-lightened hair in need of a good brush. What a funny little group we must have seemed, mismatched in so many ways.

For the next two years Minxies was where it all happened. It was a period of harmony for Emily and me, a time when we were as easy together as we'd ever been, and collectively we soon became such a firm fixture at the diner that the large candy-striped waitress treated us like proper regulars. She gave us names to match our favourite orders, so I was Miss Strawberry Milkshake and Emily was Miss Millionaire's Shortcake. Sammie was Miss Chocolate Donut, which she wasn't so keen on because she thought it made her sound fat. Minxies was *the* place to go in our little group, its American Dream charm seeing us through all manner of exam nerves and heartache, family strife and growing pains. Minxies *felt* good – it smelled good, it tasted good, it sounded good too – and it made us feel happy about ourselves, as though we were part of something grown-up and real.

It was in Minxies that Emily and I could be the best versions of ourselves together, where we could laugh and joke and sing along to the jukebox and never think a bad thought about each other. It was where we went for every celebration or commiseration, where we'd stop on the way back from shopping before a night out, so that we could plan our outfits together, pulling new purchases from our crinkly shopping bags to lay them out on the table and tell each other we would look just great. Minxies was the last place Emily and I had been together before that party at Sammie's house when I had just turned seventeen. But after that party we never returned to Minxies again, either together or alone.

'Did they miss me?' I ask Emily after Becca has cleared away the plates from our main course. Emily looks up from her wine glass, startled. 'Did Mum and Dad miss me, after I'd gone?'

She takes a slow, considered sip from her drink before reaching for the bottle and topping up our glasses, her measures coming dangerously close to spilling over. 'Well, they must have done, I'm sure.' She returns the bottle to its position at the edge of the table.

'So they never said as much?' I hadn't meant to bring this up. It must be the wine talking – I'm not used to drinking during the day. 'They never worried, or wondered where I'd gone?'

'Well, yes, but I told them what we'd agreed I would. That you'd got yourself a job in London, and wanted a fresh start, away from home. That *is* what we'd agreed, wasn't it?'

Of course she's right. That was what we had agreed – or at least what my big sister had suggested, and I had gone along with.

I remember her voice, soft and kind enough to be persuasive, as she'd knelt in the darkness at my bedside a few nights before I left home. 'You'll hurt them more if you hang around reminding them of the whole awful thing,' she had whispered. The crack of light from the street lamps beyond the curtains had lit her up momentarily, illuminating the shine of her glossy hair, the wet of her eyes. She'd moved back into darkness.

'But what if I were to talk to them? Explain it all? Maybe they'd understand? Maybe they'd see that it wasn't how it sounds.'

Emily had made a horrible scoffing sound and, even as I said it, I knew I was wrong to hope I could make them see something as terrible as this as anything other than sinful. Even if my father could forgive me, my mother's morals were so hard-wired that it was impossible to imagine her even hearing the words, let alone forgiving the actions. *Mum, I got pregnant by a boy I hardly know – and then I aborted it. I murdered an unborn child.* These were words I would never speak; I could no more bear to say them aloud than my mother could bear to hear them on my lips.

Emily was resolute. 'You didn't see her after the phone call, Jess. When the clinic phoned she was *crushed*. Haven't you seen the way she's been around us all lately? I promise you, she's not ready to talk about it yet.'

She was right, Mum had been puffy-eyed and withdrawn lately. Dad did his best to go along with the charade that all was tickety-boo, but it was clear she was depressed, and it was all down to me.

I lay there, reeling from the news that the clinic had phoned her. 'But I thought the clinic was supposed to be confidential? They even had posters saying that, on the walls! You said once I'd done it, Ems, that would be the end of it. Why did they have to tell her?' I broke into a sob – I can recall the raw pain of the emotion to this day – and I clamped my hand to my mouth to stop the loneliness and self-hatred from spilling into the darkness, my body straining to let it all out, to let my keening voice be heard.

'You're under eighteen, Jess. I guess they must have a rule about telling your parents if you're under eighteen. I didn't know, honest.'

We were silent then for a while, until Emily had stood and patted my arm and told me I'd be fine. 'Just take yourself away for six months – maybe a bit more – and then we'll see? It'll be for the best, Jess. Trust me.' And then she had left the room.

Trust me. The words pass through my head now as my big sister sits across the table from me, up-ending the last few drops of wine into her own glass. *Trust me*, she had said, and I had. Despite everything I knew about Emily, despite every little wrong she'd ever done me, I *had* trusted her.

But that was then, and this is now. 'Yes,' I reply, returning her unblinking gaze. 'You're right, Ems. That's what we agreed.'

12. **Emily**

It was nice, going out for lunch like that with Jess, but something about it has left Emily uneasy. She sits on the edge of the bed in the early evening light. Was it something in the hard edge to Jess's voice when she asked about their parents, something in the way she was so quick to accept Emily's version of events? Of course, they were drinking too, and it's quite possible that on top of her tablets and her fatigue and sorrow Emily is feeling edgy and mistrustful, imagining an atmosphere between them that isn't even there. After all, Jess has been her salvation these past few days, since the news came through about Avril. It's Jess who has kept Emily functioning when all she wants to do is curl up and die. She's kept them fed and clothed, she's prevented the house from falling into disarray, quietly buoying James enough to keep getting up and going to work, and dealing with all the problems of Chloe so that Emily doesn't have to. So why, then, does she feel so uneasy now? Is it suspicion and mistrust she feels? No, not exactly. It's something more like fear of letting herself go, of giving herself back to her sister without reservation. Perhaps it's *guilt*, a rare and honest voice whispers inside her head: guilt at the decades they've wasted apart, guilt at her own stubborn refusal to let bygones be bygones and bring Jess back to the fold years earlier.

Whatever it is, she tells herself, she's being neurotic and she ought to be grateful to Jess, not tight-minded and suspicious. As she lies back on her bed and closes her eyes, a terrifying thought occurs to her: what if Jess leaves her now? Her heart races – she can't allow that to happen, not now that she's here – Jess has become the glue in this family, the one thing that is holding them all together. She even plugged Emily's phone into the bedside charger this afternoon, insisting she must keep it switched on in case any news comes through, and of course Emily knew she was right. She can't leave them now. Emily leans over to the bedside table and snatches up her mobile phone, urgently tapping out a message, and pressing send before she has time to change her mind. She flops back against the pillows and exhales with relief.

Thanks for today, Jess. So glad you're here. Love you, Ems xxx

By Emily's standards the message is positively gushing, and that in itself makes her feel exposed. What is it with open displays of affection that spook her so? She doesn't know the answer to this, nor to so many of the other questions that hurtle through her mind at all hours these days, but she does know that Jess will appreciate it, that she will know she's needed, and that's the important message that Emily must convey.

Jess went out again a while ago. She didn't say where she was going or what she was doing, just that she'd tell Emily all about it in the morning. Perhaps she's off on another of her long walks across the island; perhaps she just needs a bit of time alone. Before she set off, Jess cooked up a big pan of chilli, taking a bowlful up to Chloe's room and plating up two more so that Emily can eat together with James when he gets back from work. He's gone in even though it's Saturday, claiming that he's got a lot to catch up on after taking off so much time over Daisy, and, while that may well be true, Emily knows he's glad to be away from her as much as possible. Jesus, this is one ugly great mess. Just one month ago, if anyone had predicted the future to Emily, she would have written them off as insane. If they had said to her, 'By mid-January, Emily, you will have slept with your husband's best friend and your baby will have been abducted. Your stepdaughter, who hates you, will have been hospitalised with alcohol poisoning and your husband's first wife will have turned up alive and well, not dead as you'd believed for the past thirteen years. Oh, and your long-estranged sister will be the one person you can really rely on, the one person you believe just might be able to get you through this nightmare if you don't go crazy first.' If someone had told her that this was what her future held, she would have laughed in their face.

Emily turns to look at the digital numbers of the clock, sees it is 7pm. Should she look in on Chloe, see if she needs anything? Part of her wants to, but the other part of her knows that Chloe's not interested in anything she has to say. She'll leave her for now, let her sleep. Yes, that's the thing to do. She emerges from the dim loneliness of her bedroom to seek out a new bottle of wine. She'll take it back upstairs with her, and, with no one here to cast judgment, she'll crawl into bed and drink it alone.

They are lying on the beach under a gently scorching sun, the sand mounded over their concealed bodies, their heads resting side-by-side on warm sand-built pillows. To passers-by they might look like a pair of tiny Egyptian princesses, prepared for internment in sarcophagi made of golden sand. Where are they? Emily tries to remember as she lies on her bed, half-dozing, and it comes to her, strangely, that it was *here*, on this very island, on a rare summer holiday over from the mainland. They can't have been very old at all, but the memory is as sharp as a photograph:

261

beyond their feet is the sea, lapping and glimmering, alive with the sounds of splashing children and laughing adults, and the low but clear tones of their own parents' voices tell her they are nearby, perhaps on a picnic blanket outside of her line of vision. She'd look, but she can't turn her head without fracturing the sand that pins her shoulders. Overhead the sun is a misty white, and as gulls and pipers squabble and soar across the skyline she must squint as her gaze follows them for fear of burning her eyes out.

'My face is stinging,' Jess says. She remembers now, how it was so often her – Emily – that Jess would turn to for help and advice, rather than Mum. Why was that? Was she more available? More approachable? Or was it, as Emily suspects, that she guarded her little sister so fiercely that Jess knew it was easier to ask *her* in the first place? 'Emi, my face is stinging.'

'Five more minutes,' Emily replies. She allows her fingers to burrow stealthily beneath the sand until the tips of her hand find those of her little sister, and they stay there like that for a while longer, until they're both pink and singed and hungry for sandwiches.

The phone rings, and Emily sits bolt upright in her bedroom, wishing she could remain on that beach with her little sister forever, warm and secure. Why doesn't anyone answer it? she wonders irritably, before remembering that it's just her and Chloe here in the house. She dashes on to the landing and picks up the extension there, a hot pain behind her right eyeball pounding with the beginnings of a hangover.

'Hello?' she barks with more aggression than she had intended. Perhaps she thinks it will be James, phoning to say he'll be late. But he's already late. It's too late to say you'll be late.

'Emily?' The voice is familiar to her, but Emily can't quite place it.

'Ye-es?' she replies with caution. It could be a trick; it could be a journalist. She can smell her own acrid breath, tainted with wine.

'Emily! It's Sammie! God, I'm so glad I finally got through to you!'

Sammie. One of her oldest friends, someone she once would have trusted with her life, a friend who was with her through school days and early adulthood, through thick and thin. Little Sammie who never topped five foot and looked like a fairy; little Sammie who bought her Converse trainers from the kids section of Bentalls, because she only took a size three and they were at least a tenner cheaper. Sammie, the one friend who had been there for her through childhood, always around in the fun times, always ready to pick her up each time her heart was broken. Why did they drift apart?

Sammie's voice starts off excitable – but now it drops, adopting the generic concerned tone Emily so despises. 'I've heard about everything that's happened, Ems. I heard about Daisy,' she says. 'I can't even begin to imagine what you're going through.'

Another overused cliché. *I can't begin to imagine how you're feeling.* Of course you can't, you thoughtless idiots. How could you ever begin to imagine, unless you'd been there yourself? Emily wonders if there's a special instruction manual these people are all consulting, a catalogue of trite phrases for the lost and grieving.

'It's been pretty dreadful,' she hears her own voice replying. 'What are the police saying? Is there any fresh news?'

Emily sighs heavily. 'Well, I expect you've seen that they suspect James's first wife now?' The shame she feels at this – at admitting to the world that she had no idea about Avril, that her husband keeps secrets from her – it's unbearable. 'You can't have missed it, Sammie – it's been all over the papers.'

There's a little pause, and she guesses Sammie can hear the jaded misery in her voice. 'I saw it online this morning,' Sammie admits. 'That's sort of what made me call. I couldn't believe it, Ems. They think she's taken Daisy, don't they? Surely that's better news, isn't it, than, well – than some complete, um, *stranger* or something . . .?' Her sentence grows weak at the end, as so often happens in conversations of this kind. She started off all right, but then she just had to keep talking, didn't she, leading the conversation into suggestions of psychopaths lurking in alleyways, evil men, murderers – all the terrible kinds of monsters that have, of course, raced through Emily's own tortured imagination.

She decides not to answer, to let Sammie sweat a bit more.

Sammie fills the gap. 'So, did you have any idea she was still alive?'

Emily laughs. 'You're not a journalist these days, are you, Sammie?'

'No, I'm not!' her friend shrieks. 'I'm sorry. Sorry, sorry, sorry! Oh, God, Emily, I don't know what to say to you! This is just about the most awful thing that's ever happened to any of us, and I know we haven't been in touch much over the years, but I just wanted to let you know I'm thinking of you. I just wanted to let you know I'm here!'

'I know,' Emily says after a short pause, and momentarily she forgives Sammie her clumsiness, and she understands that this must be a difficult conversation for anyone to have with a friend. 'Sorry, Sammie. I'm just exhausted.'

They talk now, relaxing a little, sticking to more pedestrian subjects such as Sammie's new job and the latest gossip from Emily's home town. Emily asks after Sammie's kids and Sammie reminisces about the old days, when she used to spend most afternoons with Emily and Jess because her own parents were always out at work, and Emily's mum cooked the best Victoria sponge cake. They laugh about the time flashing police sirens lit up the street outside Sammie's house because the neighbours had spotted 'youths' climbing in through the bathroom window, not realising it was Sammie and Emily, arriving home late from a party, drunk on alcopops and short of a house key.

The exchange is drawing to a natural close, when Sammie asks, 'Is Jess still staying with you?'

Sammie *knows* the answer to this, Emily thinks, her reservations rising up again, because Jess said she spoke to her on the phone only last week. 'Yes. She's been a real help.'

'That's *great*,' Sammie says, but her voice is overly bright, and Emily isn't fooled.

'What is it, Sammie?' she asks impatiently.

Sammie doesn't answer immediately, but ums and ahhs a bit, until Emily tells her to spit it out or hang up. 'OK,' she says with resignation. 'I'm just going to come out with it – and you can choose to forget it or hate me or whatever – but if I don't say something, I'll never forgive myself.'

What the hell is this? Emily's stomach tenses and she wonders if she might be sick. '*Yes?*'

'Has it occurred to you that Jess might have something to do with Daisy's disappearance?'

The silence hangs between them.

'I mean, it's just that everything was fine between you and James, and then Jess came back after all these years, and moved straight in – which was a bit of a surprise – and then within a few weeks, well, you know, Daisy –'

Emily lets her roll, lets her keep talking, jabbering away to fill the dreadful silences.

'I've been thinking about it a lot, Ems – ever since I first heard about Daisy going missing – and it's probably stupid, especially now that they think it's James's ex-wife – but even so, I just thought, well, maybe *Jess* contacted her – maybe Jess told her where James and Chloe were, out of –' and here she struggles to say the word '– out of *spite* or something. After everything that had happened between you two before. I know it's years ago, but I just –'

'Is this some kind of a joke, Sammie?' Emily's patience has run out. 'What do you mean, *everything that happened before*? Nothing happened! It was just kids' stuff, teenage squabbles, nothing more! Stupidly, we took far too long before getting back in touch – but now we have, and Jess and I are *just* fine. *Better* than fine!'

'But, Emily, at your mother's funeral, I think I might have –' Sammie starts to say, but Emily has had enough of her madness and she slams the receiver on to its cradle and returns to her bedroom.

Sammie. What a bloody nerve she's got, phoning up like that, trying to come between her and Jess. *Sammie Evans*. She always was a shit-stirrer.

13. **Avril**

I pick up a local newspaper and place it on the counter beside my basket of groceries.

'Isn't it awful about this missing baby?' I say to the shopkeeper. Her face falls into a slack study of sadness. 'Oh! It's a tragedy. I can't stop thinking about it, it's so terrible.' She speaks as she tots up my purchases, bagging them as she goes. 'Nothing like this ever happens here, on the island. I mean, don't get me wrong, all kinds of things happen here – just like everywhere else, I suppose – but this? A child missing? No, it's just dreadful.'

Another customer joins us at the till, a woman about my age, wearing a heavy Barbour jacket and mud-caked boots. 'Trouble is, it makes you look at everyone with suspicion, doesn't it? I mean, that's what the police have told us to do – question everything, look out for anyone with a child, anyone you don't know.' She nods towards the pram and smiles. 'You must've had a few double-takes, haven't you? People checking you haven't got the snatched baby there!'

She's joking, I know, and I laugh too, handing over a twenty-pound note and organising my shopping in the basket beneath the pram. 'I have!' I say and then I incline my head, inviting her to look inside the pram, where Chloe lies fast asleep, dressed head to toe in navy blue. 'But they soon forget their suspicions once they see he's a little boy!'

It's genius, I know. The idea came to me yesterday as I paused outside the window of Mothercare on the high street, drawn as I was to the sweet little bobble hats and warm winter outfits. A boy! No one will question me with a baby boy!

The two women take a good look at Chloe, smiling generously.

'So, is he yours?' the Barbour woman asks. She's obviously trying to assess my age.

'Yes. Late baby – usual story – too busy with my career for years, and then it took a while for me to fall pregnant. But he's here now! Better late than never.' I can't believe how normal I sound, how convincing, and I like this new life, this new normality.

They nod approvingly. 'Well, he's a poppet,' the shopkeeper says. 'Has he got a name?'

I regret it the moment it leaves my lips, but, thank God, they don't seem to make the connection. 'James,' I say, and I turn away because I'm blushing, feeling caught out. 'But we call him Jimmy. Jimmy.'

'Lovely!' they say, together, and it's the perfect time for me to leave, because they believe me, and we're all smiling, and outside the winter sun is shining and everything is good in the world.

14. Jess

Someone pushed a copy of the *Sun on Sunday* through the letterbox first thing this morning, and Emily has lost the plot. She's screaming on the landing, waving the paper around, demanding that James and I explain ourselves. As I rush up the stairs intending to calm her down she starts banging on Chloe's door, with James grabbing at her arm, trying to pull her away.

'I suppose you knew all about it too!' she yells into Chloe's room, and I push past Emily and snatch the paper from her hands in an attempt to pull her focus away from Chloe. She spins to face me, furious in the curtain-dark room. Behind her Chloe is sitting up in bed, pale, just woken, and utterly bemused.

James stands in the doorway beyond Emily, and his sleep-creased face is asking me, *what's up, what's happened now?*

'How could you do this to me again, Jess?' she shrieks, her hands on her face. '*My God!* I'm such an idiot! I trusted you.' She wrestles the newspaper back from my grasp, her chest heaving with the weight of her emotion, and shakes her head, as though remembering all the wrongs I've ever done her. And then she goes from enraged to exhausted in a breath, her shoulders slumping in defeat. '*I trusted you.*'

James enters the room and sits on the edge of Chloe's bed, reaching out to pat his daughter's leg beneath the covers. Chloe hasn't said a word, but I can tell that she thinks this is about Daisy, because she's running her thumb along her upper teeth in the way that she does when she's on edge, and her eyes are welling up with fresh tears.

'Emily,' James says, gently, 'we're all in the dark here. Exactly what is Jess supposed to have done? Only last night you were texting her to say thank you, telling her you loved her.'

The moment he says the words, his face shows he knows his mistake.

'And how would *you* know what I texted to my sister last night, James? How could you *possibly* know that!' She screams this, spittle flying – and I swear she looks as insane as a person ever could – and she raises the newspaper and slams it against her husband's chest. 'Because you were with her all evening? Because you were secretly meeting my sister when you said you were at work? Because you were drinking and flirting and after that, what? Screwing? Whispering sweet nothings? Planning your happily-ever-after together?'

James rolls his eyes in desperation, before turning them to the newspaper in his lap. Emily fixes her hard eyes on me and I want to deny it, to put her straight, but the words won't form in my mouth and then, more than anything, I'm distracted by the look of horror on James's face as he studies the front page of the tabloid.

'I suppose you don't remember a thing about it, Jess?' Emily says, calmer now, soft malice creeping in. 'The usual excuse, is it? Sorry, officer, I didn't see my niece being abducted because I fainted. Sorry, Emily, I don't remember fucking your husband because I "had an episode".'

She's goading me, urging me to react, and I really believe I won't, until she says the words, sweet as can be: 'Sorry, doctor, I don't know how I got pregnant, because I was off my face.'

270

I gasp, winded by her words, and I lunge at her, knocking her tiny frame to the bed as the rest of the room shrinks away and there's only me and her and the aching pain that courses between us. She's pinned to the bed by her shoulders, the full weight of me holding her there, our eyes locked in combat, and I see hatred there, pure, unadulterated hatred, and I know in that moment that she's never forgiven me. That she will never get over what happened with Simon O'Carroll.

James's grip eases me off her, and I see Chloe huddled up against her pillows, her face streaked with tears. I crawl over the tangle of bedsheets to pull her to my chest, desperate to protect her from yet more trauma. She's a kid, just a kid, and this is all wrong. *So* wrong. I think back to that day when Emily invited me to stay and, excited, I'd said yes, and I had had so many lovely ideas leaping around inside my head, ideas about how it would all go, how my life would change once I'd moved in with my big sister. This is not how I saw it unfolding; this is not the new future I'd planned. Her words pain me so much that I want to blurt it all out – scream out all her secrets for the world to hear – but I mustn't. I mustn't.

Emily is now sitting on the carpet, away from us, her thin fingers clasped around her knees. James sits on the other side of Chloe, his arm around her resting against the bare skin of mine. He holds the newspaper between us, and there we see the photograph that has sent Emily into meltdown. It's a side-column headline, telling readers to 'turn to page 5 for the full story'. But the front page photo says it all: it's me and James at Becca's Café last night, smiling at each other over an intimate table for two, a bottle of wine between us, and his fingers reaching out to gently touch my face. To an observer, I can see – in that split-second snapshot – we look like a couple in love. His five o'clock shadow and half-smile appear more seductive than shattered; my wind-messed hair might easily be confused for bedroom dishevelment. But it's not the photograph that has wreaked the worst of the damage here. It's the headline, with all its nasty innuendo:

MISSING DAISY DAD AND AUNT 'COMFORT' EACH OTHER OVER WINE

'It's a lie,' James says to Chloe. 'It's been set up to look bad. But it's not true.'

Chloe turns to me and I nod earnestly, wanting her to believe us, wanting her to know that I'm the same Jess that I've always been. That I *am* trustworthy and good.

Chloe glances at Emily, whose head is now resting on her knees, and Chloe whispers, so that only James and I can hear, 'I wouldn't mind if it was. I wouldn't blame you if it was true.'

James sighs sadly, and I leave the room. This family needs time alone.

Trustworthy. It's a word Emily used more than most as a child, as a young adult. Do we think so-and-so can be trusted, Jess? Are they loyal – are they honest – are they *trustworthy*? It's not that she herself was exactly the model of good behaviour when it came to these particular attributes, but she set a high bar when it came to anyone who entered her inner circle. She'd constantly test her friends, setting them difficult choices to make, choices that would illustrate how much they thought of her, how much they preferred her company over others, liked *her* the best. *Who wants to sit next to me?* she'd ask as we filed into morning assembly, favouring the first of her friends to leap at the chance. *Don't go into town with Sammie, Jane, come to the beach with me instead.*

Jess is much prettier than me, she announced one day over lunch in the school canteen. You've never heard a group of girls clamour so quickly to tell her she was wrong. It didn't upset me in the least; I was used to it. I was no stranger to Emily's loyalty traps, as she'd been laying them down for me for as long as I could remember. We shared a room in the years before we started at secondary school, often talking into the darkness long after lights out, long after Mum had popped her head around the backlit doorway to wish us goodnight, and God bless, and don't-forget-to-say-your-prayers. We would lie in silence for a few minutes, both pretending to pray, though each knew the other was also just waiting to hear the distant click of the living room door that told us we couldn't be overhead. Then, 'Jess?' Emily would start. 'Did you see Mrs Green's dirty fingernails today?'

'Yes.'

'Disgusting, weren't they?'

I liked Mrs Green. 'She told me she had to mend a bike puncture on the way to school this morning. It was oil. She said she couldn't wash it out.'

I could feel Emily's mood stiffen across the room from me. She hated it when I disagreed with her in any way. 'Who do you prefer, Mrs Green or *Mr Hobbs*?'

'Mrs Green.'

'You think I'll say you love Mr Hobbs if you said him.'

'I don't!' My stomach knotted. Why did she always do this? She was right, I *did* prefer Mr Hobbs, but only because he was kind, not because I loved him.

'OK, then. If you had to push one of them off a cliff, which one would it be? And you can't lie – imagine it like it's really going to happen.'

'Mrs Green,' I reply, reluctantly.

'Knew it,' she says, and I can feel her pleasure radiating silently into the room, in perfect opposition to my discomfort. 'Who would you marry – Josh Brown or William Hope?'

'Neither!'

'You have to, Jess. You know the rules.'

What rules, I thought? No one ever told me there were rules. 'Josh Brown,' I whisper, my face hot.

'Urghh,' she said, making a retching noise, judging me. 'I'd rather die. Who would you rather go on holiday with, me or Sammie Evans?'

This question told me I'd been spending too much time with Sammie. I would have to pull back a little, let Emily take centre stage next time Sammie was around. 'You, of course.' Could there be any other answer?

Now came the pause that always filled me with dread, in which Emily would come up with a final question, something more troubling, a haunting scenario for me to carry off into sleep. 'Jess? If you had to choose one of them to die – hanged like in the olden days – which would it be? Mum or Dad?'

'No!' I hissed out into the emptiness. 'No! You always do it – you always ask me a horrible one like this. I'm not answering.'

'You have to,' she replied, her ten months of seniority sounding so much greater. 'It's the rules, Jess. Which one?' When I went silent on her, refusing to play, she whispered, 'I don't know why you're being such a baby. I know which one I'd choose.' And she didn't tell me, just shifted over in her bed so I could hear from her breathing that she'd turned her back on me to go to sleep.

I lay there for what felt like hours, turning it over and over in my head, the alternative images of my parents, swinging from the gallows as I tried not to choose one of them over the other. The thing was, I knew I wouldn't sleep until the decision had been made, even if it was only ever inside my head.

I don't know why Emily took so much pleasure in testing me like that, because really, apart from that one time years later, I'd never given her reason to doubt my devotion at all.

'God, just look at it,' I say, standing beside James at the dining table, the newspaper spread out across its surface. 'No wonder she thinks there's something going on.'

James glances back over his shoulder, but he needn't worry, Emily is back in bed now, sleeping off the exhaustion of her earlier explosion. He looks back at the photograph of me and him in Becca's restaurant. 'It's not a bad picture, all things considered,' he says, rolling his eyes towards me, trying to find some small sliver of humour in the situation. 'I think I look quite handsome.'

I shake my head, still not quite believing that I'm looking at a photograph of myself in the national press. An intimate picture of James reaching out to touch my face. 'And what's that face-touching all about? Do you think they've Photoshopped it?'

'The only thing I can think is that it was when I was reaching up to take my credit card back from Becca. I bet if you zoomed out of this picture she'd be there, leaning over the top of you. Without her there, it looks as if I'm stroking your face.'

'Yes! Bastards. God, it just goes to show you can't take anything at face value, can you? Unbelievable. Of course the whole world will know that we're at it now.' I look at James, and we know it's serious – but it's also funny, horribly, absurdly funny, and we start to laugh, soft and unbelieving at first, growing in strength and hysteria until there are tears running from our eyes and we're holding on to the chair-backs for support.

'Stop it,' he whispers, checking again for signs of Emily, rubbing his face vigorously to clear his tears. 'Stop. God, you're terrible – this is serious.'

I nod, running a finger beneath my lashes to blot my mascara. 'Sorry. I know, I know. Shit – how are we going to convince Emily there's nothing going on? As if she needs this right now. Bloody hell.'

Having regained his composure, he reaches for the telephone. 'We'll get Becca to speak to her. She'll vouch for us – it's all straightforward enough, isn't it?'

'Emily will still think we planned to meet up, that we're trying to get one over on her. You know how suspicious she can be.'

'But it was completely innocent,' he says, throwing his hands up as if it was Emily he was speaking to. 'Jess, you had no idea I was going to be in there after work, and I had no idea you'd be there talking to Becca about an evening job! The newspaper makes it look like a romantic meal for two – but it was a drink, just one drink, for God's sake. You're my sister-in-law. Under the circumstances it would have been more strange if we *hadn't* stopped for a drink together.'

He flips through the business cards pinned to the notice-board until he finds one for Becca's Café, and he's poised to dial the number when the phone rings in his hand. 'Jeez!' he says, alarmed, and answers it on the second ring.

The previous lightness evaporates instantly, as James's face freezes, and he presses the speakerphone button on the handset and a woman's voice is projected into the room.

'James?' Her voice is soft. 'James, it's me.'

She doesn't say her name, but I know it's her from the expression on his face, and the familiarity of her tone. The one time she rings, and neither liaison officer is here, Cherry having been absent for the past couple of days with a family emergency of his own, and Piper having called to say he wouldn't be with us until midday. I scan the room trying to remember where I put my mobile phone, spotting it on the sideboard beside my keys. Should I call someone now, or wait to hear what she has to say?

'Hello, Avril,' James replies, gently, indicating for us to move into the kitchen so as not to alert Emily. I'm shocked by his calm exterior, by the way in which he is able to contain all the questions and emotions that must be rushing up through him right now. 'How are you, sweetheart?'

Sweetheart. DCI Jacobs had thought she might make contact, might try to speak to us now that her face is plastered all over the news, and she'd told James to speak to her as he would have done back then, to use the same language, the same way of speaking she would expect of him. So I know that he's just playing it by the book, but Jesus – *sweetheart*?

There's some hesitation before Avril replies, and I think maybe it was too much, this term of endearment, until she speaks again and it's clear that she's smiling.

'Isn't she adorable?' she asks him. 'Our Chloe? Isn't she adorable? I'd forgotten how like you she was, James.'

I can see from the stunned fear in his eyes that he has no idea if she's talking about the real Chloe, or the baby she has taken from us. Frantically, I grab a notepad and scribble the words *Just say yes!* Robotically, he replies, 'Yes, she is. She's adorable.'

He looks back at me and I shrug, my mind racing as I try to second-guess what it is she wants, how she wants James to react to her call. Surely the police have put a trace on the telephone line? Didn't Jacobs say something about that before? I don't know how these things work, I think, desperate to believe we're moving closer to Daisy with every passing second. Surely they'll be able to find her now?

'What have you been up to?' he says lightly, and it's as though he's pressed the magic button.

'Oh, James, we've been having the most wonderful time! Yesterday we took a walk at Alum Bay – you know, where they have the coloured sands – and afterwards we took a bus and ended up having lunch at a lovely little café where they played live piano music and let us sit and listen in the comfy seats long after our plates had been cleared away.'

'What did Chloe have?' he asks, and I know that he's worried. Avril has no idea what Chloe eats – what gets her to sleep, what makes her laugh or cry. Avril is a stranger. I see these thoughts and more flaming across James's face as he speaks.

'Well, I asked the waitress what she'd recommend, and she knew just what to suggest, because they have lots of young mothers bringing their babies in, apparently. She did a little bowl of butternut squash soup for Chloe – and she loved it! They do a wonderful Italian platter, James – remember the Parma ham in Tuscany?'

This is insane, I think. Is this conversation really happening? I blink at James, trying to encourage him to ask her something useful, something that might give us more clues to where she's staying. I scribble on the notepad: *Can we meet?*

'Maybe we could meet there for a coffee?' he says.

And that's when Avril's tone changes. It's as though she knows, and at the same time it seems as if she doesn't. As though she thinks she's still living that old life, that that baby really is Chloe – while at the same time she's trying not to be caught, knowing she's doing something wrong.

'That's why I called you,' she says, her voice harder now. 'I want to meet you – but not there. Do you know the Botanic Garden in Ventnor?'

James pauses, pensively rubbing his finger along the side of his nose as I scroll through the contacts on my own mobile phone, preparing to call DC Piper. 'Um, I've heard of it, but I don't think I've been. Is that where they grow all the tropical plants?'

'Yes! They have a microclimate, apparently. I'll meet you there tomorrow. There's an old hospital tunnel that runs through the cliff beneath the gardens – they have a daily tour there at 2pm. I overheard a group of walkers talking about it in the café yesterday, planning to go, so I know there'll be a small crowd. Join the tour and I'll find you.'

'But how –' James starts, but he's cut off as the line goes dead.

15. Emily

Emily knows she shouldn't take any more tablets, having only had her dose a couple of hours earlier, but she can't help herself, can't think of anything else to take away the upset of what she's just seen. Behind the closed door of her bedroom she knows they won't disturb her and she swigs back another couple of pills, washing it down with a gulp of the musty water that sits in a pint glass on her bedside cabinet. God, how she longs for a drink now. When did this happen, she wonders – when did she start fantasising about chilled white wine before she's even had her breakfast? She thinks about the way they looked at each other when they realised they were caught on the front of that newspaper; she thinks about the secrets that passed between them and the pathetic way they tried to deny it, tried to say her eyes were lying to her. Well, she's not wrong, is she? What's the expression? *The camera never lies*. Well, it's right there on the front page, clear as day, James caressing her sister's face, when they had both said they were elsewhere. For Christ's sake, Jess had even plated up a meal for James earlier that evening 'so you and James can eat together later'! Talk about covering your tracks; it had certainly had her fooled. She's such an idiot to have trusted her! Until Jess arrived, life was good and calm and predictable, and Emily wants so much to place this all at her feet, to show how her she is to blame for everything bad that has happened. Chloe's defection; James's retreat; her own infidelity. Daisy's disappearance.

She sobs now, allowing her grief for Daisy a rare appearance, and more than anything she wants to blame Jess for that, because, God knows, that's the worst thing, isn't it? That's the very worst thing, and whoever made that happen is the worst person, because that is what's at the heart of this entire breakdown: the abduction of her child. But, try as she might, she cannot blame anyone as much as she blames herself. *I made it happen, I made it happen, I made it happen.* A loop of images runs through her head, blurring and slurring together as sleep threatens to take her down: Marcus's mouth on hers; Jess's grateful smile as she emerges from the mainland ferry; the look on James's face in that newspaper photograph; the swirling handwriting of the letter in his desk drawer, from 'A' with a kiss. *It's me*, is her last coherent thought before sleep at last possesses her. *It's all down to me.*

The one thing she does feel bad about when it comes to that party at Sammie's was that Jess hadn't even wanted to come. If Emily hadn't pushed her into going, none of that business with Simon would ever have happened, and life would have turned out quite differently. Jess had been complaining of feeling 'a bit under the weather' (their mother's favourite expression) for a few days, and earlier that morning she'd had a light-headed moment in Topshop when she'd had to rest on the bottom step of the stairwell, right in front of everyone. By the time they sat down for lunch at Minxies she told Emily that she really couldn't face it, because they'd all be drinking and having a laugh and she didn't want to put a downer on Sammie's birthday if she took another turn for the worse.

'You'll be fine!' Emily told her. 'And anyway, Sammie will be really upset if you don't come. It's the end-of-year party, Jess. How can you even think of not going?'

The reality was that she didn't want to turn up at the party alone, which seemed likely as she'd been trying – unsuccessfully – to contact Simon for the past twenty-four hours. At least with Jess there she'd have someone to walk in with and to get safely home with afterwards. Maybe she could convince her to sort her hair out; it would look so much nicer if she wore it up, or if she used a few products to tame the natural waves that gave it a slightly wild look. Emily was lucky that her own hair was so straight and shiny. She hardly had to do a thing to make it look good.

'It's going to be a brilliant night – you *can't* miss it. Sammie's mum is away, and everyone's going to be there, Jess. You can't not go! Just have a lie-down for a couple of hours and you'll feel much better.'

They heard the music before they even reached Sammie's large detached house in Links Lane. It was a humid summer's evening, and the sprawling high-walled garden was already littered with beer cans and spilled bowls of peanuts and limp trails of trodden-in party streamers. Sammie, wrestling a large speaker out through the dining room window, spotted them and came rushing out of the front door to hug them, already gushing in the tipsy way she was inclined to after even the tiniest amount of alcohol.

'Have you seen how many people there are?' she hissed dramatically, but not looking at all unpleased. 'I swear there must be three times the number I actually invited.' She took Emily's budget bottle of cider and Jess's weak lagers and indicated for them to follow her inside, where there was at least the same number of bodies as there were outside. 'Grab a drink,' she instructed them as she returned to sorting the speakers out, and Emily fetched a pair of Bacardi Breezers from the vegetable drawer of the fridge where she knew Sammie would have hidden them. A cheer rose up from the garden, indicating successful relocation of the speakers, and Emily felt the thrill of anticipation rushing up through her legs, pulsing in time with the bass.

Jess was her usual reticent self, sticking close to Emily's side as they made their way back out into the garden to seek out their friends, and be seen. Emily ran her eyes over her sister, absently noting how pretty she looked, and hoped she'd be able to shake her off when Simon turned up. She had finally managed to speak to him late this afternoon and he'd promised her he would definitely be there by nine, but it was now gone half-past and there was still no sign of him. He would be with Lizard and Adrian and the other losers he hung around with, downing pints in his local before stopping off along the seafront for a pipe or a spliff and whatever it was that Lizard had managed to get his hands on this week. She tried to turn a blind eye to Simon's 'having a bit of laugh', but she hated the fact that he'd rather be with them than her. Couldn't he see that his mates were just hangers-on and users? Lizard and Adrian were invariably skint, while Simon always had a wad of cash in his back pocket to stand the next round or to sub them, knowing they had no intention of paying him back. His careless abandon with money was legendary. But of course his friends, like everyone else, knew that the O'Carrolls were loaded, and for just a few hours at his dad's haulage yard each week Simon would earn more money than most of them could dream of in a month in their part-time shop or bar jobs. He was generous with Emily too, frequently buying her jewellery and little trinkets, but, as much as that pleased her, it wasn't enough. They'd been going out together for six months now, and in Emily's mind that was plenty enough time to expect more of him, wasn't it? Six months was *serious*, anyone would agree, and surely *serious* meant arriving at parties together, returning each other's calls, evenings out without his friends – and making plans for the future. Emily and Simon hadn't done much of any of those things. The reality was, their relationship pretty much consisted of meeting up when he drunk-texted her at last orders, for a late-night fumble in his mum's Honda, parked on the drive at the back of his family home. She couldn't remember the last time they actually met up in daylight hours.

To her further irritation, Jess was already fighting off the boys. Even as they'd walked through the house, Emily could feel the attention she was gathering, as eyes turned towards her, glances that went unreturned. What was it about her? What was it that made people – boys *and* girls – want to look at her, want to be her friend? She was shy, boring even, and if she knew that someone was paying attention to her she became even more introverted. Emily on the other hand was gregarious. Fun! Why didn't they all look at her in the same way? She made eye contact, let it be known if she liked someone, let them know if she'd seen them looking. She was no less attractive than Jess – more so, she liked to think, and certainly more approachable. Even now, a pair of lads from their year group had cornered Jess, and Emily could overhear them trying out their adolescent chat and the awkward-ness of her responses. Jess was too busy unpinning the smooth bun that Emily had styled for her just an hour earlier, having complained that it was pulling her hair and making her eyes sting.

'So, you're Emily's sister? Blimey, I'd never have guessed.' This one was Alex, one of the sporty popular boys Jess always steered clear of. Beyond the garden the sun was low in the sky, casting a golden glow across the lawn, making halos of their hair. 'You're not twins, are you? You're not that much like each other.'

Jess shook her hair free, glancing up briefly so as not to appear rude. She took a sip of her drink as she stuffed the hairpins into the patch pocket on the front of her denim skirt. 'No, Emily's older. I only turned seventeen this week.'

'I would've said you look older,' Emily heard the other boy say. She didn't know his name; he was a nobody. It wasn't even true. Jess looked young for her age, especially now she'd let her hair down like a little girl, so he was clearly only saying it to get in her knickers.

Jess laughed self-consciously and looked over at Emily, silently imploring her to come and save her. She lifted the bottle to her lips again and drained its contents anxiously. At least if she gets a bit pissed she might lighten up, Emily thought – and then she saw Simon, dropping down from the wall at the end of the garden, tumbling across the grass with Adrian and gangly Lizard in a drunken tangle. Emily's heart juddered, and she lifted her arm and waved as she ran across the lawn to meet him.

He was, predictably, off his face. 'Emi-Emi-Emi!' he called out to her, like a football chant. His short cropped hair was waxed into hard little spikes that stood up at his forehead, giving him a cute rascally look that somehow conflicted with the large diamond stud he'd recently acquired in his left earlobe. 'It's real,' he'd told her when she'd first seen it last week, frowning her disapproval as he admired his reflection in the rear-view mirror of his mum's car. 'I'll get you a pair if you like,' he had added, smoothly reclining her seat as he sank his face into her neck, and then she hadn't minded his earring so much after all. Now, he slipped his hand around her small waist and pulled her against him fiercely so that their hips clashed as he kissed her wetly on the mouth. 'How's the party going?' he whispered conspiratorially as they returned to the crowd, his arm slung possessively around her, her face glowing with the pleasure of being possessed.

The nobody boy was returning from the house with another drink for Jess. Emily wanted to keep walking, to take Simon inside where they could sit together on one of the big luxurious sofas and kiss and murmur and disappear into their own searing bubble of longing. But Simon resisted, hanging back when they reached Jess, a wide smile splitting his features. He reached into Jess's group of three and with his middle finger he flicked her glass bottle like a person flicking an insect.

'Oy-oy, Little Sister,' he said, and Jess looked up at him, startled. 'What's all this?' He nodded towards her beer bottle. 'Didn't have you down as much of a drinker.'

And then the strangest thing. Jess held his gaze, and it was as if they were the only two people in the garden, as Emily and Alex and the other boy all faded into the background, morphing into hazy silhouettes against the glowing sunset sky. And in that split-second Emily knew: her little sister didn't like Simon.

'Thought you were the *good* one,' he said, and he laughed, betraying his discomfort, and Jess looked away and took a swig from her bottle, and the moment passed. 'Right, talking of drinking –' Simon said with a clap of his hands, and he broke into a jog, catching up with Lizard as he disappeared inside the house.

Emily stared after him. One minute he had been there, all over her, happy to see her – the next, he was gone.

'Do you want this?' Jess asked her, casually easing herself away from the two boys and offering Emily her drink.

Emily ran her eyes over her sister, suspicion clawing at her insides, and really, she wanted to lash out at her, to blame *her* for Simon's indifference. Why did she feel as though it was all Jess's fault that this evening wasn't working out the way she had imagined it would? Their eyes connected; Emily's were steely, Jess's confused.

'Is everything OK?' Jess asked.

Emily nodded, allowing herself to appear perplexed at such a pointless question. 'Why wouldn't I be? Look, there's Jane – and Sammie – let's see if they're up for a dance.' She grabbed Jess's drink and finished it in one long swallow, calling out to her friends and throwing her head back when they came rushing over, laughing as if she was having the best of times. She glanced back at Sporty Alex, noted how his angular jaw and scruffy sun-bleached hair were now painted amber in the low summer light, and gave him one of her biggest, shiniest smiles.

If Simon could do his own thing, so could she.

Even through her sedated slumber, Emily has been aware of the endlessly ringing phone, of the hammering on the front door, of the car-door-slamming and raised voices of the waiting press just beyond the gravel of their front drive. At some point Jess looked in on her and told Emily that the police were here again, but she couldn't lift her head, couldn't bring herself to acknowledge that she'd heard what her sister was saying, though she knew from her tone that it was important.

'DCI Jacobs is here,' she'd said, knocking softly on the door after she'd opened it. 'There's been a development, Ems. Don't you think you should get up?'

Emily had groaned a little and motioned 'no' with the slightest movement of her head on the pillow.

'I think you should,' Jess had pressed on. 'I'll leave you to get yourself sorted, and there'll be a cup of tea waiting for you when you get downstairs.'

They are down there now, she knows, but she can't face them. The endless talking, the same solemn questions put to her in a vaguely different format, the eternal expression of hope on James's face. At the next bang on the front door, she eases herself out of her bed, still fully clothed, and shuffles to the window to peer through a crack in the curtains, out into the early evening darkness of the front drive. It's gone five o'clock and yet there are dozens of the vultures out there, more than ever before, cawing

286

and preening for a follow-up to their salacious story. Jesus, what a reflection on modern society, that the press have more interest in an abduction story once it turns out that there are mucky goings-on between members of the heartbroken family. She wants to spit at them all.

Directly below her window, James has opened the front door. She's still trying to remain concealed, but if she presses close to the window jamb she can just make out the top of the journalist's head, and clearly hears their brief conversation.

'Mr King! Joe Leighton of the *Mirror* – no, please don't close the door – it's about Avril, your first wife.'

This is enough to get James's attention; he would have been expecting them to ask about his relationship with Jess. Emily wonders if they have news. Have they found her?

'What about her?' James replies, curtly.

'We understand that she's spent several years in mental institutions? Is that true? Do the police still think that Avril has Daisy?'

James must be backing off, because the journalist leans in, as if to prevent the door from closing, shouting, 'Mr King! Do you think that your ex-wife could be dangerous? Are you concerned?'

Now James steps out into full view, his broad posture challenging, and the journalist takes a defensive move backwards. The others all hang around at the edge of the drive, knowing better than to harangue us with the police here.

'Am I concerned? Of course I'm bloody concerned! Why would you even ask a question as pointless as that? Avril's unstable, for God's sake – who wouldn't be concerned?' James returns to the house, slamming the door behind him and for a few seconds the journalist remains on the spot staring after him, before his face shifts into a smirk and he returns to the pack.

In a sudden fit of rage Emily throws back the curtain and opens the window, leaning out so violently that for a moment she thinks she might fall. 'FUCK OFF!' she yells, and in a second their cameras are all trained on her, sending brutal missiles of flashlight out into the dark night, lighting up her craziness for all the world to see. She retreats as suddenly as she had appeared, stumbling out into the hallway to find James, to tell him what had happened, to make him sort it out and get these bastards off their front drive. 'James!' she shouts urgently as she rushes down the stairs, but when she gets there she finds they have a houseful.

It's DCI Jacobs who stands to greet her, not James, and she holds out her palm to offer Emily a seat at her own table. Emily's confusion is crippling; she looks from Jess to James, ignoring the greetings of Piper and Cherry and the other officer who sits at the table and she's certain that they have come to arrest her. Do they know what she's done?

'Mrs King,' the inspector says, stopping Emily's thoughts with the unexpected gentleness in her tone. *Emily.* Avril has been in contact. James is going to meet her tomorrow – and there's a good chance she'll have Daisy with her.'

16. **Avril**

How strange it was to hear his voice today. His tone was so warm and calm that I knew he wasn't angry at me for taking Chloe like I did. I knew he would be happy to hear from me. His letter had said as much, hadn't it? He trusts me; he knows I'll take good care of her.

It's raining now, but I don't mind a bit as I sit at the window watching the swirling tide beyond the Old Battery. Just out of view the waves will be charging up around the Needles, casting plumes of white foam in high arcs, back-flipping gracefully into the waters they came from. Some people live for the summer; not me. I love the winter months in England, from the crisp, frosted mornings of November to the drizzle-grey evenings of February. Winter challenges your senses in a way summer can't. Summer makes you feel good so effortlessly: warm and light. But winter dares you to be happy despite the cold and damp, and I like the physicality of that hardship, the way it forces you to experience the body over the mind.

Chloe is sleeping in her little cot drawer behind me; tomorrow she will see her daddy for the first time in, oh, how long? When did *I* last see him? So long ago, but my timelines are always getting muddled, like long strands of seaweed woven together by the turning currents, so that by the time I try to untangle them they appear as one great knotted rope of green. I remember St Justin's, and I know that was the first place I stayed in, as I remember James visiting me there. He never brought Chloe, but one time he came with his mother, and she tried to be nice to me – which I knew was a lie – and I screamed at her to get out and he agreed never to bring her again. I don't know how long I stayed at St Justin's, but I do know that by the time I was moved to Buddleia Hill my hair was no longer blonde, but instead the mousy brown colour nature gave me. When they showed me to my room I found it was much nicer than the one I had at St Justin's, where they didn't let me have many things in case I harmed myself (at least, that's what Annie from Trinidad told me). But here I had coat-hangers, a plastic toothbrush mug, a manicure set and even a bathroom mirror screwed to the wall above the sink. I wondered how long it had been since I'd really looked at my own reflection. Of course, there *were* mirrors at St Justin's, but not one in the privacy of my own room, one I could stand in front of for long minutes or hours while I tried to work out what had happened to me, where everyone had gone.

James never visited me at Buddleia Hill, and, for the first year or so, neither did anyone else. But then they matched me with a visiting volunteer called Lily, and she came once a week, without fail, even when I was just a day patient on the various occasions I tried independent living. The first occasion we met didn't go too well, because she reminded me so powerfully of James's mother that I quite lost my temper, in a way that the staff at Buddleia Hill had never seen before. I remember that clearly, unlike so many of my other memories. As Lily approached me in the common room and smiled, she extended her hand to shake mine, and her face was so much the double of James's mother that I stood up in fright, knocking my chair backwards as my heart hammered against my ribcage. 'No, no, no,' she said gently, despite my loud cries for help, and along with Ginny, my care worker, they talked me down and made me understand that Lily was someone else altogether. I miss Lily now, with her bright, intelligent eyes and her gentle sense of humour. She was always telling me about these meetings she went to – *my 'old biddy' meetings*, she called them – where they'd learn new skills, or talk about a book they'd all read, or take it in turns to bake a cake. Sometimes she'd bring me a slice, and always she'd bring me a new story to laugh about, like the time they went wall-climbing at the local sports centre and Dennis, her eighty-two-year-old would-be suitor, got stuck on the top rung. 'He was mortified,' she giggled into her hand. 'He kept apologising to me afterwards, as if he'd let me down. Poor old duffer.'

Of course, Buddleia Hill closed down five years after my first stay there, and they set me up in my own home, ten miles away, because I was well enough and they'd got my medication levels just right, apparently. On her last visit to Buddleia Hill, Lily handed me her telephone number jotted on a slip of paper, and asked me to keep in touch, to let her know how I was doing. I committed that number to memory there and then, but once I'd left Buddleia Hill I never spoke to Lily again. I think of her now, and I wish I could see her. I wish she were here with me now, watching the rain trickle down the window pane, telling me funny stories and sharing her cake.

A solitary gull soars across my horizon, a white flash against the turbulent grey seascape. Tomorrow I will see James again. We will take a walk around the Botanic Garden with Chloe, or head down the steps to Steephill Cove, and if the weather is fair we'll have a cream tea in the café there. I hope with all my heart that it will be just like it should have been before all our troubles. If it isn't, I don't know what I might do.

17. Jess

The meeting has been arranged for 2pm, so DCI Jacobs' team picks us up just before twelve to drive us to the Botanic Garden at Ventnor, where James will meet Avril at the tunnel tour. Chloe is still staying at Max's so it's just the three of us – James, Emily and me – dashing across the drive to jump into the back of DC Piper's car. When we arrive, DCI Jacobs is there waiting for us, and she steps out of her car and into the passenger seat of ours, looking back between the seats to give us our instructions. It seems Emily is too recognisable so she must stay out of sight, preferably in the car, while I am to don a hooded raincoat and join the tunnel tour at a distance from James, along with two other plain-clothed officers.

'It's low season,' DCI Jacobs explains. 'We need to make up the tour numbers or else she might get cold feet. As she's asked to meet James as part of a group tour, we can only assume she's looking for the anonymity of a crowded place. We've got plain-clothes officers stationed at all the entrances to the car park – they'll be on the lookout for her Renault – and there are several others positioned within the gardens, ready to apprehend her if she tries to leave via an unexpected route.'

Emily can barely look at me. Even now, even in adulthood, I'm tortured by not knowing what goes on behind that frosty veneer of hers. Is it fear? Or anger? Or jealousy, that I'm the one assisting the police operation? How could she possibly feel jealous of *this*? God knows, I'd rather be sitting in the warm car with her than going through the anxiety of a dark tunnel tour with James's resurrected first wife.

The tour meeting point is next to the pond near the gated tunnel entrance and I'm instructed to act naturally, keep my head down, attach myself to the two other officers and chat as if we're a group of friends. There will be others too – probably the group Avril mentioned overhearing yesterday – so it should be easy enough to mix in. And James, he must make sure he's towards the back of the tour party, so that the other officers, posing as ticket-takers and ground staff, can maintain a good view of him as Avril approaches. When she arrives with Daisy – God, please let it be with Daisy – he is to delay her, embrace her if it feels appropriate, take the child from her and wait for the police to step in. Simple.

Once DCI Jacobs is happy we're all clear on our roles, we take our positions, leaving Emily with DC Cherry for company. 'Can I get you a drink from the café?' I hear him asking her as we leave them, his stock line in conversation when left alone with her.

We pass through the visitor entrance and make our way through the palm gardens and succulents, past Japanese terraces and greenhouses, ascending fern-lined stairwells and sandy banks, and I feel as though I've entered a dream world, a warm, green, lush unreality on this otherwise rainy January afternoon. Emerging into the real light of day, we arrive at the pond, alongside several other visitors, including an elderly couple with a tartan-coated dog and a young family of four. The youngest child is lively, excited, running in and out of the puddles as her tired-looking parents look on, only their mouths smiling. We look completely ordinary, blending in with the other visitors, dressed in raincoats or sheltering under umbrellas against the persistent icy drizzle. We wait for a few minutes, and I check my watch, but we're still five minutes early, and I'm wondering how James is feeling, standing close by but unable to look in my direction for support. And then the tour guide arrives with the torches and we're entering the tunnel, vaguely listening to health and safety information about uneven floor surfaces and overhead hazards – and there's no sign of Avril.

The smell of damp stone is overwhelming, and despite the torches the darkness closes in around us, shrinking the space, causing us to huddle and bump against each other uncertainly. At a central point, the tour guide asks us all to stop as she tells us a little about the tunnel's original history as an access route for the Victorian patients of the former Royal National Hospital to the coast below, otherwise only accessible by the famously steep steps leading down to Steephill Cove. She dares us all to turn our torches off at the count of three, and we're plunged into darkness. *What if she's in here with us?* The thought is upon me before I have time to process it, and I gasp loudly, spooking the others around me, prompting a flurry of torches flickering back to life.

Behind us, back the way we came, a lone shape appears through the tunnel, alerting us with the sound of running foot-steps on damp ground, hood up, head down, jogging towards us in the flickering torchlight. *It's her*, I think, and I freeze, breath caught, unable to turn away, incapable of acting like just one of the group. As her figure grows closer, her shadow stretching and shrinking along the aged brickwork, I feel the collective tension of the others, of those of us in the know, and

I daren't look away from her, lest she vanish altogether, never to be seen again.

'Creepy, huh?' the guide says of the previous seconds of total darkness, and the hooded woman comes to a stop at the back of the group. And it's not her. It's a young woman, maybe nineteen or twenty – it's not Avril. Through the darkness I hear the low, long whisper of James's breath, the pain of his disappointment.

Now we're moving again, heading towards the pinprick of light at the other end of the tunnel that holds the promise of the sea. Perhaps she's there already; perhaps she took an alternative route via the beach, so as to fox the police and be already in place to meet James on the other side. My breath catches in my throat. But when we come out on the other side there's just a steep drop to the beach below, and no Avril. I glance casually in James's direction and see him standing at the edge of the grass bank, his face set in grave concentration, as he studies the beach below, searching for Avril. Searching for his daughter.

'OK, everyone ready to head back?' asks the tour guide, and we're in the tunnel again, returning to the other side, and this time James and I walk side by side, and in the darkness I feel the hopelessness radiating from him like heat.

At the centre of the tunnel, the guide stops us again. 'One more time for lights-out? One, two, three – lights out!'

Again, we're plunged into darkness, and I don't know why I do it, but I do – I move my hand towards James and our fingers slot together like jigsaw pieces and it feels like the most natural thing in the world. The torches light up again and our hands separate as we continue through the tunnel towards the circle of daylight beyond.

Outside, DCI Jacobs is standing at a distance and she indicates for us to return to the car park, an expression of resignation on her face.

'I don't think she's coming,' she says and she holds up today's newspaper.

DAISY DAD FEARS 'UNSTABLE' EX-WIFE

James brings his hand to his mouth, as all the colour drains from him. 'She'll never trust me now,' he says, and then he weeps.

There are certain things I do remember about the party, but I don't go there too often, taking pains to avoid that particular hole in time for fear that I'll fall further into the memory, further down into the horror of what actually happened that night. But since meeting Sammie again when I went home for Mum's funeral I can't seem to help it, and my mind trespasses there when I'm least expecting it, when I'm drifting into sleep or walking alone, as though there's a puzzle there that wants solving, one which can only be unravelled by returning to the scene of the crime. On the way home from the Botanic Garden I doze in the back of the detective's car, with Emily sitting rigidly beside me in the middle and James quietly brooding on her other side. I don't mean to think about it, but as my eyes grow heavy and the fields and hedges of the island rush past my window I find myself there again, back in that nightmare, back in that night. I remember arriving, and the magnificence of the setting sun that spread out beyond Sammie's big house, bathing the garden in golden light. I know I felt glad that I'd agreed to come after all. I remember drinking, perhaps just one or two, but not enough to get me drunk – and I remember a friendly boy who fetched me a top-up and who I know would have talked to me more if Emily had been less icy. I remember Simon turning up late, the awful disappointment that poured off Emily when he went off with his friends, and the hateful scowl she shot me when I asked if she was all right. I remember feeling light-headed and looking for somewhere to sit down for a while, and I remember walking into the downstairs bathroom and catching Emily in there with a boy called Alex. I can see it quite clearly, like a short video: they were kissing, and he had his hand up her T-shirt, and he glowered in my direction and I shut the door before Emily even noticed. I remember resting on the top step of the stairs, and again that familiar sensation of my blood slowing and my breaths growing shallow, and then there was Sammie helping me to my feet and Simon pushing past, saying, 'Shit, Jess. Overdone it a bit?' and Sammie telling him to piss off as she took me into her bedroom. And then it's as though I'm there again and I'm sitting on the edge of the bed and trying not to close my eyes as Sammie smooths my denim skirt over my knees and feels my forehead with the back of her hand. 'I'll go and find Emily,' she says, and I'm grateful. I'm scared, but it's going to be all right, because Emily is coming. My big sister is coming, and she'll make everything all right. And I desperately don't want to recall any further, but somehow I can't stop it, because here comes Simon with his hair all poking up and his flashy diamond earring, but this time he's being really *kind*, and he's sitting on the bed and offering me a glass of Coke, and I really don't want it but he says, 'The sugar will make you feel better,' and even though it tastes a bit funny I drink it all down. And then he's helping me lay my head on the pillow and I think I might sleep, but right before the memory runs out I notice Lizard in the doorway beside the *Little Mermaid* poster that Sammie won't part with, and as my eyelids grow too, too heavy – wholly unlike any episode or faint I've ever experienced before – I see the look that passes between Simon and Lizard. And it's not a kind look. It isn't kind at all.

18. Emily

So that was that. They've had their hopes raised only to have them dashed again. Emily really believed they would get Daisy back today, really, truly wanted to believe it, and she has been distraught since they arrived home, finally releasing her emotions the moment she was alone behind her bedroom door. She knows the media and public all think she's a hard cow – they probably even wish they had more reason to suspect *her* – because she's not breaking down in front of them every time they point a camera at her, because she won't play the textbook heartbroken mother. But they don't know her, do they? They know nothing about her. They don't know the spiralling darkness of the pain she feels, they don't hear her muffled cries, they don't see the pale salted circles that stain her pillowcase. What they want is a wilting Madonna, a mother driven half mad at the loss of her child. If only they knew, she thinks as she stands before the bathroom mirror, drying herself off from a long-overdue shower, her gaze drawn blankly to the hollows of her collarbone and her protruding ribs. She certainly feels half mad; she certainly feels like a woman out of her mind. Thoughts of Avril naturally follow. *That* mad bitch didn't even turn up today, and now, thanks to James and his big mouth, she may never make contact again. What did the detective tell them? *Stay away from the press.* 'They'll try to push your buttons,' DCI Jacobs had told the family, right at the very start of all this. 'They will try every trick in the book to get you to say something – anything – that will make good headlines.' *Idiot*, Emily repeats over in her head, recalling the sight of James chasing off the journalists on the front drive, giving them just the kind of juicy headline they were after. *Idiot.*

Of course, her own subsequent behaviour – leaning from the window, showering them with expletives – was not a proud moment, and she thanks God that *that* image only made it to page five. Her heart races at the very thought of it. Emily throws her towel to the bedroom floor and dresses.

Downstairs, James is out in the early evening darkness of the garden talking with DC Cherry, and as she approaches the window over the kitchen sink Emily sees they are both smoking. She has never seen James with a cigarette, though he once told her he had been a smoker in his university days. Under normal circumstances she'd be rushing out there, snatching it from his hand and grinding it beneath her heel, berating him for his childish behaviour. But not now; now she couldn't give a stuff what he does to himself. All she wants is her daughter back. All she wants is the life she once had, the good life she had *before Jess came to stay*.

Even as she thinks this, she knows it is irrational. This isn't Jess's fault – none of this is really Jess's fault. But Emily wants it to be. She wants it to be anyone's fault but her own.

There's no wine in the house, so Emily heads to the drinks cabinet in the living room to locate the vodka one of James's clients gave him at Christmas. They seldom drink spirits, James preferring lager or red wine and Emily favouring white, but they keep several bottles of spirits in for their friends who do. Marcus likes a scotch and Jan always asks for gin and tonic. Becca gave them a bottle of limoncello when she returned from a holiday in Italy a year or two back, and Jess got a bottle of Jamaican rum in for the festive season. In the living room, she averts her gaze from the Christmas tree beside the window, its dropped needles and drooping branches a terrible reminder of the passing of time, the time that has elapsed since Daisy was taken from them. The baubles and light garlands now lie on the carpet like discarded clothes, the weight of them too much for the slack branches to bear. Jess offered again to pack it down only yesterday, and James was in agreement but Emily won't hear of it.

As soon as she opens the door to the glass cabinet she knows there are bottles missing. When it comes to cans and jars and bottles James is particular, to the point of obsession, about straight lines and ordered rows. And, although it is a strange detail, Emily remembers that the front row of bottles was complete, a full row of four bottles to match the rows behind. Now, however, there are two spaces, and when she searches across the labels she sees that both the vodka and the rum are missing. She heads back to the foot of the stairs.

'Jess? Jess! Are you up there?'

She hears the sounds of James and DC Cherry returning through the back door, and Jess appears from her bedroom at the top of the stairs, bleary-eyed with afternoon sleep, and then Chloe is pushing open the front door and she's standing in the hallway with Max. Emily can hardly believe her eyes. He looks young, far younger than his nineteen years, his hair sandy-coloured, his nose freckly; disappointingly unlike the darkly seducing older man Emily had allowed herself to imagine. How dare she bring him here? Her rage is rising again, but then Jess answers her from above and she turns to reply but she can't quite remember what it was that she wanted in the first place.

James now stands in the entrance to the kitchen and Emily feels as though she's watching from a distance, standing on the outside, looking in. She sees the calm-faced husband, his arms open wide to the prodigal daughter, the daughter hand-in-hand with the usurping young male. Then there's her, the slighted mother, at the centre, conflicted and confused. And here's Jess, dropping off the bottom step to take in the scene. Jess, who knows just exactly what to do as she slips her hand into Emily's and leads her into the kitchen, asking DC Cherry if he'd mind filling the kettle, while father and daughter embrace, and no words are spoken.

It's Emily who is the first to break the silence.

'What is *he* doing here?' she asks from her position next to the island unit. She points towards Max on the far side of the dining room, where he stands at the front door, his jacket still buttoned up. 'What is *he* doing in my house?'

Chloe pulls back from James's arms and waits for him to speak. *Weak*, Emily thinks. *He's so weak.* 'Dad?' Chloe says, and it's suddenly clear to Emily that they've already spoken about this, already agreed how it's going to be.

'It's time for us all to accept that Chloe and Max are together,' James says firmly, but he doesn't look at Emily, just keeps his eyes locked on his daughter's for strength.

'But the police – the stuff he took!' Emily screeches.

James raises a hand. 'We need to put all that business behind us, Emily, because Chloe has told me how important Max is to her, and that's good enough for me. We've all been through too much to risk losing her too. I'd rather have Chloe with Max than no Chloe at all.'

Across the room Jess nods in agreement and Emily hates her for it.

Max's stance is one of remorse. He stands with his shoulders slightly bowed, his hands limply joined together in front of him.

'I'm sorry, Mr King – Chloe and me, well we didn't know each other all that well when I did that – and I guess I was just being an idiot. I really regret it. And I really care a lot about Chloe.'

James crosses the room and shakes Max's hand. The boy's face lights up, and to Emily's astonishment the two of them kind of hug, making contact in a cringingly awkward shoulder-bump. Chloe claps her hands together and Jess quietly says, 'Well done,' and Emily now knows the whole world has gone insane.

'Am I the only person in this room who thinks it's wrong that she's been staying at his place? Or that he is nineteen and she's not even *sixteen*!'

Emily searches their expressions for signs of disapproval or shame or something, but instead she sees pity.

'Ems,' Jess says gently, and her tone is so bloody patronising and their collective eyes are so full of embarrassment that it feels as though they're all in on it together, united engineers in the great scheme of her madness. 'Chloe had her birthday a week ago. Chloe *is* sixteen now.'

'You were asleep, *Emily*,' Chloe says, folding her arms across her chest. 'I told Dad I didn't want a big fuss made over it this year, but I did think you might have woken up for the cake.'

Emily is horrified at having forgotten her stepdaughter's birthday – Chloe, the girl she's baked a cake for every January for the past twelve or thirteen years. Until all this happened she's been a good mother – the best mother – and now, what would people say? One daughter kidnapped and the other ignored. This is too much. *Too much*. Her rage spills over. 'Well, that's just fine, isn't it? Max, you can screw her to your heart's content now, with absolutely no fear of prosecution! Fill your boots, young man!'

Max, to his credit, doesn't say a word, and nor does Chloe. Instead, Chloe kisses her dad and aunt, picks up her coat and disappears through the front door with Max without a backward glance for Emily. *I'm vanishing*, Emily thinks as she gazes across the room towards Jess and James. Their eyes are on each other, and they're speaking without talking, and it's as though she's disappearing as surely as Daisy did before her.

Everyone lies, don't they? At some point in the life of every single human being who walks this earth, they will construct a lie, whether large or small. No one is without sin when it comes to the art of lying. The hacks on the drive lie to them daily, hoping to extract scandalous headlines for their tabloids. Chloe's been lying for months. James, well, he's lied about the very fabric of his life: his ex-wife, his past, his secret meetings with Jess. Lies don't get much bigger than the ones her husband has told.

In her mind's eye she sees one of the corny postcards Becca has pinned up beside her till in the café. *Three things cannot be long hidden: the sun, the moon and the truth – Buddha*. But that's not true, is it? Secrets are so often the vehicles of truth, aren't they? And, unlike the sun and the moon, secrets can remain hidden for years – for decades, lifetimes even. Secrets are as good as their keepers' ability to conceal, and the fewer who know the secret, the stronger the chances of concealment. Emily knows this only too well. She knows better than to spread her secrets any further than she has to; it seems James has taken the same approach with those secrets of his own. Who is he? she wonders in her quiet moments. Who is this man she's devoted her life to? Has she ever really known him?

And Jess . . . there's so much that Emily is uncertain of there, so many little half-truths and concealed details, that there has to be more to uncover, have to be more reasons to mistrust her. So Emily is entitled to a few lies of her own, isn't she? She's no worse than any of the others, but she's damned if she'll let them in on her secrets. She's damned if she'll let them make her feel any worse than she already does.

Emily could have throttled Sammie when she came hammering on the bathroom door that night, just as she and that nice sporty boy were getting along so well, and she would have ignored her had she not been quite so insistent.

'Emily? It's *me*. I'm worried about Jess – she's looking really off-colour. Em? Are you coming out? She looks like she's about to pass out!'

'Shit,' Emily muttered into the boy's ear, and he gave a little huff of disappointment as she pushed him off and tugged down her skirt. They were on the floor of the downstairs bathroom, wedged up against the bathtub, and despite her irritation she knew she ought to think about making her excuses anyway. Alex was nice enough – handsome even – but it wasn't the most romantic of settings and the lumpy bathmat was making unsightly dents in her thighs. At any rate, Simon would go ballistic if he found out. *Shit*, she thought again, *shit shit shit*!

Sammie banged on the door again. 'Emily! Please, I'm really worried about her! Will you hurry up? She's in my room upstairs – I don't want to leave her on her own like that.'

Emily motioned for Alex to hide behind the door as she left, bringing a finger to her lips and hissing a low *shhh*. She unlocked the door, switching off the light as she left the room, and hooked her arm through Sammie's to steer her away.

'Who were you in there with?' Sammie asked, looking over her shoulder to see who might emerge from the bathroom.

'No one!' Emily replied. She did her best to look affronted.

'But Jane said she saw you go in there with a boy. That's how I knew where to find you.'

Emily halted, yanking Sammie round to face her. 'Jane's a bloody liar!' she said. 'She saw me talking to those boys earlier, and she tried to make a big deal of it then – she probably fancied them herself. God, she's *pathetic*. I'm going to have a word with her later.'

Sammie looked back again, and, sure enough, Alex appeared from the doorway of the darkened bathroom. 'Em –' she said, bobbing her head in his direction, but Emily's eyes contained such warning that Sammie was forced into silence.

She might look like a sweet little pixie, Emily always said of Sammie, but she could be a real meddler when she wanted to be. Naturally Jess disagreed with this description of their best friend, but then Jess was such a square that she never did anything worth gossiping about, did she?

At the foot of the stairs, Sammie gave her an anxious little shove, and Emily led the way, leisurely stepping over legs and beer cans and pausing to chat with some girls from their year. The light bulb on the top landing was out, but they could just make out their friend Jane, who was waiting in the queue for the toilet.

'Em?' Sammie wheedled, trying to convey her worry at the time it was taking them to get back to Jess. But Emily knew she had to nip *this* in the bud right away. She had no idea where Simon was, and if Jane was spreading nasty rumours about her she had to be stopped right now, before it got out of hand – before it reached his ears.

'Em!' Sammie repeated.

'*Wait!*' Emily snapped, reaching out to spin Jane around. Jane's smile dropped like a stone when Emily brought her face close to hers and whispered, 'Not another word, Jane. OK? Not even to Jo.' And the girl nodded fervently and pushed her way into the now vacant loo.

Along the corridor, Lizard stood stoop-shouldered outside the closed door to Sammie's bedroom, and in the moment it took for his startled eyes to meet Emily's she knew it was bad news.

In Emily's dreams there is a baby crying; it's so real, so clear that she tries desperately to rise from sleep, so that she can go to Daisy and pluck her from her crib, soothe her into peace. But Emily doesn't wake; instead she walks across the landing of her dreams and enters Daisy's nursery and gazes down on the infant whose face is broken by the slices of light that pour through the bars of her cot. And she sees it isn't Daisy at all. The face is little Jessica's, and she's crying for her big sister, and deep down Emily wants to help, but she resists because the cot is sealed in glass, and she doesn't want to cut her hands breaking it apart; she doesn't want glass splinters in their nice thick carpet.

The ringing of the telephone wrenches her from the dream, and she leaps from the bed, her breaths coming short and fast as she rushes into the hallway to grab the receiver.

'Yes?' she barks, and she wonders what the time is, who could possibly be phoning this late.

'Emily, it's DCI Jacobs.'

There's a beat while Emily processes the voice, the possible significance of her phoning so late.

'Emily, we've had a witness come forward in Portsmouth – the owner of a hair salon who says she met Avril King around the date she's thought to have travelled to the island. This woman says she cut Mrs King's hair, and she's now helping us to reconstruct the photographs for circulation tomorrow.'

'Is she sure it's her? How can she be certain?' Emily can't bear the thought of more disappointment. 'She must do dozens of haircuts every week.'

'Well, she says she's ninety per cent certain. Apparently this woman told her she was off to the island to visit her daughter – and it was a particularly memorable haircut because she went in with fairly long hair and had a close crop. Emily, these new pictures could be just the thing we need to jog someone's memory – and it gives us a firmer time frame for her movements.'

'OK, so what now?' Emily peers down the stairs to see Jess and James listening in, waiting for her update.

'We'll get these new images circulated to the press, and to all the local transport links and business networks overnight, and then we'll wait and see what follows. Trust me, Emily, no one's giving up hope just yet.'

Emily hangs up the receiver and stares at Daisy's picture on the landing wall, but the dream image obscures it, the image of little Jess trapped behind glass, with no one to help her.

19. Avril

I've never really been one for the newspapers. There's nothing good to be found there, no more than there is on the television news or the radio. It seemed to affect me more than others, to pain me more, seeping into my dreams and anxieties, causing me to wonder if the human race wouldn't be better off extinct than killing each other like savages. Years ago, I remember telling Dr Selton how the daily news so often caused me to weep, and he said, quite pragmatically, 'Well, I advise you to stop listening to it, then.' But yesterday morning as I was making my way to the Botanic Garden I stopped off at the little shop in Freshwater to buy some fruit sticks for Chloe, and there he was on the news-stand – James. It was a close-up photograph, and I was surprised by how much older he looked, and how much more serious. He looked angry, and I picked the paper up and stared at it in amazement. And then Chloe reached out her chubby little hand and made grasping movements towards it and I thought, of course, she recognises her daddy! How lovely, I thought, knowing she would be able to see him in a few hours, but when I unfolded the bottom half of the paper I saw the words: DAISY DAD FEARS 'UNSTABLE' EX-WIFE.

It was too much, and I dropped the paper and left the shop, forgetting to pay for the apple slices gripped in my hand, and I ran with the pushchair bumping over pavements and kerbs, splashing through puddles and soaking my shoes, back towards the bus stop where I'd just alighted. Daisy? The paper said 'Daisy', as if I don't know my own daughter's name! Is it a trick? I felt sick with the fear of it. I stood and stared at the pole-mounted timetable, and I knew I couldn't go now. I couldn't meet James now I knew that was what he really thought of me, could I? I felt mortified that I'd been so foolish as to think he'd want me back in his life.

An elderly man was approaching on the pavement ahead of me, and he smiled gently, and I asked, 'What's in Yarmouth?' and I pointed towards the timetable to explain myself.

'The ferries, love,' he replied. 'What are you after, then?'

I turned to look at Chloe, who was grizzling now, getting damper by the minute. 'A day trip, I suppose.'

'You wanna go over to Lymington,' he said, ''s'lovely in Lymington,' and he carried on up the path, and then the bus to Yarmouth arrived and I paid the fare, and that was that.

Last night we stayed in a nice little B&B looking out over Lymington harbour, and I thought of those early days with James, when we were young and full of hope, when we couldn't stop looking at each other, couldn't stop touching each other, perhaps to check it wasn't a dream, because surely that's all happiness really is?

The rain has eased up now and the quayside is bustling around us as we sit on a weathered old bench near the water's edge. It must be lunchtime. Does Chloe want feeding? My gaze rests on the horizon, back in the direction of the island, in the direction of James. What is he doing now, what is he thinking? Is he disappointed that I didn't come? A thought occurs to me: that perhaps he didn't say those hateful things at all, that the news

314

people have twisted it, distorted it to keep us apart. It's a terrible thought! Perhaps I should return, take the next island-bound ferry and make myself known to him? But I'm so tired, so, so tired and so profoundly sad, more sad than I've been in a very long time, and I know I won't make that journey today.

Despite the icy, sharp wind, the rhythmic shimmer and furrow of the sea's surface is soothing, like the mermaid's song. I look at Chloe, my sleeping water-baby, swaddled beneath her layers, oblivious to the evils of the world, and I feel lonely. I consider the idea of Lily, allowing the digits of her phone number to run across my thoughts; perhaps I'll call her from the B&B and see if I can meet her tomorrow? She'll help me. Lily will know what to do. And then I think about those newspaper articles, full of their bloodshed and horror, and again I wonder, wouldn't we all just be better off dead?

20. **Jess**

There's been a breakthrough! DC Cherry arrives mid-morning to tell us that the newly circulated photographs have prompted a flurry of fresh sightings, one in particular placing Avril and Daisy together on a regular basis just a few miles along the coast.

'It was actually one of your local shop-owners in Freshwater who gave us our first lead. We went in to follow up after Avril's call to you was traced back to the call box outside the store.' Cherry is smoking in the back doorway of the kitchen, while I fill the kettle and let Emily and James ask all the questions. 'Apparently Avril has been a regular customer there over the past couple of weeks, but they never suspected her because she didn't look like the woman in the original photograph.'

James shakes his head. 'Of course she didn't. That photograph was so out of focus, it could have been anyone.'

'She seemed completely normal, they said, which is encouraging. And then we got a call from the bus company that runs the service from Alum Bay, telling us that one of the drivers thinks he's picked her up – her and Daisy – on a number of occasions, which led us to suspect she must be staying at a holiday property in that area. We've had the entire team on it since the early hours, phoning round all the property agents.'

'And?' Emily asks, taking the coffee mug from me.

DC Cherry smiles, and I realise I've never seen him so animated, never heard him speak with such fervour. Perhaps he'd rather be out there investigating, instead of stuck here with us.

'You've found them?' James gasps.

'No, no – not yet,' Cherry replies, reverting to his safer expression of seriousness. 'But we *have* found the house. It's a remote coastguard's cottage, tucked away right up near the Needles. DCI Jacobs is over there now with forensics. Apparently there's no sign of them in the property itself, but we've found her car and – there are signs that they've been there recently.'

'What signs?' Emily demands, fear pulsing in her voice. '*What signs?*'

'Nothing alarming, don't worry. Baby clothes, a makeshift crib, jars of baby food, that kind of thing. And Mrs King's personal belongings are still there, so we don't think she's gone far.' DC Cherry puts his hand on James's shoulder. 'Don't look so worried, please. We think this is good news. All those things – the clothes and food – they all indicate that Daisy's being well looked after.'

One after the other I reach out to embrace Emily and James, and I'm so overjoyed at the news that I want to shout it from the rooftops. 'We're going to get her back, Ems! Oh, God, I'm so relieved!'

And then she slaps me with her words.

'What do you mean, *we*? You're not her mother, Jess. I'm her mother. You don't have any right to feel relieved.'

DC Cherry and James look stunned.

'I just meant – you know how much I love Daisy, I just –'

But she doesn't let me finish. 'You have no idea what this has been like for me, Jessica. No idea at all. Because you've never been a mother, have you? You haven't got a clue.'

320

DC Cherry has left now, instructing us to stay put and wait for news. But it's impossible. None of us can stay still. James has been pacing the ground floor, phoning Chloe, telling her to come home, checking the BBC headlines every five minutes to see if there are any updates. Emily is wide-eyed, and I know she's taken extra tablets this morning because she has that glassy look about her as she sits in her corner seat, staring at her own hands, turning them over this way and that. It's strange to see her so helpless; she was always the strong one, the decisive one. The leader. Look at her now, the way she just waits for life to happen to her, waits for others to sort things out, to bring her the solutions she wants. It's as though the loss of her child has disabled her; or perhaps rather it has given her permission to opt out, to give up all control. If I were Daisy's mother, I think, I'd be in the car right now, driving like the clappers to reach that house, to scour the coast and paths that surround the place, to find my little girl. If I were Daisy's mother, I wouldn't leave a thing to chance; I'd do everything in my power to get her back.

As though she can hear my thoughts, Emily tilts her head a fraction to appraise me. It's a tiny stand-off: me propped against the island unit, her balled up in her armchair in the corner of the dining room. Our eyes are locked in silent combat. She hates me just for being here; I hate her for her hatred. 'Wake me up when there's news,' she says to no one in particular, and she heads for the staircase and is gone.

There's something of an ending in those few words, and without warning James stops his pacing and rests his head on my shoulder, wrapping his arms up around me, at once strong and needful, and I don't want to let him go. Even when Chloe lets herself in through the back door, we don't move, but wait for her to join us, to join us in our tangled pillar of care and grief and relief and yearning.

'Shall we drive there?' I whisper, and the pair of them pull back, all eyes conferring.

'To the Needles?' James asks. 'But DC Cherry said –'

'I don't care what DC Cherry said!' I exclaim, pushing between them and snatching the car keys from the hook. 'Well?'

And then we're in the car, the three of us, hurtling along hedge-lined lanes with the windows rolled down and the sharp January air rushing in at us – and the sense of anticipation is exhilarating. We're going to find Daisy, I know it, and Chloe knows it and James knows it, and we're doing it together.

At the foot of the winding approach to the Needles we find the road blocked with police tape and we're forced to park in the Alum Bay car park, where we abandon the car, rushing past the glassblowing centre and the sand shop and the games kiosk with its Tin Can Alley and Hook-a-Duck and traditional Isle of Wight rock sticks – and James's phone rings, bringing us all to a sliding halt. He answers it.

'Jesus – Jesus, no,' he says, and I know it's Emily because I can hear her hysterical cries even from several feet away. 'Emily, calm down – please – I'm here now, I'm *at* Alum Bay. It's a mistake, Ems. The journalists are always getting these things wrong. It's got to be a mistake! I'll call you back.'

He cuts off the call, and he's suddenly so shock-pale that I don't want to ask him what she said. I don't want to know. He looks around, turning in circles as though searching for the nearest exit. 'Chloe, what's the quickest way to get down the bay?'

'Alum Bay?' she replies. 'The chair-lifts, I guess.'

And we're running again – sprinting at speed towards the old-fashioned ski-lift that ferries holidaymakers down to the coloured sands below – and Chloe's begging James to tell her what Emily said. But he refuses; he won't tell her and I know it's got to be bad. To our agony, the young man operating the

322

lift raises a flat hand as we approach, pointing to the sign at the turnstile: *The chair-lift may not operate in conditions of high wind.*

'Please,' Chloe begs. Long strands of her copper hair swirl around her head, cruelly reinforcing the turbulent weather conditions. 'It's an emergency!'

'Sorry, the wind's up at the moment. Might be OK in half an hour or so?'

James runs his hands up over his face, the panic in him mounting. In our rush to leave the house he hasn't shaved, and I notice how crumpled he looks in his unironed shirt and scuffed shoes. Emily once told me that the rigidity of his routines drove her a little mad: shoe-shining on a Sunday, ironing on a Monday, car wash on a Friday. Perhaps this change in him will please her. '*Please,*' he begs the young man, 'it really is a matter of life or death.'

An older man arrives, hands on slow hips, and he nods at the younger chap. 'What's the panic?' he asks and his casual manner is excruciating in the face of James's turmoil.

'Just tell him,' I urge James, clutching my jacket tight at the neck, willing the wind to drop from the sky. '*Just tell him!*'

'It's my daughter,' he says, finally, and he turns his back on Chloe and says slowly and quietly. 'She's the baby who's missing – and they think a body has washed up in the bay below.'

Emily's words, 'you've never been a mother', ring in my ears, rushing me back to a time I wish never to revisit, a time of secrets and lies , of another infant taken too early.

I think I knew I was pregnant almost immediately. Something shifted inside me, but it was so fundamentally connected to my terrifying loss of memory that night, and the physical marks left on me, that I failed to acknowledge it until my period was two months overdue. My breasts swelled painfully; tiredness would come upon me like an assault; my appetite changed, ranging from ravenous to sickened. I locked it away, hid it beneath layers of fear and self-loathing, until one day I caught sight of my reflection as I dried from the shower, and I was shocked at the thickening of my waist, at the rivulets of fine veins that converged across my taut stranger's breasts. *A baby*, I said quietly into the dense steam of the room, and cautiously I let my fingertips rest on the curve of my stomach, the slightest of curves, imperceptible to anyone but me. Would it be a monster, born out of violence? Somehow, I knew it would not. Already I could feel the heat of the infant, the warm, belonging glow of a nestled secret. No one need know, I told myself, but of course I was being naïve. Because Emily already knew – she'd known before I had – and before I even had the chance to think about how it might be, how my future could be a different one, she took that secret away.

I want to scream into the howling wind, *Please, not Daisy too! Please, God, don't take away another child!*

Chloe falls against me, a groan rising up through her juddering torso, and without another word the man at the chair-lift opens the turnstile, refusing our money and helping us into our chairs. James takes the first seat; Chloe and I sit side by side in the next. *A body washed ashore.* A dead baby.

'It can't be,' I tell Chloe firmly, as I grip her hand in mine, our knotted fingers turning white with the pressure of it. I fix my eyes on the vertical cable ahead. 'It *can't* be her.'

At first, as the chairs descend, all we can see are tree-tops below us, but when the wind whips beneath us, rocking our carriages like swings in a playground, my terror kicks in. There's the feeblest of bars securing us; the cable above looks ancient and salt-rusted. The carriage swings and tilts, shudders and bucks. My heart pounds, my breaths grow shallow and I think, *please, not now, please give me the strength to remain in the moment, to keep it together* – and then the trees drop away, along with my stomach, and we see them below. There on the desolate winter beach, a huddle of men and women, arranged around a dark mass of flotsam and weed, their fascinated formation concealing the central object as photographers rush down the coastal steps, clicking away, shouting for news. James's chair reaches the landing point and he jumps, hitting the sand at a run, quickly followed by Chloe and me, running, running, pushing through the assembled bodies to see the horror we know awaits us at the water's edge.

It's a doll. A limbless, sightless doll, pink and grubby, with oil-streaked blonde curls that lift and flourish on the incoming tide. Chloe drops to her knees, her forearms and face pressing into the cold sand, and she sobs with such force and volume that the gathered witnesses step away, frightened at the sight of her unbridled grief. When James and I help her to her feet, she is wet with dark sand and she forces us away, refusing our comfort.

'Chloe, sweetie, it's not her,' James says, holding his hands out beseechingly. 'It's not *her*.'

Chloe shakes her head and takes another step back. 'You don't understand,' she says between racking sobs. 'It's all my fault. It's my fault she got into the house and took Daisy. *Avril*. It's because of me she got in.'

'Of course it wasn't,' I tell her, but she waves her hands in front of her face, batting my words away.

'Yes, it was! Don't you understand? It was me who left the back door unlocked! Me and Max went back to the house when you were asleep, Jess! We came in the back when you were sleeping on the sofa – to nick some of Dad's booze – but then you started to cough and wake up so I just grabbed a couple of bottles and we legged it. And I know I didn't lock it again. We just pulled the door shut and ran.'

'It's not your fault, Chloe,' James says.

Chloe hangs her head and weeps. She looks tiny and broken and covered in sand, and I want to sweep her up inside my jacket and make it all disappear. 'Yes, it is, Dad. Yes, it fucking is.'

21. Emily

She's on her own again. After years spent complaining of never having a moment to herself – always at someone or other's beck and call – Emily realises she has wasted valuable time yearning for it. She's incomplete without others around her. She's less of a person without others to witness her existence. Where are they all? They were here when she went upstairs to lie down, and now they are gone. Perhaps Daisy has been found and they've gone to fetch her? She feels strangely detached from this possibility, and she wishes she could hate herself for it, but she doesn't. She doesn't feel very much at all. Maybe they've popped out for groceries; there's hardly anything in the house, so that's likely. She hopes they will remember wine. God, she could kill for a glass of chilled Sancerre right now, but at the same time her mouth is as dry as sand and she knows water is the thing she needs. Emily runs cold water into the kitchen sink and drinks straight from the tap, catching her craze-haired reflection in the shine of the chrome faucet. Did Jess polish it to such a high mirror shine? She must have done, unless James did it, having grown tired of the way Emily has let the place slip. These days Emily does nothing.

She hasn't just eased up a bit on keeping the place straight, she does absolutely nothing. She's gone from being one of the most well-presented people she knows – in all matters – to this. She does nothing, goes nowhere, cares about nothing. What is she now? she wonders. She lifts up her T-shirt hem, perhaps simply to confirm to herself that she's still flesh and blood. She prods at her bony ribs with a close-bitten fingernail.

'I'm nothing,' she says aloud, and still she doesn't care.

Back at home, Mum and Dad were already laying the table for lunch, both dressed in their summer Sunday best, and they looked up as though synchronised, surprised to see Emily up and about.

'I thought you two weren't feeling well,' Dad said, with a grey-furrowed look that told her he knew a lie when he heard one.

Emily let the silence hang in the air long enough for both her parents to halt what they were doing, knowing it would only be a matter of moments before they wondered where Jess was. Her neck felt hot and sweaty after her walk home from the train station, and now the house was heavy with the steam of cooking. Despite the heat of the day, her mother still insisted on the traditional Sunday roast. Farm-fed chicken, with all the trimmings. Emily was hungry, and she was sorry to think that what she was about to tell them would no doubt impact on her mother's immaculate timings.

'Where's your sister?' Dad asked, right on cue.

Again Emily was quiet, and she twisted her hands together as she tried to decide on the best opening sentence, to break it to them gently.

Her mum cautiously lowered her napkins, and looked from her husband to her elder daughter, the rose pattern of her summer dress drawing sharp attention to the pink spots that had started to rise in her cheeks. The tremor in her voice was heartbreaking. 'Emily?'

Emily pulled out a chair and sat, running flat palms down the lengths of her thighs. 'I tried to stop her,' she said finally, and she wept, and for a little while it really did feel as if she meant it. Did she mean it? Emily has often wondered in the years that have passed. Is it possible that she meant it – that she really did feel the loss of her sister?

'Emily! *Where* is Jess?' Her mother was growing panicked now, as Dad manhandled her into a seat, and he too insisted that Emily tell them everything.

'She's left,' she told them, 'I just saw her off at the train station.'

'Left where?' Dad demanded, blocking Mum's words with a stilling hand.

'London, to start with. She's met someone – I don't know who he is – but she says she loves him and she doesn't think you'd approve.'

'She can't just leave!' Mum cries out, clutching at the table-cloth, her voice shrill. 'Where in London, Emily? She must have said something about where she was going?'

'Sorry, Mum, I really tried to get it out of her. But she said they wouldn't be staying in London that long – I think they're going travelling as soon as they've got a bit of money together.'

'But she's only seventeen,' Mum whispered into a tightly clenched little fist.

'She's a young *adult*, Mum,' Emily replied, regretting her impatient tone the moment she said it. 'Sorry, that sounded awful. What I mean is, she'll be fine. She's a sensible girl, isn't she? I'm sure she'll be perfectly fine and I'm sure she'll be in touch as soon as she gets herself settled. She said to tell you that she loves you, and please don't worry about her.'

'That was it?' Dad asked. 'Jess would never simply leave without a word. That was all she said? Have you spoken to her friends? Sammie? Or Jane? Surely they'll know something.'

Emily shook her head and pushed her chair back to leave the room. 'Let me see what I can find out,' she said with calm reassurance in her voice, hoping to stall them a while. 'I'm sure she'll be back before you know it. Maybe we should give it a week before we start panicking? She'll run out of money and come home in no time – you'll see.'

She hoped that Mum wouldn't let the gravy spoil, but thought better of mentioning it, under the circumstances. In the doorway, she paused, to witness her father's arm reaching around her mother's shoulders for the first time in years, to console her as she wept for her lost daughter. Perhaps this would bring them closer together, Emily pondered, feeling hopeful again, noticing the way the sunlight sent dark outlines of Mum's Staffordshire figurines across the parquet floor. God knew they needed something to reunite them, something significant enough to mend the bridges he'd weakened after his years of infidelity. Emily left them to it, and headed straight for the living room, where she picked up the telephone receiver and called Simon.

'It's me!' she said when he answered on the fifth ring, her voice sounding young and high. She twirled the diamond stud of her free ear, still glowing with the thrill of finding Simon's gift, left discreetly on their doorstep that morning. 'What are you up to? I thought we could meet up later? Yes, of course, I *love* them, silly. I've missed you.'

With just a few notable exceptions, Emily has always been blessed with the ability to shut off her feelings at will. For the most part she can control it, through a combination of detachment and justification, and she is certain it has made for a happier existence, a calmer life. She knows plenty of people who don't share her gift, who live their lives under the reckless rule of their every emotion, destined to be soaring with happiness one minute, floored by bad news the next. People who waste weeks on misplaced guilt, feeling anxious that they've caused offence or that they've let a friend down through thoughtlessness. What is wrong with these people? Emily has often wondered, and she thinks of Jess back in their teenage years, the way in which she'd badger Emily constantly, paranoid that she'd upset her older sister. 'Is everything OK?' she'd ask, or, 'Have I done something wrong?' or 'Are you mad at me, Emi?' The response Emily would have liked to give was, *yes, of course I'm mad at you*, but she rarely spoke the words because then she'd have to articulate exactly *why* she was mad at Jessica, and really, she didn't always have an answer. From experience, she knew that 'I just am' didn't wash, because then Jess would go on and on until Emily was forced to make up an answer, and she'd end up saying something far crueller than she'd ever intended. Mostly, she would rather blank Jess for a few days, until her irritable mood had passed and she was ready to accept her sister again. And she wouldn't feel guilty, because Jess *was* annoying and everyone needed a bit of space from time to time, didn't they?

So Emily thinks of herself as fairly controlled when it comes to her feelings. But when that journalist lifted the flap of the letterbox today and called out the words, 'Emily, did you know a body's been washed up on the beach?' she found herself incapable of keeping a lid on her natural responses. She flung open the door and demanded, 'What? What did you say?' and she thought about grabbing the scrawny-bearded little bastard by the shirt, but he told her straight, 'We've got colleagues down at Alum Bay, and they say a baby's body has been washed up on the shore.' Emily saw the ravenous expression on his face. She knew he was starving for her reply, for something dripping in grief for his mucky publication, and she shoved him in the chest so hard he stumbled from the step, and she slammed the door between them.

Now, of course, she knows it was nothing. Just a doll, for God's sake, a washed-up baby doll. She hates herself for the madness she allowed to creep into her voice when she phoned James and ranted down the phone; she hates that she let herself down. And still, she sits here alone in last night's pyjamas, imagining where James is – where Jess is – contemplating what she should do next. But she doesn't have to deliberate too long, because the phone rings again and it's DCI Jacobs, and this time she has real news. Someone has reported seeing Avril on the Lymington-to-Yarmouth ferry in the past hour. She's heading this way, and, DCI Jacobs is happy to confirm, she has Daisy with her.

22. Avril

The temperature plummets in the evenings at this time of year, and so we've spent the first twenty minutes of the crossing warming up in the lounge seats near the front of the ferry, watching the sparkling lights of Lymington fade to pinpricks as we head back towards the island. There was no problem getting through the ferry terminal this time; not like on the way out, when there had been photographs of me posted up around the entrance, causing me to pull my hat down and rethink my plans. In the end, I simply walked in and attached myself to a young family, in the hope that their presence might help me to pass through unnoticed. They were a lovely family, with four rowdy girls – the father looked quite surprised when I asked if he'd mind holding my 'little boy' while I bought my ticket. But then we all got along so well, sitting together in the waiting room, chatting about children and holidays, that when it was time to board he offered to carry Chloe on for me, as I had the buggy.

Coming back today was far easier, and Chloe and I strolled right through, showing our open return tickets and boarding with ease. I guess they're not really looking for anyone travelling *to* the island. We've had a nice time, but my knuckles feel frozen to the bone, and I wish I had a cup of tea to thaw the chill. There's a café on board, but the sign says it closes early in low season, and its coffee machines and shortbread biscuits remain unreachable behind a padlocked grille. A couple of men in greasy overalls are complaining among themselves; they were gasping for a cuppa. Chloe doesn't mind, she's tucked up like a little dormouse under all those cosy blankets.

I worry that I'm procrastinating, sitting here uselessly, whiling away the journey, gazing out at my own reflection in the salty glass windows. It's rough out there, and by the lilting roll of the vessel I'd hazard a guess that a storm is coming in. Most of the other handful of passengers are travelling in ones or twos, like me; the odd businessman and shop worker, some young women dressed in uniforms or suits on their way home from work. Such ordinary activities: work, travel, life. In my thoughts we're standing out on the darkened deck, leaning far over the railings to watch the black sea smash and crawl up the hull of the boat. We'll reach out with stretched fingers, so far that we can feel the spray on our faces, so far that we can actually see below the water's surface, see the world beneath, a place of silvery fins and mermaids' tails and seaweed that flutters like silken thread. How would it feel, to let go, to plunge beneath the water, to just go with the drag and pull of the tide?

'Avril!'

I open my eyes; I hadn't realised I had closed them. I'm still in the lounge, and Chloe's beside me in her pushchair, and now there is an elderly woman resting a light hand on my shoulder. And I *know* her.

'Avril,' she says again, and when she smiles I recognise her at once. I recognise her expression, the set of her mouth, her voice

'Lily?' I can't believe my eyes. *Lily?* Lily from Buddleia Hill, my friend, my confidante. Lily with her cakes and stories; Lily with her lilting laughter and easy company. Lily who made me feel normal again. I've missed her so much. Why didn't I stay in touch? Why didn't I do that? 'Is it really you?'

She takes the seat opposite me, placing her neat little handbag on her neat little lap, and she reaches across and squeezes my hand. 'Thank goodness!' she says, and she shakes her head like this is the strangest thing. 'I thought I'd missed you – I didn't see you among the foot passengers on the way in. Goodness, it *is* wonderful to see you!'

'I've been thinking of you lately – I've been wondering –' and then I'm confused because I feel like I *have* heard her voice lately, I'm suddenly sure of it. '*Buddleia Hill*,' I say aloud, unintentionally, and I hope she doesn't think I'm deranged. 'What are you doing here?'

'Why, you asked me to come, dear!' she says, and I don't know what she means and I think I must have misunderstood, as so often happens. 'You phoned me, remember? I'm sorry I wasn't there to take your call – thank goodness you were able to leave a message!' I must seem confused because then she says, 'Don't you recall, dear? You said you'd just remembered my number and could I meet you at the ferry port the next day? You didn't leave a number to call you back on, but you sounded rather upset, so I thought I'd take my chances and come anyway. And now I'm so glad I did!' She bobs her head slowly, her bright eyes shining like eyes many years younger, and my heart aches for how much I've felt her absence, aches at the memory of my anguish when I thought I'd never see her again. 'Lily,' I say, the word now so strange on my lips. 'I've missed your visits.'

We talk for a while, and I show her Chloe, and Lily is wonderful – no fussing, no demands – and she tells me she's still a volunteer, but somewhere else since Buddleia Hill closed down. She gets out her mobile phone and shows me photographs of the trip she's just been on with her social group, three weeks on safari in Africa, watching animals in their natural habitat. 'You're lucky you caught me when you did, dear,' she says. 'I'd only got home a few hours earlier.' We reminisce about the jigsaws and needlepoint we worked on together, and we laugh about Irish Mattie in her miniskirts and Whispering Kate who would tell you she had an urgent secret, taking you aside to murmur, 'Tea, coffee, hot chocolate, squash,' before tapping her nose and moving on. I'm surprised at just how much I remember, and then I'm gripped with the fear that we'll miss the last part of the journey stuck here in the belly of the ship, and I stand too quickly, stumbling against Chloe's pushchair with the swell of the tide. I haven't decided what we'll do yet; we need to get on to the deck; we need to look down into the water and decide what to do before we draw too close to land and its solid shoreline.

'Whatever's the matter?' Lily asks, and I fear I've upset her.

'No, nothing!' I gasp, and I wheel the pushchair round to face the front windows where the lights of Yarmouth Harbour grow clearer as we sail on. 'We're going out on deck for a little while. I want to show Chloe the sea.'

'But it's so cold!' Lily protests, and she rises, hurrying on tiny patent shoes to catch up with me as I struggle to open the weighted door that leads out into the swirling bite of the Solent air. 'You'll freeze, dear!' she says, but she follows me all the same, pulling the flapping wings of her fawn coat closer to her body, hooking her handbag over the crook of her arm, where it swings against her, buffeted by the strong wind. That bag, that coat, the gentle use of 'dear' at the end of every sentence; these thoughts brush against a soft piece of my mind, and are gone like feathers on the breeze.

Between us and the harbour is an expanse of ink-dark water, its endlessness broken only by the occasional bobbing buoy, or a rogue reflection, a stray sliver of light cast out from the captain's deck above. The blackness is exquisite; my mind roams, returning to a place long, long ago, when blackness was all I dreamed of. When deep, dreamless sleep was the one thing I yearned for, having long since given up on everyday dreams. No simple ambitions of love and family for me; all I dreamt of was an ending. But then Lily came along, and somehow, with her quiet ways and her simple friendship, I began to imagine, not an ending, but a beginning. I look at her, this small-framed bird of a woman, and I know I have so much to thank her for.

Chloe is awake now and I lift her from her pushchair and I hold her high, so that she can see the light and darkness for herself, so that she can feel the elemental thrall of this space in time, before it is gone.

'Avril, no!' Lily shrieks, and her hand shoots out to grip my wrist and my mind divides, and I look into her eyes and she's no longer Lily. *She's not Lily.* She's James's mother again, and I'm terrified. I'm terrified that she's here to stop me from showing Chloe the water – that she's here to stop me from doing the right thing. 'Please, Avril,' she says. 'Think of her family – please, dear? Please?'

I clasp Chloe tight to me, so tight that she begins to cry, and I see the woman make a signal to a uniformed man, who appears magician-like from the far side of the level. He breaks into a run and at once he's there in front of me, making a barrier of his body as the harbour lights grow brighter and the ferry begins to turn. I run with the turn of the vessel, around the outer deck and into the fierce squall of the wind, so we might face the harbour as we approach and dock. The uniformed man runs with me, always between me and the sea, like some strange and silent ghost.

When I get as far as the railings will allow, the woman is still there at my side, and she's begging me to hand her Chloe but I won't, not while there's a breath left in my body. I won't let her take Chloe again; I won't let it happen. I see it all now for what it really is: Lily – Alicia – they were always one and the same, they were always James's mother, and I let myself believe otherwise, and for what? For companionship? For belonging? For love? Chloe is screaming now and I don't want to scare her, so I cradle her face to my neck and I turn all my rage towards that little woman at my side. '*I know who you are*,' I hiss, and she gasps at the violence in my voice.

'Of course, you do, dear,' she says, turning her smile on me again. 'I'm *Lily*. I'm your friend. Lily, from Buddleia House.'

The man in the uniform is still there between me and the railing, his arms now outstretched like a policeman holding back a mob. In the distance beyond him, a small crowd gathers on the high bank of the harbourside, family and friends waiting for their loved ones, no doubt. No such waiting party for me.

I turn back to the woman, and I wonder how I was ever fooled before. 'I know who you are,' I repeat, and this time my voice is calm, and I know she means me no harm. Holding on to Chloe, now resting peacefully at my shoulder, I close my eyes against the cut and slice of the January storm and once more I dream of darkness.

23. **Jess**

When the call comes through that Avril and Daisy are on the incoming ferry, we're halfway up the seemingly endless steps from Alum Bay beach, the chair-lift machinery now officially out of service in the approaching storm. After the drama of these past hours, we can hardly believe the news of this development, but it is so positive and real that it's all we can do to hang on to the hand-rail and pull ourselves upwards against the biting wind, up towards the car park above.

'How the hell did she get off the island in the first place?' I shout up to James, struggling to be heard over the gale that batters around our ears.

'She went via Yarmouth – Jacobs says they can't believe she got through . . .' James's breath is laboured as he takes the steps two at a time, desperate to get back to the car, to Daisy. 'But then I'm guessing the police presence there was probably nowhere near as strong as it would have been on the Portsmouth route. She came in on the Portsmouth ferry, so I guess they thought she'd go back on that one too. That, and she was travelling as a foot passenger, rather than by car. They said the disembarking

339

vehicle checks had been "vigorous" since they'd had Avril in their sights – but I'm guessing they took their eye off the ball with regard to the foot passengers.'

Chloe is the first to reach the top, and she stands waiting for us to catch up, her face set in a scowl of anger. '*Idiots!* I still don't understand how they could have missed them! Yarmouth is only a small place – how can you miss a kidnapper and a baby, for God's sake? There are posters up everywhere! It's been all over the news!'

James slings his arm around her, kissing the side of her head and hurrying her towards the parked car. 'It doesn't matter any more, Chlo,' he says, his face at last registering some kind of tense hope. 'We're getting her back.'

Chloe starts to cry again; but this time they're tears of relief.

I take the keys from James and climb into the driver's seat. 'I'll drop you at the ferry terminal first,' I say. The sky is already dark, the last lights of day disappearing beyond the sea's churning horizon, the vast cliffside car park now virtually deserted. The car rocks lightly as the wind blusters across the bonnet, spraying leaves and sand over the windscreen. 'Then I'll go back to fetch Emily. We can't risk her driving herself – not with all the tablets she's been taking. And I saw she had a bottle of wine in her hand when she went upstairs earlier.'

I start the engine and head out towards the Yarmouth road, seeing signs of the turbulent weather all along the dark route. Branches and leaves litter the roadside; a loosened pub banner flaps precariously across the country lane, and, on the front gravel of the Country Stores, a plastic garden bench is up-ended and travelling towards the field next door. In the half-light of the car I feel James watching me, and I turn to meet his gaze. I see how shocked he is by the day's events, and how grateful he is to hand the problem of Emily over to me. In the back seat Chloe is already calling Max, asking him to meet her at Yarmouth harbour, sharing the good news.

'I'll be as quick as I can,' I tell them both when we pull up beside the police cordon at the entrance to the quayside, and James clings to me, thanking me before rushing out with Chloe, into the night, out towards his baby daughter.

Alone, I turn the car around and head off towards my sister, leaving behind me the blinking lights of Yarmouth harbour. Emily will expect me to take her to her daughter; she'll be standing alone on the doorstep, the family home behind her empty and silent, and she'll be waiting for me to take her to Daisy without delay. She'll be nervous and hopeful, holding back the tears as she chews on her thumbnail and waits, her impatience growing by the second. But I'm afraid she's going to have to wait a bit longer. We've got unfinished business to attend to.

It was pure chance that I made contact with Sammie when I did, when, on reaching a point of change in my life, I had lighted on the idea that my old friend might be the one to help me be reconciled with my mother after so many years apart. I'd tried to contact Emily a few times in the early days, when I knew where she was living, but my letters had gone unanswered and I feared making direct contact with Mum when I'd hurt her so deeply before. Only recently I had completed a month-long retreat at an ashram in North Wales, a place recommended to me by a girl I'd met on my travels around Europe, and I'd emerged full of hope and newfound energy, my clearest goal being to find my way back home. Many of the residents at the rural retreat were there battling with addiction; others, like me, were trying to make sense of the lives they'd found themselves living, and, by the same token, trying to make sense of their past.

It's hard to explain without sounding like some New Age evangelist, but my time at the ashram taught me to value myself again, something I hadn't done for many years. The wide open countryside, the quiet community, the long hours spent in silent contemplation – these things converged to give me the clarity and space I needed to acknowledge the mistakes that I'd made, and the mistakes that had been made against me. It was time to forgive – to forgive myself, and others, to start thinking about the rest of my life – and live it. I knew that Sammie would welcome me without judgment, despite all this time of separation. She was always a good person, a kind and trustworthy friend, and I felt certain that she would still be in touch with my mother, to whom she had been so close in childhood. When I boarded the train in Wales I found myself hurtling towards London, not knowing quite where I would land next, and on arrival at Euston station I sought out the nearest internet café, where I handed over my payment details and began my search. For two hours I sat in a window booth looking out over a dreary London back street, drinking vending-machine coffee and trawling through pages of listings for the seemingly infinite number of potential Sammie/Samantha/Sam Evanses. Eventually, grudgingly, I set up a fake social media account just so I could narrow the possibilities down, and before long, to my astonishment, I found her. My heart raced, because there she was, Sammie Evans, unmarried with two children and still living in our home town, her profile picture showing her tiny frame and smiling face virtually unchanged. I had found her! Now I could reach out to her, and maybe, in turn, to Mum and Emily. Now I could go home. Everything was suddenly so clear and simple.

But when I read her latest entry, posted just days earlier, my lucid resolve shattered.

Am feeling such sadness at the loss of one of the loveliest women I've ever known. RIP Olive Tyler xxx

342

Beneath the words was a photograph of a white-haired woman sitting on a wooden bench in a rose-filled summer garden. My garden. My mum.

The funeral was held two days later. From first contact, Sammie took control, instructing me to take the next train to Fleet, where I would stay with her. In my state of uncomprehending shock I didn't put up any kind of resistance, and the day and a half leading up to Mum's service are still something of a blur to me. What I do remember is the unfettered joy I felt on seeing my sister Emily entering the church, and, despite the sadness our reunion marked, hope soared inside me as we chatted at the after-funeral tea, well past afternoon and into evening, the pair of us together again, laughing, remembering only the good things, the things we could build a future on. When Emily mooted the idea of me joining her family over on the island, I really thought I might be dreaming, or drunk on sherry and bonhomie. But, as I left Emily at the church hall, my sister hugged me with such fervent warmth that I knew she meant it. I was forgiven, and we would be together again. Sisters.

Back at Sammie's, I opened another bottle of wine and lit the fire as she fetched a platter of bread and cheese.

'Just like old times,' she said, sitting cross-legged beside me on the hearthside rug, 'except with alcohol and cheese rather than chocolate and chips.'

We'd changed into our pyjamas, and I was glad her kids were away at a friend's for the night, so that I could have Sammie all to myself now that the funeral was out of the way. I'd hardly seen her during the service; she had kept to herself at the far side, away from the family seats, and afterwards she had only said a brief hello to Emily. The initial shock of my mother's death was subsiding, and for the first time since I'd arrived we talked properly about our lives over the past years, filling in the gaps that we'd each missed in the other's experience. I knew it was only a matter of time before she asked me, but still, I was thrown when the question came.

'Why did you leave like that, Jess? Why did you leave without a goodbye?'

I looked at her face, so open and trusting, and perhaps it was the warmth of friendship, or maybe it was the wine, but I told her everything. For the very first time, I shared with another human being the reasons behind my sudden flight from home, unburdening the shame and guilt that I'd carried with me all these years, for betraying my sister, for extinguishing another life, for the pain and distress I'd caused my beloved parents.

In return, Sammie told me Emily's version, and in the space of one evening my world seemed to flip inside out.

Emily is waiting on the front drive when I arrive to collect her, her coat buttoned up, her dark hair swirling around a pale and vacant face, and it takes her a second to register my arrival and climb into the passenger seat.

'Did James call you?' I ask. 'Did he tell you? They've found Daisy?'

She nods, pulling the seatbelt across her chest, bringing her thumb to her mouth to gnaw at its ragged edges. We drive in silence for ten minutes or more, until I pull off the main road and detour out towards a coastal viewing point, dark and deserted, overlooking the unsettled waters looking out to the mainland beyond.

'What are you doing?' she asks, and they're the first words she's spoken to me. Her voice rises. 'What the hell are you doing, stopping in the middle of nowhere when Daisy could be waiting for me?' I can see her glance about nervously, fear rising to the surface. 'Jess? What are you doing?'

You wouldn't want to stand out on the cliff-front right now; you wouldn't stand a chance. In the safe security of this wind-battered car, Emily is my captive audience. Here, Emily has nowhere to run.

'I think we need to talk, Ems. We need to talk about the past.'

That night, Sammie listened, and for not even a moment did she question my version of the truth. She was always a good listener.

'I had no idea about the pregnancy,' she said, looking down into her glass, choosing her words carefully. 'No idea at all, Jess. Did Emily ever really talk to you about what happened with Simon that night?'

I stared into the flames, struggling to find the right words for something I'd never before spoken aloud. 'When I woke the next day, I was sick as a dog, and more terrified than I'd ever felt in my life – because I knew something awful had taken place with Simon at your house. Something too awful to even put into words. Emily wasn't speaking to me, and I couldn't remember a thing, so how could I even start to explain it to her? But one thing I can be certain of was that I wouldn't have encouraged him in any way – I couldn't stand the bloke – and I know I wasn't drunk!'

'You weren't!' Sammie reached out to touch my arm. '*I* know that. You'd barely had a drink, Jess. But what *do* you remember?'

'I remember feeling light-headed – and you helping me into your room – and then Simon, sitting on the edge of the bed, and his creepy little friend Lizard in the doorway – I remember him handing me a can of Coke –' I can hardly go on. 'And – and then *nothing*. Nothing until I'm stumbling in through my own front door with Emily, and then waking the next day.'

Sammie nodded for me to continue. 'It wasn't your fault, Jess.'

'But it must have been,' I replied, feeling no closer to unravelling my knotted tangle of memories. 'Emily said I was pissed out of my head. She said I might not think I'd led him on, but that we're all capable of acting out of character when we're that drunk. And how could I argue with that? She was the one who found me with him. There was no doubt about what had happened in there. She was the only other person who saw the way it was.'

Sammie fell silent, a sadness passing behind her eyes. 'She wasn't the only one there, Jess.'

I waited for her answer, still not understanding what it really meant.

'I was there too. I saw what happened to you, and, God forgive me, I never said a word.'

Beyond the windscreen, the storm continues to rage, blasting sharp pins of rainfall against the metal armour of the car. Emily has fallen silent again, refusing to be drawn into conversation unless I take her to James at the quayside.

'Did Sammie ever get through to you, Ems?' I ask now, swivelling around in my seat to look at my sister in the darkness.

'What?' she replies impatiently. She looks at me as though I'm mad.

'Did you speak to Sammie at all?' I ask again.

Emily pulls away from me, pressing herself further against the passenger door. She looks nervy.

'She's one of our only links to the past, you know?' I say, calmly. 'She knows more about me – and you – than anyone else in the world.'

Emily looks afraid. Not just a little, but a lot. She knows what I'm talking about, and I'm glad. If I had as much to lose as she does, I'd be afraid too.

'Take me to James,' Emily whispers. 'I want to see my daughter. I *want* to see Daisy.'

I fall silent, pulling the collar of my red jacket closer, suddenly feeling the cold of the wild night air, my mind hardening. 'I'm not taking you anywhere until we've done this, Emily. We're not moving until you tell me the truth.'

'What did Sammie tell you?' she asks, and I'm maddened by the question. So like Emily, so like my big sister to hedge her bets, waiting to hear just how much she has to own up to, assessing how much she can leave out.

'She told me everything. She told me about the state you found me in that night of the party. She told me that you knew it wasn't just one of my episodes – that you both thought he must have spiked my drink.'

Emily has no words. She simply shakes her head, and I continue.

'You knew all about my condition, Emily; you knew what the signs were. You'd witnessed it often enough. If I passed out, I'd usually be out for, what, a minute or two at most – but this – this was something else altogether. I tried telling you so many times afterwards, but you wouldn't have it, you insisted it was my fault that I'd ended up in there with Simon, that I'd got blind drunk and led him on. Well, I wasn't drunk. And I didn't lead him on.' There's a pause, and the wind whips up with such ferocity that it feels as though the tyres might lift from the ground. Out across the water the lights of an incoming ferry come into view: Daisy's ferry. I know my eyes are steely, moist with tears I won't let fall. 'You *knew* what happened to me in there, Emi, you knew that he – that he –'

Emily turns away now, because this is too much for her, this is more than she wants to hear –

'He raped me, Emily! He *raped* me. You know it and I know it and Sammie knew it too. And, instead of helping me, you sent me away. You arranged my abortion and then you sent me away.'

I'm breathing heavily now, my chest rising and falling beneath a clenched hand, and Emily looks alarmed, as though she's wondering if I'm all right, if I'm having one of my turns right now. But I don't want her sympathy, and my rage has nowhere to go but out.

'I was seventeen, for God's sake! You told me that Mum and Dad wanted me gone – that they knew all about Simon and the pregnancy. You said they were ashamed of me. But Sammie said they never got over me leaving – that they had no idea why I didn't make contact. She said they never stopped hoping I'd come home – that they even went to the police and reported me missing, wanting them to launch an investigation to find me. What's the truth of it, Emily? *What* did Mum and Dad know?'

'Dad was having an affair,' Emily murmurs, and I don't know why she is saying it, what it has to do with any of this. 'You thought that Mum was offhand with you specifically in those weeks before you left, that she could barely be in the same room as you. Do you remember? But she was the same with all of us – it had nothing to do with you. It was Dad with his fancy woman again, that's all. It just seemed easier to tell you it was because of you. I knew it was wrong, but I couldn't stand to be near you after what happened with Simon.' Her voice is blunt.

I lower my gaze, shaking my head in hopeless disbelief.

'They didn't know a thing about it, Jess – about the pregnancy, or the party or any of it. If it's any consolation, I never gave them any reason to think badly of you.'

'But what about the phone call from the clinic?' I ask.

'There was no phone call,' she replies, and she looks away, out into the darkness of the swirling night air. 'I made it up.'

'Why, Emily? Why would you do something like that?'

Emily's gaze remains fixed ahead. 'Because I wanted Simon back,' she says.

Now, I see Emily standing beside me on the station platform all those years before, her fingers distractedly circling the sparkling ear studs she'd put on for the first time that morning. Despite my distress, they had caught my attention, catching the summer light, and I remember thinking, they're new, they're expensive. *They look like a gift.*

'Did you get him back?' I ask.

She nods, her gaunt expression absent of feeling. 'For a while. For just a month or two, until he found someone new.'

This, this final piece of information, is *it*, I think to myself. The final injury.

24. **Emily**

She knows. This is the chilling realisation that Emily can't shake from her mind as they pull up in the car park at Yarmouth ferry terminal. It is the first clear thought she has had all day, the first thing she has been certain of in a very long time, and it courses through her thoughts as she runs along the dark and windswept pathway towards her daughter's safe return. Jess knows what happened in that bedroom at Sammie's house all those years ago. And worse still, Emily thinks, she knows that I've always known.

On the horizon, the tiniest hint of light appears, and a ferryman calls out, 'There she is!' and Emily thinks she might stop breathing until the boat draws nearer, when she can really believe that Daisy is on her way. DCI Jacobs and her team start to move about the quayside, pointing and calling out instructions. Emily barely hears a word of it. *She knows,* her mind taunts her again. This is the thought that runs through Emily's panicked mind over and over, as the cold wind bites at her. She fixes her gaze on the lights of the incoming ferry, fighting against this fresh terror that threatens to engulf her. *She knows.*

*

Along the corridor, Lizard stood outside the closed door to Sammie's bedroom, and in the moment it took for his startled eyes to meet Emily's she knew it was bad news.

'Who's in there?' she asked, her hands already wrestling him away from his post, her voice surging at him, high and frightened. She was vaguely aware of Sammie behind her, urging her to calm down, appealing to Lizard that they needed to check on Jess. But Emily was hysterical. She knew she had to get inside that room, and she lashed out at Lizard, scoring a deep red mark along his cheekbone, causing him to yelp and step aside, his hands raised in self-defence.

'*Who is in there*?' she screamed again, wanting to know – not wanting to know – and, as the door fell open and she stumbled against the end of the bed, she had all the answers she needed.

Sammie's neat pink bedspread was rucked up, and that in itself was uncharacteristic, unsettling. In the second it took for Simon to register her presence, all Emily could see of Jess was the pale skin of her motionless limbs, pinioned beneath Simon's moving hips, and her face, oh, God, her face. She was pale, her head lolled back against the pillow, one eye open but unseeing, and so, so lifeless, that in that second Emily truly believed that her sister was dead. She gasped, at once turning to check if she was the only witness to this, but she was not. It was Sammie, tiny little Sammie who rushed at Simon, grabbing him by the back of his shirt to haul him off her, dragging him to the floor with a drunken thud. In a second, Emily had kicked the door shut, tugging up the bedspread to cover her sister, everything happening with such speed that she thought she might collapse under the heart-pumping strain of it. And then she stood, stock still, and took in the scene. Simon was crumpled on the floor where he fell, not too wasted to cover his own modesty as he fumbled with his button fly. Sammie appeared suddenly terrified, standing in the centre of her own bedroom, wordlessly asking, *what now, Emi, what now*? And there was Jess, like a corpse on the bed, half-naked beneath those garish pink sheets, unmoving, unspeaking. *Unknowing.*

'What were you doing?' Emily murmured, and even now she can't be sure if she meant this for Jess or for Simon. All the power she possessed seemed to slip from her as she gazed down on her sister's helpless form. Now she turned towards Simon, addressed him directly. '*What. Were. You. Doing?*'

'Shit, Ems,' he said, rotating his earring between finger and thumb and pushing himself to standing. He hooked his fingers into his belt loops and tugged up his jeans. 'Shit, Ems, I'm sorry. Ah, fuck. Sorry, OK?'

Sorry? Didn't he know what he'd done? Had he no idea at all? 'She's my sister,' she said quietly. But it wasn't enough. Not for this. She knew that much from the look of abject horror on Sammie's face. She knew that much from the rotten pool of bile that had started to swill in her gut. '*She's my sister.*'

'Oh, man, look – I'm *sorry*,' he repeated, and so thrown was she by the innocent expression on her boyfriend's face that she started to question whether she'd got this all wrong. Hope flickered, for the briefest of moments, hope that perhaps she *had* got it all wrong. But she hadn't, had she? She knew what she had seen in this candy-pink bedroom, a room she once associated with childhood and innocence, a room now so sullied she feared she might never step foot in it again. She knew what this was.

'God, I'm out of my head, Ems. Babe? I didn't mean for this to happen. You believe me, don't you? I didn't mean it.' Simon moved towards her, reaching out a hand, a hand that moments earlier had been *on her sister*. She lurched backwards, crashing against Sammie's chest of drawers, shaking her head as hair clips and cotton buds scattered across the carpet.

'No!' she shouted. 'No, no, no!'

And he left the room. Simple as that. He shrugged, kicking Jess's discarded denim skirt to one side, and he left the room.

Sammie was leaning over the bed, stroking Jess's forehead, pulling at her eyelids and trying to bring her round. She indicated for Emily to go round the other side and help to hoist her up to a sitting position. Jess's body was like a dead weight, but she was breathing and starting to show signs of consciousness. 'We need to tell someone about this,' Sammie said, but Emily shook her head and focused on the task of pushing pillows behind Jess's slumped torso. 'This is *wrong*,' Sammie whispered fiercely. 'We can't just do nothing! You can't let him get away with it! Emi? She's your sister!'

Like a gift, reason flooded Emily's mind, and she was suddenly calm. She took control, as she always did, and she made it go away. 'Sammie, please, you've got to trust me on this one. Jess would never get over it if she thought you'd seen her like this – you know how embarrassed she gets about her fainting and all that –'

'But this isn't like that! She hasn't just fainted – look at her! She's taken something. Or they've given her something, more like.'

Emily reached across Jess to take Sammie's tiny wrist in her hand. 'Let me handle it, Sammie, OK? Whatever happened, Jess won't want anyone to hear about it. She'd be so ashamed, I don't know what she'd do – or what would happen to her. You know how the doctors are always telling us how she has to avoid stress, because of her heart. Please, Sammie. Swear you'll never breathe a word? *Please?* You said it yourself, she's my sister. And I think I know what's best for her, don't you?'

The ferry has docked, and the first of the passenger cars exits the lower deck of the ferry. DCI Jacobs turns and makes a wide sweeping motion with her arms. Emily looks around at the anxious faces of James and Chloe, at the assembled officers and harbour crew, poised for action, their breath white and smoky in the night air, and wonders if perhaps this has all been a dream. James has his arms around Chloe, warming her shoulders beneath his jacket, his face in her hair, and Jess – well, there she is now, at their side, where Emily should be. *She's taken my place*, she thinks. *I really am vanishing.* The irony of it does not escape her; to have been replaced by her vanished sister is perhaps the worst punishment of all. James has barely looked in her direction, oblivious to everything but the disembarkation point of the ferry, and she daren't approach him, so afraid is she of what her little sister may have said. Does he know about her? Does he know what she did?

Max arrives, running along the quayside to join the others, James and Chloe and Jess; he places his hands on Chloe's shoulders, and she turns to look back at him, and she looks happy. Jess smiles at him, welcoming him. It's as though Emily doesn't exist, and even now jealousy tugs at her, needling her to get her sister away from them. Away from her family. She yearns for another of her little tablets, just one, to take the edge off all this.

'There she is!' Chloe cries out, and her arm shoots up, a finger pointing in the direction of the passenger deck at the back of the ship. 'There! There's Daisy!'

And Emily doesn't know which way to turn because now she's crying, and everyone's crying – there's no one to hug her – and she can see her, really, really see her. She's real and she's safe and, even though they're separated by police tape and distance and waiting, waiting, waiting, they've seen for themselves that Daisy is really *here*. In this extraordinary moment of reconciliation, surely her sister could reach inside herself and find forgiveness? Surely, after everything they've been through together? Surely, after the passing of so much time? Emily moves closer, and tries to draw Jess's attention; she reaches out, touches her arm lightly, hopeful

355

that she'll respond in this moment of celebration and relief. But Jess flinches at her touch and leans in close to whisper, '*I know it was you, Emily. It had to be. It was you who contacted Avril, wasn't it?*'

Emily can see herself now, bent over James's desk, reading and re-reading the letter she'd found in her husband's paperwork, tears falling from her eyes as the full extent of his deceit dawned upon her. *Dear James, I can't bear the way we parted. Please, can we meet? I just want to talk to you. All my love, A x.* She'd acted rashly, immediately flipping open her husband's laptop to type 'his' reply – a simple yes to the woman, an invitation to come to his home while his family were away, to talk. She had printed the letter, adding a handwritten 'x', and rushed to the post box to send it before she could change her mind. Had she ever thought anything would come of it? She hadn't even had a name to put on the envelope, for God's sake. Of course she hadn't thought anything would come of it.

The minutes that follow Jess's words are a blur, Emily's state a nightmarish blend of horror and hope, of anticipation and alarm. She steps away from her sister, her heart hammering against her cold ribs, and fixes her attention on the upper deck of the ferry, where several figures stand. To one side, a police officer holds Daisy in his arms, and further along the railings is the woman who can only be Avril, flanked by two more uniformed officers. The flood-lights are full on, and, as the distant group starts to move towards the staircase to make their descent, another person comes into view, a small-framed woman in a neatly cut coat, a little handbag hooked in the crook of her elbow. She slips her arm through Avril's.

'Who's that with them?' Emily asks, the frightened sound of her own voice startling her as she squints against the glare of the floodlights.

It is James who answers, and his tear-streaked face reveals the strangest expression of pain and joy. 'It's my mother,' he says.

Epilogue

Jess

September

I love this new stretch of the island, so far away from the tourist trail and tricky to reach unless you're familiar with the hidden coastal paths. The tide is way out, the sun low in the sky, casting long shadows of the smallest shells and lugworm trails, dappling the glistening sand like a soft oil colour. I live for these moments alone, these hours of calm contemplation and movement, when I can make sense of all that has happened and be thankful for all that I have.

In the hours that followed Daisy's return, so much altered for all of us that, looking back now, it takes on a dreamlike quality, like a film, or a story belonging to someone else altogether. That night, when Avril was apprehended, she brought with her the strangest revelation, in the form of James's mother. It emerged that, after James had left his old life behind, his mother had remained steadfastly loyal to her daughter-in-law, visiting her at the psychiatric hospital until she was finally approved as recovered, and released into the community. I liked James's mother,

Alicia – or Lily, as she prefers – from the moment I met her. I love her quietly efficient little ways, and I love the wisdom with which she leads her life. James sobbed when she reached out to embrace him at the quayside, she so tiny and steadfast, he, in contrast, vast and needful.

Lily told us she had been searching for Avril since her release a year ago, and about how shocked she was on arriving home late at night from a long holiday abroad to find a message on her answerphone. In the message, Avril was almost incoherent, but Lily was able to make out that she wanted to meet her the next afternoon before she travelled to the island – and thank God, Lily decided it sounded important enough to drop everything and go. When she turned up to meet Avril at the ferry terminal in Lymington, she had no idea about James and his missing daughter – or that Avril was wanted by the police – until she picked up a newspaper in the waiting room and saw their faces on the front page. When she spotted Avril approaching with Daisy, she quickly alerted the security staff, and, on their instruction, held back to allow Avril to board before her while they organised backup.

It seems that lying runs in the family; Lily had convinced the nurses at Avril's hospital that she was someone else altogether, but her deception came from a good place, a place of compassion after James had himself suffered a breakdown and taken Chloe with no forwarding address. Amazingly, Lily had been funding Avril's private care at Buddleia Hill for the five years before she left, paying out a small fortune every month for the care of her beloved daughter-in-law. All these things we withhold from each other; so many secrets we tie ourselves up with in the keeping.

Avril is in a secure unit now, just across the water where Chloe can visit her, and often Chloe will take the hovercraft with Grandma Lily, who now lives on the island, just a few miles along the coast from the new family home. For years Lily had waited in hope that James or Chloe would find her again, invite her back into their lives, and now here they are, together, as close as a family could be. Chloe's visits to Avril are going well, and slowly she is filling in the history that her mother has missed out on, taking bundles of photographs and scrapbooks with her each time, excitedly returning home with the excavated tales of her parents' old lives. A few times, I've visited with her; they're so alike, Chloe and Avril, it's uncanny. Avril's doing just fine. She feels safe where she is, she's well cared for and monitored, and she has Chloe in her world. 'That's all I ever wanted,' she told me the last time I went along.

And Emily – well, she's gone. When James discovered that it was Emily who had made contact with Avril, encouraged her to come, any traces of love he still had for her vanished entirely. She tried to tell him about finding the letter he'd hidden, the letter signed 'A', to tell him that she hadn't known, *couldn't* have known who she was writing to – who she was inviting into their lives. 'I just wanted to see her – this other woman,' she pleaded. She tried to tell him that she'd thought he was having an affair, that she was only trying to put a stop to it, but James wouldn't hear another word. *She* was the one who made this happen; *she* was to blame for the agony of Daisy's disappearance; *she* was the one who had put them through the nightmare that no parent should ever face. And, almost worse still, she had tried to implicate Chloe in order to deflect suspicion from herself. That, he said, was unforgivable.

Of course, James doesn't know that it was me who moved the letter from his coat pocket to his desk drawer so that Emily was likely to find it, and I'm sure he would never have detected the hint of uncertainty I allowed to slip into my tone as I reassured my sister that her husband couldn't *possibly* be having an affair.

Such subtle shifts in tenor are barely audible to most; perhaps it's the kind of nuance only a sister would pick up on.

After much soul-searching, Emily agreed that she'd rather take some time out than have her involvement exposed to the police, and I gave her the details of my ashram in North Wales. It's been more than seven months now, and we haven't heard from her at all. It must be doing her good, some valuable time to reflect and heal. We all need that, don't we? Time to think things over.

Now as I ascend the sandy path towards my sun-bathed little cottage, I pause a moment to catch my breath, to cradle the tightening corset of my growing belly. I must slow down, I remind myself; it's only a matter of days until my due date. My thoughts are drawn back to that faraway night in December, when we were not much more than strangers, James and I, just the two of us together beneath the newly strung Christmas lights, sharing a bottle of wine as the rest of the house slept overhead. I'd never meant that to happen, but there you are. Life is full of surprises. From here I can just make them out, gathered in the evening light of the wildflower garden: James, his head tilted in concentration as he tends the smoking barbecue with Max; Chloe, tall and willowy as a flower herself, pushing little Daisy on her new wooden swing, causing her to laugh in high breathless squeals. I inhale the smoky warmth that catches on the air and marvel at my family. If Emily were here now I'd tell her how right she was all those years ago, how wise her words.

Life really *does* have a way of working itself out.

Acknowledgments

I was first introduced to editor Sam Eades by my agent Kate Shaw, in a cafe on London Bridge on a frosty December day when the trains were running late. Upon my tardy arrival, my anxiety quickly vanished as I was warmly greeted (and clearly forgiven) by Sam – an infectiously prolific reader, and a passionate champion of writers – and by the end of the meeting I knew I had to work with her on my next novel. Thanks to Kate and Sam, that wish came true. There followed late nights and early mornings, brain-twisting plot loops to navigate, details and locations to research, new worlds to bring to the page, and there are many excellent people who have supported me in those endeavours. Particular thanks go to Sam Eades and Kate Shaw who helped me to wrestle this thriller from concept to reality, being at once inspiring, encouraging and all-round great fun to work with. There are so many others who have laboured to bring my book to the shelf, in the UK and beyond: the designers and proof-readers, the marketing and digital bods, the foreign rights managers and literary scouts – I'm overwhelmed by your support. During the first part of my writing career I had the privilege of working with truly wonderful people, and I'm delighted to report that the tradition continues with my new family here at Orion/Trapeze.

Huge thanks also to the readers, reviewers and book bloggers who have cheered me on; to the booksellers, library staff, festival organisers and literary hosts I've met along the way; to friends and family who continue to coax me from my writing cave for sustenance and laughs. To Juliet West for lending me her writing space for a much-needed week of peaceful editing – to Michelle Davies for her generosity of time and knowledge – to the superb Linda McQueen for her ability to make copy editing an enjoyable part of the process – to Elaine Egan and Amy Davies for publicity and marketing brilliance – to my friends in the wider writing community – I am grateful to you all.

Most importantly, an ocean of love goes to my husband Colin, and my children, Alice and Samson. Thank you for patting me on the back at the start of each new project, when what you're probably thinking is, 'here we go again . . .'

A note on the technical aspects of this book – whilst I have researched and sought out insider knowledge in the areas of medicine, police procedure and the geography of the book's location, errors may have been made and downright liberties will have been taken. For these I take full responsibility and hope you will forgive me in the name of good fiction.

Isabel Ashdown, 2017

Reading Group Guide
Topics for discussion

1. What is the effect of hearing the story from both Jess and Emily's point of view? Could you keep track?

2. The Isle of Wight feels like an extra character in the novel. Discuss how the island setting is used in the story.

3. Do your feelings about Jess and Emily shift throughout the novel? If so, how do they change?

4. How does the author pull the wool over the reader's eyes in preparation for the first major twist? Did you see it coming? Or was it a surprise?

5. Discuss the relationship between Emily and James, and how it changes after Jess's arrival.

6. The title *Little Sister* could relate to Jess and Emily or Chloe and Daisy. How are their relationships different from one another?

7. Did you suspect who was behind Daisy's disappearance? Was each character responsible in their own way?

8. The ending is intentionally ambiguous: what does life hold for those characters? Do you think it was the right ending?

9. The relationship between sisters has often been explored. Share your favourite films/TV programmes/books about sisters.

10. What did you enjoy most or least about *Little Sister*?

Author Q & A
with Isabel Ashdown

1) Why did you choose to explore the relationship between sisters? What makes this relationship unique?

I have a little sister (who I love very much) – and, I have a big brother (ditto) – and I'm sandwiched between them, middle child of three. Neither of our parents had a sister, so in a way mine and Becky's relationship was our own to create, uninformed by strong sister role models. There's no doubt it's unique, special, and peculiarly different to relationships with other female friends and relations. There's an unspoken quality to it – you feel each other's joy and pain more intuitively – and so it seemed to me, in a story of secrets and betrayal, you might feel each other's darkness more clearly too.

2) The novel opens with a missing child. How does this event affect each family member?

How can we ever begin to imagine the horror of losing a child? In *Little Sister*, baby Daisy goes missing whilst in the care of her aunt, Jess. Unsurprisingly, guilt and blame are strong emotions at work – and with Jess and her sister Emily only recently reunited after years apart, it's only a matter of time before those emotions break through and old resentments show themselves in new ways.

3) How does the setting – The Isle of Wight – shape the story?

The Isle of Wight is a place I have great affection for. Over the years I've spent much time there, either holidaying with the family, or retreating there to walk, write and research. *Little Sister* is the second book I have firmly located there (the other being *Summer of '76*), and in both cases I felt that the island location lent something powerful to the unfolding of drama. I grew up in a small seaside town, and I guess small islands are similar in their way – when big things happen, perhaps they seem even bigger, magnified within the boundaries of the ocean, adding to the sense of claustrophobia and panic that courses through the characters at the heart of the story.

4) Tell us about your fascination with the idea of distorted memory.

Like many of us, I've spent much of my life being different things to different people – sister, daughter, mother, partner, friend – and I'm endlessly fascinated by the complexities of family relationships, and the weight of their power. We like to think we are most ourselves with family, but who's to say which version of us is the best version, the truest version, the most reliable version even? As a writer I'm often drawn to the shadows of family histories – my own included – and find myself wanting to explore the ways in which the memories and consequences of shared events can differ so wildly from person to person. That, in part, is what inspired *Little Sister*, the idea of inconsistent memory – of distorted memory – ultimately the idea of unreliable truths.

5) You move from present day into flashback in each chapter. What made you choose this style? Was it easy to keep track?

From the first word, I knew the shared histories of Emily and Jess would be fundamental to the telling of this story – it would have been impossible to relate their present day events without filling in some of the gaps of their childhood together. They were born less than twelve months apart, schooled in the same year group, competing over the same friends and attentions. I wanted to know who they were before these altered adults they had become – and so the flashbacks were a vital part of the process. It was surprisingly easy to keep track; the more I wrote about them, the more they grew in strength and clarity, a kind of organic blooming of character and feeling.

6) The book is filled with twists and turns. Did you know how the story was going to end? Or did it surprise you?

When working on a new novel I usually have a good sense of how it starts, what the big (if initially blurry) picture appears to be, and more often than not, a strong idea of where it will end. The hard bit tends to be the eighty to ninety thousand words in between! There are unsettling periods, when you're not sure where your writing will take you – and then there are those gloriously unexpected moments in the sun when a new twist or revelation shows itself to you, and your heart leaps – and you know it is a better book for it.

If you enjoyed *Little Sister*,
turn the page to read an extract from
Isabel Ashdown's second thriller

Beautiful Liars

**When two must keep a secret,
three's a crowd . . .**

Out April 2018

Prologue

It *wasn't* my fault.

I can see that now, through adult eyes and with the hindsight of rational thinking. Of course, for many years I wondered if I'd misremembered the details of that day, the true events having changed shape beneath the various and consoling accounts of my parents, of the emergency officers, of the witnesses on the rocky path below. I remember certain snatches so sharply – like the way the mountain rescue man's beard grew more ginger towards the middle of his face, and his soft tone when he said, 'Hello, mate,' offering me a solid hand to shake. *Hello, mate.* I never forgot that. But there are other things I can't remember at all, such as what we'd been doing in the week leading up to the accident, or where we'd been staying, or where we went directly afterwards. How interesting it is, the way the mind works, the way it recalibrates difficult experiences, bestowing upon them a storybook quality so that we might shut the pages when it suits us and place them safely on the highest shelf. I was just seven, and so naturally I followed the lead of my mother and father, torn as they were between despair for their lost child and protection of the one who still remained: the one left standing on the misty mountain ledge of Kinder Scout, looking down.

At first I didn't speak a word. I can see the scene now, if I allow myself to return to that remote place in my memory. I watch myself as though from a great distance: small and plump, black hair slicked against my forehead by the damp drizzle of the high mountain air. And there are my parents, dressed head-to-toe in their identical hiking gear: Mum, thin and earnest, a startled librarian-owl of a woman – and Dad, confused, his finger pushing his spectacles up his florid nose as he interprets my gesture and breaks into a heavy-footed run. Their alarmed expressions are frozen in time. There is horror there as they register that I now stand alone – no younger child to be seen; that I'm pointing towards the precipitous edge, my eyes squinting hard as I try to shed tears. There are no other walkers on this stretch of path, no one to say what really happened when my brother departed the cliff-edge, but the sharp cries of distress from the winding path far below suggest that there are witnesses to his arrival further down.

It wasn't your fault, it wasn't your fault, it wasn't your fault. This was the refrain of my slow-eyed mother in the weeks that followed, while she tried her best to absolve me, to put one foot in front of the other, to grasp at some semblance of normality. 'It wasn't your fault,' she'd tell me at night-time as she tucked the duvet snugly around my shoulders, our eyes never straying to the now-empty bed inhabiting the nook on the opposite side of my tiny childhood bedroom. 'It was just a terrible accident.' But, as I look back now, I think perhaps I can hear the grain of uncertainty in her tone, the little tremor betraying the questions she will never voice. *Did you do it, sweetheart? Did you push my baby from the path? Was it just an accident? Was it?*

And, if I were to speak with my mother now, what would I say in return? If I track further back into that same memory, to just a few seconds earlier, the truth is there for me alone to see. Now at the cliff-edge I see two children. They're not identical in size and stature, but they're both dressed in bright blue anoraks to match their parents, the smaller with his hood tightly fastened beneath a chubby chin, the bigger one with hood down, oblivious to the sting of the icy rain. 'Mine!' the smaller one says, unsuccessfully snatching at a sherbet lemon held loosely between the older child's dripping fingers. This goes on a while, and in my rational mind I think that perhaps the sweet *did* belong to the younger child, because eventually it is snatched away and I recall the sense that it wasn't mine to covet in the first place. But that is not the point, because it wasn't the taking of the sweet that was so wrong but the boastful, taunting manner of it. '*No!*' is the cry I hear, and I know it comes from me because even now I feel the rage rear up inside me as that hooded child makes a great pouting show of shedding the wrapper and popping the yellow lozenge into its selfish hole of a mouth, its bragging form swaying in a small victory dance at the slippery edge. The tremor of my cry is still vibrating in my ears as I bring the weight of my balled fist into the soft dough of that child's face and see the sherbet lemon shoot from between rosy lips like a bullet. '*No!*' I shout again, and this time the sound seems to come from far, far away. Seconds later, he's gone, and I know he's plummeting, falling past the heather-festooned rocks and snaggly outcrops that make up this great mountainous piece of land. I know it is a death drop; I know it is a long way down. I can't say I remember pushing him – but neither can I remember *not* pushing him.

So you see, I'm not to blame at all. From what I recall of that other child – my brother – he was a snatcher, a tittle-tattle, a cry-baby, a provoker. Even if I did do it, there's not a person on earth who would think I was culpable.

I was *seven*, for God's sake.